Richard Grant White

Memoirs of the Life of William Shakespeare

With an Essay toward the expression of his Genius, and etc.

Richard Grant White

Memoirs of the Life of William Shakespeare
With an Essay toward the expression of his Genius, and etc.

ISBN/EAN: 9783337055820

Printed in Europe, USA, Canada, Australia, Japan

Cover: Foto ©Raphael Reischuk / pixelio.de

More available books at **www.hansebooks.com**

MEMOIRS

OF THE LIFE OF

WILLIAM SHAKESPEARE,

WITH

AN ESSAY TOWARD THE EXPRESSION OF

HIS GENIUS,

AND

AN ACCOUNT OF THE RISE AND PROGRESS OF

THE ENGLISH DRAMA.

By RICHARD GRANT WHITE.

BOSTON:

LITTLE, BROWN, AND COMPANY.

1865.

WILLIAM HENRY SEWARD, LL. D.,

SECRETARY OF STATE.

S IR, —
I venture, without your knowledge, to inscribe this volume to you as an individual recognition of your long-continued and signal services to the Republic. Through all your public life the unrelenting foe of wrong and of oppression, one of the earliest and most earnest advocates of the cause of freedom, a statesman who recognized his responsibility to a higher law than that of state necessity, you have yet endeavored to secure the blessings of liberty to all by peaceful methods, and to obtain for all the protection of the law without the violation of the law. Called to the Department of State at a period when our foreign relations were fraught with peril and environed with difficulty, you have so administered them, that, while you calmly maintained the internal sovereignty and the external rights of the government you represented, the jealous ministers of rival nations publicly acknowledged your fairness and your candor, and were able only to cavil at those assertions of the unabated power and dignity of the Republic, which, made with unflinching confidence in an hour of unprecedented trial, touched the hearts of your countrymen as the expression of a faith

which was then in very deed the substance of things
hoped for and the evidence of things not seen, but which
events have shown to be well founded. Just men may
have misunderstood you, but your only enemies have
been the enemies of right and of your country. At the
hands of some of these, you have lately suffered in common with the good President whom we yet mourn. That
your life was sought with his was an additional testimony
to your faithfulness and your ability. Men seek to kill
only whom they fear and hate. That you escaped this
murderous attempt made by assassins who struck at your
country through you, was an occasion of rejoicing to true
men throughout the land. This book, although purely
literary in its character, may be fitly dedicated to a statesman in whom the cause of education has ever found an
advocate equally zealous and discreet, and whose pen
has gained him an enviable place in the world of letters.
That you may live long in the service of your country,
and that, while the undying interest of the subject of this
volume wins it readers, this page may do a little toward
preserving in the minds of your countrymen a memory
of how much they and freedom owe you, are the hearty
wishes of

Your grateful fellow-citizen,

R. G. W.

PREFACE.

THIS volume is the result of an endeavor to present in a narrative form what is known and may be reasonably inferred concerning Shakespeare's life, with an appreciation of his genius, and such a history of our early drama as would conduce to that appreciation and be suited to the perusal of the generality of his intelligent readers. During the last hundred and fifty years much has been written upon these subjects by men of various fitness for the task, and of widely differing degrees of ability. But unless my knowledge of this literature is imperfect, the present book, in its scope, its purpose, and its method, is without a rival among its predecessors. It is not intended for lovers of desultory gossip on the one hand, or for antiquaries and Shakespearian scholars on the other. I have undertaken to examine and to estimate the mass of material which has been accumulated by the painstaking researches of previous investigators of the facts connected with Shakespeare's life and of the earlier records of the English drama, — much of it having the slightest possible connection, and more no connection at all, with the subject, — to arrange with compactness and coherence that which seemed to me to be distinguished from the remainder by truth and significance, and so to tell the story that it might have a continuous interest for readers not especially devoted to dramatic studies.

Having given my authority in most cases for statement or hypothesis, it is not necessary that I should here repeat my acknowledgment of obligations in this regard. Little has been added, and nothing of moment, to the results either of the searches made in the last two centuries by Betterton, Malone, and Chalmers for tradition and record concerning Shakespeare, or of their investigations of the social and professional conditions under which his life must have been passed. The last two writers seemed also to have exhausted the field of research in regard to the history of the English drama and the English stage. But Mr.

Collier's later work upon those subjects, by its fulness and its systematic arrangement, supersedes
all others, either for the use of the dramatic student, or as a book of reference for the occasional
inquirer. Yet the account of the English drama
given in the following pages will be found to be
something more, as well as something less, than
an abridgment of Mr. Collier's three octavo vol-
umes.

These remarks apply only to the first and last
divisions of this volume. The second, the Essay
toward an Expression of Shakespeare's Genius,
is the endeavor of one who, having read the poet
much and his critics little, has thought his own
thoughts and trusted his own judgment upon this
subject, until, with a mingling of confidence and
diffidence which it would be difficult to explain,
he now ventures to offer his conclusions as hints
and aids to others; conscious the while that
those who can judge them best are those who
need them least.

Thus the purpose of this book is to enable its
reader to form as nearly as possible a full and
just appreciation of Shakespeare as a man, a
poet, and a dramatist. No other thought entered

my mind when I laid out my work. But I will
own that, as I wrote the following pages, I conceived the hope that those who read them might
be led to remember, and not only to remember
but to take to heart, the pregnant and all-impor-
tant truth, that with the intellectual wealth and
glory of Shakespeare and Milton and their contemporaries and antecessors, we have inherited,
not in any indirect and collateral way, but as
coheirs and equals with our blood brethren in
Great Britain, however sharp our political severance from them, those principles of liberty, that
intelligent respect for law, and that capacity of
self-government, which belong to and distinguish
the English race, which some call Anglo-Saxon ;
— that if we have attained a national prosperity
and power, a diffusion of mental culture and moral
sensibility, and a union of stability and progres-
sive force hitherto unheard of among any people,
it is only because we have transplanted here, and
developed by a normal and unconstrained growth,
the same political principles and the same laws
of social development from which spring the real
power and the true glory of the British nation ; —
that we in our Englishhood, as they in theirs, are

so subject to the same laws of moral and intellectual development that, however that development may be modified by circumstances, and though we are politically two nations with sometimes clashing interests, we are not, and indeed cannot be, other than one people ; — and that, with all our mutual emulation, inevitable as it is from the community of our origin, our mental constitution, and the similarity of our pursuits, we owe each other, if not mutual regard, at least a mutual consideration, respect, and confidence heartier than that which befits the merely formal intercourse of two nations which are called friendly because they are not at open enmity. Our common inheritance is one which each of us may enjoy to the full without diminishing the other's share, or impugning the other's title, and which we should share without envy, certainly without malice or uncharitableness. These truths are trite ; but the day will be a sad one, should it ever come, when they finally lose their vital binding force for those who read in a common mother tongue the words of William Shakespeare.

R. G. W.

New York, May 23d, 1865.

MEMOIRS OF

WILLIAM SHAKESPEARE.

T HE name and the works of William Shakespeare were widely known and highly
thought of by his contemporaries. Unlike Homer's, his figure does not loom vaguely from the
obscurity of a pre-historic period ; unlike Dante's,
it is not revealed by fitful and lurid light amid the
convulsions of society upon the verge of the dark
ages. From early manhood to maturity he lived,
and labored, and throve, in the chief city of a
prosperous and peaceful country, at a period of
high intellectual and moral development. His
life was passed before the public in days when the
pen recorded scandal in the diary, and when the
press, though the daily newspaper did not yet
exist, teemed with personality. Yet of Dante,
driven in haughty wretchedness from city to city,
and singing his immortal hate of his pursuers as
he fled, we know more than we do of Shakespeare ;
the paucity of whose personal memorials is so extreme, that he has shared with the almost mythi-

cal Homer the fortune of having the works which
make his fame immortal pronounced medleys, in
the composition of which he was but indirectly
and partially concerned; and two enthusiasts, one
in the Old England and the other in the New,
have even maintained that they were written by
the great philosophers and statesmen of his day,
who used his name as a stalking horse with which
to conceal themselves and mislead the public.*

Two generations had not followed that which
gave to the world the great poet of our race and
of mankind, when Thomas Betterton, the most
celebrated London actor of his day, journeyed
from the scene of Shakespeare's metropolitan distinction to that of his rustic youth and his rural
retirement, in the hope of finding in the latter
those traces of his private life which had been so
entirely obliterated in the former. The grateful
and reverential player, who had gained competence and reputation chiefly by performing Shakespeare's characters, gathered and preserved a few
fading but important traditions; to these the as-
siduous investigation of more than a century and
a half has added the records of a few other facts

* The accomplished and gifted lady who broached this theory
on this side of the ocean in *Putnam's Magazine* for January, 1856,
was then, doubtless, suffering from that mental aberration which
soon after consigned her to the asylum in which she died. The
Transatlantic critics are, I believe, without a similar excuse for
the strange fancy of her British rival, which they were so quick
to condemn in her as a trait of "American" extravagance.

of hardly more significance, and confirmation of some of those traditions; and this is all the faint and uncertain light which falls from the past upon the man whose works cast such a blaze of ever-brightening glory upon our literature. There have been issued, indeed, to us of the present generation, pamphlets professing to give new particulars of the life of Shakespeare, and tomes with even more pretentious titles. But from all these there has been but small satisfaction, save to those who can persuade themselves that, by knowing what Shakespeare might have done, they know what he did, or that a reflex of his daily life can be seen in parchments beginning, "This indenture made," or "*Noverint universi per præsentes.*" It is with no disrespect, nay, it is rather with thankfulness and sorrowing sympathy, that the devotee of Shakespeare, after examining the fruit of the laborious researches of men who have wasted sunlight and candles, and worn good eyes, in poring over sentences as musty as the parchments on which they are written, and as dry as the dust which covered them, will reluctantly decide that all this mousing has been almost in vain. It has incidentally resulted in the diffusion of a knowledge of the times and circumstances in which Shakespeare lived, and in the unearthing of much interesting illustration of his works from the mould of antiquity; but only those who have the taste of the literary antiquary can accept these documents, which have been so plentifully produced and so pitilessly printed, — extracts from parish registers and old account-books, inventories, including lists of the knives and spoons and pots and pans of the guzzling aldermen of Stratford; last wills and testaments, leases, deeds, bonds, declarations, pleas, replications, rejoinders, surrejoinders, rebutters, and surrebutters, — as having aught to do with the life of such a man as William Shakespeare. They have, most of them, told us nothing, and only serve to mark and mock our futile efforts. For, although we do know something of Shakespeare's life, yet, compared with what we long to know, and what it would seem that we should be able to discover, our knowledge is, as knowledge often is, only the narrow boundary which marks the limit of a wide waste of ignorance. We do not know positively the date of Shakespeare's birth, or the house in which he first saw the light, or a single act of his life from the day of his baptism to the month of his obscure and suspicious marriage. We are equally ignorant of the date of that event, and of all else that befell him from its occurrence until we find him in London ; and when he went there we are not sure, or when he finally returned to Stratford. That he wrote the plays which bear his name we know ; but, except by inference, we do not know the years in which they were written, or even that in which either of them was first performed. We do not know that he laid his fathei or his mother in the grave, or stood by the dying bedside of his only son, or that he gave the sanction of his presence to the marriage of his best-loved daughter. Hardly a word that he spoke has reached us, and not a familiar line from his hand, or the record of one interview at which he was present. Yet from the few facts which have been ascertained, and the vague and sometimes incongruous traditions which have been preserved concerning him, from the circumstances in which he must have been placed, and the mention of and allusion to him by some of his contemporaries, we may discover what manner of man this player-poet was, and learn, though imperfectly, his life's almost uneventful story.

Warwickshire, in Old England, seems to have been the favorite haunt, if it were not the ancestral soil, of a family whose name more than any other in our tongue sounds of battle and tells of knightly origin. It is possible, indeed, that *Shakespeare* is a corruption of some name of more peaceful meaning, and therefore mayhap (so bloody was ambition's very lowest step of old) of humbler derivation; for in the irregular, phonographic spelling of antiquity it appears sometimes as *Chacksper* and *Shaxpur*. But upon such an uncertain foundation it is hardly safe even to base a doubt; and as the martial accents come down to us from the • verge of the fourteenth century, we may safely assume that a name thus spoken in chivalric days was not without chivalric significance.*

The Shakespeares, however, seem never to have risen to the rank of heraldic gentry, or to have established themselves firmly among the landholders of the county. An old register of the Guild of Saint Anne of Knolle in Warwickshire, which goes back to 1407, shows that, among many

---

* The manner in which the name is spelled in the old records varies almost to the extreme capacity of various letters to produce a sound approximating to that of the name as we pronounce it. It appears as Chacksper, Shaxpur, Shaxper, Schaksper, Schakesper, Schakspere, Schakespeire, Schakespeyr, Shagspere, Saxpere, Shaxpere, Shaxpeare, Shaxsper, Shaxspere, Shaxespere, Shakspere, Shakspear, Shakspeere, Schakspear, Shackspeare, Shackespeare, Shackespere, Shakspeyr, Skaksper, Shakespere, Shakyspere, Shakeseper, Shakespire, Shakespeire, Shakespear, Shakespeare, Shakaspeare; and there are even other varieties of its orthography. But Shakespeare himself, and his careful friend Ben Jonson, when they printed the name, spelled it *Shake-speare*, the hyphen being often used; and in this form it is found in almost every book of their time in which it appeared. The final *e* is mere superfluity, and might with propriety be dropped; but then we should also drop it from Greene, Marlowe, Peele, and other names in which it appears. There seems, therefore, to be no good reason for deviating from the orthography to which Shakespeare and his contemporaries gave a kind of formal recognition. As to the superior martial significance of this name to all others, we have, indeed, Breakspeare, Winspeare, Shakeshaft, Shakelance, Briselance, Hackstaff, Drawswerde, Curtlemace, Battleman, and some others of that sort; but in this regard they all must yield to that which was an attribute of Mars himself as long ago as when Homer wrote : —

Μαίνετο δ', ὡς ὅτ' Ἄρης ἐγχέσπαλος.
Iliad, O. 605.

Shakespeares in whose eternal welfare the brothers and sisters were led to concern themselves,
there was a Prioress Isabella, whose soul was
prayed for in 1505 (did player William know it
when he wrote *Measure for Measure?*), and a Lady
(" Domina") Joan, who seems to have been living
in 1527; but these trifling distinctions are the
highest which have been discovered in connection
with the name.

Little need we care, however, what was the
condition of those Shakespeares who were moul-
dering in the earth before he without whom they
would never have been heard of appeared upon it.
Who his paternal grandfather was, we do not surely know; but there is hardly a doubt that he was
one Richard Shakespeare, farmer, of Snitterfield,
a village near Stratford on Avon. This Richard
Shakespeare was a tenant of Robert Arden, a
gentleman of ancient family but moderate estate,
who lived at Wilmecote, three miles from Stratford, and who tilled a part of his patrimonial fields,
and let a part to humbler husbandmen. The
Ardens had been high among the gentry of Warwickshire since a time long before the Conquest,
at which period Turchill de Arden was military
governer, *vice-comes* (or viscount, then not an he-
reditary dignity) of Warwick Castle. The family
took its name from the wooded country, called
Arden or Ardern, which lay in the northern and
western part of that county, of which at one time

they had no small part in their possession.* Robert Arden's branch of this family held lands in
Snitterfield as far back, at least, as the early part
of the fifteenth century; and he inherited his
property there in direct succession. Two of the
family had held places of some honor and responsibility in the household of King Henry VII., —
Sir John Arden, who was squire of the body, and
his nephew Robert, who was page of the bedchamber, to that shrewd and thrifty monarch, in
whose service they both prospered. This John
Arden did not escape great peril of marriage in
his youth. For when he was about eighteen
years old he was carried off bodily by a certain
Richard Bracebridge of Kingsbury, who threatened him with his daughter Alice. As to which
proposition, indeed, the lad's father had no small
difference with the lady's. "Howbeit," says Dugdale, who tells the story, "at length, by a reference to Sir Simon Mountfort of Colshill, Knight,
and Sir Richard Bingham (the Judge who then
lived at Middleton), it was determined that the
marriage should be solemnized betwixt them, and,
in consideration of two hundred marks portion,
a convenient jointure settled; and also that, for
the trespass done by the same Richard Brace-

---

* The name Ardern, or Wood, was given at first to a forest-
covered tract, which extended from the Avon to the Trent on the
north, and the Severn on the west; but it was retained at a very
early period by that part only which lay within Warwickshire.

bridge in so taking away the young gentleman, he should give to the before specified Walter Arden the best horse that could by him be chosen in Kingsbury Park." *

Robert Arden, the page of the bedchamber, was grandfather to the Robert Arden who let his land to Richard Shakespeare, — a fact in which we may be sure that landlord and tenant took some pride, because, as we shall see, it was so well remembered by their grandson. Of the family affairs and fortunes of Richard Shakespeare, nothing of interest is known ; but among the Shakespeares of Snitterfield were two, John and Henry, who were of the age which his sons might be, and who were brothers. There appears to have been but one family of the name in the place, and there is hardly room for doubt that they called him father. Henry Shakespeare's name will come up again ; but our concern is with the fortunes of his brother John, who appears to have been a man of thrift and capacity, and withal, as such men are apt to be, somewhat ambitious. Robert Arden had no son to inherit his name, his property, and his bedchamber honors ; but he had seven daughters. The youngest of these, Mary, who seems to have been her father's favorite, John Shakespeare won to look on him with liking ; and so he married into the landlord's family, and allied his blood to that of the Ardens, with their high old English

* Dugdale's *Antiquities of Warwickshire*, (fol., 1656,) p. 678.

1*

pedigree, stretching past the Conqueror away beyond the reign of the Confessor. And to us of
English race it is a matter of some interest to
know that Shakespeare came of pure English
blood, and not upon his mother's side of Norman,
as some have concluded, because of her gentle
and ancient lineage, and because, to use the words
of one of them, Arden "sounds like a Norman
name." But *Ardern*, which became Arden, is
Celtic, and the name was given to the northern
part of Warwickshire by the ancient Britons.
And as there has even been a book written to
show that Shakespeare was a Celt, it may be well
to say here, that the Turchill* de Arden who is
above mentioned was the first of his family who
assumed a surname. His father's name was Al-
win, which, like his own, was common enough of
old among the English. He called himself, from
the place in which he lived, Turchill de Ardern ;
but the Normans called him Turchill de Warwick,
because of the office which he held under Edward
the Confessor, and which the Conqueror allowed
him to retain in spite of his English, or possibly
Danish blood, because, like many other powerful
Englishmen, he had not helped Harold, and did
not oppose Duke William's title.† For it should

---

* The *ch* is hard in this name, which was often written *Tur-
kill*.

† "This Turchill resided here at Warwick, and had great possessions in this county when William Duke of Normandy invaded

always be remembered that, according to the loose dynastic notions of that day, the Norman bastard had some claim to the throne of England, and that it was the land of a divided people that he successfully invaded. From this people, who swallowed up their conquerors (like themselves, of Teutonic family), and imposed upon them their language, their customs, and their very mental traits, came the man in whose origin we have so great an interest; and, to all intents and purposes, from this people only, even on the mother's side; for the Ardens, in spite of their position, seem to have intermarried almost altogether with English families.*

But to return to the humbler members of the Arden family, with whom we have more immediate concern. Whether Robert Arden consented to the marriage of the daughter who has given

England and vanquisht King Harold; and though he were then a man of especial note and power, yet did he give no assistance to Harold in that battail, as may be easily seen from the favor he received at the hands of the Conqueror. . . . . And though he had so much respect from the victorious Norman as to possess these during his life, yet is it most clear that his son [Siward] enjoyed none of them as his heir, but by the favor of the Conqueror. . . . . By which instance we may partly see how hardly the native English were dealt with; viz., not to enjoy their inheritances though they did not at all oppose the Conqueror's title, as by that trust committed to this Turchill for enlarging of Warwick Castle may be inferred." — Dugdale's *Antiquities of Warwickshire*, pp. 302, 303.

* See Dugdale's *Antiquities of Warwickshire*, passim.

him a consequence in the eyes of posterity that
he little dreamed of, or whether the pedigree and
the charms of the fair Mary were the only motives
of John Shakespeare's choice, we cannot tell; because the wedding did not take place until after,
and probably not until a full year after, the death
of the young lady's father, by which event she became the inheritress of a pretty fortune in possession and in reversion. Her father had bequeathed
her a farm, of between fifty and sixty acres, in
Wilmecote, called Ashbies, with a crop upon the
ground, and £6 13s. 4d. in money, beside her
share in what was left after legacies were paid;
and she had also a reversionary interest of far
greater value than Ashbies in a stepmother's
dower estate at Snitterfield, and in some other
land at Wilmecote. The small sum of money set
down to the young heiress (though in the end she
doubtless had much more) may excite a smile,
until we remember that money had then nearly
six times its present value, and also how very little
of actual money is got, or in fact needed, by agricultural people, even of comparatively large possessions.

Robert Arden died about the 1st of December, 1556, and the first child of John Shakespeare
and Mary Arden was baptized on September
15, 1558. Joan Shakespeare received her name
in the Church of the Holy Trinity, the parish
church of Stratford on Avon, where her father

had for some years been settled, and had become a prosperous and rising man. When he went thither, we do not know; but he was there, and a householder in Henley Street, in 1552. His chief occupation seems to have been that of a glover; for he is so styled in a law document issued in June, 1556. But he was also engaged in husbandry, and in company with another person; for on the 19th of November in the same year he brought a suit against Henry Field, who unjustly kept from him eighteen quarters of barley. John Shakespeare's private and public fortunes advanced steadily and rapidly for twenty years from the time when he first appears in Stratford. It is true that he could not write his name; but that was no disgrace, and little impediment, at a time when men much above him in social position were equally incapable. In 1556 he purchased the copyhold of two houses, one with a garden and croft, and one — that in Henley Street — with a garden only. In the course of the next year he acquired other property (how considerable for a man in his station, we have already seen) by his marriage. In this year he was regarded as of sufficient substance and importance to be marked as one of the jury of the court-leet, upon which he served soon afterward; and at this date he was also appointed ale-taster, — an office of which, in spite of its humble name, the mighty consumption of that fluid in Old England must

have made the duties arduous, though pleasant,
and the perquisites acceptable. He must have
given the burgesses of Stratford cause to speak
well of him over the liquor that they loved; for
in 1557 they elected him one of their number, and
they were only fourteen. The next year saw him
a constable, and also the father of the girl who
was called after him; and in 1559 he was re-
elected one of the keepers of the Queen's peace
in Stratford. About this time he appears to have
dropped his glover's trade. It was, indeed, quite
inconsistent with the notions of propriety in that
day that the husband of an Arden and an heiress
should be an artisan; and this consideration could
not but have its weight with the young burgess,
now that he had land and beeves. The year 1561
saw him made an affeeror in the spring, and before
the leaves began to fall, elected chamberlain. It
was the duty of an affeeror to impose fines upon
offenders who were punishable arbitrarily for mis-
demeanors to which no express penalty was attached by statute, — an office only to be filled by
a man of discretion and integrity; and as John
Shakespeare, according to the date when he is
with good reason believed to have been born, was
at this time but thirty or thirty-one years old, his
appointment to this office by the court indicates,
not only soundness of character on his part, but
somewhat unusual ripeness of judgment. He
served as chamberlain two years, in the second

of which another daughter was born to him, who
was called Margaret. But Mary Arden's little
family did not thrive like her husband's business.
A few months lightened the young mother's arms,
to lay a load upon her heart. Margaret as well
Joan died in early infancy.

To the now childless couple there came consolation and a welcome care in their first-born son,
whom, on the 26th of April, 1564, they christened
and called William. The Reverend (or, as he was
then called, Sir) John Breechgirdle probably performed that office. Of the day of William Shakespeare's birth there exists, and probably there was
made, no record. Why should it have been otherwise? He was only the son of a Warwickshire
yeoman, a burgess of a little rural town. And
there were two score at least of children born that
year in Stratford, who, in the eyes of their parents
and of the good townsfolk, were of just as much
importance, and of whose appearance in the world
no other note was taken than such as tells us of
his advent, — the entry of their christening in the
parish register. As yet it was not the custom to
record upon the blank leaves of the Bible the
dates of life and death in humble families; and
had John Shakespeare owned a Bible, neither he
nor even his higher-born wife could have written
the words to read which, if they had endured,
men would have made a pilgrimage. All unsus-

pecting what he was whom she had borne and whom she cherished in her bosom, the mother of William Shakespeare could have looked on him only as the probable inheritor of his father's little wealth, the possible recipient of his father's little honors, or mayhap, in some moment of high hope, the occupant of a position like that of his maternal grandfather. And had he become a peer instead of a player, the day of his birth might have been no less uncertain. Tradition says it was the 23d of April; and the old custom of christening the third day after birth, though it was far from universal, if it did not give rumor a hint, gives tradition some support.

A court roll tells us that in 1552 John Shakespeare lived in Henley Street; and another, that he bought the copyhold of a house in that street in 1556. Tradition points out a house in Henley Street, which we know belonged to John Shakespeare, as the birthplace of his illustrious son, who himself became its owner; and the probability of the truth of this tradition amounts, to all intents and purposes, to certainty. Neglect, subdivision, and base uses had reduced this house at the beginning of the present century to a very forlorn and unsightly condition. But as late as 1769 it preserved enough of its original form to show that William Shakespeare was born and passed his childhood and his adolescent years in a home which was not only pretty and picturesque, but very comfortable and unusually commodious for a man in his father's station in the middle of the sixteenth century.　For in the reign of Elizabeth domestic architecture was in its infancy.　Something had been done for the household comfort of noblemen and gentlemen of large estate; but almost nothing for the homes of that large class, composed, in the words of Agar, of those who have neither poverty nor riches, but food convenient for them, and which now gives the architect his chief employment.　Old abbeys, priories, and granges, recently sequestered, and newly-built halls, were taking the place of cold, crumbling castles as dwellings for the rich; and between these and the humble farm-house or village cot, often built, as the haughty Spaniard wrote in the reign of Elizabeth's sister, "of sticks and dirt," there was no middle structure.　People corresponding in position to those whose means and tastes would now insure them as much comfort in their homes as a king has in his palace, and even simple elegance beside, then lived in houses which in their best estate would seem at the present day rude, cheerless, and confined, to any man not bred in poverty.　In 1847 the Shakespeare house passed into the hands of an association, under whose care it has been renovated; but unfortunately, like some of the Shakespeare poetry, not restored to a close resemblance to its first condition; though that was perhaps in both cases

B

impossible. Whether it was in this house that
John Shakespeare and his wife, with their only
precious child, stayed out the plague which visited Stratford in 1564, or whether they fled to
some uninfected place, we do not know. But
families did not move freely in those days, or
easily find house-room; and on the 30th of August in that year John Shakespeare, as the Stratford register tells, was at a hall or meeting, held
in a garden, probably for fear of infection. On
this occasion he gave twelvepence for the relief
of poor sufferers. The highest sum given was
seven shillings and fourpence, the lowest, sixpence; and there were but two burgesses who
gave more than twelvepence. In September he
gave sixpence more, and in October eighteen-
pence. It may be assumed as quite certain, then,
that the Shakespeares remained at Stratford during the plague, thus leaving William, like any
other child, in peril of the pestilence. They
passed through a period of fearful trial. The
scourge made Stratford desolate. In six months
one sixth of their neighbors were buried. But
although around them there was hardly a house
in which there was not one dead, there was a
charm upon their threshold, and William Shakespeare lived.

In the next year the father was chosen one of
the fourteen aldermen of the town; and in 1568
he was made high bailiff, which office he filled

one year. He continued to prosper, and in 1570 he took under his cultivation yet other lands, a farm called Ington, at the then goodly rent of £8. The year 1571 saw him chief alderman; and in 1575 he bought two freehold houses in Henley Street, with gardens and orchards. William Shakespeare, therefore, at ten years of age, was the son of one of the most substantial and respected men of Stratford, who was one of its fourteen burgesses, and who had rapidly attained, step by step, the highest honors in the gift of his townsmen. He was styled *Master* Shakespeare, — a designation the manly style of which we have belittled into *Mister*, voiding it at the same time of its honorable significance. As high bailiff and chief alderman he sat as justice of the peace, and thus even became "worshipful." There has been much dispute as to what was his occupation at this time; his glover's trade having been before abandoned. Rowe, on Betterton's authority, says that he was "a considerable dealer in wool." John Aubrey the antiquary, or rather *quid-tunc*, says that he was a butcher; in a deed dated 1579, and in another seventeen years later, he is called a yeoman; and his name appears in a list of the gentlemen and freeholders of Barlichway Hundred in 1580. One of his fellow-aldermen, who was his predecessor in the office of bailiff, was a butcher; but with our knowledge of his landed possessions and his consequent agricultural occu-

pation, we may be pretty sure that his nearest
approach to that useful business was in having
his own cattle killed on his own premises. Wool
he might well have sold from the backs of his own
flocks without being properly a wool-dealer. But
what was his distinctive occupation is a matter
of very little consequence, except as it may have
affected the early occupation of his son, and of
not much, even in that regard. He was plainly
in a condition of life which secured that son the
means of a healthy physical and moral development, and which, if he had lived in New England
a century or a century and a half later, would
have made him regarded, if a well-mannered man,
as fit company for the squire and the parson and
the best people of the township, and emboldened
him perhaps to aspire to a seat in the General
Court of the Colony.

II.

Stratford on Avon, where William Shakespeare
was born and bred, is a place the antiquity of which
is so great as to be uncertain. It was known as
Stratford or Streatford, i. e. Street-ford, three hundred years before the Conquest. Having its origin probably in a wayside ale-house, boatman's
cabin, or blacksmith's forge at a ford of the Avon
River, on which it stands, it grew slowly to an
insignificant size through long centuries. The
Avon is one of those gently flowing rural streams

which, unvexed by factories, undisturbed by traffic, and spanned by solid bridges which have sounded to the tread of mail-clad men, make the soil of England rich and her landscapes beautiful. The ford, which was the nucleus of the town, and gave it half its name, was on the high road or street which gave the other half, and which stretches from the hamlet of Henley in Arden through Stratford across the Avon on towards London; and thus the names of Shakespeare's native place, of the street on which stood his boyhood's home, and of his mother's family, were happily associated. Stratford is now a clean and quiet little place, containing about four thousand inhabitants, who seem to live comfortably enough without trade or manufactures. But in itself it has no attraction; and towards the end of the reign of that shrewd and selfish termagant whom our forefathers called Good Queen Bess, it would have appeared to modern eyes unsightly. It then contained about fifteen hundred inhabitants, who dwelt chiefly in thatched cottages, which straggled over the ground, too near together for rural beauty, too far apart to seem snug and neighborly; and scattered through the gardens and orchards around the best of these were neglected stables, cow-yards, and sheep-cotes. Many of the meaner houses were without chimneys or glazed windows. The streets were cumbered with logs and blocks, and foul with offal, mud, muck-heaps, and reeking stable refuse, the

accumulation of which the town ordinances and
the infliction of fines could not prevent, even before the doors of the better sort of people. The
very first we hear of John Shakespeare himself,
in 1552, is that he and a certain Humphrey Rey-
nolds and Adrian Quiney "*fecerunt sterquina-
rium*" in the quarter called Henley Street, against
the order of the court; for which dirty piece of
business they were "*in misericordia*," as they well
deserved. But the next year John Shakespeare
and Adrian Quiney repeated the unsavory offence,
and this time in company with the bailiff himself.
This noisome condition of their streets, however,
did not indicate a peculiar carelessness of dirt
among the Stratford folk, at a time when in noblemen's houses, and even in palaces, the great halls,
in which the household ate, were offensive, because
the rushes with which the floors were strewed, by
way of carpet, remained until they became mouldy,
and beneath were bones and crusts, dogs' refuse,
that were left there to decay. Launce gives us a
glimpse of the habits and manners of those days,
in that touching remonstrance which he addresses
to Crab, upon his sad misbehavior when he was
presented to Madam Silvia. But, with the strange,
sad incongruity of early times, although squalor
and discomfort thus pervaded the little town of
Stratford, it had public structures beautiful and
venerable, — such as now-a-days would not be
erected in a place of fifty times its size. Now, a

rich river-side city of fifty thousand inhabitants, nearly all of whom are comfortably, and a large proportion of them elegantly, housed, is content to be approached over a serviceable wooden bridge, resting on strong, but homely, stone piers; the people worship according to their choice in various, perhaps pretty, but almost surely unpretending churches; if there be other market than the butchers' and hucksters' stalls scattered through the streets, it presents no other attractions than those of convenience and cleanliness; and there is no private dwelling so superior and lofty, that it looks down upon the others round it as the homes of an inferior caste. But the little nest of plaster-walled, thatch-roofed cottages, most of them of a single floor, in which William Shakespeare was born, was approached by a noble stone bridge of fourteen arches, built at his own expense by Sir Hugh Clopton, a Stratford grandee and Mayor of London. The single parish church was a collegiate foundation, and had had a chantry of five priests. In size it was superior to, and in general appearance not unlike, the largest church in the United States, its namesake Trinity, in New York. Its interior walls were decorated with rude but striking fresco paintings, representing, among other subjects, some groups of the Dance Macabre, otherwise known as the Dance of Death; and around its aisles and chancel end were monuments and effigies of departed great folk of that neigh-

borhood.   There was the Chapel of the Guild of
the Holy Cross, a fine, well-proportioned building
of the earlier Tudor style of ecclesiastical architecture, and some parts of it very much older,
which, after the dissolution of religious houses by
that conscientious Protestant, Henry VIII., had
been used by the endowed and incorporated
Grammar School of Stratford.   The walls of this
building were also decorated with paintings of
sacred and historical subjects.   In the open place,
where the markets and the fairs were held, was a
market cross with clock and belfry, from the steps
of which the public crier performed his clamorous
duty.   Hard by the Chapel of the Guild was the
Great House, or New Place, a grand mansion
then a hundred years old, and more, built by Sir
Hugh Clopton, of bridge memory, who lived and
died there ; and near the Great House was the
college, a fine monastic structure, which had been
converted into a dwelling, and where lived one
John a Combe, a wealthy gentleman who lent
money upon interest and good security.   From
the narrow limits of the town the country stretched
away, with gentle undulations, into a broad expanse
of meadows and cornfields, bright with grass and
grain, laced with little brooks and divided by the
ever stone-bridged Avon, dotted with old clumps
of trees, darkened with remnants of the ancient
forest, enlivened with rustic hamlets, and adorned
with parks and gardens.   Clopton House, old,

manorial, and substantial, the home of Sir Hugh's
·family, was only two miles off; and about four
miles distant, on another road, was Charlecote, a
new country-seat built by Sir Thomas Lucy, in
the form of an E, to please his royal mistress, in-
satiable of flattery. Only nine miles away was
the county town, and the grand old feudal pile of
Warwick Castle, dating back to the time of Alfred,
of which William Shakespeare's maternal ancestor
had been governor; and five miles farther was
Kenilworth, not quite so old, but not less magnifi-
cent, where the Earl of Leicester, the Queen's
favorite, was lately come as lord, and where within
a few years he had spent £60,000, or according
to our present measure of value $1,500,000, in
making the place grand and beautiful.

It was in such a town and amid such a country
that William Shakespeare passed his early years;
and a glance at them has been worth our while;
for when he left them for a wider, busier, and more
varied field of observation, marvellous as were the
flexibility of his nature and the range and activity
of his thought, his memory never lost the forms,
nor did his soul cast off the influences, which had
surrounded him in boyhood. As to the people of
Stratford, they were much like others of their class
and condition; simple folk, contentedly looking
after their fields, their cattle, and their little trade,
not troubling themselves about the great world
which lay beyond their ken, but somewhat over-

ready to take the law of one another upon small
provocation, and strongly inclined to Puritanism.
If they had one trait which seems more prominent
than any other, it was a great capacity for liquor,
which they tested on every possible occasion.
The sums which they spent in providing themselves and each other, and the strangers within
their gates, with ale possets, claret, and sack and
sugar, must have been no small proportion of the
yearly outlay of the town. And yet perhaps in
this respect they were but of their day and generation.

What was the education of William Shakespeare were a question indeed of interest to all
reasonable creatures, and to those who think that
education makes great men, of singular importance. But of his teachers we know nothing,
save of one, — his father. What were his mother's traits of character, and whether she had
transmitted any of them to her son, we cannot
tell. In which ignorance there is a kind of bliss to
those people who have taken up the novel notion
of the day, that men of mark derive their mental
and their moral gifts, not from the father, but the
mother. A fungus fancy, which must have sprung
up while men could forget that Philip the Great
of Macedon was eclipsed by his son Alexander;
that there was a family of Scipios, all eminent;
that Hamilcar, one of the master generals and

statesmen of antiquity, would have come down to us as the great Carthaginian, had his abilities and his fortunes not been surpassed by those of his son Hannibal; that Charles Martel, a born king of men, who founded a great monarchy, was father to Pepin, who, with the new-created power which he inherited, inherited also the ability to preserve, to consolidate, and extend it, and whose son was the central figure of the Middle Ages, the imperial Charlemagne; that Henry II., great after the fashion of his time and of the Plantagenets, transmitted all his energy, his craft, and his military genius to his son Richard the Lion-hearted, great also after the Plantagenet fashion, and who equalled him in most of his qualities and surpassed him in others; that strong-minded, strong-willed Henry VIII. had his strong-minded, strong-willed daughter Elizabeth by that weak coquette, Anne Boleyn; that his great Lord Chancellor, Sir Thomas More, was son to Sir Thomas More, Justice of the King's Bench, a man "of excellent wit and judgment," yet surpassed by his son in these points, as in others; that William, the great Prince of Orange, was succeeded by his son, Prince Maurice of Nassau, one of the two great captains of his day; that William Pitt, called "the Great Commoner," who became Earl of Chatham, had for his son the other William Pitt, the greater commoner, while Chatham's most formidable rival, Henry Fox,

who raised himself to be first Lord Holland,
transmitted his talents, though not his titles or
his lands, to his yet more eminent son, Charles
James Fox; and that Julius Scaliger would have
been the first of scholars and critics, had not the
splendid abilities of his son, Joseph Scaliger, made
him the second. The Mendelssohn who came
between Moses the scholar and Felix the musician used smilingly to say that he was the son
of the great Mendelssohn and the father of the
great Mendelssohn. But this single case would
prove nothing, even if it were true that the mid-
dleman had a woman of mark for his wife. Intellect, like gout, sometimes skips a generation,
yet none the less follows the blood; but sometimes it is also inherited by immediate descent.
The truth is, that upon the very interesting
subject of transmitted qualities in the human
race, we know almost nothing. But we do know
that, in Shakespeare's own words, "good wombs
have borne bad sons"; and even a little observation will discover that the converse is equally
true, and that mothers, as well as fathers, of vicious character or feeble intellect have had children born to them upon whose moral integrity
or mental endowments they have looked with
perplexity and wonder.*

* Whoever thinks this subject of sufficient interest and moment to examine it, could not fail, I am sure, to add many similar
and perhaps more striking examples to those above mentioned,

Mary Arden may have been such a woman as it would please us to imagine the mother of William Shakespeare; but the limits of our knowledge oblige us to look upon him during childhood only under the tutelage of the father, whose good sense and strong character are shown by his rapid and steady rise of fortune and his advancement among his townsmen. His son was taught, we may be sure, to fear God and honor the King,* and, in the words of the Catechism, to learn and labor truly to get his own living, and do his duty in that state of life to which it had pleased God to call him; for that was the sum and substance of the

which have occurred to me only as I have been writing. In the brief annals of this Republic we find the two Adamses, John and John Quincy, father and son; and Daniel Webster, the equal in intellectual capacity of any statesman of his generation, had for his sire a man of such singular ability and great force of character, that we cannot be sure that his son surpassed him, except by reason of a higher culture and a wider field of labor. From the memoir of his life by George Nesmith, we learn that he went through with honor an amount of public service rarely rendered by a single individual. He was a "Selectman" in Salisbury nine years, Town-Clerk three years, Representative four years, Senator four years, a Delegate to two State Constitutional Conventions, Elector for President when Washington was first chosen to that office, a county magistrate thirty-five years, and a Judge of the Court of Common Pleas fifteen years, which office he held at the time of his death in 1806. Judge Webster also filled several offices in the village church, was elected chairman of the town-meeting in Salisbury forty-three times; he served in the "Old French War," was a captain during the Revolution, and a colonel in 1784.

* "*Moriamur pro rege nostro,*" — as applicable to Elizabeth of England as to Maria Theresa of Hungary.

home-teaching of our forefathers. For book instruction, there was the Free Grammar School of
Stratford, well endowed by Thomas Jolyffe in the
reign of Edward IV., — forever therefore let his
name be honored! — where, unless it differed from
all others of its kind, he could have learned Latin
and some Greek. Some English too; but not
much, for English was held in scorn by the
scholars of those days, and long after. The only
qualifications for admission to this school were
residence in the town, seven years of age, and
ability to read. That the sons of the chief alderman of Stratford went there, we could hardly
have entertained a doubt, even had not Betterton
learned the tradition that William had been bred
there for some .time. The masters of the school
between 1572 and 1580 were Thomas Hunt, the
parson of the neighboring village of Luddington,
and Thomas Jenkins. Had either the Englishman or the Welshman known when they breeched
Shakespeare *primus* that he would have his revenge in making the one sit for his portrait as
Holofernes, and the other as Sir Hugh Evans,
they would doubtless have taken out their satisfaction grievously in advance upon the spot.
Could any one with power of conviction upon his
tongue have told them what he was whom they
were flogging, they would have dropped the birch
and fled the school in awe unspeakable. There is
better discipline, even for a dull or a vicious boy,

than beating ; but, aside from question of the kind
of training to which he was subjected, it was well
perhaps for William Shakespeare that his masters
knew only what he then was.   Insight of the
future would not always bring good fortune.

At school Shakespeare acquired some knowledge of Latin and of Greek.   For not only does
Ben Jonson tell us that he had a little of the
former and less of the latter, but his very frequent
use of Latin derivatives in their radical sense
shows a somewhat thoughtful and observant study
of that language ; and although he has left fewer
traces of his personal feelings and experience upon
his works than any modern writer, he wrote one
passage bearing upon this subject, and telling a
plain story.   Warwick, pleading to King Henry
IV. in extenuation of the fondness of Prince Hal
for wild associates, says : —

> "My gracious lord, you look beyond him quite.
> The Prince but studies his companions,
> Like a strange tongue ; wherein, to gain the language,
> 'T is needful that the most immodest word
> Be look'd upon and learn'd ; which once attain'd,
> Your Highness knows, comes to no farther use,
> But to be known and hated."
>
> *Second Part of King Henry IV.*, Act IV. Sc. 4.

Genius does not teach facts ; and every man who
has himself been through the curriculum will see
that the writer of that passage had surely, at least,
passed through the same course before the days
of expurgated classics.   Jonson's phrase, " small

Latin and less Greek," has been generally taken
as meaning a mere smattering of the first, and
nothing at all of the second; but without sufficient reason, in my opinion. So does Edward
Bathurst, B. D., in his memoir of his friend Arthur
Wilson, the author of *The Inconstant Ladie*, written before 1646, say that " He had little skill in
the Latin tongue and less in the Greek, a good
readiness in the French and some smattering in
the Dutch";* and yet, according to the same
authority, Wilson had been a fellow-commoner of
Trinity College, Oxford, where he had been regular and studious; and by his own account he
could, at a pinch, speak Latin.† Little and much
are comparative terms, the value of which can be
determined only when we know the standard according to which they are used. Jonson's scholarship, though not profound or various, seems to
have been somewhat thorough and exact, and
Bathurst was probably a man entirely given up
to study. Both, we may be sure, would speak
very lightly of the Latin and Greek of many men
now-a-days who have well earned their degree of
Master of Arts, and who can make good use of
their academical acquirements. From report and
from the evidence of his works we may reasonably
conclude that William Shakespeare read, as boys

---

* " Character of Wilson," &c., in the Appendix to *The Inconstant Ladie*. Ed. 1814, p. 156.

† " Observations of God's Providence in the Tract of my
Life." *Ibid.*, p. 128.

read, the easier classical Latin authors at Stratford Grammar School, and added to them the favorite of that day, old Baptista Mantuan, whom
he quotes in *Love's Labor 's Lost*, and that he retained enough of what he learned to have thereby
a finer insight and more thorough mastery of
English, if not to enjoy Virgil and Terence in the
original. It is true, as Farmer has shown, that
his works furnish evidence undeniable that in preparing himself to write upon Greek and Roman
subjects he used the existing translations of the
classics. But how many who for years have spent
a part of every day in the study of Greek and
Latin do the same, when college exercises are
driven out of mind by the duties and labors for
which college studies are but discipline, and turn
laboriously from translation to original only when
they wish to examine some particular passage
closely. When, in *The Taming of the Shrew*,
Tranio quotes a passage from Terence, he is in-
accurate, and gives it not as it appears in the text
of the Latin dramatist, but as it is misquoted in the
Latin Grammar of William Lilly, whose accidence
was in common use among our forefathers when
Shakespeare was a boy, and held its place indeed
much longer.* But, even if this showed that

---

* "Quid agas? nisi ut te redimas captum quam queas
Minimo."
Eunuchus, Act I. Sc. I.

"Redime te captum quam queas minimo."
The Taming of the Shrew, Act I. Sc. I.

Shakespeare had not read Terence, which it does
not, it surely does show that he had studied Master Lilly's book, which, be it remembered, is itself
not in English, but in Latin, after the strange,
pedantic fashion of the times when it was written.
The scene between Sir Hugh and William, in
The Merry Wives of Windsor, is as surely evidence of the writer's knowledge of the Latin grammar. "*Singulariter, nominativo, hic, hæc, hoc,*"
does not lie very far beyond the threshold of that
elementary book ; but the question which elicits
the declension, "What is he, William, that does
lend articles?" by which the pragmatic parson
tries to trip the poor boy up, although borrowed
from Lilly, shows an intelligent acquaintance with
the rudiments of the Latin language.

Italian and French, we may be sure, were not
taught at Stratford Grammar School ; but this is
the most convenient occasion on which to say that
Shakespeare appears to have learned something
of them before he became too busy a man to
study. It was probably in his earlier London
years. Both these languages, and especially the
former, were much in vogue among the cultivated
people of that period. Shakespeare was likely to
be thrown into the society of those who taught
them ; and their instructions he might well re-
quite, if he were sparing of money, by orders of
admission to the theatre, which have been held
to pay many a larger debt in later times. He

has left several traces of a knowledge of Italian,
which might be great or small, scattered through
his plays; but in two passages there are indications of an acquaintance with two Italian poets,
which, though hitherto passed by, cannot, I think,
be mistaken. When Othello, in the dawning of
his jealousy, chides Desdemona for being without
the handkerchief, his first love-token, he tells her:

> "There's magic in the web of it.
> A sibyl, that had number'd in the world
> The sun to course two hundred compasses,
> In her prophetic fury, sew'd the work."

The phrase "prophetic fury" is so striking, so
picturesque, and so peculiar, that in itself it excites remark, and remains upon the memory as
the key-note of the passage; but when we regard
it as applied to mood in which a web was woven
or embroidered, all these characteristics are much
enhanced. Now in the *Orlando Furioso* there is
the following passage about a tent which Cas-
sandra gave to Hector, and which descended
through Cleopatra to Constantine, who gave it
to Melissa:—

> "Eran de gli anni appresso che duo milia
> Che fu quel ricco padiglion trapunto.
> Una donzella de la terra d' Ilia
> Ch' avea il furor profetico congiunto
> Con studio di gran tempo e con vigilia,
> Lo fece di sua man, di tutto punto." *
>
> Canto XLVI. St. 80.

* Thus rendered by Rose:—

> "Two thousand tedious years were nigh complete,
> Since this fair work was fasioned by the lore

Here we have the identical thought, and, in their Italian form, the identical words, *furor profetico*, used in the description of a woman, sibyl-like, if not a sibyl, weaving a cloth of magic virtues. There is, too, in both passages, the idea of a great lapse of time, though in one it is applied to the weaver and in the other to the thing woven. It would seem impossible that this striking coincidence of thought, of incident, and of language could be merely accidental; and there was no other translation of the *Orlando Furioso* into English in Shakespeare's time than Sir John Harrington's, published in 1591, and in that the phrase "prophetic fury," or any one like it, does not occur.*

Again, when Iago, distilling his poison into Othello's ears, utters the often quoted lines, —

"Who steals my purse, steals trash; 't is something, nothing;
'T was mine, 't is his, and has been slave to thousands;
But he that filches from me my good name
Robs me of that which not enriches him,
And makes me poor indeed," —

he but repeats with little variation this stanza of Berni's *Orlando Innamorato*, of which poem, to this day, there is no English version: —

Of Trojan maid, warmed with prophetic heat;
Who 'mid long labor, and 'mid vigil sore,
With her own fingers all the storied sheet
Of the pavilion had embroidered o'er."

* See Harrington's *Orlando Furioso in English*, Canto XLVI. St. 64, ed. 1591.

> "Chi ruba un corno un cavallo un anello,
> E simil cose, ha qualche discrezione,
> E potrebbe chiamarsi ladroncello ;
> Ma quel che ruba la reputazione,
> E de l' altrui fatiche si fa bello,
> Si puo chiamare assassino e ladrone ;
>   E tanto più odio e pena è degno
>   Quanto più del dover trapassa il segno." *

Canto LL St. 1.

Now, when we consider that the faculty and habit of assimilating what he read was one of Shakespeare's mental traits, and that both these passages of his, so identical in thought and in expression with others in two Italian poets who wrote on kindred subjects, occur in a play founded upon an Italian novel which had not been rendered into our language in his day, can we reasonably doubt that he was sufficiently an Italian scholar to read Ariosto, Berni, and Giraldi Cinthio in the original ? †

---

* As no English translation has been made of the *Orlando Innamorato*, I must ask the reader who cannot command the original to be content with this rendering of the above stanza : —

> The man who steals a horn, a horse, a ring,
>   Or such a trifle, thieves with moderation,
> And may be justly called a robberling ;
>   But he who takes away a reputation,
> And pranks in feathers from another's wing,
>   His deed is robbery, assassination,
> And merits punishment so much the greater
> As he to right and truth is more a traitor.

† Mr. Halliwell in his Life of William Shakespeare, p. 190, quotes from a MS. entitled *The New Metamorphosis*, which was

The consideration of this subject has diverted
us from the course of Shakespeare's life, and has
given us an anticipatory glance of one of its few
landmarks; which, however, are so well known,
that I have not sought and shall not seek solici-
tously to follow them in due order.

John Shakespeare's prosperity hardly lasted to
his eldest son's adolescence. Betterton heard a
tradition, that the narrowness of his circumstances and the need of his son's assistance at
home forced him to withdraw William from
school; and the evidence of town registers and
of court records corroborates the story. In 1578,
when the young poet was but fourteen years old,
his father mortgaged the farm at Ashbies for
forty pounds to Edmund Lambert. That this
step was taken, not to raise money for a venture
in trade or for a new purchase, but on account of
serious embarrassment, is shown by a concur-

---

written "by J. M. Gent. 1600," the following lines, which he, not
having Berni's stanza in mind, naturally regards as an imitation
of the passage of *Othello* in question, and therefore, of course,
as evidence that that play was written before the date of the
MS. : —

> "The highwayman that robs one of his purse
> Is not soe bad; nay, these are ten times worse!
> For these doe rob men of their pretious name,
> And in exchange give obloquy and shame."

But J. M.'s lines are, on the contrary, a manifest imitation of
Berni's, rather than Shakespeare's; and if they have any bearing at all upon the question of the date of *Othello*, (which in my
opinion they have not,) they show that it was written after 1600.

rence of significant events, all pointing in the
latter direction.   In the same year when his fellow-aldermen assessed themselves 6s. 8d. each towards the equipment of pikemen, billmen, and
an archer, he is set down as to pay only 3s. 4d.
Again in that year when the aldermen paid 4d.
each a week for the relief of the poor, it was ordered that John Shakespeare should not be taxed
to pay anything.   In March, 1578–9, the inhabitants of Stratford having been assessed for the
purchase of arms, he failed to contribute his
quota.   In October, 1579, he sold his wife's share
in the Snitterfield property, and in 1580 a reversionary interest in the same, — the latter for forty
pounds.   Six years afterwards his little wealth
had found such wings that, a distraint having
been issued against him, the return made upon it
was, that he had nothing upon which to distrain ;
whereupon a writ of *capias* was issued against his
person, — he who as high bailiff had but a short
time before issued such writs against others.*
He seems even to have been in hiding about this
time ; for the town records show that in 1586 he
was deprived of his alderman's office, the reason
given being that " Mr. Shaxpere dothe not come
to the halles when they be warned, nor hathe not
done of longe tyme " ; and it appears, on the
same authority, that he had thus absented him-

* The Shakespeare Society of London was in possession of
two such writs.

self for seven years. But before March of the
next year he had been arrested, and was imprisoned or in custody, doubtless for debt, according
to the barbarous and foolish practice of which our
brethren in the mother country have not yet rid
themselves. This we know by his suing out a
writ of *habeas corpus* in the Stratford Court of
Record. Perhaps he suffered this indignity on
account of his kindness to his brother Henry, before mentioned, who had much money trouble,
and for whom he became surety to one Nicholas
Lane for ten pounds. Henry not having duly
paid this sum, Lane sued John Shakespeare for
it in February, 1587. To follow his sad fortunes
yet further, in 1592 a commission, upon which
were Sir Thomas Lucy and Sir Fulke Greville
with six others, which had been appointed to inquire into the conformity of the people of Warwickshire to the established religion, with a
special eye to Jesuits, priests, and recusants, reported many persons "for not comming moneth-
lie to the churche, according to hir Majestie's
lawes"; and among them was John Shakespeare.
But the commissioners specially note as to him
and eight others, that "it is sayd that these last
nine coom not to churche for fear of processe for
debtte."

Thus low in fortune and estate had sunk the
once prosperous high bailiff of Stratford, in the
veins of whose children ran the blood of men who

had owned half the county through which he skulked, a bailiff-hunted debtor. Those very children added largely to his anxiety and his cares. For since Margaret's death six had been born to him: William; Gilbert, born in 1566; a second Joan, in 1569; Anne, in 1571; Richard, in 1573-4; and Edmund, in 1580. Rowe, upon Betterton's authority, says that John Shakespeare had "ten children in all." But Betterton only reported tradition; and the Stratford parish register, better authority on such a point, records the baptism of no more than eight, two of whom, as we have seen, died before their father reached the height of his prosperity; and Anne died at the beginning of his troubles. At her burial there were both pall and bell, for which it has been discovered that eight pence were paid, while other children buried in the same year (1579) were honored with only half the ceremony, the bell, at half the price. This has been accepted as evidence that John Shakespeare had money to spare. He doubtless meant that it should be so regarded; and he deceived even posterity. As long as funeral ceremonies are deemed important, they will be the last as to which poverty will compel retrenchment. In 1579 John Shakespeare had not abandoned the struggle to keep up appearances. Had his purse been fuller, or his position lower, he might have been willing to save the four pence. But a few years later five little mouths to feed,

five little backs to clothe, were quite enough to
harass the poor man who could not keep his
own body out of a debtor's prison, and to cause
him to abandon any ambitious projects which he
might have formed for his eldest son, and call him
from his studies to contribute something to his own
support, and perhaps to that of the family.

The traditions of the townsfolk upon this subject were surely therefore in the main well
founded, though in their particulars they were
discordant.   Rowe, speaking for Betterton, says,
that "upon his leaving school he seems to have
given entirely into that way of living which his
father proposed to him," which, according to the
same authority, was that of a dealer in wool.
Gossiping John Aubrey, who says that John
Shakespeare was a butcher, adds : "I have been
told heretofore by some of the neighbors that
when he was a boy he exercised his father's
trade ; but when he kill'd a calfe he wold
doe it in a high style, and make a speeche."
Aubrey, who died about 1700, probably received
this precious information from the same source
through which an old parish clerk of Stratford,
who was living in 1693, and was then more than
eighty years old, derived a similar story, that
Shakespeare had been "bound apprentice to a
butcher."   Aubrey also records, on the authority
of an unknown Mr. Beeston, that William Shakespeare "understode Latin pretty well, for he had

been many years a schoolmaster in the country."
The only point upon which these loose traditions
are of importance is that upon which they all conform to probability, that William Shakespeare was
obliged to leave school early and earn his living.*

* Isolated passages in Shakespeare's plays have been gravely
brought forward to sustain each of these traditions as to his early
occupation, — surely a wise and penetrative method of getting at
the truth in such a matter. Let us see. When we read a passage like this in *King Henry the Sixth*, —

> "Who finds the heifer dead and bleeding fresh,
> And sees fast by the butcher with an axe,
> But will suspect 't was he that made the slaughter?"—

what way to avoid concluding that the writer had been himself a
butcher? Consider, too, the profound inner significance of this
passage in *Love's Labour's Lost*, in which Holofernes describes
Sir Nathaniel: "He is too picked, too spruce, too affected, too
odd, as it were, too peregrinate, as I may call it. . . . He draweth out the thread of his verbosity finer than the staple of his
argument." Is there not a goodly part of the wool-stapler's art,
as well as of the art of rhetoric, compressed into that last sentence by the power of Shakespeare's genius? And is it not thus
made clear that he was practically initiated into the mysteries
of long and short staple before he wrote this, one of the earliest
of his plays? But, again, ponder the following lines in *King
Henry the Sixth*, written when the memory of his boyish days
was freshest, and see evidence that both these traditions were
well founded : —

> "So, first the harmless sheep doth yield his fleece,
> And next his throat, unto the butcher's knife."

Certainly these lines could have been written only by a man who
was *both* the son of a considerable dealer in wool, and a butcher,
who killed calves in high style, making a speech. Who, appreciating rightly the following passage in *Hamlet*, can have a doubt
about this matter?

Utterly ruined, however, as John Shakespeare was, he seems never to have been driven out of his house in Henley Street, or to have lost his property in it; though how this could be in the case of a man as to whom the return upon an execution was "no effects," it is not easy to conjecture.

> "Our indiscretion sometimes serves us well
> When our deep plots do fall; and that should teacn us
> There's a divinity that shapes our ends,
> Rough-hew them how we will."

Upon which thus discourse two acute and learned commentators. George Steevens speaks: —

"Dr. Farmer informs me that these words are merely technical. A woolman, butcher, and dealer in *skewers* lately observed to him that his nephew (an idle lad) could only *assist* him in making them. 'He could *rough-hew* them, but I was obliged to shape their ends!' To shape the ends of wool-skewers, i. e. to *point* them, requires a degree of skill; any one can *rough-hew* them. Whoever recollects the profession of Shakespeare's father will admit that his son might be no stranger to such terms. I have frequently seen packages of wool pinn'd up with skewers."

What a revelation at once of the unknown outer and that more mysterious inner life of Shakespeare! Lucky wool-man, butcher, and dealer in skewers! to furnish thus a comment upon the great philosophical tragedy, and proof that you and its author were both of a trade. Fortunate Farmer, to have heard the story! and most sagacious Steevens, to have penetrated its hidden meaning, recollecting felicitously that you had seen packages of wool pinned up with skewers! But, O wisest, highest, and deepest-minded Shakespeare! to have remembered, as you were propounding, Hamlet-wise, one of the great unsolvable mysteries of life, the skewers that you, being an idle lad, could but rough-hew, leaving to your careful father the skill-requiring task of shaping their ends! — ends without which they could not have bound together the packs of wool with which you loaded

But what was William Shakespeare doing in all those years through which his father was descending into the vale of poverty, whither we have followed him to the lowest depth? We have passed over thereby some events of great importance to the son, whom his father's trials seem not

carts at the door in Henley Street, or have penetrated the veal of the calves you killed in such high style and with so much eloquence, and which loaded the tray you daily bore on your shoulder to the kitchen-door of New Place, yet unscheming to become its master!

Yet I would not insist too strongly upon this evidence that Shakespeare's boyhood was passed as a butcher's and wool-stapler's apprentice; because I venture to think that I have discovered like evidence in his works that their author was a tailor. For in the first place I have found that the word "tailor" appears in his plays no less than twenty-seven times! "Measures" occurs nearly thrice as often; "shears," no less than six times; "thimble," thrice; "goose," no less than twenty-seven times! And when we see that in all his thirty-seven plays "cabbage" occurs but once, and then with the careful explanation that it means roots, and is "good cabbage," must we not regard such reticence upon this tender point as touching confirmation of the theory sartorical? His plays abound with like evidence. He says of the use to which his favorite hero Prince Hal will put the manners of his wild companions, that

> "Their memory
> Shall as *a pattern or a measure* live
> By which his Grace must meet the lives of others."

He makes one of the Two Gentlemen of Verona, as his severest censure of the other, reproach him with being badly dressed: —

> "Ruffian, let go that rude uncivil touch,
> Thou friend of *an ill fashion!*"

And how unmistakably he gives us in *Hamlet* a reminiscence of a highly ornamented style of children's clothing: —

to have chastened into sobriety. In estimating Shakespeare's character, the fact that he left among his neighbors the reputation of having been somewhat irregular in his youth cannot be lightly set aside. Nor is it at all strange that such a reputation should have been attained in the early years of a man of his lively fancy, healthy organization, and breadth of moral sympathy. It is from tradition that we learn that during his father's misfortunes he was occasionally engaged in stealing deer ; but we know on good evidence that about that time he also got himself married in no very creditable fashion. While he was sowing his wild oats in the fields round Stratford, he naturally visited the cottage of Richard Hathaway, a substantial yeoman of Shottery, who seems to have been on terms of friendship with John Shakespeare. This Richard Hathaway had,

> "The canker galls the infants of the Spring
> Too oft before *their buttons* be disclosed."

What more natural than that a tailor, vexed with the memories of peevish customers, should make the incensed Northumberland compare himself to a man who is "impatient of his fit "? And yet this evidence, so strong and cumulative, must not be too much relied upon. For who but a publisher, anxious about the health and the progress in her work of a popular authoress, could have written thus in *Twelfth Night?*

> "Lady, you are the cruell'st she alive,
> If you will lead these graces to the grave
> And leave the world *no copy*."

The subject expands illimitably before me, and I resign it to the followers of Farmer and of Steevens, and to the Germans.

among other children, a daughter named Anne, who might have dandled William Shakespeare in his infancy upon her knee; for she was eight years old when he was born, in 1564. Whether or no Anne Hathaway had a fair face and a winning way which spontaneously captivated William Shakespeare, or whether he yielded to arts to which his inexperience made him an easy victim, we cannot surely tell. But we do know that she, though not vestally inclined, as we shall see, remained unmarried until 1582, and that then the woman of twenty-six took to husband the boy of eighteen. They were married upon once asking of the banns; and the bond given to the Bishop of Worcester for his security in licensing this departure from custom was given in that year, on the 28th day of November.* About those days

---

* "Noverint universi per præsentes nos ffulconem Sandells de Stratford in comitatu Warwici, agricolam, et Johannem Rychardson ibidem agricolam, teneri et firmiter obligari Ricardo Cosin generoso, et Roberto Warmstry notario publico, in quadraginta libris bonæ et legalis monetæ Angliæ, solvend. eisdem Ricardo et Roberto, hæred. execut. vel assignat. suis, ad quam quidem solucionem bene et fideliter faciend. obligamus nos et utrumque nostrum per se pro toto et in solid. hæred. executor. et administrator. nostros firmiter per præsentes sigillis nostris sigillat. Dat. 28 die Novem. anno regni dominæ nostræ Eliz. Dei gratia Angliæ, Franc. et Hiberniæ reginæ, fidei defensor, &c. 25.

"The condicion of this obligacion ys suche, that if herafter there shall not appere any lawfull lett or impediment, by reason of any precontract, consangui[ni]tie, affinitie, or by any other lawfull meanes whatsoever, but that William Shagspere one thone partie, and Anne Hathwey of Stratford in the dioces of Worces-

there was great need that Anne Hathaway should provide herself with a husband of some sort, and that speedily; for in less than five months after she obtained one she was delivered of a daughter. The parish register shows that Susanna, the daughter of William and Anne Shakespeare, was baptized May 26th, 1583.

There have been attempts to turn aside the obvious bearings of these facts upon the character of Anne Hathaway. But it is a stubborn and unwise idolatry which resists such evidence as this, — an idolatry which would exempt Shakespeare,

ter, maiden, may lawfully solennize matrimony together, and in the same afterwardes remaine and continew like man and wiffe, according unto the lawes in that behalf provided: and moreover, if there be not at this present time any action, sute, quarrell, or demaund, moved or depending before any judge ecclesiasticall or temporall, for and concerning any suche lawfull lett or impediment: and moreover, if the said William Shagspere do not proceed to solemnizacion of mariadg with the said Anne Hathwey without the consent of hir frindes: and also, if the said William do, upon his owne proper costes and expences, defend and save harmles the right reverend Father in God, Lord John Bushop of Worcester, and his offycers, for licensing them the said William and Anne to be maried together with once asking of the bannes of matrimony betweene them, and for all other causes which may ensue by reason or occasion thereof, that then the said obligacion to be voyd and of none effect, or els to stand and abide in full force and vertue."

To this instrument are attached the rude marks of Sandells and Richardson, and a seal which bears two letters, R, and another, imperfect, which seems to be an H. This seal is conjectured to be that of the bride's father, who at the execution of the bond had been dead five months.

and not only him, but all with whom he became connected, from human passion and human frailty. That temperament is cruel, and that morality pharisaic, which treats all cases of this kind with inexorable and indiscriminating severity, and that judgment outrageously unjust which visits all the sin upon the weaker and already suffering party. Yet if in the present instance it must be that one or other of this couple seduced the other into error, perhaps where a woman of twenty-six is involved with a boy of eighteen, for the honor of her sex the less that is said about the matter the better. Besides, Anne Hathaway rests under the implied reproach of both the men whose good opinion was to her of gravest moment. Her father, like Mary Arden's, had died about a year before her marriage; but while Mary Arden had special legacies, and was assigned to the honorable position of executrix by her father's will, Anne Hathaway was passed over even without mention by her father, who yet carefully and minutely remembered all but one of his other children. And to look forward again, — which we well may do, for Shakespeare's wife will soon pass entirely from our sight, — when her husband was giving instructions for his will, he left her only his second-best bed, the one that probably she slept upon. It is true, as Mr. Knight has pointed out, that she was entitled to dower, and that so her livelihood was well provided for; it is true also, that a bed

with its furniture was in those days no uncommon
bequest. But William Shakespeare's will was one
of great particularity, leaving little legacies to
nephews and nieces, and also swords and rings
as mementoes to friends and acquaintance; and
yet his wife's name is omitted from the document
in its original form, and only appears by an after-
thought in an interlineation, as if his attention
had been called to the omission, and for decency's
sake he would not have the mother of his children
unnoticed altogether. The lack of any other bequest than the furniture of her chamber is of small
moment in comparison with the slight shown by
that interlineation. A second-best bed might be
passed over; but what can be done with second-
best thoughts? And second-best, if good at all,
seem to have been all the thoughts which Shakespeare gave her; for there is not a line of his
writing known which can be regarded as addressed to her as maid or matron. Did ever poet
thus slight the woman that he loved, and that too
during years of separation?

The cottage in which Anne Hathaway lived is
still pointed out in Shottery. It is a timber and
plaster house, like John Shakespeare's, standing
on a bank, with a roughly paved terrace in front.
The parlor is wainscoated high in oak; and in the
principal chamber is an enormous and heavily
carved bedstead. Though a rustic and even rude
habitation when measured by our standard, it was

evidently a comfortable home for a substantial yeoman in the time of Queen Elizabeth, and is picturesque enough for the cradle of a poet's love. But it never can be looked upon without sadness by those who rightly estimate the sorrow and the shame which there were born to William Shakespeare, — sorrow and shame which not all the varied successes of his after-life could heal and obliterate, and his sufferings from which find frequent expression both in his plays and sonnets. True, he was of all poets the most dramatic, and therefore the most self-forgetful; but his trouble he did not forget.   His works are full of passages, to write which, if he had loved his wife and honored her, would have been gall and wormwood to his soul; nay, which, if he had loved and honored her, he could not have written.   The nature of the subject forbids the marshalling of this terrible array; but did the "flax-wench" whom he uses for the most degrading of all comparisons do more "before her troth-plight" than the woman who bore his name and whom his children called mother?*   It is not a question whether his judgment was justifiable, but of what he thought and felt.

And even if Anne Hathaway's fair fame, if indeed it was ever fair, remained untarnished, the marriage at eighteen of such a man as her boy husband proved is one of the saddest social events

* *The Winter's Tale*, Act I. Sc. 2.

that can be contemplated. Not because it was singular in all its circumstances or its consequences ; for, alas ! in most of them it is too common. A youth whose person, whose manner, and whose mental gifts have made him the admired favorite of some rural neighborhood, captivated ere he is well a man by some rustic beauty, or often by his own imagination, married and a father before he should be well beyond a father's care, or bound as much in honor, according to the matrimonial code, as if he were married, developing into a man of mark and culture, attaining social position and distinction which would make him the welcome suitor of the fairest and most accomplished woman of the circle into which he has risen by right of worth and intellect, yet tied to one who is inferior to him in all respects, except perhaps in simple truthfulness, and who does not — poor creature, who cannot if she would — keep pace with him ; and all this the consequence of a boyish passion, which opposition might have confirmed, but which tact and a little time — so little ! — might easily have dissipated : this case, so pitiable ! — so pitiable for both parties, even most pitiable for her, — we see too often. But add to all this that the man was William Shakespeare, and that he met his fate at only eighteen years of age, and that the woman who came to him with a stain upon her name was eight years his senior, and could we but think of their life and leave out the world's interest in him, should we not wish that one of them, even if it were he, had died before that ill-starred marriage? But chiefly for him we grieve ; for a woman of her age, who could so connect herself with a boy of his, was either too dull by nature or too callous by experience to share his feelings at their false, unnatural position. Who can believe that the well-known counsel upon this subject which he put into the Duke Orsino's mouth in *Twelfth Night* * was not a stifled cry of anguish from his tormented, over-burdened soul, though he had left his torment and his burden ·so far behind him? It is impossible that he could have written it without thinking of his own experience; the more, that

---

* "*Duke.*   Thou dost speak masterly :
My life upon 't, young though thou art, thine eye
Hath stay'd upon some favor that it loves ;
Hath it not, boy?
    Vio.   A little, by your favor.
    Duke. What kind of woman is 't ?
    Vio.   Of your complexion.
    Duke. She is not worth thee then.   What years, i' faith?
    Vio. About your years, my lord.
    Duke. Too old, by Heaven!   Let still the woman take
An elder than herself; so wears she to him,
So sways she level in her husband's heart.
For, boy, however we do praise ourselves,
Our fancies are more giddy and unfirm,
More longing, wavering, sooner lost and worn,
Than women's are.
    Vio.   I think it well, my lord.
    Duke. Then let thy love be younger than thyself,
Or thy affection cannot hold the bent."
                       Act II. Sc. 4.

the seeming lad to whom it is addressed is about his years, and the man who utters it about Anne Hathaway's, at the time when they were married.

After considering all that has been said, which is quite all that can reasonably be said, about the custom of troth-plight in mitigation of the circumstances of Shakespeare's marriage, I cannot regard the case as materially bettered. It has been urged that Shakespeare put a plea for his wife into the mouth of the Priest in *Twelfth Night*, where the holy man says to Olivia that there had passed between her and Sebastian

> "A contract of eternal bond of love,
>   Confirm'd by mutual joinder of your hands,
>   Attested by the holy close of lips,
>   Strengthen'd by interchangement of your rings ;
>   And all the ceremony of this compact
>   Sealed in my function, by my testimony."
>
> Act V. Sc. I.

But what this was is shown by Olivia's language at the time when it took place, in a passage which the apologists leave out of sight.

> "Blame not this haste of mine. If you mean well,
>   Now go with me, and with this holy man,
>   Into the chantry by: there, before him,
>   And underneath that consecrated roof,
>   ·Plight me the full assurance of your faith ;
>   That my most jealous and too doubtful soul
>   May live at peace. He shall conceal it,
>   Whiles you are willing it shall come to note ;
>   What time we will our celebration keep
>   ·According to my birth. — What do you say ?"
>
> Act IV. Sc. 3.

This plainly was a private marriage, in church and by a priest; indissoluble and perfect, except that it lacked consummation and celebration according to the lady's birth. As to troth-plight, its import depends entirely upon that to which troth is plighted. The closing words of the binding declaration in the marriage ceremony of the Church of England are, "and thereto I plight thee my troth."

The marriage between William Shakespeare and Anne Hathaway took place in December, 1582. The ceremony was not performed in Stratford; and no record of it has been discovered. But there is a tradition in Luddington, a little village not far off, that it took place there; and the story derives some support from the fact that Thomas Hunt, Shakespeare's schoolmaster, was curate of that parish. Susanna, the first child born in this wedlock, was baptized May 26th, 1583; and Hamnet and Judith, twins, were baptized February 2d, 1584-5. William Shakespeare and his wife had no other children; and soon after the latter event their household married life was interrupted for many years by the departure of the youthful husband from Stratford. The eldest son of a ruined man just degraded from office, having four brothers and sisters younger than himself, and a wife and three children upon his hands before he was twenty-one, there were reasons enough for him to go, as he did, to London, if he could get money there more rapidly than at Stratford. But tradi-

tion assigns a particular occasion and other motive
for his leaving home.   Betterton heard, and Rowe
tells us, that he fell into bad company, and that
some of his wild companions, who made a frequent
practice of deer-stealing, drew him into the rob-
bery of a park belonging to Sir Thomas Lucy, of
Charlecote.   For this, according to Rowe's story,
he was prosecuted by the knight, and in revenge
lampooned him in a ballad so bitter that the prosecution became a persecution of such severity that
he was obliged to flee the country, and shelter himself in London.   There is what may perhaps be accepted as independent authority for the existence
of this tradition.   The Reverend William Fulman, an antiquary, who died in 1688, bequeathed
his manuscript biographical memorandums to
the Reverend Richard Davies, Rector of Sapper-
ton in Gloucestershire, and Archdeacon of Lich-
field, who died in 1708.   To a note of Fulman's,
which barely records Shakespeare's birth, death,
and occupation, Davies made brief additions, the
principal of which is, that William Shakespeare
was "much given to all unluckinesse in stealing
venison and rabbits, particularly from S^r —— Lucy, who had him oft whipt and sometimes imprisoned, and at last made him fly his native country,
to his great advancement : but his revenge was so
great that he is his Justice Clodpate, and calls him
a great man, and that in allusion to his name bore
three louses rampant for his arms."   Davies may

have heard this story in Stratford; but considering the date of his death, 1708, and that of Betterton's visit to Warwickshire, 1675, and Rowe's
publication of his edition of Shakespeare's Works,
1709, it is not at all improbable, to say the least,
that the story had reached the Archdeacon directly or indirectly through the actor.* But Capell tells us that a Mr. Thomas Jones, who lived
at Tarbick, a few miles from Stratford, and who
died there in 1703, more than ninety years of age,
remembered having heard from old people at Stratford the story of Shakespeare's robbing Sir Thomas Lucy's park.† According to Mr. Jones their
story agreed with that told by Rowe, with this addition, — that the lampoon was stuck upon the
park gate, and that this insult, added to the injury
of the deer-stealing, provoked the prosecution.
Mr. Jones had written down the first stanza of

* Betterton was born in 1635, and went upon the stage in 1656
or 1657. The veneration for Shakespeare with which he was imbued by the study of his plays was the motive of his pilgrimage
to Stratford. We may be quite sure that the journey was undertaken after 1670, for in that year Shakespeare's granddaughter,
who must have known much that Betterton did not discover, died
in Shakespeare's house; and it could hardly have been after
1675, for at that time the great actor was grievously afflicted with
a disease, — the gout, — which compelled him to retire from the
stage, and from which he suffered until it caused his death, in
1710. Betterton had been taught to play some of Shakespeare's
principal characters by Sir William Davenant, who had seen them
performed by actors of the Black-friars Theatre, who had been instructed by the poet himself. See Downes's *Roscius Anglicanus*.

† *Notes and Various Readings*, &c., Vol. II. p. 75.

this ballad, and it reached Capell through his own grandfather, a contemporary of Jones. A similar account of a very old man living near Stratford, and remembering the deer-stealing story and the ballad, is given by Oldys, the antiquarian, in his manuscript notes. Oldys and Capell plainly derived their information from the same source, though possibly through different channels; and the stanza of the ballad is given by both of them in the same words, with the exception of a single syllable. These are the lines according to Oldys, with the addition of "O" in the last line, which appears in Capell's copy, and which plainly belongs there : —

> "A parliemente member, a justice of peace,
> At home a poor scare-crowe, at London an asse,
> If lowsie is Lucy, as some volke miscalle it,
> Then Lucy is lowsie whatever befall it :
>   He thinks himself greate,
>   Yet an asse in his state
> We allowe by his ears but with asses to mate.
> If Lucy is lowsie, as some volke miscalle it,
> Sing O lowsie Lucy, whatever befall it."

The phrase "Parliament member," if we must accept it as having been originally written in the first line of this lampoon, is inconsistent with its genuineness ; for in Shakespeare's time, and long after, the phrase was Parliament man. But as the verses were handed down orally, a conformity to the more recent custom in this respect would creep in easily and unnoticed.

This story enriches with a rare touch of real life our faint and meagre memorials of Shakespeare. Not sufficiently well established to be beyond the assaults of those who think it scorn that the author of *King Lear* and *Hamlet* should have stolen deer and written coarse lampoons, it yet may well be cherished, and its credibility maintained, by those who prize a trait of character and a glimpse of personal experience above all question of propriety. In Queen Bess's time deerstealing did not rank with sheep-stealing; and he who wrote, and was praised for writing, *The Comedy of Errors* and *Troilus and Cressida* when he was a man, may well be believed, without any abatement of his dignity, to have written the Lucy ballad in his boyhood. Malone thought that he had exploded the tradition by showing that Sir Thomas Lucy had no park, and therefore could have no deer to be stolen; and the lampoon has been set aside as a fabrication by some writers, and regarded by all with suspicion. But it appears that, whether the knight had an enclosure with formal park privileges or not, the family certainly had deer on their estate, which fulfils the only condition requisite for the truth of the story in that regard; for Sir Thomas Lucy, son of Shakespeare's victim, sent a buck as a present to Harehill when Sir Thomas Egerton entertained Queen Elizabeth there in August, 1602.* I think that there is a

* *Egerton Papers*, pp. 350, 355.

solution to the question somewhat different from any that has yet been brought forward, and much more probable.

The first scene of *The Merry Wives of Windsor* certainly gives strong support to the tradition; so strong, in fact, that it has been supposed, with some reason, to have been its origin. In that scene Shakespeare makes Justice Shallow (who, in the words of Davies, is his clodpate, or, as we should say, his clownish or loutish, justice) bear a dozen white luces, or pikes, in his coat of arms, which bearing gives the Welsh parson the opportunity for his punning jest that "the dozen white louses do become an old coat well." * The Lucys bore punning coat-armor, three luces, *hariant;* and the allusion is unmistakable. In that scene, too, the country gentleman who is so proud of the luces in his old coat bursts upon the stage furious at Falstaff for having killed his deer. Now, in Shakespeare's day, as well as long before, killing a gentleman's deer was almost as common among wild young men as robbing a farmer's orchard

* Some critics have attributed the transformation of *luces* to *louses* to Sir Hugh's incapacity of English speech; but this is to rob the Welshman of his wit. The pronunciation of *u* as *ow* is no trick of a Welsh tongue, or of any other, I believe; but "louse" was pronounced like "luce" or "loose" by many people. So the ballad tells us that "lousy is Lucy as some volke miscall it." There is a similar variation as to the name Toucey, which some pronounce *Toosey*, giving the first syllable the vowel sound of *too* and *you*, others *Towsey*, with the sound of *how*, *thou*.

among boys. Indeed, it was looked upon as a sign of that poor semblance of manliness some-times called spirit, and was rather a gentleman's misdemeanor than a yeoman's; one which a peas-ant would not have presumed to commit, except, indeed, at risk of his ears, for poaching at once upon the game- and the sin-preserves of his bet-ters. Noblemen engaged in it; and in days gone by the very first Prince of Wales had been a deer-stealer. Among multitudinous passages illustra-tive of this trait of manners, a story preserved by Wood in his *Athenæ Oxonienses* fixes unmistak-ably the grade of the offence. It is there told, on the authority of Simon Forman, that his patrons, Robert Pinkney and John Thornborough, the lat-ter of whom was admitted a member of Magdalen College in 1570, and became Bishop of Bristol and Worcester, "seldom studied or gave themselves to their books, but spent their time in fencing-schools and dancing-schools, in stealing deer and conies, in hunting the hare and wooing girls." * In fact, deer-stealing then supplied to the young members of the privileged classes in Old England an excite-ment of a higher kind than that afforded by beat-ing watchmen and tearing off knockers and bell-pulls to the generation but just passed away. A passage of *Titus Andronicus*, written soon after Shakespeare reached London, is here in point. Prince Demetrius exclaims:—

* Vol. I. p. 371.

> " What, hast thou not full often struck a doe,
>   And cleanly borne her past the keeper's nose ? "

Whereupon Steevens, wishing to discredit the
play as Shakespeare's, remarks: "We have here
Demetrius, the son of a queen, demanding of his
brother if he has not often been reduced to practise the common artifices of a deer-stealer, — an
absurdity worthy the rest of the piece."   Probably
Steevens had never read in the old chronicle of
Edward of Caernarvon, the first Prince of Wales,
that "King Edward put his son, Prince Edward,
in prison because he had riotously broken into the
park of Walter Langton, Bishop of Chester, and
stolen his deer."   The Prince did this at the instigation of his favorite, that handsome, insolent rake,
Piers de Gaveston ; and he had previously begged
Hugh le Despencer to pardon his "well-beloved
John de Bonynge," who had in like manner broken
into that nobleman's park.   What was pastime
for a Prince of Wales and his companions in the
fourteenth century, might well be regarded as a
venial misdemeanor on the part of a landless
knight, and a mark of spirit in a yeoman's son, in
the sixteenth.

But he with the "three louses rampant" on
his coat makes much more than this of Falstaff's affair.   He will bring it before the Council, he will make a Star-Chamber matter of it, and
pronounces it a riot.   And, in fact, according to
his account, Sir John was not content with steal-

ing his deer, but broke open his lodge and beat his men. It seems then, that, in writing this passage, Shakespeare had in mind not only an actual occurrence in which Sir Thomas Lucy was concerned, but one of greater gravity than a mere deer-stealing affair; that having been made the occasion of more serious outrage.

Now, Sir Thomas Lucy was a man of much consideration in Warwickshire, where he had come to a fine estate in 1551, at only nineteen years of age. He was a member of Parliament twice; first in 1571, and next from November, 1584, to March of the following year; just before the very time when, according to all indications, Shakespeare left Stratford. Sir Thomas was a somewhat prominent member of the Puritanical party, as appears by what is known of his Parliamentary course. For instance, during his first term he was one of a committee appointed upon "defections" in religious matters, one object of the movers of which was "to purge the Common Prayer Book, and free it from certain superstitious ceremonies, as using the sign of the cross in baptism," &c. He was, on the other hand, active in the enforcement and preservation of the game privileges of the nobility and gentry, and served on a committee to which a bill for this purpose was referred, of which he appears to have been chairman. This took place in his last term, 1584 to 1585, — the time of his alleged persecution of

William Shakespeare for poaching. Charlecote,
his seat, being only three miles from Stratford,
and he being a man of such weight and position
in the county, he would naturally have somewhat
close public relations with the towns-people and
their authorities. That such was the case, the
records of the town and of the county furnish
ample evidence. Whenever there was a commission appointed in relation to affairs in that
neighborhood, he was sure to be on it ; and the
Chamberlain's accounts, as set forth by Mr. Halliwell, show expenses at divers times to provide
Sir Thomas with sack and sugar, to expedite or
smooth his intercourse with the corporation. But
in spite of mollifying drinks, the relations of the
Lucy family with the Stratford folk were not
always amicable. Mr. Halliwell's investigations
have shown that the Lucys were not unfrequently
engaged in disputes with the corporation of that
town. Records of one about common of pasture
in Henry VIII.'s time are still preserved in the
Chapter House at London ; and among the papers at the Rolls' House is one containing "the
names of them that made the ryot uppon Master Thomas Lucy, esquier."

Here are all the conditions of a very pretty
parish quarrel. A puritanical knight, fussy about
his family pretensions and his game, having he-
reditary disagreement with the Stratford people
about rights of common, — a subject on which

they were, like all of English race, sure to be tenacious, — after having been left out of Parliament for eleven years, is re-elected, and immediately sets to work at securing that privilege so dearly prized by his class, and so odious to all below it, — the preservation of game for the pastime of the gentry. The anti-puritan party and those who stand up stoutly for rights of common vent their indignation to the best of their ability ; one of their number writes a lampoon upon him, and a body of them, too strong to be successfully withstood, break riotously into his grounds, kill his deer, beat his men, and carry off their booty in triumph. The affair is an outbreak of rude parish politics, a popular demonstration against an unpopular man ; and who so likely to take part in it as the son of the former high bailiff, who, we know, was no puritan, and whose father, ambitious, and, as we shall see, even pretending to a coat of arms, had most probably had personal and official disagreements with, and received personal slights and rebuffs from, his rich, powerful, arrogant neighbor, — or who so likely to write the lampoon as young Will Shakespeare? There could hardly have been two in Stratford who were able to write that stanza, the rhythm of which shows no common clodpole's ear, and which, though coarse in its satire, is bitter and well suited to the occasion. That it is a genuine production, — that is, part of a ballad written

E

at the time for the purpose of lampooning Sir Thomas Lucy, — I think there can be no doubt: it carries its genuineness upon its face and in its spirit. That Shakespeare wrote it, I am inclined to believe. But even were he not its author, if he had taken any part in a demonstration against Sir Thomas Lucy, and soon after was driven, by whatever circumstances, to leave Stratford for London, where he rose to distinction as a poet, rumor would be likely soon to attribute the ballad to him, and to assign the occasion on which it was written as that which caused his departure ; and rumor would soon become tradition.* That Shakespeare meant to pay off a Stratford debt to Sir Thomas Lucy in that first scene of *The Merry Wives*, and that he did it with the memory of the riotous trespass upon that gentleman's grounds, seem equally manifest. That he had taken part in the event which he commemorated, there is

---

* The stanza given above is plainly one, and not the first, of several. Others have been brought forward as the remainder of the lampoon ; but they are too plainly spurious to be worthy of notice. The story of the deer-stealing is said by Mr. Fullom, in his *History of William Shakespeare*, to be confirmed by a note, entered, about 1750, in a manuscript pedigree of the Lucy family, by an old man named Ward, who derived his information from family papers then in his hands. But this date is nearly fifty years after the publication of the story in Rowe's Life, and so is of little or no value. According to the same authority Sir Thomas Lucy ceased his prosecution of Shakespeare, and released him, at the intercession of the Earl of Leicester.

not evidence which would be sufficient in a court
of law, but quite enough for those who are satisfied with the concurrence of probability and
tradition; and I confess that I am of that number.

From 1584, when Shakespeare's twin children—Hamnet and Judith—were baptized, until
1592, when we know that he was rising rapidly to
distinction as a playwright in London, no record
of his life has been discovered; nor has tradition
contributed anything of importance to fill the
gap, except the story of the deer-stealing and its
consequences. What was he doing in all those
eight years? and what before the former date?
For he was not born to wealth and privilege, and
so could not, like the future Bishop of Bristol and
Worcester, spend all his time in stealing deer
and wooing girls. Malone, noticing the frequen-
cy with which he uses law terms, conjectured that
he had passed some of his adolescent years in an
attorney's office. In support of his conjecture,
Malone, himself a barrister, cited twenty-four
passages distinguished by the presence of law
phrases; and to these he might have added many
more. But the use of such phrases is by no
means peculiar to Shakespeare. The writings of
the poets and playwrights of this period, Spenser, Drayton, Greene, Beaumont and Fletcher,
Middleton, Donne, and many others of less note,

are thickly sprinkled with them.* In fact, the
application of legal language to the ordinary affairs of life was more common two hundred and
fifty years ago than it is now; though even now-
a-days the usage is much more general in the

* There are two passages in Shakespeare's works which are
so remarkable for the freedom with which law phrases are scattered through them, that it is worth while to give them here.
The first is the well-known speech in the grave-digging scene of
Hamlet: —

"*Hamlet.* — There's another. Why may not that be the skull
of a lawyer? Where be his quiddits now, his quillets, his *cases*,
his *tenures*, and his tricks? Why does he suffer this rude knave,
now, to knock him about the sconce with a dirty shovel, and will
not tell him of his *action of battery?* Humph! This fellow
might be in 's time a great buyer of land, with his *statutes*, his
recognizances, his *fines*, his *double vouchers*, his *recoveries*. Is this
the *fine* of his *fines*, and the *recovery* of his *recoveries*, to have
his fine pate full of fine dirt? Will his *vouchers* vouch him no
more of his *purchases*, and *double ones*, too, than the length and
breadth of a pair of *indentures?* The very *conveyances* of his
lands will hardly lie in this box; and must the *inheritor* himself
have no more? ha?"—Act V. Sc. 1.

The second is the following Sonnet (No. XLVI.), not only the
language, but the very fundamental conceit of which, it will be
seen, is purely legal : —

"Mine Eye and Heart are at a mortal war
    How to divide the conquest of thy sight;
    Mine Eye my Heart thy picture's sight would *bar*,
    My Heart mine Eye the freedom of that right.
    My Heart doth *plead* that thou in him dost lie
    (A closet never pierc'd with crystal eyes);
    But the *defendant* doth that *plea* deny,
    And says in him thy fair appearance lies.
    To 'cide this title is *impanelled*

rural districts than persons who have not lived in them would suppose. There law shares with agriculture the function of providing those phrases of common conversation which, used figuratively at first, and often with poetic feeling, soon pass into mere thought-saving formulas of speech, and

> A *quest* of thoughts, all tenants to the Heart,
> And by their *verdict* is determined
> The clear Eye's *moiety*, and the dear Heart's part;
> As thus: Mine Eye's due is thine outward part,
> And my Heart's right, thine inward love of heart."

It would seem, indeed, as if passages like these must be received as evidence that Shakespeare had more familiarity with legal phraseology, if not a greater knowledge of it, than could have been acquired except by habitual use in the course of professional occupation. But that he is not peculiar even in this crowding of many law-terms into one brief passage, take this evidence from *The Miseries of Enforced Marriage*, a poor play written by George Wilkins, an obscure contemporary playwright: —

> "*Doctor*. Now, Sir, from this your *oath and bond*,
> Faith's pledge and *seal* of conscience, you have run,
> Broken all *contracts*, and the *forfeiture*
> Justice hath now in *suit* against your soul:
> Angels are made the *jurors*, who are *witnesses*
> Unto the *oath* you took; and God himself,
> Maker of marriage, He that hath *sealed the deed*
> As a firm *lease* unto you during life,
> *Sits now as Judge* of your transgression:
> The world *informs against you* with this voice, —
> If such sins reign, what mortals can rejoice?
> "*Scarborow*. What then ensues to me?
> "*Doctor*. A heavy *doom*, whose *execution 's*
> Now *served upon* your conscience," &c.
>
> *D. O. P.*, Vol. III. p. 91, ed. 1825.

which in large cities are mostly drawn from trade
and politics.*

There are reasons, however, for believing that
Shakespeare had more than a layman's knowledge
of the technical language of the law. The familiarity with that language manifested by other playwrights and poets of his day precludes us, indeed,
from accepting the mere occurrence of law phrases
in his works as indications of a distinctive professional training. On the other hand, we have direct
contemporary evidence that many dramatic authors of the Elizabethan period (1575 – 1625) were
bred attorneys or barristers. Thomas Nash, a
playwright, poet, and novelist, whose works were in
vogue just before Shakespeare wrote, in an " Epis-

---

* And yet Lord Chief Justice Campbell could cite these lines
from the exquisite song in *Measure for Measure* as among the evi-
dences of Shakespeare's legal acquirements : —

> " But my kisses bring again
> *Seals* of love, but *sealed* in vain."

If Shakespeare's lines smell of law, how strong is the odor of
parchment and red tape in these, from Drayton's Fourth Eclogue
(1605) ! —

> " Kindnesse againe with kindnesse was repay'd,
> *And with sweet kisses couenants were sealed.*"

Surely a man must be both a Lord Chancellor and a Shakespearian commentator to forget that the use of seals is as old as the
art of writing, and perhaps older, and that the practice has furnished a figure of speech to poets from the time when it was
written, that out of the whirlwind Job heard, " It is turned as clay
to the *seal*," and probably from a period yet more remote.

tle to the Gentleman Students of the Two Universities," with which, according to the fashion of the time, he introduced Greene's *Menaphon* (1587) to the reader, has the following paragraph : —

"It is a common practice, now-a-days, amongst a sort of shifting companions that run through every art and thrive by none, to leave the trade of Noverint, whereto they were born, and busy themselves with the endeavors of art, that could scarcely Latinize their neck-verse, if they should have need; yet English Seneca, read by candle-light, yields many good sentences, as, *Blood is a beggar*, &c. ; and if you intreat him fair in a frosty morning, he will afford you whole Hamlets, — I should say, handfuls of tragical speeches. But, oh, grief! *Tempus edax rerum,* — what is that will last always ? The sea, exhaled by drops, will, in continuance, be dry; and Seneca, let blood line by line and page by page, at length must needs die to our stage."

It has most unaccountably been assumed that this passage refers to Shakespeare, chiefly, it would seem, if not only, because of the phrase, "whole *Hamlets,* — I should say, handfuls of tragical speeches," — which has been looked upon as an allusion to Shakespeare's great tragedy. That Shakespeare had written this tragedy in 1586, when he was but twenty-two years old, is improbable to the verge of impossibility ; and Nash's allusion, if indeed he meant a punning sneer at a play, (which is not certain,) was doubtless to an old, lost dramatic version of the Danish story upon which Shakespeare built his *Hamlet.* But on the contrary, it seems clear that Nash's object

was to sneer at Jasper Heywood, Alexander
Nevil, John Studley, Thomas Nuce, and Thomas
Newton, — one or more of them, — whose *Seneca,
his Tenne Tragedies translated into Englysh*, was
published in 1581. It is a very grievous performance; and Shakespeare, who had read it thoroughly, made sport of it in *A Midsummer Night's
Dream*. Indeed, Nash introduces the passage
above given by this paragraph, which has been
hitherto omitted in noticing the subject: "I will
turn my back to my first text of studies of delight,
and talk a little in friendship with a few of our
trivial translators."

Upon the leaving of law* for dramatic literature the passage in question is plainly of general
application. Such a change of occupation Nash
says was common; and his testimony accords
with all that we know of the social and literary
history of that age. There was no regular army
in Elizabeth's time; and the younger sons of gentlemen not rich and of well-to-do yeomen flocked
to the church and to the bar; and as the former
had ceased to be a stepping-stone to power and
wealth while the latter was gaining in that regard,
most of these young men became attorneys or
barristers. But then, as now, the early years of
professional life were seasons of sharp trial and

---

* Attorneys were called *noverints* because of the phrase *Noverint universi per presentes* (Know all men by these presents) with
which many legal instruments then began.

bitter disappointment. Necessity pressed sorely, or pleasure wooed resistlessly; and the slender purse wasted rapidly away while the young lawyer awaited the employment that did not come. He knew then, as now he knows, the heart sickness that waits on hope deferred; nay, he felt, as now he sometimes feels, the tooth of hunger gnawing through the principles and firm resolves that partition a life of honor and self-respect from one darkened by conscious loss of rectitude, if not by open shame. Happy (yet, it may be, O unhappy) he who now in such a strait can wield the pen of a ready writer! For the press, perchance, may afford him a support which, though temporary and precarious, will hold him up until he can stand upon more stable ground. But in the reigns of Good Queen Bess and Gentle Jamie there was no press. There was, however, an incessant demand for new plays. Play-going was the chief intellectual recreation of that day for all classes, high and low. It is not extravagant to say that there were then more new plays produced in London in one month, than there are now in both Great Britain and the United States in a whole year.

To play-writing, therefore, the needy and gifted young lawyer turned his hand at that day, as he does now to journalism; and of those who had been successful in their dramatic efforts, how inevitable it was that many would give themselves up

4

to play-writing, and that thus the language of the plays of that time should show such a remarkable infusion of law phrases ! To what, then, must we attribute the fact, that of all the plays that have survived of those written between 1580 and 1620 Shakespeare's are most noteworthy in this respect ? For no dramatist of the time, not even Beaumont, who was a younger son of a Judge of the Common Pleas, and who, after studying in the Inns of Court, abandoned law for the drama, used legal phrases with Shakespeare's readiness and exactness. And the significance of this fact is heightened by another, — that it is only to the language of the law that he exhibits this inclination. The phrases peculiar to other occupations serve him on rare occasions by way of description, comparison, or illustration, generally when something in the scene suggests them ; but legal phrases flow from his pen as part of his vocabulary and parcel of his thought. The word "purchase," for instance, which in ordinary use meant, as now it means, to acquire by giving value, applies in law to all legal modes of obtaining property, except inheritance or descent. And in this peculiar sense the word occurs five times in Shakespeare's thirty-four plays, but only in a single passage in the fifty-four plays of Beaumont and Fletcher. And in the first scene of the *Midsummer Night's Dream* the father of Hermia begs the ancient privilege of Athens, that he may dispose of his daughter either to Demetrius or to death, —

"according to our law
Immediately provided in that case."

He pleads the statute; and the words run off his tongue in heroic verse as if he were reading them from a paper.

As the courts of law in Shakespeare's time occupied public attention much more than they do now,—their terms having regulated "the season" of London society,*—it has been suggested that it was in attendance upon them that he picked up his legal vocabulary. But this supposition not only fails to account for Shakespeare's peculiar freedom and exactness in the use of that phraseology,—it does not even place him in the way of learning those terms his use of which is most re. markable ; which are not such as he would have heard at ordinary proceedings at *nisi prius*, but such as refer to the tenure or transfer of real property,—"fine and recovery," "statutes merchant," "purchase," "indenture," "tenure," "double voucher," "fee simple," "fee farm," "remainder," "reversion," "forfeiture," &c. This conveyancer's jargon could not have been picked up by hanging round the courts of law in London two hundred and fifty years ago, when suits as to the title to real property were comparatively so rare. And beside, Shakespeare uses his law just as freely in his early plays, written in his first London years, as in those

---

* Falstaff, for instance, speaks of "the wearing out of six fashions, which is four terms or two actions."

produced at a later period.*   Just as exactly
too ; for the correctness and propriety with which
these terms are introduced have compelled the admiration of a Chief Justice and Lord Chancellor.†
Again, bearing in mind that genius, although it
reveals general truth, and facilitates all acquirement, does not impart facts or acquaintance with
technical terms, how can we account for the fact
that, in an age when it was the common practice
for young lawyers to write plays, one playwright
left upon his plays a stronger, sharper legal stamp
than appears upon those of any of his contemporaries, and that the characters of this stamp are
those of the complicated law of real property?

* Thus, in *Henry the Sixth*, Part II., Jack Cade says, "Men shall
hold of me *in capite*: and we charge and command that wives be
as free as heart can wish or tongue can tell"; — words which indicate acquaintance with very ancient and uncommon tenures of
land. In the *Comedy of Errors*, when Dromio of Syracuse says,
"There's no time for a man to recover his hair that grows bald
by nature," (wise words, and fatal to many hopes,) his master replies, "May he not do it by *fine and recovery*?"   Fine and
recovery was a process by which, through a fictitious suit, a transfer was made of the title in an entailed estate.   In *Love's Labor's
Lost*, almost without a doubt the first comedy that Shakespeare
wrote, on Boyet's offering to kiss Maria (Act II. Sc. 1), she de-
clines the salute, and says, "My lips are no common, though several they be."   Maria's allusion is plainly to tenancy in common
by several (i. e. divided, distinct) title.

† These are Lord Campbell's words: "While novelists and
dramatists are constantly making mistakes as to the law of marriage, of wills, and of inheritance, to Shakespeare's law, lavishly
as he propounds it, there can neither be demurrer, nor bill of exceptions, nor writ of error."

Must we believe that this man was thus distinguished among a crowd of play-writing lawyers, not only by his genius, but by a *lack* of special knowledge of the law? Or shall we rather believe that the son of the late high bailiff of Stratford, a somewhat clever lad, and ambitious withal, was allowed to commence his studies for a profession for which his cleverness fitted him, and by which he might reasonably hope to rise at least to moderate wealth and distinction, and that he continued these studies until his father's misfortunes, aided perhaps by some of those acts of youthful indiscretion which clever lads as well as dull ones sometimes will commit, threw him upon his own resources, — and that then, law failing to supply his pressing need, he turned to the stage, on which he had townsmen and friends? One of these conclusions is in the face of reason, fact, and probability; the other in accordance with them all.

But the bare fact that Shakespeare was an attorney's clerk, even if indisputably established, though of some interest, is of little real importance. It teaches us nothing about the man, of what he did for himself, thought for himself, how he joyed, how he suffered, what he was in his mere manhood. It has but a naked material relation to the other fact, that he uses legal phrases oftener, more freely, and more exactly than any other poet.

III.

Somewhere, then, within the years 1585 and 1586, Shakespeare went from Stratford to London, where we next hear of him as an actor and a mender of old plays. That he went with the intention of becoming an actor, has been universally assumed; but perhaps too hastily. For he had social ambition and high self-esteem; and in his day to become an actor was to cast the one of these sentiments aside, and to tread the other under foot. Betterton's story, told through Rowe, is, that Shakespeare was "obliged to leave his business and family for some time, and shelter himself in London." In so far as this may be relied upon, it shows that Shakespeare had business in Stratford, and that he sought only a temporary refuge in the metropolis. Probably it was with no very definite purpose that he left his native place. Poverty, persecution, and perhaps a third Fury, made Stratford too hot to hold him; and he might well flee, vaguely seeking relief for the present and provision for the future. He would naturally hope to live in London by the business which he had followed at Stratford. Such is the way of ambitious young men who go from rural districts to a metropolis. And, until every other means of livelihood had failed him, it was not in this high-minded, sensitive, aspiring youth to assume voluntarily a profession then scorned of all men. We may

be sure that, if he sought business as an attorney
in London, he did not at once obtain it.   Shakespeare although he was, no such miracle could be
wrought for him; nay, the less would it be wrought
because of his being Shakespeare.   He doubtless
in these first days hoped for a publisher; and not
improbably this purpose was among those which
led him up to London.   Let who will believe that
he went that journey without a manuscript in his
pocket.   For to suppose that a man of poetic
power lives until his twenty-first year without
writing a poem, which he then rates higher
than he ever afterward will rate any of his work,
is to set aside the history of poetry, and to silence those years which are most affluent of
fancy and most eager for expression.

With *Venus and Adonis* written, if nothing
else, — but I think it not unlikely a play, —
Shakespeare went to London and sought a patron.   For in those days a poet needed a patron
even more than a publisher; as without the former he rarely or never got the latter.   Shakespeare found a patron; but not so soon, we may
be sure, as he had expected.   Meantime, while he
waited, the stage door stood ajar invitingly, and
he was both tempted and impelled to enter.   For
that natural inclination to poetry and acting
which Aubrey tells us he possessed had been
stimulated by the frequent visits of companies of
players to Stratford, at whose performances he

could not have failed to be a delighted and
thoughtful spectator. Indeed, as it was the custom for the mayor or bailiff of a town visited by
a travelling company to bespeak the play at their
first exhibition, to reward them for it himself, and
to admit the audience gratis, it may safely be assumed that the first theatrical performance in
Stratford of which there is any record had John
Shakespeare for its patron. For it was given in
1569, the year in which he was high bailiff; and
the bailiff's son, although he was then only five
years old, we may be sure was present. Between
1569 and 1586 hardly a year passed without several performances by one or more companies at
Stratford. But natural inclination and straitened
means of living were not the only influences
which led Shakespeare to the theatre. Other
Stratford boys had gone up to London, and some
of them had become players. Thomas Greene,
one of the most eminent actors of the Elizabethan
period, he who gave his name to *The City Gallant*,
which was known and published as " Greene's
Tu Quoque," was in 1586 a member of the company known as " The Lord Chamberlain's Servants,"
to which Shakespeare became permanently attached. Greene was of a respectable family at
Stratford, one member of which was an attorney,
who had professional connections in London,
and was Shakespeare's kinsman. Burbadge, Sly,
Heminge, and Pope, who all bore Warwickshire

names, were on the London stage at the time of Shakespeare's arrival at the metropolis.* If Shakespeare went to London relying upon the good offices of friends, we may be sure that he looked more to his townsman, Greene the attorney, than to his other townsman, Greene the actor. But in that case, considering how shy attorneys are apt to be of the sort of young man who steals deer and writes verses, it is not at all surprising that the player proved to be the more serviceable acquaintance.

Many circumstances combine to show that it was in 1586 that William Shakespeare became connected with the London stage ; a few month's variation — and there cannot be more — in the date, one way or the other, is of small importance. Betterton heard that "he was received into the company at first in a very mean rank," and the octogenarian parish clerk of Stratford, before mentioned, told Dowdall, in 1693, that he "was received into the play-house as a serviture." These stories have an air of truth. What claim had this raw Stratford stripling to put his foot higher than the first round of the ladder ? In those days that round was apprenticeship to some well-established actor ; and as such a servitor probability and tradition unite in assuring us that

* See the Remarks on the Preliminary Matter to the Folio, Vol. II. pp. xxxvi., xlvii., xlviii. of the author's edition of Shakespeare's Works.

William Shakespeare began his theatrical career.
There is a story that his first occupation in London was holding horses at the play-house door;
but it was not heard of until the middle of the
last century, and is unworthy of serious attention.

Theatres had increased rapidly in London during the few years preceding Shakespeare's arrival.
Not long before that time public acting was confined almost entirely to the court-yards of large
inns, or to temporary stages which were erected
in the open air or in booths; although sometimes
the use of a large hall was obtained by the generosity of a nobleman or a corporation, or that of a
churchyard, or even a church, by the paid conni-
vance of the rector.   The public authorities, more
especially those who were inclined to Puritanism,
exerted themselves in every possible way to repress the performance of plays and interludes.
They · fined and imprisoned the players, even
stocked them, and harassed and restrained them
to the utmost of their ability.   But, like all such
restrictive, persecuting folk, they began their
work at the wrong end to warrant any hope of
its accomplishment.   They punished the players
when they should have disciplined the public.
Had they been able to root out the taste for dramatic entertainment, and checked the demand for
it, they might have let the poor players go quietly
on with their performances, sure that they would

soon come to an end. But the taste grew into a fierce appetite, and pervaded all classes of society; and the supply of the needful food was an inevitable necessity. The strait-laced aldermen of London would neither be mollified by the art of the player nor learn sufficient wisdom from experience to devote their energies to regulating that which they could not stop; and in 1575 the players were interdicted from the practice of their art (or rather their calling, for it was not yet an art) within the limits of the city.

Among the men who suffered from this new ordinance was James Burbadge, a Warwickshire man. He is said to have been a carpenter; but he added to the gains of his craft what he could get as one of a cry of players; and mayhap, like that other artisan actor, Nick Bottom, he had "simply the best wit of any handy-craft-man" in his city. Certainly whatever wit he had was put to good use; for, as he could not play in London, he determined to play just outside of it, and to use his skill as a carpenter in building that then unheard-of thing in England, a play-house. Borrowing the good round sum of £600 from a rich father-in-law, he leased a plot of ground and the buildings upon it in the suburb of Shoreditch for twenty-one years, with the privilege of putting up a theatre; and partly by altering, partly by building, as we have seen under similar circumstances in New York, he soon had his play-house finished. And thus the oppression of an artisan player caused the erection, in 1575, of the First English Theatre, — indeed the first modern theatre; for, setting aside the ruined structures of antiquity, in no other country at this time had there been built a house for the especial purpose of dramatic performances. Burbadge's house was called inevitably "The Theatre." It had no other name; and no other was needed. The enterprising dramatic carpenter's venture proved so profitable, that, resolving, like a Yankee showman of world-wide notoriety, to be his own opposition, he built within a year another theatre in Moorfields, which he called "The Curtain"; and to these two he added, in 1576, a third, destined to immortal fame. This was in the liberties of the late dissolved monastery of the Blackfriars. Like "The Theatre," it was constructed by the alteration of dwelling-houses. Its site is now in the heart of London, near Printing-House Square; and even then, though outside the city proper, it was one of the most thickly-built quarters of the town, and one inhabited by the better sort of folk, and even by the nobility. These people, aided by the Mayor of London, did all they could to get the Privy Council to forbid the erection of the new theatre in their elegant and orderly neighborhood. But it is worthy of special notice that all this aristocratic and high official influence failed of the object to which it was directed. The love

of the whole people for the drama was too strong
and too vivid in its manifestation to make it
politic, even in those days of arbitrary power, to
restrict that individual liberty of which our race
is so jealous, in favor of the few who were averse
to stage plays or annoyed by the surroundings of
a play-house. In 1586 the houses above named
were the principal theatres of London; but there
were three or four other buildings, near the bank
of the river, one of which was called "The Rose,"
which were used by players, tumblers, mounte-
banks, and bear-baiters promiscuously. Paris
Garden, which some time afterward became a
theatre, was entirely devoted to the cruel sports
of the baiting ring.

These theatres were occupied by companies of
players, each of which was under the patronage
and protection of some distinguished nobleman.
The most esteemed of these companies were the
Queen's, the Earl of Leicester's, the Lord Admi-
ral's (Earl of Nottingham), the Earl of Pembroke's, the Earl of Sussex's, and the Children
of the Royal 'Chapel and of St. Paul's. The
company which played at the Blackfriars, and of
which James Burbadge was the leading man, was
the Earl of Leicester's. This company had played
at Stratford several times in Shakespeare's boyhood. The playwrights whose works were then
most in vogue, and who were all attached to one
or other of these companies, and were actors of

more or less repute, were George Peele, Robert
Greene, Christopher Marlowe, John Lyly, Thomas
Kyd, Thomas Nashe, Thomas Lodge, Henry
Chettle, and Anthony Munday.   Of these only
the first four possessed any marked superiority
over their fellows ; and of the four only Marlowe's
pen obtained for him any other place in the
world's memory than that of having been a contemporary of Shakespeare.

Tradition and the custom of the time concur in
assuring us that Shakespeare's first connection
with the stage was as an actor ; and an actor he
continued to be for twenty years or more.   But
although Aubrey tells us that "he did act exceeding well," he seems never to have risen high in
this profession.   Betterton, or perhaps Rowe,
heard that the top of his performance was the
Ghost in his own *Hamlet ;* and Oldys tells a story,
that one of his younger brothers, who lived to a
great age, being questioned as to William, said
that he remembered having seen him act the part,
in one of his own comedies, of a long-bearded,
decrepit old man, who was supported by another
person to a table, where they sat among other
company, one of whom sang a song.   If this were
true, Shakespeare played Adam in *As You Like
It.*   And it is consistent with all that we know of
him that he should play such parts as this and the
Ghost, which required judgment and intelligent
reading rather than passion and lively simulation.

It is not probable that Shakespeare, when he had found that he could labor profitably in a less public walk of his calling, ever strove for distinction or much employment as an actor. We know from one of his sonnets how bitter the consciousness of his position was to him, and that he cursed the fortune which had consigned him to a public life.* If he ever had comfort on the stage it must have been in playing kingly parts, which are assigned to him in the lines of Davies.†

But although Shakespeare began his London life as a player, it was impossible that he should long remain without writing for the stage ; and so it happened. With what company he became first connected, there is no direct evidence ; but his earliest dramatic employment seems to have been as a co-worker with Greene, Marlowe, and Peele for the Earl of Pembroke's players. There are good reasons for believing that, in conjunction with one or more of these playwrights, he labored on *The First Part of the Contention betwixt the Two Famous Houses of York and Lancaster, The True Tragedy of Richard Duke of York, A Pleasant Conceited History of the Taming of a Shrew, Titus Andronicus*, an early form of *Romeo and Juliet*, of which there are some remains in the quarto edition of 1597, and probably some other pieces which have been lost.‡ It would have

* Sonnet CXI.   † See page 138.
‡ See the Essay on the Authorship of *King Henry the Sixth*,

been strange, indeed almost unprecedented, if a young adventurer going up to London had immediately found his true place, and taken firm root therein. But little as we know of Shakespeare's period of trial and vicissitude, we do know that it was brief, and that within about three years from the time when he left his native place he attached himself to the Lord Chamberlain Hunsdon's company (previously known as the Earl of Leicester's), of which the Burbadges, father and son, were prominent members, and that he became a shareholder in this company, and remained an active member of it until he finally retired to Stratford.

Shakespeare immediately showed that unmistakable trait of a man organized for success in life, which is so frequently lacking in men who are both gifted and industrious, — the ability to find his work, and to settle down quickly to it, and take hold of it in earnest. He worked hard, did everything that he could turn his hand to, — acted, wrote, helped others to write, — and seeing through men and things as he did at a glance, he was in those early years somewhat over-free of his criticism and his advice, and, what was less endurable by his rivals, too ready to illustrate his principles of art successfully in practice. He came soon to be regarded, by those who liked and

Vol. VII., and the Introduction to *Titus Andronicus*, Vol. IX., *The Taming of the Shrew*, Vol. IV., and *Romeo and Juliet*, Vol. X. of the author's edition of Shakespeare's Works.

needed him, as a most useful and excellent fellow, a very factotum, and a man of great promise;
while those who disliked him and found him in
their way, and whose ears were wounded by his
praises, set him down as an officious and conceited upstart. He saw at once the coarse, unnatural, feeble, and inflated style of the men
whom he found in possession of public favor, and
he treated them to a little good-natured ridicule,
of which we find traces in some of his plays, as in
Hamlet and *A Midsummer-Night's Dream*, and in
some of his burlesque bombastic characters, as in
Pistol and Nym. Now, men may love their enemies and do good to them that hate them; but
men will never love their critics, or do anything
but evil to them that ridicule them. As to criticism men are unwise; but in regard to ridicule
they have some reason. Accusation of crime is
trifling in comparison. Say that a man has murdered his mother; and if he has not done the
deed, your slander will recoil upon your own head,
bringing him consolation in your infamy. But
make him ridiculous, and he simply is ridiculous,
and there is an end; except that he is your enemy for life. Ridicule can neither be refuted nor
explained away. For which reason, although it is
a fair weapon against words and acts, (however
poor a test of truth,) against persons it is the fit
resort of cowardice and malice;—a distinction,
however, which many men cannot or will not

make ; and consequently an author often resents
the ridicule of his writings as if it were directed
against himself. This was Shakespeare's experience. But not content with criticism and carica-
ture, he began to outstrip his victims in favor with
the public. Now, such conduct is always resented
as an insult. There is no surer, as there can be
no sadder, evidence to a man that he is rising in
the world's consideration, than an outcry from the
little souls around him that he is receiving that of
which he is not worthy. How they strive by pro-
tests (always in the interests of truth), by sneers,
and by all the little artifices of detraction, even
silence, to show that he is as small as they are,
only showing the while how much he is their
superior! Goodness divine and wisdom infinite
could not escape such scoffing. "Is not this the
carpenter's son? is not his mother called Mary?
and his brethren James, and Joses, and Simon,
and Judas, and his sisters, are they not all with
us? Whence then hath this man all these
things? And they were *offended* in him."

That such was Shakespeare's lot we are not left
to conjecture, hardly to infer. One of the playwrights whom he found in high favor when he
reached London, and with whom, as a youthful
assistant, he began his dramatic labors, stretched
out his hand from beyond the grave to leave a record of his hate for the man who had supplanted
him, and who, he saw, would supplant his com-

panions, as a writer for the stage. The drunken debauchee, Robert Greene, dying in dishonorable need, left behind him a pamphlet written on his death-bed, and published after his burial. It was called *A Groatsworth of Wit bought with a Million of Repentance*, and was better named than its author, or its editor, Henry Chettle, probably supposed. But Greene, though repentant, with the repentance of sordid souls when they are cast down, was not so changed in heart that he could resist the temptation of discharging from his stiffening hand a Parthian shaft, barbed with envy and malice, and winged with little wit, against young Shakespeare. In the pretended interests of truth and friendship, he warned his companions and co-workers, Marlowe, Lodge, and Peele, that the players who had all been beholden to them, as well as to him, would forsake them for a certain upstart crow, beautified with their feathers, who supposed that he was able to write blank verse with the best of them, and who, being in truth a Johannes Factotum, was in his own conceit the only Shake-scene in the country.* Greene was right, as his surviving friends ere long discovered. Their sun had set ; and it was well for them that they all died soon after. They could not forgive

* See the passage in question, given verbatim and in full, and its significance with regard to Shakespeare's early labors set forth, in the Essay on the Authorship of *King Henry the Sixth*, Vol. VII. pp. 408-412 of the author's edition of Shakespeare's Works.

Shakespeare his superiority; but he forgave at
least one of them his envy; for when, a few years
after, he wrote *As You Like It*, he made Phebe say
of Marlowe, quoting a line from *Hero and Leander*,

> "Dead Shepherd, now I find thy saw of might,
> 'Who ever loved that loved not at first sight?'"

Greene sank into his grave, his soul eaten up with
envy as his body with disease; but he was spared
the added pang of foreseeing that his own name
would be preserved in the world's memory only
because of his indirect connection with the man
at whom he sneered, and that he would be chiefly
known as his slanderer. Had he lived to see his
book published, he would have enjoyed such base
and pitiful satisfaction as can be given by revenge.
His little arrow reached its mark, and the wound
smarted. As the venom of a sting. often inflicts
more temporary anguish than the laceration of a
fatal hurt, such wounds always smart, although
they rarely injure; and few men are wise and
strong enough to bear their suffering in dignity
and silence. Whether, if Greene had been alive,
Shakespeare would have publicly noticed his at-
tack, can only be conjectured; but I feel sure that
he would have been kept from open wrangle with
such an assailant by his reticence and self-respect.
Yet, although he was above petty malice and re-
crimination, he was sore and indignant; and he,
and others for him, protested against the wrong
which had been done him in Greene's pamphlet.

He did not protest in vain; for Chettle, Greene's editor, although he treated with great contempt a like complaint of disrespect on the part of Marlowe, whom Greene had also slurred, apologized to Shakespeare in a tract called *The Kind Heart's Dream*, which he published immediately afterward, saying that, although he was personally guiltless of the wrong, he was as sorry as if the original fault had been his own to have offended a man so courteous, so gifted, and one who, by his worth and his ability, had risen high in the esteem of many of his superiors in rank and station.* Greene died in the autumn of 1592, and his pamphlet and Chettle's were both published in the same year. Thus Shakespeare, within six or seven years of his departure from Stratford a fugitive adventurer, had won admiration from the public, respect from his superiors, and the consequent hate of some, and, what is so much harder of attainment, the regard of others, among those who were his equals, except in his surpassing genius.

These two pregnant passages, which we owe to the malice of a disappointed rival, are the first public notice of Shakespeare, and our earliest authentic record of his presence in London.† By

* See Chettle's apology in full and verbatim in the Essay on the Authorship of *King Henry the Sixth*, Vol. VII. p. 410, as above.

† In 1835 Mr. John Payne Collier published a small volume entitled *New Facts regarding the Life of Shakespeare*, in which he brought to notice six documents as having been found at Bridgewater House among the papers of Lord Ellesmere, who was

this time he had produced, in addition to his con-
tributions to partnership plays and to old ones
partly rewritten, *The Comedy of Errors, Love's La-*

Chancellor in the reigns of Elizabeth and James I. One of these
documents was an unsigned certificate or memorandum, intended
apparently for the Privy Council, exculpating the players at the
Black-friars Theatre from a charge of having meddled in matters
of state and religion, which had been brought against the theatres generally in 1589. Among the names of the players mentioned in this paper as sharers in the theatre appears that of
William Shakespeare, which stands twelfth on the list. The document is as follows : —

"These are to sertifie yor right honorable Ll., that her Ma^{tis}
poore playeres James Burbidge Richard Burbidge John Laneham
Thomas Greene Robert Wilson John Taylor Anth. Wadeson
Thomas Pope George Peele Augustine Phillippes Nicholas Tow-
ley William Shakespeare William Kempe William Johnson Bap-
tiste Goodale and Robert Armyn being all of them sharers in the
blacke Fryers playehouse haue neuer given cause of displeasure,
in that they haue brought into their playes maters of state and
Religion, vnfitt to be handled by them or to be presented before
lewde spectators neither hath anie complainte in that kinde ever
beene preferrde against them, or anie of them Wherefore, they
trust most humblie in yor Lls consideracion of their former good
behauiour being at all tymes readie and willing to yeelde obedience to any comaund whatsoever yor Ll in yor wisdome may
thinke in such case meete, &c.

"Nov. 1589."

Until recently this memorandum was received as genuine ; and
were it so, it would show us that, within three years after his arrival at London, William Shakespeare had advanced from the
position of servitor, apprentice, or hired man in the Lord Chamberlain's company to that of a sharer in the receipts of the company, not that of a proprietor of the theatre. But suspicion of
the genuineness of the documents brought forward by Mr. Collier having been excited, this, among the others, was carefully

bor's Lost, and *The Two Gentlemen of Verona*, his earliest original productions. He was already thriving, with prosperity in prospect. But he had

examined by the most eminent palæographists in London, some of them holding high official positions, and all pronounced it a forgery. The facts in regard to the investigation of the character of these documents will be found in Mr. N. E. S. A. Hamilton's *Inquiry*, &c., 4to, London, 1860 ; Dr. Mansfield Ingleby's *Complete View of the Shakespeare Controversy*, London, 1861 ; Mr. Duffus Hardy's *Review of the Present State of the Shakespearian Controversy*, London, 1860 ; and in *The Shakespeare Mystery*, in the *Atlantic Monthly*, Sept., 1861. It is possible, though very improbable, that the judgment pronounced by such high palæographic authorities may be incorrect ; but the documents are put by this decision out of question as evidence of the bare and meagre facts in Shakespeare's life which they profess to establish.

In Spenser's *Teares of the Muses*, printed in 1591, a passage beginning with the lines, —

> "And he, the man whom Nature selfe had made
> To mock her selfe, and Truth to imitate,
> With kindly counter under mimick shade,
> Our pleasant Willy, ah, is dead of late," —

has been held to refer to Shakespeare ; chiefly, it would seem, because of the name, Willy. But that, like "shepherd," was not uncommonly used merely to mean a poet, and was distinctly applied to Sir Philip Sidney in an Eclogue preserved in Davidson's *Poetical Rhapsody*, published in 1602. And the *Teares of the Muses* had certainly been written before 1590, when Shakespeare could not have risen to the position assigned by the first poet of the age to the subject of this passage, and probably in 1580, when Shakespeare was a boy of sixteen in Stratford. Indeed, the notion that Spenser had him in mind would not merit even this attention, were it not that my readers might suppose that I had passed it by through inadvertence. All that ingenuity and persistent faith can urge in support of it the reader will find in Mr. Knight's and Mr. Collier's biographies of the poet.

literary ambition which play-writing did not satisfy (for that he did as a conveyancer draws deeds,
— as business) ; and he had a poem written ; so
he still looked about for a patron. Now, there
was at this time in London a nobleman of high
rank and large wealth, Henry Wriothesley, Earl
of Southampton, who had a genuine love of letters, and who was just upon the threshold of a
lordly life. As yet he had not exhibited in any
marked degree the high spirit, the fine capacity
of appreciation, the graciousness, and the generosity which made him afterward admired and loved
of all men at the court of Queen Elizabeth. For
at the publication of Greene's pamphlet he was
but nineteen years old, and Shakespeare was nine
years his senior. Loving literature and the society of men of letters, he had a special fondness
for the drama, and, being a constant attendant upon the theatre, he saw much of Shakespeare and
his plays ; and there can be no doubt that he was
one of those " divers of worship " whose respect
for the poet's " uprightness of dealing " and admiration of his " facetious grace in writing " Chettle
assigns as one reason for his apology to a man
whom, it is very easy to see, he did not think it
prudent to offend.* Shakespeare must have had

---

* The meaning of the word " facetious " in this well-known passage has been very generally misunderstood, and by none more
completely than by Miss Bacon, who rested her misapprehension
of Shakespeare's rank among his contemporaries much on Chet-

some acquaintance with Southampton at this time, and have felt that he was in his Lordship's favor. For to him he determined to dedicate his *Venus and Adonis*, although he had not asked permission to do so, as the dedication shows ; and in those days, in fact at any time, without some knowledge of his man and some opportunity of judging how he would receive the compliment, a player would not have ventured to take such a liberty with the name of a nobleman. In the next year (1593) the closing of the London theatres on account of the plague afforded a favorable occasion for the publication of the poem, and it was printed by Richard Field, a Stratford man. It immediately won its author a high literary reputation. Before a year had passed a new edition was called for ; a third was published in 1596, and two others within nine years of its first appearance. Southampton must have been a churl not to be gratified at the homage of such a poet ; and being a man whose rank was the mere pedestal, and whose

tle's use of this epithet, upon which she rung a never-ending change of sneers. But "facetious" here has no reference to that light comic vein of speech to which it is now exclusively applied. It was used in Shakespeare's time in a sense combining our terms "felicitous" and "fastidious" in regard to style. Thus Thomas Sackville, Earl of Dorset, a grave statesman as well as an accomplished man of letters, who in his very youth wrote only serious and sententious works, is said by Naunton to have been "so facete and choice in his phrase and style" when drafting state papers, that his secretaries could rarely please him.

wealth the mere adornment, of his real nobility, he acknowledged Shakespeare's compliment in a manner both munificent and considerate. Tradition tells us the former ; a second dedication, the latter. In the dedication of his *Venus and Adonis*, which we must not forget that Shakespeare regarded as his first appearance as an author, he expressed a fear that he might offend the young Earl by connecting his name with the first heir of his invention ; but he promised that, if his patron were only pleased, he would devote all the time that he could steal from the daily labor of playing and play-writing to some graver labor in his honor. Such a work, we may be sure, he then already had in mind ; for in the very next year appeared the *Lucrece*, a grave and even tragic poem, showing much greater maturity of thought and style than its predecessor, and dedicated also to Southampton. But the tone of the poet toward the patron is now very different from what it was a year before ; although it is still tainted with that deference of simple manhood to privilege, which, in the time of Elizabeth, Englishmen of Shakespeare's rank, no matter what their age, their ability, or their character, must needs pay to English lads of Southampton's. How is it now, except among those Englishmen who have never bowed again under the yoke of privilege which their forefathers cast off in the days when Milton was our mouthpiece and Cromwell our leader ?

It is evident from this dedication, that the Earl
had done something more than seem pleased with
its predecessor. Shakespeare speaks in it of a
warrant which he had of his patron's honorable
disposition that makes him sure of acceptance,
and adds, "What I have done is yours; what I
have to do is yours; being part in all I have, devoted yours." This is not flattery, or even deference: words of acknowledgment could not be
stronger. On this evidence alone it is plain that
something had passed between Shakespeare and
the Earl which had bound the former entirely to
the latter by lasting ties of gratitude. Again circumstance and tradition strengthen and eke out
each other. A story reached Rowe through Davenant (would that so excellent a thing had been
preserved in a cleaner vessel!) that Southampton
gave Shakespeare a thousand pounds to make a
purchase of importance. Now, it so happened
that in 1594 the Globe Theatre was built by the
company to which Shakespeare belonged, in all
the property of which we know that he became a
large owner. The sum which the Earl is said to
have given to Shakespeare is so very large, — being equal to thirty thousand dollars at our present
rate of value, that, while the world has willingly
believed the substance of the story, many have
doubted the correctness of its details. And yet,
remembering the customs of those times, the
more we consider how splendid a fellow young

Southampton was, how munificent to men of letters, how whole-hearted to his friends, the more
we shall be ready to receive the story of his generosity to Shakespeare without abatement. We
know that the Earl of Essex gave Bacon — then
only Mr. Francis Bacon, a rising young barrister
— an estate worth eighteen hundred pounds, —
nearly twice as much as Southampton's reported
gift to Shakespeare. And the story that Sir
Philip Sidney, on reading the first stanza of *The
Faerie Queene*, which had been sent to him in
manuscript, directed fifty guineas to be given to
the author, which he doubled on reading the second, and raised to two hundred as he went on, at
least shows the way in which the higher class of
Englishmen of noble birth treated the higher
class of men of letters in the days of Queen
Elizabeth. This story is probably not true, because Sidney was not rich ; but Southampton
was. When only eight years old he inherited
large estates, which, being well cared for during
his minority, made him one of the wealthiest of
his class when he came of age. He used his
money with discriminating liberality. John Florio, George Chapman, Thomas Nash, and Francis
Beaumont, all sing his praises. Florio says, in
the dedication of his *World of Words* to the Earl
of Rutland, the Earl of Southampton, and the
Countess of Bedford, in 1598: "In truth I acknowledge an entyre debt, not onely of my best

knowledge, but of all ; yea of more than I can or
know to your bounteous lordship, most noble,
most vertuous and most Honorable Earle of Southampton, in whose paie and patronage I have lived
some yeeres ; to whom I owe and vow the yeeres
I have to live. But as to me and manie more, the
glorious and gracious sunneshine of your honour
hath infused light and life." "Who," asks Beaumont, "lives on England's stage and knows him
not ?" Chapman calls him, in his *Iliad,* "the
choice of all our country's noblest spirits"; and
Nash says, "Incomprehensible is the height of
his spirit," and calls him "a dear lover and cher-
isher as well of the lovers of poets as of poets
themselves." Nor should we be troubled about
any loss of manly dignity on Shakespeare's part
by the acceptance of such a gift. For there need
be no doubt that there was a genuine friendship
between these men, in spite of their difference of
rank. Nay, wise Francis Bacon would say, by
very reason of that difference. "There is little
friendship in the world," (thus he closes his essay
Of Followers and Friends,) "and least of all between equals, which was wont to be magnified.
That that is, is between superior and inferior
whose fortunes may. comprehend the one the
other." In those days there might be such
friendship between a peer and a player, because
then classes were sharply defined, and rank meant
something ; and therefore the creature now called

"snob" did not exist. Henry VIII., who defied
the Pope, could be a frequent guest at the table
of simple Sir Thomas More, and afterward be-
head him. Queen Elizabeth could on one day
complain to a proud Earl, when he saluted her,
that he did not put his knee well to the ground,
and on another go in state to dine with the rough
sailor Francis Drake, in his little ship, the Golden
Hind. She could do the one because she could
do the other. If the Earl had left Shakespeare a
thousand pounds by will, no objection would have
entered any mind ; and must a man die before he
can do another a substantial service ? Does dignity require us to insist that a friend shall lose
the pleasure of benefiting us, and we be released
from the obligation of gratitude ? Does one
friend ever lower himself by accepting freely
what another freely gives, and can afford to give,
for friendship's sake ? In countries where land
and wealth and privilege pertain to a comparatively small class, such gifts are but noble, though
inadequate, attempts to do away some of the
wrongful consequences of established inequality ;
and although it is more manly and independent
to enjoy rights, than to receive compensation for
the lack of those rights by way of favor, we must
judge Southampton's literary friends by the social canons of an aristocracy in the sixteenth
century, and not by those of a democracy in the
nineteenth.

Between 1592 and 1596 Shakespeare produced, in addition to his *Lucrece, King Richard the Third, A Midsummer-Night's Dream, The Merchant of Venice, King Richard the Second,* and some of his Sonnets; probably also *Romeo and Juliet* and (with the name "Love's Labor's Won") *All's Well that Ends Well,* in earlier forms than those in which they have come down to us; — works, which, although none of them exhibited his genius in its full height and power, effectually established his supremacy among his contemporaries as a poet and a dramatist. England now began to ring with his praises. His brother dramatists made their lovers long for his *Venus and Adonis* by which to court their mistresses; other poets made their chaste heroines compare themselves to the Lucretia whom he had "revived to live another age"; they sung of his "hony-flowing vein," and that he had given new immortality even to the goddess of love and beauty; and some of them paid him the unequivocal compliment of plagiarism.* Even Spenser, then at the height of his fame and his court favor, having in mind Shakespeare's two

* See Willoughby's *Avisa,* 1594; Drayton's *Matilda,* 1594; Barnefield's *Poems in Divers Humors,* 1598; Heywood's *Fair Maid of the Exchange,* 1607, but written some years before; *Phillis and Flora,* by R. S., 1598; and Nicholson's *Acolastus his Afterwitte,* 1600. In "A Letter from England to her Three Daughters," reprinted in the *British Bibliographer,* (Vol. I. pp. 274–285,) and which forms the second part of a book called *Polimanteia,* published in 1595, there is a marginal note, "All praise worthy Lucretia Sweete Shakespeare."

martial histories and his name, generously paid the young poet this pretty compliment in *Colin Clout's come Home again*, written in 1594 : —

> " And there, though last not least, is Ætion ;
> A gentler Shepheard may no where be found;
> Whose muse full of high thought's invention
> Doth, like himselfe, heroically sound." *

Nay, in this interval Colin Clout's mistress, the imperial Elizabeth herself, distinguished him by her favor, won, or acknowledged, by the exquisite compliment in *A Midsummer-Night's Dream*. For we know upon Ben Jonson's and Henry Chettle's testimony, and from tradition, that she did delight in him ; and it is not in mortal woman, . least of all was it in Elizabeth, to know of such a compliment, and not to hear it and be captivated.†

* It may be worth while to say, that if Shakespeare's name had been Shaksper or Shakspere, as some would have it, this compliment would have been impossible.

† These well-known lines are from Jonson's verses in memory of Shakespeare, which were published in the folio of 1623 : —

> " Sweet Swan of Avon, what a sight it were
> To see thee in our waters yet appeare,
> And make those flights upon the banks of Thames,
> That so did take Eliza and our James."

On the death of Queen Elizabeth, Chettle, in his *England's Mourning Garment*, thus reproached Shakespeare that his verse had not bewailed his own and England's loss : —

> " Nor doth the silver-tongued Melicert
> Drop from his honied Muse one sable tear,
> To mourne her death that graced his desert,
> And to his lines opened her royal eare.
> Shepheard remember our Elizabeth,
> And sing her rape done by that Tarquin, Death."

Having this evidence of his reputation, and other of an equally pleasing and satisfactory character as to his increase in wealth, we can afford to be very indifferent in regard to the trustworthiness of a document about which there has been much ado, and the only interest of which consists in the fact that it enumerates Shakespeare among the owners of the Black-friars Theatre, and names him fifth among eight; but which, after a life of thirty years of antiquarian glory, has been "done to death by envious tongues" as spurious.* A like fate has befallen a memoran-

---

* This document exists in the State Paper Office at West-minster. (London.)   It was brought to public notice by Mr. Collier in his *History of English Dramatic Poetry*, &c., 1831. (Vol. I. p. 297.)   It professes to be an answer to a remonstrance by thirty inhabitants of the Liberty of the Black-friars, "some of them of honor," against the repairing of the Black-friars Theatre. The remonstrance was said by Mr. Collier to be "preserved in the State Paper Office"; but it is not to be found there.   This reply is so genuine in appearance, that it was given in fac-simile even by Mr. Halliwell, in his great folio edition of Shakespeare's Works, although that gentleman was one of the first to pronounce many of the Collier Shakespeare MSS. spurious.   It is as follows :—

"To the right honorable the Lords of her Mat[les] most honora-ble privie Counsell.

"The humble petition of Thomas Pope Richard Burbadge John Hemings Augustine Phillips Willm Shaksepeare Willim Kempe Willim Slye Nicholas Tooley and others, seruaunts to the right honorable the L. Chamberlaine to her Mat[ie].

"Sheweth most humbly that yor petitioners are owners and players of the priuate house or theater in the precinct and libertie of the Blackfriers, wch hath beene for manie yearse vsed and oc-cupied for the playing of tragedies commedies histories enter-

dum which would otherwise show us that at this
time Shakespeare lived in the part of London
called Southwark.   Malone speaks of a certain

ludes and playes.   That the same by reason of hauing beene soe
long built hath falne into great decaye and that besides the repa-
ration thereof it hath beene found necessarie to make the same
more conuenient for the entertainement of auditories comming
thereto.   That to this end yor petitioners haue all and eche of
them putt downe sommes of money according to their shares in
the saide theater and whch they haue justly and honestlie gained
by the exercise of their qualitie of Stage-players but that certaine
persons (some of them of honour) inhabitants of the said precinct
and libertie of the Blackfriers have as yor petitioners are en-
fourmed besought yor honorable Lps not to permitt the saide priuate house anie longer to remaine open but hereafter to be shut
vpp and closed to the manifest and great injurie of yor petitioners
who have no other meanes whereby to maintaine their wiues and
families but by the exercise of their qualitie as they have heretofore done.   Furthermore that in the summer season yor petitioners are able to playe at their newe built house on the Bankside
callde the Globe but that in the winter they are compelled to
come to the Blackfriers and if yor honorable Lps giue consent
vnto that whch is prayde against yor petitioners thay will not
onely while the winter endureth loose the meanes whereby they
nowe support them selues and their families but be vnable to
practise them selues in anie playes or enterluds when calde upon
to performe for the recreation and solace of her Matie and her
honorable Court, as they have beene heretofore accustomed.
The humble prayer of yor petitioners therefore is that your
honble Lps will graunt permission to finishe the reparations and
alterations they have begunne and as your petitioners have hitherto been well ordred in their behauiour and just in their deal-
inges that yor honorable Lps will not inhibit them from acting at
their aboue named priuate house in the precinct and libertie of
the Blackfriers and your petitioners as in dutie most bounden
will ever praye for the increasing honour and happinesse of yor
honorable Lps."

paper which was before him as he wrote, which belonged to Edward Alleyn, the eminent and public-spirited player, and from which it appeared

This document being in a public office, upon a grave suspicion of its genuineness, Sir John Romilly, Master of the Rolls, ordered a palæographic examination of it to be made ; and there is now appended to it the following certificate : —

"We, the undersigned, at the desire of the Master of the Rolls, have carefully examined the document hereunto annexed, purporting to be a petition to the Lords of her Majesty's Privy Council, from Thomas Pope, Richard Burbadge, John Hemings, Augustine Phillips, William Shakespeare, William Kempe, William Slye, Nicholas Tooley, and others, in answer to a petition from the inhabitants of the Liberty of the Black-friars ; and we are of opinion that the document in question is spurious.

"FRA. PALGRAVE, K. H., Deputy Keeper of H. M. Public Records.

FREDERIC MADDEN, K. H., Keeper of the MSS., British Museum.

J. S. BREWER, M. A., Reader at the Rolls.

T. DUFFUS HARDY, Assistant Keeper of Records.

N. E. S. A. HAMILTON, Assistant, Dep. of MSS., British Museum.

"30th January, 1860."

The following professed copy of a letter from the Earl of Southampton, concerning Shakespeare, is now pronounced spurious with an equal weight of authority.

"My verie honored Lord. The manie good offices I haue receiued at your Lordship's hands, which ought to make me backward in asking further favors, onely imbouldeneth me to require more in the same kinde. Your Lordship will be warned howe hereafter you graunt anie sute, seeing it draweth on more and greater demaunds. This which now presseth is to request your Lordship, in all you can, to be good to the poore players of the Black Fryers, who call them selves by authoritie the servaunts of his Majestie, and aske for the protection of their most gracious Maister and Sovereigne in this the tyme of their troble. They are threatened by the Lord Mayor and Aldermen of London, never friendly to their calling, with the distruction of their

that in 1596 Shakespeare lived in Southwark, near the Bear Garden. Malone makes this statement in his *Inquiry into the Authenticity of Certain Papers*, which were forged by that scapegrace William Ireland ; and eminent palæographers and Shakespearian scholars will have it that there

meanes of livelihood, by the pulling downe of their plaiehouse, which is a priuate theatre, and hath neuer giuen occasion of anger by anie disorders. These bearers are two of the chiefe of the companie ; one of them by name Richard Burbidge, who humblie sueth for your Lordship's kinde helpe, for that he is a man famous as our English Roscius, one who fitteth the action to the word, and the word to the action most admirably. By the exercise of his qualitye, industry, and good behaviour, he hath be come possessed of the Blacke Fryers playhouse, which hath bene imployed for playes sithence it was builded by his Father, now nere 50 yeres agone. The other is a man no whitt less deserving favor, and my especiall friende, till of late an actor of good account in the companie, now a sharer in the same, and writer of some of our best English playes, which, as your Lordship knoweth, were most singularly liked of Quene Elizabeth, when the companie was called uppon to performe before her Maiestie at Court at Christmas and Shrovetide. His most gracious Maiestie King James alsoe, sence his coming to the crowne, hath extended his royal favour to the companie in divers waies and at sundrie tymes. This other hath to name William Shakespeare, and they are both of one countie, and indeede allmost of one towne : both are right famous in their qualityes, though it longeth not of your Lo. grauitie and wisedome to resort vnto the places where they are wont to delight the publique eare. Their trust and sute nowe is not to bee molested in their way of life, whereby they maintaine them selves and their wives and families, (being both maried and of good reputation) as well as the widows and orphanes of some of their dead fellows.

     " Your Lo most bounden at com.

" *Copia vera*."   "H. S."

was contamination in the subject, and that the following brief memorandum, which Mr. Collier brought forward as the paper to which Malone referred, is also spurious.

"Inhabitantes of Sowtherk as have complaned
this ——— [o]f Jully, 1596.

        Mr. Markis
        Mr. Tuppin
        Mr. Langorth
        Wilson the pyper
        Mr. Barett
        Mr. Shaksper
        Phellipes
        Tomson
        Mother Golden the baude
        Nagges
        Fillpott and no more and soe well ended."

It may be that this is a delusion, deliberately contrived. If it be, the rogue has baited his trap so well that he shall have me a willing prey. I cannot easily believe that such a genuine-seeming glimpse of real life is artificial; and I am loath to lose those neighbors of William Shakespeare upon whom his calm and searching glances fell, and who watched with curiosity the handsome player-poet as he went in and out on his way to and from the Black-friars. I sympathize too heartily with the writer as he shuts his ears against Wilson the piper, who had the real Lincolnshire drone, — I have Falstaff's word for it, — and as he tosses off Fillpot with such a round Amen of thankfulness. I mourn the vanishing Nagges, whom I think of as a humble kind of Silence, or perhaps Goodman Verges, and feel injured at the assertion that Mother Golden — Mrs. Quickly in the flesh, and plenty of it — is a myth; than which nothing could be more deplorable, except, indeed, that she were virtuous.

The last five years of the sixteenth century are among the most interesting and important in the history of Shakespeare's life. He was then rapidly attaining the independent position which he coveted, and for which he labored; while growth, culture, and experience were uniting in the development of those transcendent powers which reached their grand perfection in the next decade. To those years may be confidently assigned the production of *Romeo and Juliet* in its second and final form, *King John*, the two Parts of *King Henry the Fourth*, the first sketch of *The Merry Wives of Windsor*, *Much Ado about Nothing*, *Twelfth Night*, *King Henry the Fifth*, *As You Like It*, and *Hamlet*. They were probably produced in this order, the first in 1596, the last in 1600. The man who could put those plays upon the stage at a time when play-going was the favorite amusement of all the better and brighter part of the London public, gentle and simple, was sure to grow rich, if he were but prudent; and Shakespeare was prudent, and even thrifty. He knew the full worth of money. He felt the truth

told in the simile of Franklin (in the large grasp
of his worldly wisdom the Bacon of democracy),
that it is hard for an empty sack to stand upright.
And he saw that pecuniary independence is absolutely necessary to him who is seeking, as he
sought, a social position higher than that to
which he was born.   Therefore he looked after
his material interests much more carefully than
after his literary reputation.   The whole tenor of
his life shows that he labored as a playwright
solely that he might obtain the means of going
back to Stratford to live the life of an independent gentleman.   His income now began to be
considerable ; and there are yet remaining records of the care with which he invested his
money, and his willingness to take legal measures
to protect himself against small losses.   It is not
pleasant to think of the author of *The Merchant of
Venice* going to law to compel the payment of a
few pounds sterling : it would be revolting, if the
debtor's failure were because of poverty.   But as
we have to face the fact, we may find comfort in
the certainty that a man of that sweetness of disposition which is attributed to him by his contemporaries, could not have been litigious, and in
the probability that he knew too much of human
nature and of the law to commence a suit, unless
to protect himself against fraud, or to decide a
legal liability.   He who so pitilessly painted Shy-
lock could not but have felt the truth of the maxim, *Summum jus, summa injuria.*

Filial piety, unhappily, is not always a sign of generosity of soul ; for hard masters, cruel creditors, and selfish friends are sometimes devoted sons ; but it is pleasant, in remarking upon Shakespeare's thrift, to record that one of the earliest uses of his prosperity seems to have been the relief of his father from the consequences of misfortune. The little estate of Ashbies, part of Mary Arden's inheritance, which had been mortgaged to Edmund Lambert in 1578, should have been released by the conditions of the mortgage on the repayment of the mortgage-money on or before the 29th of September, 1580. The mortgagors tendered the money, forty pounds ; but they owed Lambert more, upon another obligation ; and he, having possession, and knowing John Shakespeare's inability to incur law expenses, refused to release Ashbies unless the other debt, for which it was not given as security, was discharged also. But in 1597, John Shakespeare and his wife ventured upon that most trying and expensive of all legal proceedings, a chancery suit, to compel John Lambert, the son and heir of Edmund, to restore the estate. There can be no reasonable doubt that the money necessary to this proceeding, and the prompting to undertake it, came from William Shakespeare, incited by filial love and attachment to ancestral fields.

Previously to this date, — how long we do not know, but it was certainly some months before

October, 1596, — John Shakespeare applied to
the Heralds' College (and, if we are to believe
the records, not for the first time) for a grant of
coat-armor, by which he, then a yeoman, might
attain the recognized position of a gentleman.
Such applications were then customarily made by
men who deemed themselves of sufficient importance to enter the pale of gentry. The arms, if
granted, were of value; for they were an official
and universally recognized certificate of a certain
social standing, which those to whom they were
granted were required to show that they were
in condition creditably to support. It has been
conjectured that John Shakespeare made this application at the instigation and with the means —
for the honor cost money — of his now prosperous
son. But in the circumstances of the case, and
in certain evidence which William Shakespeare
himself unconsciously left upon the subject, there
seems to be ground for more than a guess that he
was the real mover in this matter.

To John Shakespeare, a man now past middle
life, and without property or position, this empty
honor would have brought only such distinction
as a man having the good sense of which his
career was evidence must have seen was most un-
enviable. But sustained by the money and the
influence of his son, prosperous and in favor with
powerful members of the nobility, he could bear
up against ridicule. And as far as the son him-

self was concerned, aside from the fact that he
was a player, to whom the heralds would have refused coat-armor, there was a reason, very cogent
to a man ambitious of social advancement at that
time, why the application should be made by the
father. For, the arms being granted to John
Shakespeare, William inherited them, and became a gentleman, not by grant or purchase, but
by descent,— an important advantage where the
social scale is graduated by degrees in heraldic
gentry. But to these reasons add Shakespeare's
own evidence. It is in that scene of *King Lear*
in which the crazy King, his Fool, and the sham-
madman Edgar are left together in the farm-
house.* The Fool asks his uncle, "Tell me
whether a madman be a gentleman or a yeoman"; and he, forlorn alike of royalty and reason, with an indirection that has a grand touch of
heart-break in it, answers, "A king, a king!"
But then the Fool rejoins, "No; he's a yeoman
that has a gentleman to his son. *For he's a mad
yeoman that sees his son a gentleman before him.*"
Now, entirely as Shakespeare avoided mingling
himself with any of the creatures of his imagination, it is absolutely impossible that he should
have put this mere sententious moralizing into
the Fool's mouth without a distinct recollection
of the process by which he became the son of a
gentleman, as well as the grandson of one on

* Act III. Scene 6.

the mother's side. Well-deserved ridicule is now heaped, even in Europe, upon weak people who go to the heralds to have arms hunted up for them, or granted to them; and we may think it small business for the man to whose mental grandeur this memoir is one of a thousand feeble witnesses, thus to go about to make himself a gentleman by inheritance. And he himself had a keen appreciation of the essential absurdity of the whole affair. Let any one who doubts read the passage in *The Winter's Tale*, written years after, in which the Clown, having, with his father, received grace at court, announces to Autolycus, that he is "a gentleman born," and has been so "any time these four hours"; that he was a gentleman born before his father; and that on the occasion in question they wept,—and these, he adds, "were the first gentleman-like tears that ever we shed."

Why then, with this perception of the factitious nature of heraldic gentry, should Shakespeare have desired its possession? From the most sensible and reasonable of motives;—simply because at his day it brought with it more or less of that which every man who is by nature fitted to be a gentleman prizes above all other things, except his self-respect,—consideration. Consideration; —something different from respect, esteem, or love, or even fear; any, and possibly all, of which may pertain to him who has not the other, and who, if he be sensitive, and the least lacking in self-reliance, will therefore fret internally;—something the assurance of which, even at the end of a diplomatic note, is a rampart of respectful intercourse. Congreve has been laughed at because he was offended that Voltaire visited him as a poet and a man of letters, and Gray subjected to a like ridicule, because, when residing at Cambridge, he desired to be regarded, not as a professional scholar and writer, but as a gentleman who was fond of literary pursuits. But, society in Europe being what it was in their day, Congreve and Gray were right.* Nay, even now and here, such a feeling, in a certain degree, is but becoming. Men of letters who are also gentlemen cannot fail to see that distinction in their calling sometimes wins, and justly wins, only an attention different in degree, but not much in kind, from that which is lavished upon a mountebank or a medium. For between what a man can do to amuse, and even to instruct, and what he is, there' is great difference. He may be wonderfully clever, learned, wise,—may have that mysterious gift which we call genius,—and yet be one whom we would not willingly see within the limit

---

* Nevertheless it is rather ridiculous to turn men of letters into noblemen. Among people who must have lords it was well to make dukes of General Churchill and General Wellington, a baron of Judge Murray and an earl of the ex-Premier John Russell; but a baron in virtue of brilliant historical essays was in a position only a little less absurdly false than a baronet might be in virtue of charming idyls.

of our social circle. Society is not purely an affair of intellect, or even of moral worth.

It was, then, for this social consideration that William Shakespeare labored and schemed ; that he, the Stratford fugitive, might return to his native place and meet Sir Thomas Lucy as a prosperous gentleman. But Sir Thomas, I think, with that scorn of new men which, it may well be feared,.is very general, even in republics, endeavored to check one of his aspirations, — this one for coat-armor. The arms were granted, but not until three years after they had been applied for, and in fact not until that time after a grant of them had been drafted. A draft dated October 20th, 1596, of a grant to John Shakespeare of the right to bear a golden silver-headed spear upon a black band in a golden shield, with a white falcon grasping a golden spear for a crest, still exists in the College of Arms ; and from this the grant actually issued in 1599 differs only by the addition of the right to bear the Arden arms impaled ; impaling, or bearing a second coat upon the left half of the shield being the heraldic mode of recording marriage with an heiress of the family whose coat is thus displayed. And these documents, both sketch and grant, also tell the story of the application for the arms. For they were made, as they record, upon the ground that "John Shakespere, nowe of Stratford upon Avon in the counte of Warwik gent., whose parent, great grand-

father, and late antecessor, for his faithefull and
approved service to the late most prudent prince
King H. 7. of famous memorie, was advaunced and
rewarded with lands and tenements geven to him
in those parts of Warwikeshere," was, like his ancestors of some descents, in good reputation and
credit, and also that he had married the daughter
and one of the heirs of Robert Arden of Wilmecote. Now, John Shakespeare's great-grandfather
had nòt been thus distinguished and rewarded by
Henry VII. ; but his wife's, and therefore his son's,
ancestor had ; and of those bedchamber honors
that son was evidently not forgetful, and determined to obtain the fullest advantage. If there be
littleness in this, it was the age that was in fault,
and not the man who conformed to prejudices
which, as we have seen, he really scorned, but was
not strong enough to override.

The delay of three years in the granting of these
arms must have been caused by some opposition to
the grant ; the motto given with them, *Non sans
droict*, (Not without right,) itself seems to assert a
claim against a denial ; and who so likely to make
this opposition as the great neighbor of the Shakespeares, the Parliament member and justice of
peace, Sir Thomas Lucy ? There is record of censure after they were granted. The herald princi-
pally concerned in conferring them, Sir William
Dethick, Garter King at Arms, was called to account for having granted arms improperly, and the

grant to John Shakespeare was among the causes of complaint. His justification rested, in a great measure at least, upon the allegation upon the margin of the draft of 1596, that John Shakespeare "sheweth a patent thereof under Clarence Cook's hands in paper xx years past"; and in the grant of 1599 it is expressly stated that John Shakespeare had "produced this his auncient cote of arms heretofore assigned him whilst he was her Majesties officer and baylefe" of Stratford. Because no record of this grant is known to exist, it has been hitherto supposed that no such grant was made. But it is not at all improbable that John Shakespeare, when he was bailiff and in the height of his prosperity, made application to the heralds for arms at the time of one of their visitations, and that the matter went as far, at least, as the draft of a grant and a sketch, or, as it was called, a trick, of the arms, and that, the matter being spoken of in the neighborhood, the final grant was stopped at the instance of an old county family like the Lucys, who were particular about what Mrs. Page of Windsor would have called the article of their gentry. For in the famous first scene of the comedy in which she appears, where the bearer of the coat with the luces is ridiculed, his particularity about the antiquity of that coat is made even more of than his anger at the stealing of his deer. He is Robert Shallow, Esquire, Justice of Peace and *coram*, and *cust-alorum*, and *ratalorum* too; and a

gentleman born, who writes himself *armigero* in
any bill, warrant, quittance, or obligation ; and he
has done it any time these three hundred years ;
all his successors that have gone before him, and
all his ancestors that come after him may give the
dozen white luces in their coat. For, mind you, it
is an old coat ; and although this ignorant, low-
bred Welsh parson will mistake a luce for the
familiar beast to man, and have it *passant*, you
are to know that the luce is the fresh fish, and
that the salt fish is an old coat, and that the
upstart bailiffs in yonder dirty little town are not
to be bearing silver-headed tilting-spears upon
golden shields, and getting within the pale of gentry by marrying poor gentlemen's daughters, and
by heraldic puns upon their names, when their
betters, by punning on *their* names can only bear
fresh fish, which are subject to unpleasant misapprehension and mispronunciation, and have to be
salted to keep and attain the honors of antiquity.
If Shakespeare had two causes of quarrel with the
man of the luces, he settled the two accounts
rarely in that short scene of his only comedy of
English manners; which he wrote in 1598, between the date at which the confirmation of his
father's arms was drafted and that at which it
was granted.

IV.

Shakespeare was now able to take an important step toward establishing himself handsomely in his native place. In 1597 he bought of William Underhill the Great House, or New Place, as it was called in Stratford, a mansion built of brick and timber, about a hundred and fifty years before, by Sir Hugh Clopton, the benefactor of the town. It cost Shakespeare sixty pounds sterling (equal to about $1500); a small outlay for the dwelling of a man of its new possessor's means and capacity of enjoyment. We know from the fine levied at the sale, that the premises included the Great House itself, two barns, two gardens, and two orchards. But from contemporary legal documents we learn that in 1550 the house was so much in need of repair as to be almost in decay. This was doubtless the reason why it was sold for so small a price. Its owner in the early part of the last century, Sir Hugh Clopton, a lineal descendant of its builder, told Theobald that Shakespeare "repaired and modelled it to his own mind"; and this family tradition is supported by the record of the payment in 1598 of "x *d*" to Mr. Shakespeare for "a lod of ston," which was probably at the thrifty poet's disposal on account of the extensive alterations at New Place. No representation of the house as it was in Shakespeare's time is known to exist, it having been

6

again much altered by Sir John Clopton in 1700 ;
yet its size was not enlarged, and an existing representation of it in its last condition shows that it
was a goodly mansion.   But its new master took
possession bereaved and disappointed.   The death
of his only son, Hamnet, in the twelfth year of his
age, 1596, left him without a descendant to whom
he might transmit, with his name, the houses and
lands and the arms which he had obtained by such
untiring labor.   Shakespeare having money to in-
vest, of course there was no lack of applicants for
the pleasure of placing it for him to his advantage. ·
Of these was one Master Abraham Sturley, a Puritan of the first water.   He begins a long letter,
written at Stratford, January 24th, 1559, to a friend
in London, (probably Richard Quiney, whose son
afterward married Shakespeare's daughter,) with
a pious ejaculation, and then passes promptly to
business, urging his correspondent to quicken an
intention which Shakespeare was known to have
to lay out some of his superfluous money in Stratford property, and especially to recommend to him
a purchase of the tithes of Stratford and three
other parishes, as profitable to himself, beneficial
to the town, and likely to gain him many friends.*

* "Most loveinge and belovedd in the Lord. In plaine Eng-
lishe we remember u in the Lord, & ourselves unto u. I would
write nothinge unto u nowe, but come home. I prai God send u
comfortabli home. This is one speciall remembrance ffrom ur
ffather's motion. It semeth bi him that our countriman, Mr.
Shakspere, is willinge to disburse some monei upon some od

The recommendation, as we·shall hereafter see, appears to have had some effect. There is another letter of this time, written also to Richard Quiney, which contains an obscure mention of a money transaction with Shakespeare.* And the fact is somewhat striking in the life of a great poet, that the only letter directly addressed to Shakespeare which is known to exist, is one which asks a loan of £30. It is from Richard Quiney, who at the writing was in London, and is as follows; for this money transaction belongs in full to Shakespeare's history.

"Loveinge Contreyman, I am bolde of yo", as of a ffrende, craveinge yo"" helpe wth xxx^{li}, uppon Mr Bushells & my securytee, or Mr Myttens with me. Mr Rosswell is nott come to London as yeate, & I have especiall cawse. Yo" shall ffrende me muche in helpeinge me out of all the debtts I owe in London, I thanck god, and muche quiet my mynde wch wolde not be indebeted. I am now towardes the Cowrte, in hope of answer for the dispatche of my Buyse-nes. Yo" shall nether loose creddytt nor monney by me, the Lorde wyllinge; & nowe butt perswade yo"" selfe soe, as I

yarde land or other att Shottri or neare about us; he thinketh it a veri fitt patterne to move him to deale in the matter of our tithes. Bi the instructions u can geve him theareof, & by the frendes he can make therefore, we thinke it a faire marke for him to shoote att, & not impossible to hitt. It obtained would advance him in deede, and would do us much good. Hoc movere, et quantum in te est permovere, ne necligas, hoc enim et sibi et nobis maximi erit momenti. Hic labor, hoc opus esset eximiae et gloriae et laudis sibi." &c., &c.

* "Yff yow bargen with Wm. Sh—— or receve money there-for, brynge your money home that yow maye."

hope, & yo˙ shall nott need to feare; butt with all hartie
thanckfullnes I wyll holde my tyme & content yo˙˙ frend,
& yf we Bargaine farther, yo˙ shall be the paie m˙ yo˙˙ selfe.
My tyme biddes me to hasten to an ende, & soe I comitt
thys [to] yo˙˙ care & hope of yo˙˙ helpe. I feare I shall nott
be backe this night ffrom the Cowrte. haste. the Lorde be
w˙˙ yo˙ & w˙˙ us all. amen. From the Bell in Carter Lane,
the 25 october 1598.

"Yo˙˙ in all kyndenes,

"RYC. QUYNEY."

This letter is addressed " To my loveing good
ffrend and countreyman Mr. Wm. Shackespere
delr thees."

It is impossible to disguise the fact that Quiney
offers an approved indorsed note to the author
of *Hamlet;* but it is gratifying to observe that he
applies to him as a friend. The motive which he
touches is not interest, but the helping him out
of trouble ; and though the sum was not a small
one, — half the price of New Place, — he plainly
feels that Shakespeare had both the ability and
the willingness to spare it. There is another letter of this period, dated November 4th, 1598, addressed to the same Richard Quiney by Abraham
Sturley again. The first part, with which only we
have concern, begins, "All health happiness of
suites and wellfare be multiplied unto u and ur
labours in God our ffather by Christ our Lord,"
and ends, with no less fervor, " O howe can you
make dowbt of monei who will not bear xxx-tie or
xl. s towardes sutch a match!" But its chief in-

terest to us is, that the writer of these beatitudes has heard that "our countriman Mr. Wm. Shak. would procure us monei, wc. I will like of." It is pleasant thus to see that Shakespeare's townsmen, even the staid and sober men among them, respected and looked up to him, and leaned confidently upon the support of his influence and his purse. And this marvellous "Mr. Wm. Shak." then had real property in London, as well as in Stratford, besides his theatrical possessions; for in October of 1598 he was assessed on property in the parish of St. Helen's, Bishopsgate, £5 13s. 4d.

In 1598 Ben Jonson's first and best comedy, *Every Man in his Humour,* was produced at the Black-friars, and the author of *King Henry the Fourth* and *Romeo and Juliet* might have been seen for twopence by any London prentice who could command the coin, playing an inferior part, probably that of Knowell, in the new play. But, according to tradition, Shakespeare not only played in •Jonson's comedy, — he obtained Ben his first hearing before a London audience. The play had been thrown aside at the Black-friars with little consideration, as the production of an unknown writer; but Shakespeare's attention •having been drawn to it, he read it through, admired and recommended it, and then and thereafter took pains to bring the author's works before the public. Jonson's honest love for

Shakespeare may well have had its spring in gratitude for this great service, which having been performed by one dramatic author for another, who was his junior, indicates both kindness and magnanimity.

The year 1598 was one of great professional triumph to Shakespeare. We may safely accept the tradition first mentioned by John Dennis a century later, that in that year he was honored with a command from Queen Elizabeth to let her see his Falstaff in love, which he obeyed by producing in a fortnight *The Merry Wives of Windsor* in its earliest form.* In that year, too, the greatness and universality of his genius received formal recognition at the hands of literary criticism. Francis Meres published in 1598 a book called *Palladis Tamia, Wits Treasury*, which was a collection of sententious comparisons, chiefly upon morals, manners, and religion. But one division or chapter is "A comparative discourse of our English Poets with the Greeke, Latine, and Italian Poets." Meres was a Master of Arts in both Universities, a theological writer, and the author of poetry which has been lost. His comparative discourse makes no pretence to analysis or æsthetic judgment. Indeed, according to the modern standard, it can hardly be regarded as criticism;

---

* See this tradition, and the facts which bear upon it, discussed in the Introduction to *The Merry Wives of Windsor*, in the author's edition of Shakespeare's Works.

but it may be accepted as a record of the estimation in which Shakespeare was held by intelligent and cultivated people when he was thirty-four years old, and before he had written his best plays. In this book Shakespeare is awarded the highest place in English poetical and dramatic literature, and is ranked with the great authors of the brightest days of Greece and Rome. It is true that other poets and dramatists are compared by Meres to Pindar, Æschylus, and Aristophanes, to Ovid, Plautus, and Horace, and that, like all who have judged their contemporaries, he bestows high praise upon men whose works and names have perished from the world's memory. But in his comprehensive eulogy Shakespeare has this distinction, that while he shares equally all other praise, it is said of him, that, "as Plautus and Seneca are accounted the best for comedy and tragedy among the Latins, so Shakespeare among the English is the most excellent in both kinds for the stage." * There is ample evidence

---

* The following are all the passages of this chapter of the *Palladis Tamia* in which Shakespeare's name appears. They have never been all reprinted before.

"As the Greekes tongue is made famous and eloquent by Homer, Hesiod, Euripedes, Æschylus, Sophocles, Pindarus, Phyloclides, and Aristophanes; and the Latine tongue by Virgile, Ouid, Horace, Sicilius Italius, Lucanus, Lucretius, Ausonius, and Claudianus, so the English tongue is mightily enriched and gorgeously invested in rare ornaments by sir Philip Sidney, Spencer, Daniel, Drayton, Warner, Shakespeare, Marlow, and Chapman."

that this appreciation of Shakespeare was general, and that, although his contemporaries could hardly have suspected that his genius would overshadow all others in our literature, they regarded

"As the soule of Euphorbus was thought to liue in Pythagoras, so the sweete wittie soule of Ouid liues in mellifluous and hony-tongued Shakespeare; witnes his *Venus and Adonis*, his *Lucrece*, his sugred sonnets among his priuate friends," &c.

"As Plautus and Seneca are accounted the best for Comedy and Tragedy among the Latines: so Shakespeare among y⁰ English is the most excellent in both kinds for the stage; for Comedy, witnes his *Gĕtlemĕ of Verona*, his *Errors*, his *Loue labors lost*, his *Loue labours wonne*, his *Midsummers night dreame*, & his *Merchant of Venice*: for Tragedy his *Richard the 2. Richard the 3. Henry the 4. King Iohn, Titus Andronicus* and his *Romeo and Iuliet*."

"As Epius Stolo said, the Muses would speake with Plautus tongue, if they would speak Latin; so I say the Muses would speak with Shakespeare's fine-filed phrase, if they would speak English."

"And as Horace saith of his, Exegi monumentū ære perennius, Regaliq; situ pyramidum altius; Quod non imber edax; Non Aquilo impotens possit diruere, aut innumerabilis annorum series et fuga temporum; so say I severally of Sir Philip Sidneys, Spencers, Daniels, Draytons, Shakespeares, and Warner's workes."

"As Pindarus, Anacreon, and Callimachus among the Greekes, and Horace and Catullus among the Latines, are the best lyrick poets; so in this faculty the best amōg our poets are Spencer (who excelleth in all kinds), Daniel Drayton, Shakespeare, Brettō."

"As these tragicke poets flourished in Greece, Æschylus, Euripedes, Sophocles, Alexander Aetolus, Achæus Erithriæus, Astydamas Atheniēsis, Apollodorus Tarsensis, Nicomachus Phrygius, Thespis Atticus, and Timon Apolloniates; and these among the Latines, Accius, M. Attilius, Pomponius Secundus and Seneca; so these are our best for tragedie; the Lord Buck-

him as a poet and a dramatist beyond comparison among his countrymen.   Shakespeare's plays
filled the theatre to overflowing when even Jonson's would hardly pay expenses.* •It was not

hurst, Doctor Leg of Cambridge, Dr. Edes of Oxford, Maister
Edward Ferris, the Authour of the *Mirrour for Magistrates*,
Marlow, Peele, Watson, Kid, Shakespeare, Drayton, Chapman,
Decker, and Beniamin Iohnson."

"The best poets for comedy among the Greeks are these:
Menander, Aristophanes, Eupolis Atheniensis Alexis, Terius,
Nicostratus, Amipsias Atheniensis, Anaxādrides Rhodius, Aris-
tonymus, Archippus Atheniēsis, and Callias Atheniensis; and
among the Latines, Plautus, Terence, Næuius, Sext. Turpilius,
Licinius Imbrex, and Virgilius Romanus; so the best for comedy
amongst us bee Edward Earle of Oxforde, Doctor Gager of Oxforde, Maister Rowley, once a rare scholler of learned Pem-
brooke Hall in Cambridge, Maister Edwardes, one of her Maies-
ties Chappell, eloquent and wittie John Lilly, Lodge, Gascoyne,
Greene, Shakespeare, Thomas Nash, Thomas Heywood, Anthony Mundye, our best plotter, Chapman, Porter, Wilson,
Hathway, and Henry Chettle."

"As these are famous among the Greeks for elegie, Melan-
thus, Mymnerus Colophonius, Olympius Mysius, Parthenius
Nicæus, Philetas Cous, Theogenes Megarensis, and Pigres Hali-
carnasœus; and these among the Latines, Mecænas, Ouid, Ti-
bullus, Propertius, T. Valgius, Cassius Seuerus, and Clodius
Sabinus; so these are the most passionate among us to bewaile
and bemoane the perplexities of loue; Henrie Howard Earle of
Surrey, sir Thomas Wyat the elder, sir Francis Brian, sir Philip
Sidney, sir Walter Rawley, sir Edward Dyer, Spencer, Daniel, •
Drayton, Shakespeare, Whetstone, Gascoyne, Samuell Page
sometimes fellowe of *Corpus Christi* Colledge in Oxford, Church-
yard, Bretton."

* See the following lines from the verses of Leonard Digges,
prefixed to the edition of Shakespeare's Poems published in 1640.

"So have I seen, when Cæsar would appear,
  And on the stage at half-sword parley were

6*   I

until the moral and literary decadence of the
Restoration, and the establishment of the exotic
and artificial standards of the so-called Augustan

> Brutus & Cassius, O how the audience
> Were ravish'd ! with what wonder they went thence !
> When, some new day, she would not brook a line
> Of tedious, though well-labour'd Catiline ;
> Sejanus too, was irksome : they priz'd more
> 'Honest' Iago, or the jealous Moor.
> And though the Fox & subtil Alchymist,
> Long intermitted, could not quite be mist,
> Though these have sham'd all th' ancients, & might raise
> Their author's merit with a crown of bays,
> Yet these sometimes, even at a friend's desire,
> Acted, have scarce defray'd the sea-coal fire,
> And door-keepers : when, let but Falstaff come,
> Hal, Poins, the rest — you scarce shall have room,
> All is so pester'd : let but Beatrice
> And Benedick be seen lo ! in a trice
> The cock-pit, galleries, boxes, all are full,
> To hear Malvolio, that cross-garter'd gull.
> Brief, there is nothing in his wit-fraught book,
> Whose sound we would not hear, on whose worth look,
> Like old coin'd gold, whose lines, in every page,
> Shall pass true current to succeeding age."

In *The Return from Parnassus*, a comedy acted certainly before the death of Queen Elizabeth by the students of St. John's
College, Cambridge, but the earliest known copy of which was
printed in 1606, there is this tribute to the native superiority of
Shakespeare : —

"*Kemp.* Few of the ◆niuersity pen plaies well; they smell
too much of that writer Ovid, and that writer Metamorphosis,
and talke too much of Proserpina and Jupiter. Why, heres our
fellow Shakespeare puts them all downe ; I and Ben Jonson too.
O, that Ben Jonson is a pestilent fellow : he brought up Horace
giuing the poets a pill : but our fellow Shakespeare hath giuen
him a purge that made him beray his credit."

age of English literature, that he was thought to have equals, and even superiors. In spite of Shakespeare's manifest and generally acknowledged superiority, under which Jonson, conscious both of larger learning and more laborious effort, fretted a little, there was warm friendship between the two men, which lasted through Shakespeare's life, and the memory of which inspired and softened gruff Ben when his friend had passed away. There was never more generous or more glowing eulogy of one man by another than that in Jonson's verses which appeared among the preliminary matter to the first folio; and in the well-known passage in his *Discoveries*, written in his later years, the crusty critic, though he must carp at the poet, breaks out into a hearty expression of admiration and cherished love of the man.*

* "I remember the Players have often mentioned it as an honour to Shakespeare, that in his writing (whatsoever he penn'd) he never blotted out line. My answer hath beene, would he had blotted a thousand. Which they thought a malevolent speech. I had not told posterity this, but for their ignorance, who choose that circumstance to commend their friend by, wherein he most faulted. And to justifie mine own candor, (for I lov'd the man, and doe honour his memory (on this side idolatry) as much as any.) Hee was (indeed) honest, and of an open and free nature: had an excellent *Phantsie*, brave notions, and gentle expressions: wherein he flow'd with that facility, that sometime it was necessary he should be stop'd. *Sufflaminandus erat*, as Augustus said of Haterius. His wit was in his owne power, would the rule of it had beene so too. Many times he fell into those things, could not escape laughter: As when he said in the person of Cæsar

In 1599 Shakespeare received a not very welcome tribute to his poetic eminence. A bookseller named Jaggard, who, even in those days of extremest license in his craft, was distinguished by his disregard of the rights of literary property and literary reputation, printed a volume of verses under the unmeaning title *The Passionate Pilgrim*, upon the title-page of which he impudently placed Shakespeare's name, although but a part of its meagre contents were from his pen, and that part had been surreptitiously obtained. Shakespeare was much offended that Jaggard made so bold with his name. This we know on the testimony of Heywood, who in a second edition saw two of his own compositions also attributed to the favorite of the hour, and who publicly claimed his own.* Shakespeare, although offended at the personal liberty, seems to have been careless of any possible injury to his reputation. No evidence of any public denial on his part is known to exist ; and it was not until after the publication of the third edition of the volume, in 1612, that his name

one speaking to him, *Cæsar thou dost me wrong.* Hee replyed : *Cæsar did never wrong, but with just cause ;* and such like ; which were ridiculous. But hee redeemed his vices, with his virtues. There was euer more in him to be praysed, then to be pardoned." *Discoveries. De Shakespeare nostrat.* Lond., fol., 1640, p. 97.

* These were two poetic epistles, from Paris to Helen and from Helen to Paris. See the postscript to Heywood's *Apology for Actors*, 1612. *The Passionate Pilgrim* was printed only on one side of each leaf, to eke out the volume.

was taken from the title-page. In 1600 he was made for a time to father *Sir John Oldcastle;* but the publisher appears to have been speedily undeceived, or compelled to do justice; for Shakespeare's name was omitted from some part of the impression. We know from Henslow's Diary that *Sir John Oldcastle* was written by Munday, Drayton, Wilson, and Hathway, jointly. The removal of Shakespeare's name from the title-page was more probably owing to their pride and jealousy than to Shakespeare's. An edition of *King Henry the Fifth* was published in this year, which shows from internal evidence that the bookseller was so eager to put this work of Shakespeare's before the public that he used a version obtained by surreptitious means, and so mangled as to be almost without connection from page to page. A misfortune, which we may well believe was more seriously regarded by Shakespeare than any liberty with his reputation, fell upon him also in this year, through the plot which cost Essex his head, and his friend and Shakespeare's patron, Southampton, his liberty during the remainder of Elizabeth's reign.

The latter years of John Shakespeare's checkered life seem to have been passed in tranquil though humble ease, through the filial care of his distinguished son. He died in September, 1601, as we know by the record of his burial on the 8th of that month; being then, if we set him down

as twenty-one or twenty-two years old when we
first hear of him at Stratford, somewhat more than
seventy years of age. His house in Henley Street,
and probably such other real property as he may
have owned at the time of his death, descended
to William, who, though the possessor and occu-
pier of the Great House which had doubtless im-
pressed his youthful imagination by its magnitude
and its village pre-eminence, clung to the memories of his humbler home, and always kept it in
his possession. During the next year he added
to his landed estate one hundred and seven acres
of land in the parish of Old Stratford, which
he bought from the brothers William and John
a Combe. He also bought a cottage in Henley
Street from Walter Gettey; and from Hercules
Underhill, a messuage with two barns, two orchards, and two gardens. He was not in Stratford at the time of the completion of the first of
these purchases, in which he was represented by
his brother Gilbert. In this year, while he was
thus rapidly acquiring that landed interest in his
native county without which no man in his day
could maintain a respectable position as a gentleman of family, the burgesses of Stratford passed
an ordinance forbidding the exhibition of plays
of any kind in the chamber, the guild-hall, or any
part of the house or court, — a proscription which
was made more rigid in 1612. Is it strange that
under these circumstances Shakespeare did not

show much solicitude about the careful publication of his dramas and the perpetuation of his fame as a playwright?

The death of Elizabeth in 1603, which gave our fathers, instead of a royal family that tyrannized firmly and sagaciously, one that was at once despotic, feeble, and vacillating, and whose monstrous outrages upon the rights of Englishmen contributed mainly to the founding of an English nation upon this continent, produced a change in Shakespeare's professional position, traces of which remain in the mother country until this day. One of King James's earliest warrants under the privy seal of England made the company of which Shakespeare was a member "His Majesty's servants"; a designation which has since always pertained to the performers at the leading theatre of London. In this warrant Shakespeare's name appears second, Laurence Fletcher's being first.*

---

* It is, verbatim et literatim, thus : —

"By the King.

"Right trusty and welbeloved Counsellor, we greete you well, and will and commaund you, that under our privie Seale in your custody for the time being, you cause our letters to be derected to the keeper of our greate seale of England, commauding him under our said greate Seale, he cause our letters to be made patents in forme following. James, by the grace of God, King of England, Scotland, Fraunce, and Irland, defendor of the faith, &c. To all Justices, Maiors, Sheriffs, Constables, Headboroughes, and other our officers and loving subjects greeting. Know ye, that we of our speciall grace, certaine knowledge, and

And in this year, too, if we could believe in the
authenticity of a letter professing to be written by
the poet Daniel to Sir Thomas Egerton, and which
Mr. Collier brought to light in 1835,* Shakespeare

meere motion have licenced and authorized, and by these presentes doe licence and authorize, these our servants, Lawrence
Fletcher, William Shakespeare, Richard Burbage, Augustine
Phillippes, John Hemmings, Henrie Condell, William Sly, Robert Armyn, Richard Cowlye, and the rest of their associats, freely
to use & exercise the arte and faculty of playing Comedies, Tragedies, Histories, Enterludes, Moralls, Pastoralls, Stage plaies, and
such other like, as that thei have already studied or hereafter
shall use or studie, as well for the recreation of our loving subjects, as for our solace and pleasure, when we shall thinke good
to see them, during our pleasure. And the said Comedies, Tragedies, Histories, Enterludes, Moralls, Pastoralls, Stage plaies, and
such like, to shew & exercise publiquely to their best commo-
ditie, when the infection of the plague shall decrease, as well
within theire now usuall howse called the Globe, within our county of Surrey, as also within anie towne halls, or mout halls, or
other convenient places within the liberties & freedome of any
other citie, universitie, towne, or borough whatsoever within our
said realmes and dominions. Willing and commaunding you,
and every of you, as you tender our pleasure, not only to permit
and suffer them heerin, without any your letts, hinderances, or
molestations, during our said pleasure, but also to be ayding or
assisting to them, yf any wrong be to them offered. And to al-
lowe them such former courtesies, as hathe bene given to men of
their place and qualitie : and also what further favour you shall
shew to these our servants for our sake, we shall take kindly at
your hands. And these our letters shall be your sufficient warrant and discharge in this behalfe. Given under our Signet at
our mannor of Greenewiche, the seaventeenth day of May in the
first yere of our raigne of England, France, and Ireland, & of
Scotland the six & thirtieth.

                              "Ex per Lake."

* *New Facts regarding the Life of Shakespeare.*

applied for the office of Master of the Queen's
Revels, which, through Sir Thomas Egerton's influence, was given to Daniel. The genuineness
of this letter, in which the allusion to Shakespeare
is slight and incidental, has been disputed on
purely palæographical grounds. But it may also
be questioned whether Shakespeare would have
applied at this time for such an office as that of
Master of the Queen's Revels, which would have
occupied much of his time and attention; for he
was now at the height of his reputation, and was
gathering a profit from his professional labors for
the loss of which the position of Master of the
Queen's Revels would not have been a recompense. If indeed he did apply for it, the world
has reason to be thankful at his disappointment.
For it is to the first ten years of the seventeenth
century that we owe the great tragedies, *Troilus
and Cressida, Othello, King Lèar, Timon of Athens, Macbeth, Julius Cæsar, Antony and Cleopatra,*
and *Coriolanus,* with *Cymbeline, All 's Well that
Ends Well, Measure for Measure,* and Shakespeare's part in *Pericles* and *The Taming of the
Shrew,* of which all but *Pericles* and *The Taming
of the Shrew* were quite surely written after 1603.

In that year Ben Jonson's *Sejanus* was produced at the Black-friars, and the author of *Hamlet* might have been seen playing a subordinate
part in it. But about this time he appears to
have retired from the stage, where, as we have

seen, he had gained but little distinction at much
sacrifice of feeling, and to have confined his labors
for the theatre to the more congenial occupation
of play-writing.   Chettle, it is true, says that
Shakespeare was excellent in the quality he professed ; but in that commendation, "quality" may
include play-writing as well as play-acting ; and
mayhap it refers with some vagueness to both.
According to a contemporary epigram by Davies
(in *The Scourge of Folly*), which has been previously mentioned, Shakespeare played kingly
parts ; and in so doing offended his new master,
and marred his fortunes.   The verses are not
clear, as the reader will see.

> " *To our English Terence, Mr. Will Shakespeare.*
>
> " Some say, good Will, which I in sport do sing,
>   Had'st thou not plaid some kingly parts in sport,
>   Thou had'st bin a companion for a king,
>   And beene a king among the meaner sort.
>
> " Some others raile ; but raile as they thinke fit,
>   Thou hast no rayling, but a raigning wit :
>   And honesty thou sow'st, which they do reape,
>   So to increase their stocke, which they do keepe."

It cannot be that Shakespeare in playing kingly
parts ventured to take off " God's vicegerent upon
earth."   The temptation to do so must have been
great ; but he was too prudent to indulge in a sport
so expensive and so dangerous.   It is difficult to
see how the mere decorous performance of kingly
parts could have offended James ; and yet we must
remember that he was as petty and capricious as

he was tyrannical. Nevertheless the king was attacked through the players; of which the following very direct evidence has been found in a treatise on hunting preserved among the Sloane MSS. The writer, having censured the players for lack of decorum, thus continues: "What madnesse is it, I saye, that possesseth them under faigned persons to be censureing of their soveraigne: surely though these poets for many years have, for the most part, lefte foles and devills out of their playes, yet nowe on the suddayne they make them all playe the foles most notoriouslye and impudently in medlinge with him (in waye of taxacion) by whome they live and have in manner there very being." In this grovelling and blasphemous style it was the fashion to speak of a man who was about as mean and sordid a creature as ever lived.

There is a story which was first printed in Lintot's edition of Shakespeare's Poems, published in 1710, that King James wrote with his own hand an amicable letter to Shakespeare, which was once in the hands of Davenant, as a creditable person then living could testify; and conjecture, ever ready, has made Macbeth's prophetic vision of kings the occasion of the compliment. It is well to have a more creditable person than Davenant to corroborate such a story; and Oldys, in a manuscript note to his copy of Fuller's *Worthies*, says that the Duke of Bucking-

ham told Lintot that he had seen this letter in
Davenant's possession. If Oldys meant George
Villiers, the last Duke of Buckingham, which is
possible, he added not much to our security for
the mere existence of such a letter; but if he
meant John Sheffield, the first Duke of the County of Buckingham, which is also possible, we
can the more readily believe that Davenant produced such a letter as that in question, although
even then we lack satisfactory evidence of its genuineness. Davenant is poor authority for any
story about Shakespeare. This one, however, is
more probable than another which places Shakespeare in royal company. It was unheard of till
late in the eighteenth century, and is to the effect
that Queen Elizabeth, being at the theatre one
evening when Shakespeare was playing a king,
bowed to him as she crossed the stage. He did
not return the salutation, but went on with his
part. To ascertain whether the omission was an
intentional preservation of assumed character, or
an oversight, the Queen again passed him, and
dropped her glove. Shakespeare immediately
picked it up, and, following the royal virgin, handed it to her, adding on the instant these lines to a
speech which he was just delivering, and so aptly
and easily that they seemed to belong to it.

> "And though now bent on this high embassy,
>   Yet stoop we to take up our cousin's glove."

The Queen, it is said, was highly pleased, and

complimented him upon his adroitness and his courtesy. In judging the credibility of this story, it should be remembered that in Shakespeare's time the most distinguished part of the audience went upon the stage, during the performance, in what must have been a very confusing manner. But the anecdote is plainly one made to meet the craving for personal details of Shakespeare's life. In addition to its inherent improbability, Shakespeare well knew what the author of the verses seems not to have known, — that kings cannot go on embassies. Empty compliment and his share of payment to the company for services rendered seem to have been all the benefit that Shakespeare obtained from royal favor. There is not the least reason for believing that either the strong-minded woman or the weak-minded man in whose reigns he flourished recognized his superiority by special distinction or substantial reward.*

* Mr. Peter Cunningham's Extracts from the Accounts of the Revels at Court include the following entries of the performance of Shakespeare's plays before King James, between 1604 and 1611 : —

The Plaiers.		The Poets which mayd the plaies.
By the Kings Ma^{tis} plaiers.	Hallamas day being the first of Novembar, A play in the Banketinge House att Whithall called the Moor of Venis. [Nov. 1st, 1604.]	
By his Ma^{tis} plaiers.	The Sunday ffollowinge, A Play of the Merry Wives of Winsor. [Nov. 4th, 1604.]	

On the 5th of June, 1607, Susanna Shakespeare,
who was her father's favorite daughter, and who
seems to have been a superior woman, was married to Dr. John Hall, a physician of good repute
in his county.   On the 31st of December of the
same year, Edmund Shakespeare was buried in
the parish of St. Saviour's, Southwark.   He was

The Plaiers.		The Poets which mayd the plaies.
By his Matie plaiers.	On St. Stivens night in the Hall a Play called Mesur for Mesur. [Dec. 26th, 1604.]	Shaxberd.
By his Matie plaiers.	On Inosents Night The Plaie of Errors. [Dec. 28th, 1604.]	Shaxberd.
By his Matie plaiers.	Betwin Newers day and Twelfe day a Play of Loves Labours Lost. [1605.]	
By his Matie plaiers.	On the 7 of January was played the play of Henry the fift. [1605.]	
By his Matie plaiers.	On Shrovsunday A play of the Marchant of Venis. [Mar. 24th, 1605.]	Shaxberd.
By his Matie plaiers.	On Shrovtusday A Play cauled the Merchant of Venis againe commaunded by the Kings Matie. [Mar. 26, 1605.]	Shaxberd.

[Accounts from Oct. 31st, 1611, to Nov. 1st, 1612.]

By the Kings players.	Hallomas nyght was presented att Whithall before ye Kinges Matie a play called the Tempest. [Nov. 1st, 1611.]
The Kings players.	The 5th of November: A play called ye winters nightes Tayle. [1611.]

a player of no distinction, who probably had followed his brother to London and obtained a place
in the Black-friars company by his influence.

The inducements presented to Shakespeare by
his Puritan townsman Sturley, as early as the
year 1597, to the purchase of tithes in his native
place, were insufficient at the time, or he had not
the needful money at hand; for he then acquired
no interest in them. But he seems to have entertained the project favorably, and to have formed
the design of making an investment of this kind;
for in 1605 he bought the moiety of a lease,
granted in 1544, of all the tithes of Stratford,
Old Stratford, Bishopton, and Welcombe; for
which he paid down in cash £440. This is the
most important purchase he is known to have
made. The consideration was equal to between
eleven and twelve thousand dollars of our money.

The natural desire of transmitting an honorable name and a fair estate to descendants seems
to have been strong in Shakespeare, and his
hopes, sadly disappointed by the early death of
his only son, must have been a little dashed again
by the event which made him first a grandfather,
— the birth, in February, 1607–8, of a daughter to
his daughter Susanna, the wife of Dr. Hall. She
brought her husband no other children. In September following Mary Arden died, having survived her husband seven years. Shakespeare's
mother must have been about seventy years old

at her death, which took place probably in the old home in Henley Street, to which she had gone fifty years before as John Shakespeare's wife, and where the son was born to whom she doubtless owed her undisturbed residence in that house of hope and of sad and tender memories. We do not know that he was present at her funeral; and he seems to have set up no stone to tell us where she or his father lay. But the same is true with regard to his son Hamnet; and it is reasonable to suppose that his own death prevented the completion of designs for a tomb for the family. The next month, October of this same year, 1608, affords us, though in the most formal and unsatisfactory manner, our nearest approximation to a record of a social gathering at which he was present. On the 16th, he was sponsor at the baptism of the son of Henry Walker, an alderman of Stratford. The boy was called after his godfather, who remembered him in his will by a legacy of xx. s. in gold. So that, after all, as Shakespeare's mother's funeral took place on the 6th of the previous month, we may be pretty sure that he performed for her the last offices, and that he was remaining at Stratford in temporary and much coveted seclusion when he was asked to be William Walker's godfather.

In 1605, when he was forty years old, he had produced his great tragedy, *King Lear*, the most admirable and wonderful work of human genius.

Of this drama the bookseller obtained a copy in 1608, and in that year published three editions of it, the high reputation of its author, as well as the public admiration of this particular work, having been shown not only by the unusual demand which the bookseller was called upon to supply, but by the means which the latter took to make it clear upon the title-page that this was "Mr. William Shakespeare *HIS* Tragedy of King Lear."

For anxious souls who are concerned upon the subject of Shakespeare's taxes, there is a comfortable memorandum preserved at Dulwich College, which professes to give the names of all those who in April, 1609, were rated and assessed for a weekly payment toward the relief of the poor of the Clink Liberty in Southwark. Among fifty-seven names are those of Philip Henslow, Edward Alleyn, and Mr. Shakespeare, who are each assessed weekly at vj. *d.* But, alas! this invaluable evidence also is impeached as spurious; and judging from the fac-simile of it which has been published, it is certainly but a clumsy, and sometimes careless, imitation of seventeenth-century writing. But for this loss there is recompense in the authenticity of a court record, by which we know that in August, 1608, Shakespeare sued John Addenbroke of Stratford, got a judgment for £6, and £1 4*s.* costs, and that, Addenbroke being returned *non est inventus*, Shakespeare sued his bail, Thomas Hornby, the proceedings lasting until

June, 1609. Four years before, Shakespeare had
sued one Philip Rogers in the Stratford Court of
Record for £1 15s. 10d. He had sold Rogers malt
to the value of £1 19s. 10d., and had lent him
2s., of which the debtor had paid but 6s. And
so Shakespeare brought suit for what is called in
trade the balance of the account, which represented about $40 of our money. These stories
grate upon our feelings with a discord as much
harsher than that which disturbs us when we
hear of Addison suing poor Steele for £100, as
Shakespeare lives in our hearts the lovelier as
well as the greater man than Addison. But Addison's case was aggravated by the fact that the
debtor was his long-time friend and fellow-laborer.
Debts are to be paid, and rogues who can pay
and will not pay must be made to pay ; but the
pursuit of an impoverished man, for the sake of
imprisoning him and depriving him both of the
power of paying his debt and supporting himself
and his family, is an incident in Shakespeare's life
which it requires the utmost allowance and consideration for the practice of the time and country
to enable us to contemplate with equanimity,—
satisfaction is impossible.

The biographer of Shakespeare must record
these facts, because the literary antiquaries have
unearthed and brought them forward as " new particulars of the life of Shakespeare." We hunger,
and we receive these husks ; we open our mouths

for food, and we break our teeth against these stones. What have these law-papers, in the involved verbiage of which dead quarrels lie embalmed, in hideous and grotesque semblance of their living shapes, their life-blood dried that lent them all their little dignity, their action, and their glow, exhaling only a faint and sickly odor of the venom that has kept them from decay,—what have these to do with the life of him whom his friends delighted to call sweet and gentle? Could not these, at least, have been allowed to rest? The parties to them have been two centuries in their graves. Why awake from slumber the empty echoes of their living strife?

It is almost as remote from the purpose of true biography, though it is somewhat more satisfactory, to ascertain the amount of the income which Shakespeare so laboriously acquired and so jealously guarded. That the basis of a calculation might not be lacking, the indefatigable (and ever successful) Mr. Collier produced from the manuscripts at Bridgewater House a memorandum which professes to state the value of Shakespeare's property in the Black-friars. The reader will remember the fruitless opposition of the Lord Mayor and Aldermen of London to the establishment of this theatre. Neither their animosity nor their efforts ceased with their first failure. They neglected no opportunity, no means, to attain their end. Finally, in 1608, Sir Henry Mon-

tagu, the then Attorney-General, gave an opinion
that the jurisdiction of the corporation of London
extended over the Liberty of the Black-friars, and
there was another attempt to dislodge Richard
Burbadge, William Shakespeare, and their fellows.
Either through lack of title or of influence, it was
in vain. The players could not be ousted. Then,
if we could accept the evidence of Mr. Collier's
document, the Mayor and Aldermen thought of
buying out the men whom they could not turn
out, and had an estimate made of the value of the
Black-friars theatrical property, which proved to
be in the bulk worth £7,000, of which sum Shakespeare's shares and wardrobe property absorbed
£1,433 6s. 8d. According to this memorandum
Shakespeare's income from his four shares was
£133 6s. 8d.; the rent of a wardrobe and properties set down as worth £500 could not have been
less than £50; which makes the Black-friars income £183 6s. 8d. Reckoning a like return from
the Globe, we have £366 13s. 4d.; and remembering that Shakespeare had other property, and
also a productive pen, Mr. Collier, whose calculation this is, certainly rather underrates than
overrates his income at £400 — equal to about
$10,000 now — yearly. But alas! this paper, like
so many others brought to light by the same hand,
and like the professed Southampton letter which
refers to the same circumstances, has been pronounced spurious by high, though perhaps not

infallible, authority.* Yet the conclusions based upon it are sustained by a letter of unquestioned

---

* The following is a copy of the memorandum in question. It has been pronounced spurious by Sir Frederic Madden, Mr. T. Duffus Hardy, Mr. N. E. S. A. Hamilton, Professor Brewer (as to whose official positions see the note on p. 107), Mr. Richard Giardner, M. W. B. D. D. Turnbull, and Mr. Halliwell.

"For avoiding of the playhouse in the Blacke Friers.

Impr	Richard Burbidge owith the Fee and is alsoe a sharer therein. His interest he rateth at the grosse summe of 1000li for the Fee and for his foure Shares the summe of 933li 6s 8d	1933 li 6s 8d
Item	Laz Fletcher owith three shares wch he rateth at 700li that is at 7 years purchase for eche share or 33li 6s 8d one year with an other.	700 li
Item	W. Shakspeare asketh for the wardrobe and properties of the same playhouse 500li, and for his 4 shares, the same as his fellowes Burbidge and Fletcher 933li 6s 8d	1433 li 6s 8d
Item	Heminges and Condell eche 2 shares	933 li 6s 8d
Item	Joseph Taylor one share and an halfe	350 li
Item	Lowing one share and an halfe	350 li
Item	foure more playeres with one halfe share unto eche of them	466 li 13s 4d
	Suma totalis	6166. 13. 4.

Moreover, the hired men of the Companie demaund some recompence for their greate losse and the Widowes and Orphanes of players who are paide by the Sharers at diuers rates & proporcōns soe as in the whole it will coste the Lo. Mayor and Citizens at the least } 7000 li "

Here may conveniently be added another document from the same source, which rests under even graver imputations against its genuineness. It professes to be a draft or abridged transcript of a warrant, appointing Robert Daiborne, William Shakespeare, and others, instructors of the Children of the Queen's Revels. But aside from the palæographic condemnation of the paper, its contents have been shown by Mr. Halliwell (in his

authenticity in the State Paper Office at London.
Mr. John Chamberlain, writing to Sir Dudley

Curiosities of Shakespearian Criticism, p. 22) to be entirely incongruous with the circumstances under which it professes to have been written.

" Right trusty and welbeloved, &c., James, &c.   To all Mayors, Sheriffs, Justices of the Peace, &c.   Whereas the Queene, our dearest wife, hath for her pleasure and recreation appointed her servaunts Robert Daiborne, &c. to provide and bring upp a convenient nomber of children, who shall be called the Children of her Majesties Revells, knowe ye that we have appointed and authorized, and by these presents doe appoint and authorize the said Robert Daiborne, William Shakespeare, Nathaniel Field, and Edward Kirkham, from time to time to provide and bring upp a convenient nomber of children, and them to instruct and exercise in the quality of playing Tragedies, Comedies, &c., by the name of the Children of the Revells to the Queene, within the Blackfryers, in our Citie of London, or els where within our realme of England.   Wherefore we will and command you, and everie of you, to permitt her said servaunts to keepe a convenient nomber of children, by the name of the Children of the Revells to the Queene, and them to exercise in the qualitie of playing according to her royal pleasure.   Provided alwaies, that no playes, &c. shall be by them presented, but such playes, &c. as have received the approbation and allowance of our Maister of the Revells for the tyme being.   And these our lres. shall be your sufficient warrant in this behalfe.   In witnesse whereof, &c., 4° die Janij. 1609.

Bl Fr and globe
Wh Fr and parish garden } All in & neere London
Curten and fortune
Hope and Swanne

" Proud povertie.   Engl tragedie.
Widow's mite.   False Friendes.
Antonio kinsmen.   Hate and love.
Triumph of Truth.   Taming of S.
Touchstone.   K. Edw 2.
Grissell.   Stayed."

Carleton at the Hague in 1619, mentions that the death of the Queen hinders the players from the exercise of their calling, and adds, "One speciale man among them, Burbadge, is lately dead, and hath left, they say, better than £300 land." Now, if Burbadge, who was but an actor, could acquire landed property to the value of £300 yearly, surely Shakespeare might well receive £100 more from all his sources of income. A chancery suit upon which Shakespeare was obliged to enter, apparently in 1612, for the protection of his interests in the tithes of Stratford and neighboring parishes, shows us that his receipts from that quarter were £60 (now full $1500) yearly.* To

I here remark upon a hitherto unnoticed but very significant and suspicious fact in connection with this paper, and one of a very unpleasant nature for Mr. Collier. It will be observed that the list of plays which follows the essential part of the paper, and which is followed by the memorandum "Stayed," ends with "K. Edw 2." According to the fac-simile made by a fac-similist of high repute in London, this list is in a single column, and between the title of the last play and the word "Stayed" there is a blank space about two inches wide. Now, in the copy of this paper given in Mr. Collier's Life of Shakespeare (p. ccxxix.) "K. Edw 2" is followed by the name of another play, "Mirror of Life." Whence did Mr. Collier derive the name of that play, which does not exist upon the document itself as it appears in the Bridgewater MSS.? From a draft from which the Bridgewater MS. was written out? How else? For it must be noted that this is not an instance of error in reading or copying, but an absolute interpolation. See the Southampton letter above referred to, on pp. 107, 108 of this volume.

* The Bill, which may be found at full length in Mr. Halliwell's *Life of Shakespeare*, furnishes the following single paragraph of interest : —

finish all that need be said about mere business transactions, in March, 1612–3, Shakespeare, in connection with "William Johnson citizein and vintner of London and John Jackson and John Hemynge gentlemen," purchased from "Henry Walker citizein and minstrell" a house and the land attached, not far from the Black-friars theatre; paying for it £140, of which £60 were left on bond and mortgage.   Mr. Collier has reasonably conjectured that Shakespeare joined in this purchase to serve his fellow-actor, Heminge; and that, Heminge and the two other purchasers not being able to discharge the amount which he had paid and assume the mortgage, the property fell to him.   The deed of conveyance has a peculiar interest as bearing one of the four certainly authentic signatures of Shakespeare.   It is now preserved in the library of the city of London, at Guildhall.

Shakespeare had been about eighteen years in London, and with the approach of his fortieth year was attaining the height of his reputation, when a club was established there, which owes a

" . . . . and your oratour William Schackspeare hath an estate and interest of and in the moyty or one half of all tythes of corne and grayne aryseing within the townes, villages and ffields, and of and in the moity or half of all tythes of wool and lambs, and of all small and privy tythes, oblacions and alterages arisinge or increasing in Old Stratford, Bishopton, and Welcome, being in the said parishe of Stratford, or within the wholl parishe of Stratford uppon Avon aforesaid, for and during all the residue of the said terme, beinge of the yearly value of threescore pounds."

wide celebrity and perpetual fame chiefly to him, although there is no evidence that he was one of its members. It was founded by Sir Walter Raleigh, and met at the Mermaid, — a favorite tavern in Bread Street. Here Raleigh himself, Jonson, Beaumont, Fletcher, Selden, Colton, Carew, Donne, and others their chosen companions, met for social and convivial enjoyment; and that they did not admit Will Shakespeare of their crew, who can believe? Yet our confidence that he sat with them round that board which Beaumont celebrates in his well-known lines,* can only rest upon the moral impossibility that he should have been absent. There all students of the literature and manners of those days have reasonably agreed in placing the scene of the wit combats between Shakespeare and Jonson, the fame of which had reached Fuller's time, and caused him to imagine

* " What things have we seen
Done at the Mermaid! heard words that have been
So nimble, and so full of subtle flame,
As if that every one from whom they came
Had meant to put his whole wit in a jest,
And had resolv'd to live a fool the rest
Of his dull life; then when there hath been thrown
Wit able enough to justify the town
For three days past, wit that might warrant be
For the whole city to talk foolishly
Till that were cancell'd, and, when that was gone,
We left an air behind us which alone
Was able to make the two next companies
Right witty, though but downright fools, more wise."

Letter to Ben Jonson.

7*

the encounter of the two like that between a
Spanish great galleon and an English man-of-
war; Jonson, like the former, built far higher in
learning, and solid, but slow in his performances;
Shakespeare, like the latter, less in bulk, but
lighter in movement, turning and tacking nimbly,
and taking every advantage by the quickness of
his wit and invention. This, however is only Fuller's imagination. We have no testimony as to
the quality or the style of wit exhibited by either
of these redoubted combatants; and all the pretended specimens of their colloquial jests and
repartees that have reached us are so pitiably
tame and forced, that they are plainly foolish fab-
rications.

We all are sure that Shakespeare must have
been one of this Mermaid club, because of his certain acquaintance with some, and his very probable acquaintance with all of its members, and because of the qualifications which made him the
most desirable of men as one of such a social
circle. For he was not only a great poet, a successful playwright, and an influential man in his
company, but, according to all accounts, a charming companion. What, then, may we conclude,
was Shakespeare's social life in London, while
from earliest manhood to maturity he rose by his
connection with literature and the drama from
obscurity to the highest distinction attainable by
those means in that day?

We have seen that at twenty-eight years of age he enjoyed the acquaintance and had won the respect of men very far above him in social position. It could not have been that his intercourse with that class of society was confined to casual meetings at the theatre and convivial gatherings at the tavern. Men of his gifts, rating him merely at contemporary estimation, are too rare in any society not to be welcomed if there are not special reasons for their exclusion. Nay, they sometimes make their way into the most fastidious circles, even when they are needy and debauched, or uncouth and domineering. And in the time of Queen Elizabeth such association was more open to them than it is in our day, from the very fact that then the grades of society were so distinctly marked, and the position of every man so exactly known, that there was no apprehension on the one part, or hope on the other, of any confusion of class and rank. Difference in social position and in occupation was then indicated unmistakably in the every-day dress and even the holiday costume of the wearer. Peasant, yeoman, artisan, tradesman, and gentleman could then be distinguished from each other almost as far as they could be seen. Except in cases of unusual audacity, neither presumed to wear the dress of his betters. But to these rigid and exclusive rules of demarcation the poets, and especially the players, were, in a certain degree, exceptions. Even in dress they assumed a license which was made the subject of remark and satire, and rustled through the streets in silks and satins, with swords and plumed hats, like noblemen. The reasons for this peculiarity were partly the fact that their intellectual culture gave them the taste, and in some degree a claim, to assume the habit and manners of the higher classes, partly because their ranks were in some measure recruited from those of the poorer gentry, and partly also from the habit which the players at least (and many of the poets were players) acquired on the stage of bearing and dressing themselves like gentlemen.

Belonging to the exceptional class, yet by nature not of it, Shakespeare was exceptional in it, and shared its privileges without contamination of its vulgar vices, and so without suffering all its disabilities. And beside, the very company of which he was a member enjoyed, and seems to have deserved, peculiar consideration. Authority nearly contemporary assures us that " all those companies got money and lived in reputation, especially those of the Black-friars, who were men of grave and sober behavior." In this respect, as well as in all others, we may be sure that he was *primus inter pares.* We can see by the impression which he left upon his contemporaries, that to a native dignity of soul and gentleness of disposition he united a courtesy of bearing that made him in fact the gentleman, to be acknowledged as

which seems to have been his chief desire. In
the phraseology of modern society, he was eminently presentable in any circle. Being such a
man, being distinguished as he was, and having
early won the personal esteem of influential noblemen, it can hardly be but that he was received
into the high and cultivated society of the metropolis. Once there, we may be sure he met with
ladies who were more than willing that he should
yield to that fascination of soul and sense which
the personal and mental charms of beautiful and
high-bred women exert upon men of sensitive organization. What effect this experience must have
had upon him, almost every man can measurably
judge. We know how Robert Burns, that inspired
peasant, was bewildered by a brief draught of like
intoxication. But over Burns Shakespeare had
not only the advantage of superior genius. Self-
poised, reserved, instinct with tact (this is no more
than inference, but inference which to me is moral
certainty), he was no inspired peasant, and bore
himself so unexceptionably that no woman, whatever her rank or her refinement, who looked on
him with favor, was put to shame by his weak-
ness, his extravagance, or even his eccentricity.
That there should be such women was inevitable.
Tradition tells us that he went yearly to Stratford,
where he left his wife and children. This may
well have been. The interests which he looked
after so carefully would be likely to take him into

the society of his wife as often as once in a twelve-
month. Tradition also tells us, that on his way
back and forth on these dutiful journeys he used
to stop in Oxford, at the Crown Tavern, which
was kept by John Davenant, a grave and melancholy citizen who had to wife a beautiful and
charming woman. Sir William Davenant, who
was born in February, 1605–6, was her son; and
Shakespeare, it is said, was his godfather. And
the story goes that one day an old townsman,
seeing Will running homeward in great haste
"to see his godfather Shakespeare," told him to
be careful lest he took God's name in vain. This
may all be true; but a story essentially the same
is not uncommon in very old jest-books. Indeed,
the humorous quibble is so apparent and so invit-
ing, that, if the tale is not as old as the custom
of having fathers, it is only because it cannot be
older than that of having godfathers. Now Sir
William Davenant gave countenance to this report
of his origin; but what credit shall be given to
the testimony of a man who would welcome an
aspersion upon his mother's reputation for the
sake of being believed to write, by inheritance,
"with the very spirit of Shakespeare," as he said
he thought he did. Davenant was morally a poor
creature, and in this he only did his kind.

Another story is also told of Shakespeare's fortunes with the sex. Having been long current as
a tradition, it was afterwards found recorded in

Manningham's diary among the Ashmolean MSS., under the date, March 13th, 1601. It is, that a woman, "a citizen," seeing Richard Burbadge, the great actor of the day, play Richard III., was so carried away by her admiration that she asked him to visit her after the play, — an invitation to supper from ladies to favorite actors being then not uncommon. Shakespeare overheard the appointment, (the custom of admitting spectators upon the stage during the performance must again be remembered,) and, resolving to supplant his friend, went to the rendezvous before him, announced himself as the crook-backed tyrant, and was as successful as his own hero in winning female favor under adverse circumstances. Burbadge arrived soon after, and, sending word that Richard III. was at the door, received for answer, from a source as to which he could have had no doubt, that "William the Conqueror was before Richard III."

But it was not by adventures of this kind that a soul like Shakespeare's could be satisfied ; nor was it under the influence of women of this sort that with the advance of years a striking change took place in the traits of his female characters. For it is remarkable that in his earliest plays, those written when his Stratford reminiscences were freshest, the women are the reverse of lovable and gentle. But after a few years of London life had widened his observation and mitigated his

experience, there came such a change over his
creatures of this kind, that it is praise enough of
any, the fairest now and sweetest, to say she is
like one of Shakespeare's women.   Surely not to
chance, and as surely to no evolution from the
depths of moral consciousness, is due the difference between the women in *Henry the Sixth, The
Comedy of Errors, Titus Andronicus,* and *Love's
Labor's Lost,* and those in the later plays.   Nor
could it have been merely the fruit of maturing
judgment.   For very young men, and, most of all,
very young poets, are sure to see women with the
mind's eye only through the soft lustre of those
charms which bewilder even the better instructed,
though perhaps not wiser, apprehension of prosaic age.*   Shakespeare's mind, like Raphael's,
furnished forth his own ideals ; but there can be
no reasonable doubt that it was in the high-bred,
cultivated women into whose society his noble and
worshipful admirers took him that he found his
female models.†   From among these women did

* I have always thought Kent's reply to Lear's inquiry as to his
age a superlative touch of penetration.

"*Lear.*   How old art thou ?

"*Kent.*   Not so young, sir, to love a woman for singing ; nor
so old, to dote on her for anything : I have years on my back for-
ty-eight."

† During the slow progress of these Memoirs from manuscript
into type Miss Bunnett's translation of Dr. Gervinus's voluminous
Shakespeare Commentaries has reached me.   In his comments
upon *Much Ado About Nothing* he says : " We have before drawn
attention to the fact, that in the plays belonging to Shakespeare's

he go forth with heart unscathed? Among them all, was there not one who felt that, although she perhaps was of noble birth, that player, though not . her lord, was master of her heart? Of the many courtly dames who then gave up all, even their good name, for men they loved, was there not one who knew the worth of Shakespeare? He with a painter's eye for beauty, and a poet's soul of passion, who could read women's hearts as in a mirror, alive to all the charms of cultivated society, and illustrating them in his person, and with a rustic wife eight years older than himself away off in Stratford, — he with honey upon his tongue as well as in his pen, of such winning ways that men called him sweet, and gruff Ben Jonson's heart went out to him, — handsome and well-shaped too, — is it in man's nature, is it in woman's nature, that he should not have loved and been beloved in London? Let only those who

early period there is a remarkable preponderance of bad women : the poet's own experience appears at that time to have inspired him with no advantageous opinion of the female sex." Afterward Gervinus adds, speaking of the author's second period : "Shakespeare must at that time in London, in the wider circle of his acquaintance, in his contact with the higher classes, have become intimate with women who withdrew him suddenly from his former ill humor with the sex, into a devoted admiration of them." (Vol. I. p. 588.) While I cannot but be gratified at the support which my views thus receive from the learned German philosopher, it is only just that I should say that they are not appropriated from him without acknowledgment ; they having been written out, and even partly put in type, long before his *Shakespeare Commentaries* made their appearance.

K

have thoughtfully read his sonnets answer. For whatever may have been the motives of those . mysterious compositions, which alternately beguile us with their seeming revelations of a simple fact, and baffle us with the sudden presentation of impossibility, there beats beneath their artificial surface a pulse of passion so profound, there comes from behind their impenetrable veil a cry of anguish so personal as well as so human, that reason seeks in vain to stifle the intuitive conviction that in them we are face to face and eye to eye with the man Shakespeare, reading, though but vaguely comprehending, the inmost secrets of his heart. They may not be the record of his soul's experience, but they surely are its witness. They may possibly have been written for others, but they are of himself. They lack entirely the dramatic element, and tell an individual story ; and no such living, fleshly birth as they ever took life from another's joy, or was brought forth by vicarious suffering.

To what period of Shakespeare's life we are to assign these sonnets cannot be decided. He had written some sonnets before 1598, because in that year Meres mentions certain "sugared sonnets among his private friends." But were .they these? These tell of a dear, a trusted, and a faithless friend, of a mistress loved in spite of reason and in the teeth of conviction. Are these the sort of literary exercises that Shakespeare would be likely to hand around among his curious, criticising friends? Or if they revealed the secrets of another's heart, would *he* be inclined to have them submitted to such publicity? The date of their publication makes it certain that these sonnets were all written before Shakespeare was forty-five years old; and they probably were produced between his thirtieth and his fortieth year. Thomas Thorpe's dedication tells us absolutely nothing of their origin; only that there was a secret about it that has never been revealed. Could either of those other persons whom they concern have become so reduced as to make merchandise of them, or have been so small-souled as to seek notoriety through their publication? Sadder, stranger things have happened. The mystery of these sonnets will never be unfolded; yet in an attempt to trace the course of Shakespeare's life they cannot be passed by, although they tell us nothing surely, except that they express the inmost thoughts and feelings of one who, however wise and prudent he might have been, was in his affections and his passions little more self-restrained than David, little less wise than Solomon.

V.

We are as ignorant, upon direct evidence, of
the exact date at which Shakespeare at last withdrew from London to live at ease in Stratford,
as we are of that at which he fled from Stratford
to enter upon a life of irksome toil in London.
But all circumstances which bear upon this question point to some time in the year 1611. He
retired from active life a wealthier man than he
could reasonably have hoped to become when he
entered it. He had achieved a fame and attained
a social standing which must have been very far
beyond his expectations; and he had won the favor and enjoyed the society of men of high rank
and great public distinction. But yet even to
William Shakespeare, with his surpassing genius,
his worldly wisdom, his prudence and his thrift,
all culminating in a success which made him the
mark of envy at the end, as he had been at
the beginning of his career, life was unsatisfy-
ing.* He returned to Stratford a disappointed
man.

* The following passage in a tract called *Ratsei's Ghost, or the
Second Part of his Mad Prankes and Robberies*, of which only one
copy is known to exist, plainly refers, first to Burbadge and next
to Shakespeare. The book is without date, but is believed to
have been printed before 1606. Gamaliel Ratsey, who speaks, is
a highwayman who has paid some strollers 40s. for playing before
him, and afterward robbed them of their fee. The author was

Circumstances not pleasant, we may be sure, had limited his family to three children born at two births before he was of age, and heaviest among his household sorrows was the loss of the only boy his wife had brought him. He had no son to bear his name, to inherit his property, to glory in his fame, and to be the third gentleman of his family. His daughters, rustic born and rustic bred, were not fitted for circles in which they might otherwise have been sought as wives by men of the position to which their father had raised himself. He saw them married rather late

probably some inferior player or playwright to whom Shakespeare had been chary of his money or his companionship.

"And for you, sirrah, (says he to the chiefest of them,) thou hast a good presence upon a stage, methinks thou darkenst thy merit by playing in the country: get thee to London, for if one man were dead, they will have much need of such as thou art. There would be none, in my opinion, fitter than thyself to play his parts: my conceit is such of thee, that I durst all the money in my purse on thy head to play Hamlet with him for a wager. There thou shalt learne to be frugal (for players were never so thrifty as they are now about London), and to feed upon all men; to let none feed upon thee; to make thy hand a stranger to thy pocket, thy heart slow to perform thy tongue's promise; and when thou feelest thy purse well lined, buy thee some place of lordship in the country; that, growing weary of playing, thy money may there bring thee to dignity and reputation: then thou needest care for no man; no, not for them that before made thee proud with speaking their [thy] words on the stage. Sir, I thank you (quoth the player) for this good council: I promise you I will make use of it, for I have heard, indeed, of some that have gone to London very meanly, and have come in time to be exceeding wealthy."

in life to simple village folk, and he resigned himself to simple village society, — wisely, perhaps, but yet, we may be sure, not without a pang and that sense of wrong which afflicts so many of us at the unequal and incongruous distribution of means and opportunities. It must have been with bitterness of soul that he saw the disappearance of his hopes of being the head of a family ranking among the gentry of England.

Rowe says that the latter part of his life was spent, as all men of good sense will wish theirs may be, in ease, retirement, and the conversation (i. e. the society, the intercourse) of his friends. He adds, that "his pleasurable wit and good nature engaged him in the acquaintance and entitled him to the friendship of the gentlemen of the neighborhood." And Mr. Fullom tells us that the Lucys have lately discovered that his quarrel with their family was made up, and that he lived on pleasant terms with Sir Thomas, the son of his ancient enemy.* But this story, though not very improbable, rests on vague and untrustworthy evidence. William Shakespeare, retired from the stage, and living in a fine mansion, upon a handsome fortune, in his native town, seems to us a man whose acquaintance might well have been courted by the gentlemen of the neighborhood. But we must remember the social canons and the class limitations of his time, and take also

---

* Fullom's *History of William Shakespeare*, p. 314.

into consideration that, when he abandoned authorship and the theatre, he divided the ties which had bound him not only to a profession which he disliked, but to a social circle into which that profession had introduced him. Thereafter his personal relations and social position depended merely upon his personal character and his social importance ; and he inevitably fell into the place which could be filled by one who, although a pleasant companion, a poet of reputation, and a highly respectable, prudent man, was yet barely within the nominal pale of gentry ; and who yet, being within it, could not be treated as a yeoman. William Shakespeare the great play-writer and poet, omnipotent at the Black-friars and the Globe, and living a bachelor's life in London, was socially a very different person from William Shakespeare the retired actor, assuming the position of a gentleman, and living at Stratford with his rustic wife and daughters. To the gentlemen of the county round he was merely one of the newest sort of new men. And although, from what we know of his business affairs, it is probable that on his retirement to Stratford he sold all his theatrical property, and withdrew from any connection with the theatre, except such as consisted in the writing of two or three plays, yet it cannot have been that, in a community so pervaded with the leaven of Puritanism as Warwickshire around Stratford was, and where, as we have already seen, in 1602, and again in 1612, the most stringent measures were taken by the corporation of the town to prevent the performance of any plays, the profession which had brought Shakespeare his wealth and his eminence did not tell against his social advancement, except among the liberal and generous-minded few. Again I remark, that it is to this prejudice and to Shakespeare's desire to stand with the world as a gentleman of substance and character, and not as an actor and playwright, that we must attribute his neglect of his dramas after they had discharged their double function of filling his pockets and giving his brain employment and his soul expression. Indifference to the literary fate of their works was common among the playwrights of that day; but to this custom was added, in Shakespeare's case, a motive. The Reverend John Ward, who was made Vicar of Stratford in 1662, records a tradition that Shakespeare in his retirement supplied the stage with two plays every year, and lived at the rate of £1000. This is quite surely but a gross exaggeration of the facts, both as to the rate of his expenditure and the amount of his dramatic labor. We have seen that his income was about £400, though it was rather over than under that then handsome sum; and only three of his plays, *The Tempest, The Winter's Tale*, and *Henry the Eighth*, were produced after his retirement to Stratford. The last of these was brought out at the Globe Theatre, as a spectacle piece, on the 29th of June, 1613 ; and during its performance the theatre took fire from the discharge of the chambers during one of the pageants, and was burned to the ground. It is an interesting coincidence, that the first performance of the last play that came from Shakespeare's pen was the occasion of the destruction of that " wooden O " in which he had won so many of his imperishable laurels.

Shakespeare is said to have put his poetical . powers to use during his later Stratford years in writing epitaphs for friends and neighbors. Such an employment of his pen would have been natural. The following verses upon the tomb of Sir Thomas Stanley in Tonge Church are attributed to him by Dugdale in his *History of Warwickshire.* It is possible that he wrote epitaphs no better.

> " *Written upon the east end of the Tomb.*
> " Ask who lies here, but do not weep ;
> He is not dead, he doth but sleep.
> This stony register is for his bones ;
> His fame is more perpetual than these stones :
> And his own goodness, with himself being gone,
> Shall live when earthly monument is none.

> " *Written on the west end thereof.*
> " Not monumental stone preserves our fame,
> Nor sky-aspiring pyramids our name.
> The memory of him for whom this stands
> Shall outlive marble and defacer's hands.
> When all to time's consumption shall be given,
> Stanley, for whom this stands, shall stand in heaven."

8

Rowe tells us of a tradition that John a Combe, of whose residence and habits something has been said in the earlier part of these memoirs, told Shakespeare laughingly, at a sociable gathering, that he fancied he meant to write his epitaph if he happened to outlive him, and begged the poet to perform his task immediately. Upon which Shakespeare gave him these now well-known verses : —

> "Ten in the hundred lies here in-grav'd ;
> 'T is a hundred to ten his soul is not sav'd :
> If any man ask, Who lies in this tomb ?
> Oh ho, quoth the Devil, 't is my John a Combe."

Much the same story had reached Aubrey's ears, and was of course duly recorded. But according to Aubrey the epitaph was written at a tavern on occasion of the funeral of its subject, and was in these words : —

> "Ten in the hundred the Devil allows,
> But Combe will have twelve, he swears and he vows.
> If any one ask, Who lies in this tomb ?
> Ho ! quoth the Devil, 't is my John a Combe."

Rowe says that the sharpness of the satire so stung the man that he never forgave it. This, at least, is untrue. Shakespeare and his wealthier neighbor of Stratford College were good friends to the end of the latter's life. John a Combe's will is extant, and in it Shakespeare is remembered by a bequest of five pounds, and Shakespeare himself left his sword to Thomas, John a Combe's nephew. It must be remembered that in those times all interest was called usury, i. e. money paid for the *use* of money, and John a Combe's will is that of a man of true benevolence and mindful friendship. He forgives debts, makes wide and generous provision for the poor, and re-members with much particularity a large circle of friends among the knights, esquires, and gentle-men of his neighborhood.* This jest, turning upon ten in the hundred (the usual interest at that time), and a hundred to ten in favor of the Devil, was an old and a common one among our fore-fathers; and consequently it has been generally supposed that this epitaph is a fabrication which was foisted upon Shakespeare. But I am inclined to think that he did crack this innocent joke upon his friend, using, as he would be likely to use, an

---

* Mr. Halliwell discovered among the Ashmolean MSS. one "written," as he says, "not many years after the death of Shake-speare," in which this version of the above anecdote appears:—

" *On John Combe, a covetous rich man, Mr. Wm. Shak-spear wright this att his request while hee was yett liveing for his epitaphe.*

"Who lies in this tombe?
Hough, quoth the devil, tis my sone John a Combe.
Finis.

" *But being dead and making the poor his heires, hee after wrightes this for his epitaph.*

"Howere he lived judge not,
John Combe shall never be forgott
While poore hath memmorye, for he did gather
To make the poore his issue: he their father,
As record of his tilth and seedes,   ·
Did crowne him in his later needes.
Finis. W. Shak."

old, well-known jest, and giving it a new turn upon
the money-lender's name. For Shakespeare was
not always writing *Hamlet*. "'T is my John a
Combe" involves of course the sharp punning
jest, 't is my John ha' come.*

A project for the enclosing of some common
lands near Stratford brings Shakespeare forward
in 1614 as a man of weight and consideration in
his neighborhood. It touched his interests in his
own acres and in his tithes so closely, that he said
to one of the numerous Greenes of Stratford, that
"he was not able to bear the enclosing of Wel-.
combe." His kinsman Greene, the attorney, who
was clerk of Stratford, records in his note-book
this almost the only speech of Shakespeare which
has been authoritatively handed down to us.
Shakespeare took all possible measures to secure
his threatened interests ; and there exists an agreement between him and William Replingham, who
appears to have been one of the movers in the
affair, by which the latter agrees to make good
any damage which the former may receive by the
proposed enclosure.† The corporation of Strat-

---

* Mr. Hunter says that the verses are "allusive to the double
sense of the word *Combe*, as the name of the person there interred, and also the name of a certain measure of corn"; and
this explanation has been hitherto accepted. What point is there
in likening John a Combe to a measure of corn?

† " *Coppy of the articles with Mr. Shakspeare.*

"Vicesimo octavo die Octobris, anno Domini 1614. Articles

ford were also opposed to this measure, alleging
that it would press heavily upon the poorer classes, already distressed by a destructive fire which

of agreement made [and] indented between William Shackespeare of Stretforde in the County of Warwick gent. on the one
partye, and William Replingham of Great Harborow in the County of Warwick gent. on the other partie, the daye and yeare above
said.

"*Item*, the said William Replingham for him, his heires, exec-
utors and assignes, doth covenaunte and agree to and with the
saide William Shackspeare his heires and assignes, That he, the
said William Replingham, his heires or assignes, shall uppon reasonable request, satisfie, content, and make recompense unto him
the said William Shackespeare or his assignes, for all such losse,
detriment, and hinderance as he the said William Shackespeare, his
heirs and assignes, and one Thomas Greene gent. shall or maye
be thought in the viewe and judgement of foure indifferent persons, to be indifferentlie elected by the said William and William
and their heires, and in default of the said William Replingham,
by the said William Shackespeare or his heires onely, to survey
and judge the same to sustayne or incurre for or in respecte of
the increasinge of the yearlie value of the tythes they the said
William Shackespeare and Thomas doe joyntlie or severallie hold
and enjoy in the said fieldes or anie of them, by reason of anie
inclosure or decaye of tyllage there ment and intended by the
said William Replingham; and that the said William Replingham and his heirs shall procure such sufficient securitie unto the
said William Shackespeare and his heires for the performance
of theis covenauntes, as shall bee devised by learned counsell.
In witnes whereof the parties abovsaid to theis presentes inter-
changeablie their handes and seales have put, the daye and yeare
first above wrytten.

"Sealed and delivered in the presence of us,
> "THO. LUCAS,
> JO. ROGERS,
> ANTHONIE NASSHE,
> MICH. OLNEY."

took place in that town in 1613, but which seems
to have left Shakespeare's property untouched.
In the autumn of 1614, Thomas Greene was in
London about this business; and by one of his
memorandums we know that Shakespeare arrived
there on the 16th of November of that year, probably upon the same errand. Greene's memorandums show that he was in constant communication with his "cosen Shakespeare" upon this subject, and that the corporation counted much upon
their distinguished townsman's influence in the
matter.* He remained in London until after the
23d of December in that year. From the same
authority we hear of him in the negotiations of
1615, with regard to the same affair, which was
not settled until 1618; and this testimony as to
his thrift and his care for his material interests is
the last known contemporary record of the life of
the great poet of all time.

---

* "1614. Jovis, 17 No. My cosen Shakspear comyng yes-
terdy to Town, I went to see him how he did. He told me that
they assured him they ment to inclose no further than to Gospell
Bush, and so upp straight (leavying out part of the Dyngles to
the ffield) to the gate in Clopton hedg, and take in Salisburyes
peece; and that they mean in Aprill to survey the land, and then
to gyve satisfaccion, and not before; and he and Mr. Hall say
they think ther will be nothyng done at all."

"23. Dec. A hall. Lettres wrytten, one to Mr. Manyring,
another to Mr. Shakspear, with almost all the company's hands
to eyther. I also wrytte myself to my cosen Shakspear the cop-
pyes of all our acts, and then also a not of the inconvenyences
wold happen by the inclosure."

His younger daughter, Judith, was married on the 11th of February, 1615–6, to Thomas Quiney, a vintner of Stratford, and son of the Thomas Quiney who in 1598 had asked Shakespeare to lend him £30. On the 25th of the following March he executed his will, which an erased date shows that he had intended executing on the 25th of the preceding January; and on the 23d of April, 1616, William Shakespeare, of Stratford on Avon, in the county of Warwick, Gentleman, died.

Of the cause of his death we only know what Vicar Ward aforesaid heard and noted down half a century after the event. His account is: "Shakespeare, Drayton, and Ben Jonson had a merrie meeting, and it seems drank too hard, for Shakespeare died of a feavour ther contracted." We shrink from the thought of such a close of Shakespeare's life. But looking back upon the manners of the time, and considering its convivial habits, and the inordinate quantities of wine and strong ale then drunk by all who could procure them, we must admit that to die of fever after festivity might have been the fate of any man Men now living can remember when no person entered a house, at any time, the family of which were not very poor, without being offered and ex- pected to drink some spirituous liquor; cake and wine having been brought forward even to our mothers at morning calls. And Spence tells us

in his *Anecdotes*, on the authority of Pope, that
Cowley the poet died as Ward says Shakespeare
died, but from potations in more reverend, though
perhaps not more worshipful company. He and
Dean Sprat, afterward Bishop of Rochester, "had
been together," Spence says, "to see a neighbor
of Cowley's, who (according to the fashion of
those times) made them too welcome. They did
not set out for their walk home until it was too
late, and had drunk so deep that they lay out in
the fields all night. This gave Cowley the fever
that carried him off. The parish still talk of the
drunken Dean." And in the Chamberlain's accounts of Stratford, among the frequent charges
for sack and sugar, claret, and beer, for such worshipful folk as Sir Fulke Greville and Sir Thomas
Lucy, and even Lady Lucy, is one in 1614 for
"on quart of sack and on quart of clarett wine
geven to a preacher at the New Place," Shakespeare's own house. These considerations make
the alleged excess at such a merry meeting of
poets as that recorded in Ward's diary a venial
sin, and the sad consequences, though uncertain,
not improbable.

Shakespeare's remains were interred the second day after his death, the 25th of April, in
Stratford church, just before the chancel rail.
Above his grave, on the north wall of the church,
a monument was erected, at what exact date we
do not know ; but it was before 1623, as it is

mentioned by Leonard Digges in his verses prefixed to the first folio edition of Shakespeare's
plays. The monument shows a bust of the poet
in the act of writing. Upon a tablet below the
bust is the following inscription:—

> JUDICIO PYLIUM, GENIO SOCRATEM, ARTE MARONEM,
> TERRA TEGIT, POPULUS MAERET, OLYMPUS HABET.
>
> STAY PASSENGER, WHY GOEST THOU BY SO FAST,
> READ, IF THOU CANST, WHOM ENVIOUS DEATH HATH PLAST
> WITHIN THIS MONUMENT, SHAKESPEARE, WITH WHOME
> QUICK NATURE DIDE; WHOSE NAME DOTH DECK YS TOMBE
> FAR MORE THEN COST; SITH ALL YT HE HATH WRITT
> LEAVES LIVING ART BUT PAGE TO SERVE HIS WITT.
>
> OBIIT ANO. DOI. 1616.   AETATIS 53. DIE 23 AP.

The last line of this inscription, and a tradition
unheard of until Oldys wrote his notes in Lang-
baine, have raised the question whether Shakespeare died on the same day of the month on
which he is supposed to have been born. But what
matter whether he lived a day more or less than
fifty-two full years? He had lived long enough.
His work was done, and he had tasted, nay, had
drained, life's cup of bitter sweet. Dugdale
tells us that his monument was the work of Ge-
rard Johnson, an eminent sculptor of the period;
others have attributed it to Thomas Stanton; and
experts have supposed that the face was modelled
from a cast taken after death. Be this as it may,
the bust must be accepted as the most authentic
likeness that we have of Shakespeare. It was
originally colored after life. The eyes were light

8*   L

hazel, the hair and beard auburn, the complexion fair; the doublet was scarlet; the tabard, or loose gown without sleeves thrown over the doublet, black; the neck and wristbands white; the upper side of the cushion green, the under, crimson; its cord and tassels, gilt. The colors were renewed in 1749; but in 1793 Malone, tastelessly and ignorantly classic, had the whole figure painted white by a house-painter. A flat stone covers the grave. Upon it is the following strange inscription:—

> GOOD FREND FOR IESVS SAKE FORBEARE
> TO DIGG THE DVST ENCLOASED HEARE
> BLEST BE YE MAN YT SPARES THES STONES
> AND CURST BE HE YT MOVES MY BONES.

A Mr. Dowdall, in an existing letter to Mr. Edward Southwell, dated April 10th, 1692, says that these lines were written by the poet himself a little before his death. Dowdall plainly records a tradition which possibly may have been well founded. It is more probable, however, that to prevent the removal of Shakespeare's remains to the charnel-house of the church, in compliance with a custom of the day and place, when time made other demands upon the space they occupied, some member of his family, or some friend, had this rude, hearty curse cut upon his tombstone. Tradition, not traceable higher than 1693, says his wife and daughters earnestly desired to be laid in the same grave with him, but that "not one, for fear of the curse above said, dare touch his gravestone." It has had one good effect, at least. It has kept at Stratford those relics which but therefor would probably have been removed to Westminster Abbey.

Shakespeare's wife and his two daughters — Susannah, married to Dr. Hall, and Judith, married to Thomas Quiney — survived him. His granddaughter, Elizabeth Hall, who also was living at the time of his death, was twice married; first, to Thomas Nash, an esquire, of Stratford, and afterward to Mr. John Barnard of Abington in Northamptonshire, who was knighted by Charles II. in 1661; but she had no children. Judith had three sons, who died unmarried; and with Lady Barnard, who died in 1669–70, Shakespeare's family became extinct. His property was strictly entailed upon the male issue of his daughter Susannah, which failed to appear. The entail was broken by legal contrivance; and soon after the death of Lady Barnard, the estate which he had gathered with so much labor and solicitude was dispersed. New Place, which was the home of his later years, was distinguished, in Lady Barnard's time, by the brief residence there of Queen Henrietta Maria, during the troubles of the Great Revolution. Mr. and Mrs. Nash entertained the Queen there for three weeks, in June, 1643, when, escorted by Prince Rupert and his troops, she was on her progress to join King Charles at Oxford, —

an incident which would have been well-pleasing
to Mistress Nash's grandfather. Afterward, as we
have already seen, New Place fell into the hands
of Sir Hugh Clopton, a descendant of its builder,
who renovated and altered it; and it was finally
bought by the Reverend Francis Gastrell as his
residence. He lived there several years, much
annoyed by curious pilgrims to his house and to
his garden, in which there was a mulberry-tree,
which, according to the tradition of the town,
Shakespeare planted with his own hands. This
reverend gentleman was wealthy enough to indulge in that very expensive. luxury, a high temper. So at last he gave his vexation vent by cutting down the mulberry-tree,* and afterward, in
1759, having quarrelled with the magistrates about
assessments, he razed his house to the ground,
and left the place, a petty ecclesiastic Erostratus,
hooted and execrated by the Stratford people.
Thus, within less than one hundred and fifty years
of his death, all traces of Shakespeare had disappeared from his native village, except his birthplace and his tomb.

This is all that we know by authentic record,
by tradition, and by inference, of him who stands

---

* The wood of this tree was bought by a watchmaker of Stratford, who made it into boxes and similar articles. It must have
attained an enormous size; for there is enough of it extant to
make a line-of-battle ship. But my piece and yours, reader, are
genuine.

alone in the highest niche of literary fame. But
this is much. It seems little only because of his
greatness. Of many men not to be thought of
in comparison with him we know indeed much
more; and in these days, when every man seems,
like Pepys, to be his own Boswell, we are likely
to know all; but of many who occupy a place
only second to his, we know much less. The
causes of our ignorance of Shakespeare's life are
partly the Puritanism which developed itself in the
mother country.during his life, and the consequent
political convulsions which came so soon after his
death, and lasted so long; partly the frivolous
and grovelling taste of the literary and dramatic
school which came in with the Restoration, and
prevailed for more than half a century, and which
cared little about the works and less about the life
of William Shakespeare; partly, too, we may be
sure, a desire on his part, characteristic of all cultivated people of English race, to keep personal
affairs from publicity. But the total effect of these
causes is small in comparison with the results of
the indifference which prevailed among people
of all ages and countries, until within the last
hundred or hundred and fifty years, to the personal character and private lives of poets, paint-
ers, scientific men, and generally of all public persons not concerned in government. When men
have control over the lives and fortunes of their
fellow-citizens in peace, and are able to plunge

two nations into war, the world follows their movements with prying, wondering eyes; but heretofore when they only amused, or even instructed, they must have achieved fame, and a generation or two must have passed away before the world at large concerned itself about their personal histories. We know more of the lives of brutal, selfish soldiers, and of crafty, selfish churchmen, who had no thought or purpose beyond the attainment or the preservation of power and place for themselves and their adherents, than we do of men whose quiet, thoughtful labors have blessed and delighted millions from generation to generation. Of Shakespeare we know more than the Greeks knew of Æschylus, the father of their tragedy, or of Aristophanes, the father of their comedy, two centuries after they died. Public functions partially preserved the personal history of Sophocles from similar obscurity. Of Molière, the greatest and most original of French dramatic writers, we have very meagre personal accounts; and it is remarkable that not a page of his manuscripts is known to be in existence. The personal history of Shakespeare's great contemporary, Bacon, is well known; but had he not become successively the King's Attorney-General, Sir Francis Bacon, Lord Verulam, Viscount St. Albans, and Lord High Chancellor of England, Master Bacon might have written his Essays and worked out his *Novum Organon* in happy, unobserved obscurity, and the world might have begun to inquire into his every-day life only after it had discovered that he was the greatest philosopher and the worldly-wisest man of modern times. We are yet more ignorant of Shakespeare's fellow-craftsmen than we are of him. · Of Beaumont and Fletcher, both born in the rank of gentry, one the son of a Judge, the other of a Bishop, we know little more than that they wrote their plays and lived in the society of the most intelligent men of their day. Chapman's associations and what he did are discovered only by indirect collateral evidence; but eminent as he was, and highly esteemed as he appears to have been, nothing is recorded of his personal history. We are obliged to infer the year of his birth from the record of his age upon his portrait; and time has left us no guide-post to his birthplace. The minor stars of the Elizabethan galaxy, the Greenes, Peeles, Marlowes, Websters, Fords, and such like, left hardly a trace behind them which their own pens had not written. Ben Jonson, who lived to see all the poets of the Elizabethan period in their graves, and to be an object of literary and almost antiquarian interest to a new generation and a new school, left more materials for his memoirs than any contemporary poet. But it is only with his later years that we are thus acquainted. Of his youth and early manhood we are not less ignorant than we are of Shakespeare's.

How difficult it is to trace the vestiges of a life not passed in the performance of important public duty is shown by our ignorance of the youth and early manhood of the last great English ruler of England, Oliver Cromwell : — last English ruler ; for since his time his place has been occupied, not filled, by certain Scotch and German men and women, sons and daughters of Scotch fathers and German fathers and mothers, not always even born in the British purple. Although he came, on both sides, of families of knightly rank and landed estate, and made himself in effect absolute monarch of England and of Scotland south of the Grampians, the little that we know of him before he rose, at mature years, into notice in public life, is gathered from obscure tradition and official mention. We know more of William Shakespeare, yeoman's son and player, before he was forty years old, than we do of Oliver Cromwell, country gentleman and Lord Protector, at the same age. The same degree of doubt exists as to the occupation of the father of each of them, and the same uncertainty as to how and where they passed certain years of early life ; the debatable period being longer in the case of the Protector. The same truth in biography is illustrated by a striking deficiency in the biography of Washington. We are well and authoritatively informed as to the small details of his daily life after he entered the service of the revolted Colonies; but his own nephew, to whom were open all family papers and records, and who was in communication with many of the friends and neighbors of his illustrious uncle, was unable to discover the date of his marriage, although his wife, Mrs. Custis, was one of the richliest dowered widows in all Virginia.* Instead, therefore, of our ignorance of Shakespeare's life being in itself at all remarkable, we have reason for congratulation, that from one source or another we have learned so much upon a subject which interests us so greatly, but about which his generation and its successor were so indifferent.

Unlike Dante, unlike Milton, unlike Goethe, unlike the great poets and tragedians of Greece and Rome, Shakespeare left no trace upon the political, or even the social, life of his era. Of his eminent countrymen, Raleigh, Sidney, Spenser, Bacon, Cecil, Walsingham, Coke, Camden, Hooker, Drake, Hobbes, Inigo Jones, Herbert of Cherbury, Laud, Pym, Hampden, Selden, Walton, Wotton, and Donne may be properly reckoned as his contemporaries; and yet there is no proof whatever that he was personally known to either of these men, or to any others of less note among the statesmen, scholars, soldiers, and artists of his day, except the few of his fellow-craftsmen whose acquaintance with him has been

---

* George Washington Parke Custis's *Recollections of Washington*, p. 502.

heretofore mentioned in these Memoirs. This, partly from the loss of evidence, and partly, perhaps, because he was not personally acquainted with any of these men. It is a common mistake to suppose that, even in these days of free intercourse, eminent persons who are contemporaries and countrymen must needs be brought into contact. Their personal relations, like those of other persons, are governed by prudential reasons and social influences, — greatly also by mere accident.

Shakespeare's character, entirely free from those irregularities which are usually, but unreasonably, regarded as almost the necessary concomitants of genius, seems to have been of singular completeness and of perfect balance. Of his transcendent mental gifts, the results of the daily labor by which he first earned his bread and then made his fortune remain as evidence; and what else we know of him shows him to us in the common business and intercourse of life, upright, prudent, self-respecting, — a man to be respected and relied upon. An actor at a time when actors were held in the lowest possible esteem, he won the kind regard and consideration of those who held high rank and station: a poet, he was not only thrifty but provident. Though careful of his own, he was not only just, but generous, to others. His integrity was early noticed; and Jonson says "he was indeed honest, and of an open and free nature." Surpassing all his rivals, after the recoil of the first surprise he was loved by all except tne meanest souls among them; and such men only love themselves. "Sweet" and "gentle" are the endearing epithets which they delighted to apply to him. In his position, to have produced this effect upon high and low he must have united a native dignity to a singular kindness of heart, evenness of temper, and graciousness of manner. His ready wit and his cheerfulness in social intercourse are particularly mentioned in tradition. To these qualities it is plain that he added a sympathy that was universal,—a gift which more than any other wins the love of all mankind. And, indeed, it is to the effect of this moral quality that we owe the complete and multitudinous manifestation of his intellectual greatness. The Reverend Mr. Davies, writing after 1688, says that "he died a Papist." If he became a member of the Church of Rome, it must have been after he wrote *Romeo and Juliet*, in which he speaks of "evening mass"; for the humblest member of that Church knows that there is no mass at vespers. The expression used by Davies implies, indeed, that Shakespeare died in a faith in which he had not been educated. But his report is improbable. In the overmuch righteousness of the puritanical period in which Shakespeare's last years were passed, a moderate degree of cheerfulness and Christian charity, to say nothing of conformity to the Church of England, might easily have brought the reproach of Papistry upon men less open to that suspicion than a retired player. Shakespeare, although he seems to have been a man of sincere piety, seems also to have been without religious convictions. His works are imbued with a high and heartfelt appreciation of the vital truths of Christianity; but nowhere does he show a leaning towards any form of religious observance, or of church government, or toward any theological tenet or dogma. No Church can claim him; no simple Christian soul but can claim his fellowship. Such as this imperfect record shows was William Shakespeare; a man who adorned an inferior and dignified an equivocal station in life, and who raised himself from poverty and obscurity to competence and honorable position by labors which, having their motive, not in desire of fame, but in duty and in manly independence, have placed him upon an enduring eminence to which in these after ages sane ambition does not aspire.

AN ESSAY

TOWARD THE EXPRESSION OF SHAKESPEARE'S GENIUS.

———◆———

"May I express thee unblam'd?"

ESSAY.

THE student of language, or the mere intelligent observer of the speech of his own day, cannot but notice how surely men supply themselves with a word when one is needed. The new vocal sign is sometimes made, but is generally found. A lack is felt, and the common instinct, vaguely stretching out its hands, lays hold of some common, or mayhap some half-forgotten or rarely used word, and, putting a new stamp upon it, converts it into current coin of another denomination, a recognized representative of new intellectual value. Purists may fret at the perversion, and philologers may protest against the genuineness of the new mintage; but in vain. It answers the needs of those who use it, and that it should do so is all they require. A good example of the perversion of a word from its true etymological meaning is the modern use of "several." This adjective not long ago conveyed only the idea of severance, and was generally applied but to two objects of one kind. Thus in old plays it is very common to find two personages directed to

enter by several doors, — meaning by two, or as
we now say, with less etymological correctness,
different doors; for the two doors may not differ
at all, but be exactly alike. But the need was felt
of a word which should mean a greater number
than a few, or some, and less than many; and by
general unexpressed consent "several" was put to
that service; so that the unlearned reader of the
present day, who finds two persons directed in an
old play to enter by several doors, is for the moment puzzled as to the mode in which the instruction is to be obeyed.

The word "talent," in the sense of mental faculty, affords an example both of appropriation and
perversion. Its appropriation took place about
three centuries ago; but its perversion has been
gradually going on within the memory of men yet
living, and is perhaps hardly yet completed. And
there is this singularity in its history, that it was
taken at about the same time into the vocabularies of several languages of divers origin; into
all those in fact which felt the influence of the
Christian Scriptures at the time of the revival
of learning. Christ's parable of the servants who
received a different number of talents in trust
during their master's absence, in which the word
is used with its original meaning of a sum of
money, but figuratively to signify those personal
gifts and advantages for the use of which each
man is responsible, is the source of the word as it

appears in all the languages of civilized Christendom; it having been taken into them in its purely metaphorical signification.* But at first it was used to mean the natural bent of the mind; and in fact, until the present generation, it was synonymous with "genius," a word which in its application to the mind or soul is, in our tongue at least, of later introduction. The earlier, as well as the later lexicographers of the English, French, and Italian languages, give definitions of these words which are really identical; and Crabb himself, although his function is that of nice discrimination, can divide them no further than by saying that "genius is the particular bent of the intellect which is born with a man," and that "talent is a particular mode of intellect which qualifies its possessor to do some things better than others"; thus furnishing as perfect an example as could be given of distinction without difference. But since the author of the Synonymes issued the last edition of his work, 1837, the usage of intelligent people has been drawing

---

* There is a fidgety dislike on the part of some persons to the word "talented," which some British critics brand as an "Americanism"; and even Dr. Richardson is betrayed into saying, "Dr. Webster has the word 'talented,' and it has been too hastily used in common speech here." There is no ground whatever of objection to the participial adjective, which does not apply to the noun. If "talent" be correctly used to mean mental gifts, it is as correct, as English, to say "a talented man," as to say "a moneyed corporation," or "a landed aristocracy."

a sharp line of demarkation between these two words. One, "genius," has been raised, and the other, "talent," has been degraded, from their former common level. The next lexicographer who does his work with nicety and thoroughness must define "genius" as original creative mental power, and "talent" as that inferior and more common, though sometimes more expanded and more beneficent faculty, which puts to new use facts already known, principles already discovered, methods of thought or expression already established, or which in literature and the arts of design produces by labor and taste rather than by new conception.

Genius may be of high or low order; talent may be great or small; genius may be pestilent, talent beneficent. But the former in its lower grades is not approached in kind by the latter in its larger developments, any more than a poor diamond is rivalled by a fine quartz crystal, or a living spring, from which flows but a thread of water, by a reservoir which supplies the daily needs of millions. Genius is as unmistakable in Gustave Doré's drawing on wood for book illustration, as in Raphael's Sistine Madonna; while all the canvas which Giulio Romano covered with paintings in the grand style — some of them, in drawing and composition, not unworthy of his master — only made it manifest that he was a man of talent, who had studied. The throng of perfect,

polished figures which Canova left behind him
only bear multiplied witness to his talent; but the
few worn and broken marbles of the Parthenon
proclaim a genius before which we stand mute in
delight and wonder. We can see how taste and
skill, culture and application, might produce many
Canovas; but who does not feel that what we
bow down to in the Theseus and the Parcæ is
something which, although it may be cultivated
and developed, cannot be acquired? Meyerbeer
is an instance of a musician whose compositions,
though rich and varied, and sometimes really
grand masterpieces too of skill, are the productions of only a great and highly cultivated talent.
But had Schubert written only his Serenade, he
would have shown that in his soul burned the native fire of genius. The apothegm *poeta nascitur,
non fit*, is true only if by poet we mean no other
than the poet of genius.   But so we do not mean ;
and we have crowned, and worthily crowned, a
made poet with bays, and left a born poet to live
by gauging the liquor that soothed his grief and
quickened his inspiration. Perhaps Gray affords
the most signal example of poetic talent developed and cultivated to its utmost capability and
perfection ; and his *Elegy in a Country Church-
yard*, the most admired instance of an exquisite
work of poetic art produced by taste and fine
susceptibility and labor, — in a word, by talent.
But certainly the highest manifestation of genius

in poetry is Shakespeare, who indeed united in himself genius in its supremest nature and talent in its largest development; adding to the peculiar and original powers of his mind a certain dexterity and sagacity in the use of them which are frequently the handmaids of talent, but which are rarely found in company with genius.

There are two great divisions of genius. One supplies the needs and expresses the spirit of its age; the other finds its inspiration in elemental truth, and deals only with that which is eternal. Of the three great poets of the world, (if we pass by the author of the Book of Job,) Homer, working in the simplest elements of human nature, and limited less than any one of his successors by artificial modes of thought and forms of life, himself a mere voice, chanting an unconscious epic in the dim twilight beyond the farther verge of history, and telling the story of man's youth before his anxious eye had been turned inward, belongs pre-eminently to the universal type of genius, and therefore appeals directly to both instructed and uninstructed minds; while of those who found their inspiration in their own experience, Dante the chief, as much politician as poet, making a hell for his foes and a heaven for his friends, cannot be fully understood without some knowledge of the period and the country in which he lived. Hence it is that even among his countrymen Dante is and always must remain the poet of the instructed few; while unlearned men of all bloods and all ages find in the barrier of a foreign tongue their only hindrance to perusing with a common delight the ever fresh and ever living page of Homer. But Shakespeare presented as simply and directly as Homer to the universal mind of man the perennial truth of unchanging nature. This seems to have been perceived by his very contemporaries. Ben Jonson, in the only line of his eulogy of Shakespeare which is generally known, and which, continually cited, is almost as often destructively misquoted, expresses this appreciation of his beloved friend and fellow. It will be recognized by nearly every reader, in these words:

"He was not for an age, but for all time."

But this was not what Jonson wrote. He said of Shakespeare,

"He was not of an age, but for all time";

and the almost universal substitution of the one preposition for the other shows a failure to appreciate Jonson's meaning, and degrades a most remarkable expression of the high quality of Shakespeare's genius into a clever antithetical utterance of the commonplace eulogy that his fame would endure forever. Jonson said, and the context as well as the line itself shows his meaning, that Shakespeare was not a man of his age, but that what he wrote was for, adapted to, all time. The

voice of more than two centuries has confirmed
this far-reaching and discriminating judgment.
Yet it but partly told the truth ; for Shakespeare
alone of all great poets attained the highest and
rarest combination of power, and united in himself the two kinds of genius.   He was both of his
age and for all time.   Only his race could have
produced him, (for a Celtic, a Scandinavian, or
even a German Shakespeare is inconceivable,) and
that race only at the time when he appeared.

The English or so-called Anglo-Saxon race is
distinguished by a sober earnestness and down-
rightness of character, which manifests itself even
in its narrative, dramatic, and poetical literature ;
and our greatest poet, universal although he was,
marked himself peculiarly ours by raising his diz-
zy pile of fancy and imagination upon the broad
and solid foundation of English common-sense.
The eminence of the rugged and solid English
mind in all departments of poetry is a noteworthy
intellectual phenomenon.   It seems akin to one
observable in music, where we see that the most
brilliant vocalization is that of large and robust
voices carefully trained and painfully broken in to
flexibility ; and in fact, that the dazzling effects of
rapid movement are in direct ratio to the physical
inertia which has, or which seems to have been,
overcome. No trill like that of the heroic-voiced
Jenny Lind, which had the weight and the
steady beat of an antique pendulum, although it

quivered like the reflection of sunlight from water.
But Shakespeare not only thought and spoke as
an Englishman, and so was always truly national,*
(although of his plots not historical only one is
English,) he thought and spoke only as an Englishman could think and speak in the Elizabethan
era. Before that period our forefathers were too
rude, and since we have become, on both sides of
the water, too lettered a folk, though not too learned, for such an utterance. Who can conceive of
Hamlet or *King Lear* or the *Merchant of Venice*
being written by a contemporary of John Skelton,
by a dramatist of the Restoration, by one of the
wits of Queen Anne's reign, or by either king or
subject in Johnson's realm of letters? Had any
man been moved to write them at either of those
periods, the public would not have listened to them,
produced as new compositions. In the style and

---

* Nation has come to mean the people under one government.
As, for instance, the British nation is composed of English,
Scotch, Welsh, and Irish people; and the nation which is called
most improperly, but it would seem inevitably, American, is composed of the same peoples, with a still greater predominance of
the English element, to which within the last twenty years there
has been a considerable addition of Germans. Owing to peculiar political, social, and material conditions, the assimilation of
the minor elements goes on much more rapidly here than in the
mother country; and the English or Anglo-Saxon race, stub-
bornly preserving its own characteristics, as it ever has done, ab-
sorbs here those who flee to it for refuge, as in the mother country it absorbed its nominal conquerors. But there is no other
word than "national" suited to the sentence above written:
"ethnical" will not serve the purpose.

in the vocabulary of the so-called Augustan age of English literature, or in the Johnsonian period, such writing would have been impossible. Yet bearing thus plainly the mark of the time as well as of the race which produced them, these writings have as their chief distinction, that whatever they possess of beauty is beautiful, and whatever they tell of truth is true to all mankind forever. The attempt to explain such an intellectual phenomenon seems indeed presumptuous. We may rightly admire what we cannot fully understand; we may apprehend what we cannot comprehend, and comprehend that which we cannot express; and I own that I shrink back as I essay to measure with my little line and fathom with my puny plummet the vast profound of Shakespeare's genius.

Individual organization determines preference; but organization and circumstances together determine choice, which is preference moved by will, or preference in action. Happily both these joined to make a dramatist of Shakespeare. Circumstances took him to London to earn his bread; circumstances made the theatre the aptest field for his labor; and his organization fitted him supremely for the dramatic function. Yet, had he been born in the present day, it may at least be questioned whether he would have chosen the drama as his profession; for in contemporary Eng-

lish literature, indeed upon our very stage, there is
no indigenous drama. One great cause of this, however, is the fact, that Shakespeare has so entirely
covered the field that there is neither room for
new dramatic literature nor need of it; only for
intrigue, incident, by-play, the scene-painter, and
the tailor. Perhaps he might have chosen journalism, but more probably trade; for competency
was the sole object of his exertion. It is clear
from what we know of him, that he would have
made an influential journalist, or a first-rate merchant. But living in the reign of Elizabeth, he
went to London to become an actor and write
plays for a London audience.

Never, perhaps, did imaginative works, written
to please the public of a great city, have less of a
town air, of that urban quality which, for instance, is so striking in Pope's poems, in Addison's essays, and in the plays of their period and
of Dryden's, than is to be found in Shakespeare's
dramas. They have local allusions, it is true, but
these are comparatively few; and were they many,
this would not touch the point. They are so free
from city taint, that in this respect they might
have been written at a country-seat by one who
had never passed its boundaries or made himself
acquainted with the tone of the metropolis. Yet
it was only in London that those plays could
have been written. London had only just before
Shakespeare's day made its metropolitan suprem-

acy felt, as well as acknowledged, throughout
England.   As long as two hundred years after
that time the county of each member of Parliament was betrayed by his tongue ; but then the
speech of the cultivated people of Middlesex and
its vicinity had become for all England the undis-
puted standard.   Northumberland, or Cornwall,
or Lancashire, might have produced Shakespeare's
mind ; but had he lived in any one of those coun-
ties, or in another, like them remote in speech as
in locality from London, and written for his rural
neighbors instead of the audiences of the Black-
friars and the Globe, the music of his poetry would
have been lost in sounds uncouth and barbarous to
the general ear, and the edge of his fine utterance
would have been turned upon the stony rough-
ness of his rustic phraseology.   His language
would have been a dialect which must needs have
been translated to be understood by modern English ears, with the loss of that heavy discount
which is always paid at the desk of the broker in
literary exchange.   For us of after days, and so
for the perpetuity and diffusion of Shakespeare's
fame, he appeared at a most propitious period of
the history of our race, not only as to its language,
but as to its political and social condition.   As to
language, there was then a freedom from critical
and scholastic restraint which has never since
existed, united to a copiousness of vocabulary,
which, except in the direction of philosophy and

science, has not been materially enlarged. The English language, even the English of London, although Chaucer and Spenser had used it, was regarded then in England itself as unfit for the use of scholars. English literature held no admitted place in the realm of letters; and the English people were of small consideration in Europe. Andrew Borde, a physician of Henry the Eighth's time, in his *Book of the Introduction of Knowledge*, says: "The speche of Englande is a base speche to other noble speches, as Italion, Castylion, & Frenche; howbeit the speche of Englande of late dayes is amended." And Lilly, Shakespeare's contemporary, makes his Euphues, in describing England, speak of "the English tongue, which is, as I have heard, almost barbarous."

We are accustomed to think of London as the capital of a great kindred empire, which is in letters as well as in arms and commerce one of the five or six great powers of the civilized world. We measure its importance by the fact of its being the time-honored literary metropolis of the great kingdom and the great republic whose tongue it speaks. But at the time of Shakespeare's arrival there, although that time was the glorious reign of Queen Elizabeth, London was only the chief city of the southern part of a little island which then contained the whole English race, — a race which had not yet taken its

appointed place among the nations. Haughty
Spain, splendid in the spoil of the Indies, France,
chivalric and courtly, and Italy, rich in art, in literature, and learning, looked down upon us as
rude islanders who spoke an uncouth tongue, — a
people not much to be regarded, but not to be
interfered with or offended, because, as Euphues
says, English folk "are impatient in their anger
of any equall ; readie to revenge an injurie, but
never wont to proffer any ; they never fight without provoking, and once provoked they never
cease." It would seem that in some respects at
least the traits of race have not changed during
three centuries, on either side of the water. Indeed, as a people it was not until the beginning of
Elizabeth's reign that we attained to the full maturity of our English-hood. The great civil wars,
which involved three generations, though lasting
but thirty years, and which ended by placing the
Tudors on the throne, were not only the expir-
ing throes of feudalism, they were the pangs of a
new birth, and that birth was the English nation.
Until after the reign of Henry the Seventh the
people of England, although politically bound together, were as little penetrated by that unity of
feeling and character which we call the genius of
a nation as could possibly be in a community
mainly of one origin, which had lived for nearly
a thousand years in one small country, isolated
from other peoples by the sea, and for six cen-

turies under one government. Yet up to that period the habits and tone of thought, even among the governing and cultivated classes, those which held most frequent communication with each other and felt most the influence of the court, were so unlike, for instance in Northumberland, Kent, and Cornwall, that they might have served to distinguish alien and hostile populations. But during the long and tranquil reigns of the first Tudor and of his immediate successor the English people became knit together through peaceful intercourse, and by assimilation of thought and manners among the superior classes. And even among the yeomanry and peasantry the Wars of the Roses, by disturbing the inertness and local isolation of people otherwise tied to the soil on which they lived, and ignorant of their own countrymen beyond their own narrow neighborhood, by sending them in large bodies through the land, thus mingling their blood and measurably assimilating their dialects by attrition, did much to establish the condition of a true nationality.

The nation whose various elements were thus upheaved by the ploughshare, and intermingled by the harrow of war, lay fallow under the genial skies of the long succeeding days of peace, gaining strength and unity for the new growth which was to enrich it for the first time throughout its borders with an indigenous and common harvest. To this people thus made approximately homogeneous, the Reformation came and completed the enfranchisement which the destruction of feudalism had but partly accomplished. The English character did not completely attain its ideal type until after it had freed itself from the fetters of feudality and cast off the yoke of Rome. During the century which succeeded the latter event it seems to have been more purely and absolutely, and at the same time unconsciously and generously, English, than the influences of party politics, the entangling interests of an extended empire, and the artificial preservation of a dead form of society, have permitted it to be since that period. Then from this people, thus interfused, thus tried and purified, thus invigorated by repose, in the first flush and strength of its perfected and awakened nature, there sprang an array of men glorious in arts and arms, in learning and in literature, in commerce and in statesmanship. The rich intellectual product of the Elizabethan era was like nothing that the world has seen, except the outburst of genius in Greece after the Persian war, which produced Pericles, Sophocles, Euripides, Aristophanes, Thucydides, Socrates, Plato, and Phidias. It was this period, celebrated under the name of the princess whose reign filled the greater part of it, and which extended from about 1575 to 1625, which produced the men who changed the position of the English people before the world; and chief

among them, though not then reckoned of them,
was William Shakespeare.

Not until the beginning of the nineteenth century did Shakespeare's own race acknowledge,
with one consent, that the rustic-bred playwright
was the greatest of poets, and one of the wisest, if
not the wisest, of men. It took us two hundred
years to bring ourselves with unanimity to the
simple acceptance of that miracle. We literally
brought ourselves to it ; for the professed scholars
and critics rather hindered than helped our progress to that large appreciation, in which they
were ever behind the people. In fact Shakespeare's supreme popularity dates from his own
day ; and in this respect it was not exceptional,
but conformed to a rule which is almost universal.
The judgment of posterity may reverse, or it may
confirm, enhance, and diffuse the approval of contemporaries ; but in literature the man who fails
to please those to whom he addresses himself has
failed forever. We have contemporary testimony
to the fact that Shakespeare's plays were regarded
by the public of his own day as incomparably superior to those of all his rivals ; and it may be
doubted whether a remarkable appreciation of
them which was printed in the bookseller's Ad-
dress to the Reader of *Troilus and Cressida*, in
1609, that "they serve for the most common commentaries of all the actions of our lives," has been
more than decorated and illustrated, amplified and

weakened, by all subsequent criticism. It was the demand of succeeding ages for these dramas, the delight in them which was constantly felt and expressed, broadening, deepening, strengthening, with each generation, and the moral and intellectual influence which they exerted, which compelled the critics to undertake to account for this extraordinary phenomenon in literature. The literary history of the seventeenth century, during the first sixteen years of which Shakespeare was alive, shows a demand for his plays by the reading public unapproached in the case of any other author. The fondness grew. It included all classes of readers, from the most thoughtful to those who merely sought in books a momentary pastime. In the first half of the eighteenth century the demand of the public for Shakespeare's plays was at least fourfold greater than that for any other book, notwithstanding the great number already issued from the press, and in spite of the fact that the most admired and elegant writer of the early part of that period had devoted his best powers to the diffusion of a taste for the works of our great epic poet, while he hardly mentions those of the greater dramatist. Yet the literary men of his own day who praise Shakespeare, almost without exception, leave his plays unnoticed, and limit their eulogy to his *Venus and Adonis* and his *Lucrece;* and the critics of the eighteenth century, yielding personally, as we can see, to the spell of

his genius, were yet reluctant, doubtful, and troubled with many scruples when they came to account for all the admiration of which they themselves and their labors were living witnesses.
True, one of them, himself a poet, Pope, passed
in happy phrase one of the most penetrative judgments that has been uttered upon him, when he
said: "The poetry of Shakespeare is inspiration
indeed. He is not so much an imitator as an instrument of Nature; and it is not so just to say
that he speaks for her, as that she speaks through
him."   But he, like all his contemporaries and immediate successors, thought it necessary to praise
and blame with alternate breath, and to point out
deformities manifold and monstrous in this be-
witching but untutored and half-savage child of
nature.   Yet at this very time the intelligent love
of Shakespeare was so deeply rooted in the English mind that his words and thoughts pierced,
like multitudinous fibres, the intellectual being of
the people; and while these men and their little
rhymes and their bulbous sentences might have
lived or perished, and no harm been done, and little notice taken, he could not have been uptorn
without a disturbance of the whole English nature, and a destruction of no small part of the
phraseology of common life.

This being true as to the relative position of our
own critics to our own spontaneous appreciation
of Shakespeare, still more is it true with regard to

the relations of foreign critics to that appreciation.
Some people, who ought to have known better,
have more than half admitted that the German
critics taught us to understand our own poet.   I
am unwilling to believe this of the English race in
Europe ; I know that it is not true of that part of
it which is in America.   Here at least there is, and
always has been, a class of people so large and so
diffused through society that it cannot be rightly
called a class, who do not know that there are German critics, who have little acquaintance with any
criticism, to whom Schlegel is unrevealed and
Coleridge is but a name, and who would quietly
smile at the notion that "at last" we understand
Shakespeare, because some learned people have
said very profound sayings about his revelations
of "the inner life."   I have an abiding faith which
no criticism that I have yet seen has shaken, that
most of those who read Shakespeare worthily and
lovingly understand what he meant as thoroughly
as Coleridge did, or as Gervinus does, with all their
metaphysics and philosophy.   All honor to them
for what they have written ; which is in itself admirable, and which it would not be well lightly to
undertake to rival or to imitate.   But we must
be careful not to confound perception with expression, or comprehension with power of analysis.
Newton saw no better, rejoiced no more in the
beauty of color, than other people, because he
analyzed the sunbeam.   The ignorant monk, who

would have roasted him as a sorcerer, illuminated
missals with an intuitive mastery of the harmonies of the prism which he could not have attained
by all his experiments or explained by all his theories. Shakespeare himself, who seems to have
seen and understood all mental relations and conditions, saw this, and, as if with an eye of favor
upon the millions who would read him with simple
pleasure, made Birone say of the astronomers:

> "These earthly godfathers of heaven's lights,
> That give a name to every fixed star,
> Have no more profit of their shining nights
> Than those that walk and wot not what they are."

It was by no strange feature or striking peculiarity in the construction of his works that Shakespeare commanded the attention and won the
applause of his contemporaries. In their design,
as in their very means and methods, his plays
were like those of his immediate predecessors,
which themselves were the fruits of a slow and
compact growth. He affected no novelties, es-
sayed no surprise. He did just what others did,
but did it incomparably better, supremely best.
He did not even seek to awaken interest by origi-
nality in the stories of his dramas. Beginning
his career by working over old plays, and performing his labor in company with others, when he
came to be an independent writer and the sole
author of plays, he still used old chronicles and

plays and stories, the subjects of which were familiar to many of his audience; and he adopted the forms of the old plays with little variation. This he did, not only for convenience and expedition, but because the public for which he wrote was more easily interested by dramas with the subjects of which they were acquainted, than by those the subjects of which were entirely new.

That which first distinguished Shakespeare from the little throng of dramatists among whom and with some of whom he first labored, was the character of his thought and the language in which he clothed it, — in a word, his style. It is this which first strikes the attention of the reader of the present day when he takes up Shakespeare's works. It is this by which we are enabled to distinguish his writing from that of other dramatists in the same play, as in the First and Second Parts of *King Henry the Sixth*, the *Taming of the Shrew*, and *Pericles*. The distinction can be made with a very great degree of certainty by any one qualified by natural gifts and practice for such investigations, even with regard to Shakespeare's earliest writing. It is not that Shakespeare is all fine gold and others are all dross; but when we know that of several mines one produced gold, another silver, and another lead, and when we find gold and dross, or silver and dross, or lead and dross, or gold and silver and lead together, we need not be in much doubt as to the distribution of the ownership.

Purely English as Shakespeare was in what we may call the externals of his dramatic art, he was in no respect more so than in his style. In the earlier half of the sixteenth century Italian literature had begun to exercise a modifying influence upon that of England, and especially upon English poetry. Surrey, Spenser, Sidney, Daniel, Jonson, Beaumont, Fletcher, Drayton, Milton, all show the effect of this influence. In Shakespeare's writings it does not appear, except, perhaps, in his erotic pastoral poem, *Venus and Adonis*. His very sonnets are free from any traits of Italian spirit or versification. He went to Italian literature, in his time the great mint and treasure-house of fiction; but it was only for the raw material of a tragedy like *Othello*, or a comedy like *The Merchant of Venice*. He doubtless read Italian well enough to master the works of the early Italian novelists; but although the literature of that language could not but have insensibly enlivened his genius and enriched his stores of thought, it had no perceptible effect upon his mental tone, his turn of expression, or his choice of imagery. He is as free from the influence of this as he is from that of classic literature, — the imitation of which was in vogue with the regularly educated writers of his day. His vocabulary, at once his means of thought and medium of expression, is merely that of his time, that which was used by his dramatic contemporaries and by the

translators of the Bible. ˙ Writing for the general public, he used such language as would convey his meaning to his auditors, — the common
phraseology of his period. But what a language
was that! In its capacity for the varied and
exact expression of all moods of mind, all forms
of thought, all kinds of emotion, a tongue un-
equalled by any other known to literature! A
language of exhaustless variety; strong without
ruggedness, and flexible without effeminacy. A
manly tongue; yet bending itself gracefully and
lovingly to the tenderest and the daintiest needs
of woman, and capable of giving utterance to
the most awful and impressive thoughts in homely words that come from the lips and go to the
heart of childhood. It would seem as if this
language had been preparing itself for centuries
to be the fit medium of utterance for the world's
greatest poet. Hardly more than a generation
had passed since the English tongue had reached
its perfect maturity; just time enough to have it
well worked into the unconscious usage of the people, when Shakespeare appeared, to lay upon it a
burden of thought which would test its extremest
capability. He found it fully formed and developed, but not yet uniformed and cramped and disciplined by the lexicographers and rhetoricians, —
those martinets of language, who seem to have
lost for us in force and flexibility as much as they
have gained for us in precision. The phrase-

ology of that day was notably large and simple among ordinary writers and speakers. Among the college-bred writers and their imitators, there was too great a fondness for little conceits; but even with them this was an extraneous blemish, like that sometimes found in the ornament upon a noble building. Shakespeare seized this instrument, to whose tones all ears were open, and with the touch of a master he brought out all its harmonies. It lay ready to any hand; but his was the first to use it with absolute control; and among all his successors, great as some are, he has had, even in this single respect, no rival. No unimportant condition of his supreme mastery over expression was his entire freedom from restraint—it may almost be said from consciousness—in the choice of language. He was no precisian, no etymologist, no purist. He was not purposely writing literature. The only criticism that he feared was that of his audience, which represented the English people of all grades above the peasantry. These he wished should not find his writing incomprehensible or dull: no more. If we except the translators of the Bible, Shakespeare wrote the best English that has yet been written; but they who speak of it as remarkably pure, that is, as having a notably small admixture of Romance words, utter mere vague, unwarranted encomium. In the sixteenth century there were probably more Romance words adopted into our

language than there had been before, or have been
since, if we exclude words of technical or quasi-
technical character.   These words Shakespeare
and the translators of the Bible used at need with
unconscious freedom.   The vocabularies both of
the Bible and of Shakespeare's plays show forty
per cent of Romance or Latin words, which, with
the exception just named, is probably a larger
proportion than is now used by our best writers ;
certainly larger than is heard from those who
speak their mother tongue with spontaneous idio-
matic correctness.* So many Latin words having
been adopted into the English language in the
Elizabethan era, and English having been up to
that period almost excluded from literature, the
Latin element then retained much of its native
character ; to which fact is due, in some measure,
Shakespeare's use of words of Latin origin in
their radical signification.   But although he uses
them thus oftener than any of his contemporaries,
we may be sure that it was the result of no yielding to the constraints of scholarship.   In brief,
words were his slaves, not he theirs ; and if one
could serve his purpose better than another, he
did not stop to ask the birthplace or to trace the
lineage of his servant.   He will compose verse
after verse almost wholly of Anglo-Saxon mono-
syllables ; and this equally in passages descriptive,

* See Lectures on the English Language, by the Hon. George
P. Marsh, LL.D., pp. 124, 125.

dramatic, and lyric, and of the utmost dissimilari-
ty of sentiment.

> "The moon shines bright.— In such a night as this,
> When the sweet wind did gently kiss the trees,
> And they did make no noise, — in such a night,
> Troilus methinks mounted the Trojan walls,
> And sighed his soul toward the Grecian tents,
> Where Cressida lay that night."

> "Howl, howl, howl, howl! — O, you are men of stone!
> Had I your tongues and eyes I 'd use them so
> That heaven's vault should crack. — She 's gone forever!
> I know when one is dead, and when one lives:
> She 's dead as earth. — Lend me a looking-glass:
> If that her breath will mist or stain the stone,
> Why, then she lives."

> "Vex not his ghost!   O, let him pass: he hates him
> That would upon the rack of this tough world
> Stretch him out longer."

> "Take, O take those lips away
>   That so sweetly were forsworn,
> And those eyes, the break of day,
>   Eyes that do mislead the morn.
> But my kisses bring again, — bring again,
> Seals of love, but sealed in vain, — sealed in vain."

On the other hand, he will make two Latin
words fill an entire verse, except perhaps one syllable.

> "He and Aufidius can no more atone
> Than violentest contrariety."

> "You shout me forth
> In acclamations hyperbolical."

> "No, this my hand will rather
> The multitudinous seas incarnadine."

> " This supernatural soliciting
>   Cannot be good, cannot be ill."

> " Think'st thou to catch my life so pleasantly
>   As to prenominate in nice conjecture
>   Where thou wilt hit me dead ? "

These brief passages furnish us five verses, each composed, except a monosyllable or two, of two Latin words, and each of these verses preceded or followed, or both preceded and followed, by one made up of short native words.

Shakespeare discriminates with exquisite nicety between the fitness of romance and of native words. He writes of Cleopatra:

> " Age cannot wither
>   Nor custom stale her infinite variety."

But in *Pericles* he makes the Prince, speaking of the obtaining of the beautiful prize who has tempted so many men to their destruction, say, — not

> " To gain such infinite felicity," —

but, counter-changing, in the herald's phrase, his Anglo-Saxon and his Latin,

> " To compass such a boundless happiness."

To an English ear "boundless happiness" means more, comes more directly home, than "infinite felicity"; while on the other hand "compass," though strictly inapplicable to anything boundless, conveys an idea of encircling, which is most appropriate to the occasion. Again, Shakespeare mingles words of native and of foreign origin which are synonymous, so closely as to subject him to the charge of pleonasm, — a charge which can, for the like reason, be brought against the noble liturgy of the Church of England. He has, for instance, in *King John*, "infinite and boundless reach," in *Measure for Measure*, "rebate and blunt his natural edge," and in *Othello*, "to such exsufflicate and blown surmises." It is thus manifest that Shakespeare was secure in his use of words, and thoughtless except as to their power to serve his present purpose. So that there can be no more futile objection to a reading in his plays, than that the doubtful word occurs in no other passage of his writing. For if he had occasion to use a word but once, or, for that matter, to make it for his single need, he would have used or made it without hesitation. Yet his intuitive knowledge of the peculiar value of words of various derivation is continually manifest. That he was keenly sensible of the ludicrous effect of long Latin words in certain situations is manifest, not only from such instances as Costard's conclusion, that remuneration is "the Latin word for three farthings," and Bardolph's definition of accommodated, "that is when a man is as they say accommodated, or, when a man is, being, whereby, a may be thought to be accommodated, which is an excellent thing," but from such usage as that in Sir Toby Belch's rejoinder to Maria's remonstrance against his rois-

tering behavior, — "Tilly vally, am I not consan-
guineous?" — where the use of the Latin word and
the abstract idea has a humor which would be lost
had he said, "Am I not her kinsman?"

Shakespeare's freedom in the use of words was
but a part of that conscious irresponsibility to
critical rule which had such an important influence upon the development of his whole dramatic
style. To the working of his genius under this
entire unconsciousness of restraint we owe the
grandest and the most delicate beauties of his
poetry, his most poignant expressions of emotion,
and his richest and subtlest passages of humor.
For the superiority of his work is just in proportion to his carelessness of literary criticism.
His poems, the least excellent of his writings,
were written for the literary world; and it is
upon them that his contemporaries, in passing
literary judgment, found his reputation. His sonnets, which occupy a middle place, were written
for himself or for his private friends, and were obtained for publication in some indirect way. His
plays were mere entertainments for the general
public, written, not to be read, but to be spoken;
written as business, just as Rogers wrote money
circulars, or as Bryant writes leading articles.
This freedom was suited to the unparalleled richness and spontaneousness of his thought, of which
it was in fact partly the result and itself partly
the condition. Ben Jonson had these traits of his

friend's genius in his mind when he wrote that passage in his *Discoveries* in which he tells us that he "had an excellent phantsy, brave notions, and gentle expressions; wherein he flow'd with that facility that it was sometimes necessary he should be stopp'd. *Sufflaminandus erat*, as Augustus said of Haterius. His wit was in his own power; would the rule of it had been so too." The whole of the passage of Seneca from which Jonson quotes, is so notably applicable to Shakespeare that it deserves to be preserved entire.

"Itaque divus Augustus optime dixit: Haterius noster sufflaminandus est. Adeo non currere, sed decurrere videbatur; nec verborum tantum illi copia, sed etiam rerum erat; quotiens velles eandem rem, et quamdiu velles, diceret." — *Excerpta Controversiarum*, Lib. IV. Præf.

We, with our dictionaries and our books of synonymes, our thesauruses of words and phrases to facilitate literary composition, our Blairs and our Kameses, may think, some of us, that we have smoothed the road to literary excellence, when we have but cumbered our movement and distracted our attention. After all, the secret of the art of writing is to have somewhat to say, and to say just that and no other. We think in words, and when we lack fit words we lack fit thoughts. When we strive to write finely for the sake of doing so, we become bombastic or inane. Oldisworth, quoted by Dr. Johnson in his Lives of the Poets, says of Edmund Neale (known under the assumed name of Smith), who had a great reputation in his own day: "Writing with ease what could easily be written moved his indignation. When he was writing upon a subject he would seriously consider what Demosthenes, Homer, Virgil, or Horace, if alive, would say upon that occasion, which whetted him to exceed himself as well as others." Which I take it is one principal reason why, although the world yet hears something of Demosthenes, of Homer, of Virgil, and of Horace, it has long ceased to hear anything of Neale. It must not be supposed, however, that Shakespeare, in the composition of his plays, was guided by no written law, because in his day in England no literary law had yet been written. In *The Garden of Eloquence*, by Henry Peacham, published in 1577, there are forms and figures of speech described and classified and named to the number of two hundred and more, with apt rules to use them withal. But not seeking to square his work by these rules, Shakespeare wrote in his marvellous fashion, because, if he wrote at all, it was just as easy for him to write in that way as in any other. When Lear says,

> "Down, thou climbing sorrow,
> Thy element 's below," —

the critics of the last century, walking through the clipped verdure and formal alleys of the Garden of Eloquence, point out, with dignified complacency, that "here is a most remarkable proso-

popœia." So there is, if they must have it so.
But it comes from Shakespeare's pen as a matter
of course; as if no other thought, no other words,
could have occurred to him on that occasion.
And what cared he what Homer or what Virgil
would have said? But it is always thus with him.
Unlike other great writers, he does not seem to
scatter his riches with a lavish hand: they drop
from him like fatness from the clouds of heaven;
as if, with the intellectual riches of a god, he had
a godlike serenity in their possession and their
bestowal.

Notwithstanding Shakespeare's copiousness of
thought and affluence of imagery, no remark
upon his style could be more erroneous than that
so often made by his critics, that he does not repeat himself. It has even been attempted to
regulate his text upon this assumption. But
Shakespeare did not hesitate to repeat his own
thoughts or words, or, for that matter, those of
other .writers, when to do so served his present
purpose. Examples are scattered all through his
plays. For instance, the same feeling is expressed
in nearly the same words by characters as radically unlike as King Lear, Justice Shallow, and
Othello. The first two in their feebleness, the
last in constraint, revert to their former prowess.
Lear says:

> "I have seen the day when with my good biting falchion
> I would have made them skip."

Shallow:

"I have seen the time with my long sword I would have made your four tall fellows skip like rats."

Othello:

"I have seen the day
When, with this little arm and this good sword,
I have made my way through more impediments
Than twenty times your stop."

In no respect was Shakespeare's art classical. He was essentially a Goth; and his style corresponded entirely to the character of his mind. English is a Gothic language; yet there can be classical English, as we have been shown by Addison and Goldsmith. In the former of these eminent writers we find the perfection of ease, clearness, harmony, and dignity. So we do in Shakespeare, except that some passages, from compression of many thoughts, from neglect of elaboration, and sometimes from corruption, lack clearness. But it is not thus that Shakespeare's style is to be defined. It is not to be defined at all; it is a mystery. Addison's sound sense, the eminently graceful character of his mind, and his lambent humor, were individual qualities which marked his thought; but as to his style, it can be easily analyzed; its elements can be detected and their proportions declared. But you cannot take certain qualities of style and combine them in certain proportions, by certain rules, and make your Shakespeare's mixture. A nameless something, not grace, not harmony, not strength, which yet

mingles with them all in Shakespeare, would be
lacking.   Addison's perfect style has been perfect-
ly imitated.   There have been men, there might
be many men, who could produce, not what would
properly be called an imitation of it, but the thing
itself.   But the man has never yet written, except
Shakespeare, who could produce ten lines having
that quality which, for lack of other name, we call
Shakespearian.

It is, however, not only in this nameless charm
and happy audacity that Shakespeare differs from
those writers of our language whose styles may be
regarded as models of correctness.   He is often
undeniably incorrect, in consequence partly of the
syntactical usage of his day, which upon minor
points had not yet attained a complete logical conformity to the very principles then recognized, and
partly of his own neglect to revise carefully that
which he wrote so fluently.   Such of his occasional
errors as are not of the former kind appear exclusively in his plays: they are not found in the poems
which he carefully prepared for perusal.   Perhaps
it is safe to say that it is not among those great
imaginative writers who are affluent in thought and
free in style that we are to look for a grammati-
cally faultless use of language; but rather among
didactic writers, who are constipated and precise,
and who occupy a place in the second or third
grade, or one yet lower.   The pages of Walter
Scott, who in imagination and richness of re-

source stands nearer (if any can be near) to Shakespeare than any other writer in our language,
are marked with instances of inaccuracy of style,
as well as of statement, which we pass by almost
unnoticed as we are borne along upon the strong,
swift current of his narrative.   But whatever may
be the general truth in this respect, it is certain
that in Shakespeare's plays we find not a few
such passages as the following, which there is
no reason for doubting came as we have them
from his pen.

"No more of this, Helena: go to, no more, lest it be thought
you rather affect a sorrow than to have."
All's Well, &c., Act I. Sc. I.

"Achievement is command, ungain'd beseech."
Troilus and Cressida.

"He hath, and is again to cope your wife."
Othello, Act IV. Sc. I.

These would serve as fit school exercises in
faulty syntax, of which alone they are examples.
But in that grand rejoinder to the desperate
Othello, in which Emilia, noble though not un-
tainted soul, rises to the serenest height of conscious self-sacrifice, —

"Thou hast not half the power to do me harm
As I have to be harm'd," —

the grandeur and the pathos of this truly woman-
ly utterance reach our hearts through a confusion
not only of syntax, but of logic; "power" being
used in the first part of the sentence in the sense

of ability, and understood in the latter in the
sense of capacity,—inaccurately, because power
is an attribute of action, not of reception. But
the hand which should undertake to rectify these
errors in construction by rule and plummet would
find that it had strength enough only to bring
down the noble though irregular structure in a
ruin that would overwhelm the rash endeavor
with disgrace and ridicule.

There is, however, a vagueness in some passages of Shakespeare's poetry which is intentional, and which is a result of the highest art, —
a vagueness which magnifies an image, generally
of terror, that would be belittled by being drawn
with sharper outline. This is a trait of Gothic
art, and is not peculiar to Shakespeare, or indeed
to poetry ; for it finds its place in Gothic architecture. Schiller has been much praised, and
somewhat over-praised, for his use of the indefinite neuter pronoun "it" in his ballad, *The Diver*,
to indicate the fabled polypus, which, however, he
immediately describes.* But Shakespeare, who
seems to have been beforehand with most modern
poets in all their happiest devices, had in this
effect anticipated and surpassed Schiller, and had
availed himself of our indefinite dread of unknown
horrors in the recesses of the sea, not only, like
Schiller, to leave upon the mind a vague image of

---

* "It saw—a hundred-armed creature—its prey."
                              Sir E. Bulwer Lytton's Translation.

the unknown creature itself, but to heighten our
dread of, and aversion to, unnatural crime.　How
indefinite the comparison when Lear exclaims:

> "Ingratitude, thou marble-hearted fiend,
> More hideous when thou show'st thee in a child,
> Than the sea-monster!"

What is *the* sea monster?　Yet how much more
of horror is suggested by that definite indefinity,
than if the comparison had been in terms to a
crocodile or a kraken!*　And in other modes,
and for other reasons than the heightening of an
image, Shakespeare is sometimes vague, and in
expressing abstract thought or simple emotion
purposely indefinite.　He is aided in his effects
of this kind by a singular felicity in framing
phrases which convey ideas by mere suggestion,
and which at once fill mind and ear with a satisfaction, the reason for which escapes close analy-

---

* I will here remark that the happy comparison made by
Swift, so often quoted, and always as his, of those able and well-
informed men who are yet hesitating speakers, to a full church,
which, from its very fulness, is emptied more slowly than if the
congregation were a small one, was taken by the Dean from
Shakespeare.　And it shows how little the *Lucrece* is read, that
this appropriation has not been pointed out before.

> "Her maid is gone, and she prepares to write,
> First hovering o'er the paper with her quill.
> Conceit and grief an eager combat fight;
> What wit sets down is blotted straight with will;
> This is too curious good, this blunt and ill:　　·
> 　Much like a press of people at a door
> 　Throng her inventions, which shall go before."

sis. What, for instance, is the exact meaning of the last two lines of this passage from one of Macbeth's soliloquies?

> "Present fears
> Are less than horrible imaginings.
> My thought, whose murder yet is but fantastical,
> Shakes so my single state of man, that function
> Is smother'd in surmise, and nothing is
> But what is not."

Yet there is no doubt that it leaves upon the mind just the impression which Shakespeare intended to make; and that probably the intelligent reader of sensitive organization but uncritical mind is placed by it more in sympathy with the poet's mood than some of those who have harder heads and subtler intellects. So as to the phrase "blood-boltered Banquo," it may be safely doubted if any modern reader on first meeting with the passage knew positively the meaning of "boltered"; but it may be as safely believed that few readers, except those who read a play as the mathematician did, to see what it all proves, did not receive from the sound of the phrase, and a vaguely attributed sense, the impression intended by the poet.

Akin to this power in Shakespeare is that of pushing hyperbole to the verge of absurdity; of mingling heterogeneous metaphors and similes which, coldly examined, seem discordant; in short, of apparently setting at naught the rules of rhetoric, without paying the penalty by the critics in such case made and provided. Thus, when Cleopatra, about to send a message to Antony, says,

> "Give me ink and paper.
> He shall have every day a several greeting,
> Or I 'll unpeople Egypt,"—

how needlessly extravagant is the hyperbole in regard to the number of messengers, three hundred and sixty-five of whom would have conveyed a several greeting to Antony every day for a year! But it is really reflective in its effect; it is a revelation of Cleopatra's character; and as a measure of her feeling toward her lover, and of her consciousness of absolute power, it is in keeping. Of both mixed metaphor and apparently discordant simile, where is there a more flagrant seeming example than the following passage from the *Tempest*, the beauty of which, as a whole, is transcendent?

> "The charm dissolves apace:
> And as the morning steals upon the night,
> Melting the darkness, so their rising senses
> Begin to chase the ignorant fumes that mantle
> Their clear reason."

Now if the beauty and propriety of metaphor depended upon the exact, the material and mechanical conformity of images, what a hotchpot would be here! Indeed, a learned and generally judicious critic of the last century has selected this very passage as a shocking example of mixed metaphor, in which " so many ill-sorted things are joined that the mind can see nothing clearly." And if it were necessary to the beauty and the force of the metaphor that we.should picture to ourselves a figure of the dawn stealing upon a figure of the darkness, and at the same time melting it up in a pot, and that we should see a likeness between this process and the equally incomprehensible one of senses rising up and running after uninstructed fumes which were casting a mantle over reason, it need hardly be said that the passage would be ridiculous. But not thus does the mind receive the impression of a metaphor. And in this passage, as in hardly any other in the range of poetry, is the tender glory of the dawning day gently dispelling the darkness that covers the face of nature brought up before the mind; and it is to this image, not sharply defined, but seen as if in a mental twilight, that Prospero compares his charm's dissolving. It should ever be remembered, too, in our judgment of a poet's, and especially a dramatic poet's, fancies and expressions of emotion, that they are to be looked upon from his plane of vision. If we do not rise with him to the point to which he has risen, much that has to his eye due proportion will to us seem monstrous. To one who stands upon a mountain-top, objects, the size and opposite character of which strike the eye of him who remains upon the plain, are dwarfed into insignificance or blended into harmony. There is in a play, which, though not the greatest ·production of Shakespeare's genius, displays more completely than any other all the qualities of his style, — *The Second Part of Henry the Fourth,* — a passage which in its resistless sweep and majestic imagery is not surpassed by any other of his writing, and which is an extreme example at once of the vagueness, the mingling of metaphor, and the extravagance with which he could dare to write, and splendidly succeed. Northumberland, after several speeches, during which he, with rapidly rising emotion, is led to the certain knowledge of his son Hotspur's death, enraged with grief, thus closes his outbreak of wrath and sorrow : —

> "Now bind my brows with iron, and approach
> The ragged'st hour that time and spite dare bring
> To frown upon the enrag'd Northumberland.
> Let heaven kiss earth : now let not nature's hand
> Keep the wild flood confin'd ; let order die ;
> And let this world no longer be a stage
> To feed contention in a ling'ring act ;
> But let one spirit of the first-born Cain
> Reign in all bosoms, that, each heart being set
> On bloody courses, the rude scene may end,
> And darkness be the burier of the dead ! "

How big this is with strong emotion ! how turbulent with grand and multitudinous impersonation ! The very abstract subjects are all endowed with life and passion. Yet no clear images are left upon the mind ; the attributed actions are in

themselves preposterous, impossible; and the im-
precation of the end of all things upon occasion
of the death of one man in battle shows, by attaining it, that there can be a limit even to extravagance. But what reader, except a rhetori-
cian of the last century, ever attempted to form an
image of a personified heaven kissing a personified earth? How great a loss would be the knowledge of what the wild flood is which nature keeps
confined! Who ever supposed that Shakespeare
meant that a stage could properly be said to feed
anything, much more feed contention? The truth
is, that in such passages as that in question, when
they are the work of a hand strong enough to
carry the reader with the writer, the mind does
not take the personifying words in their strict
sense. That sense, as in the phrases, "Let heaven
kiss earth," "let order die," "to feed contention,"
is only suggested, and gives a certain color and intensity to expression. And in Northumberland's
speech, the quick opposing changes of impersonation perturb the passage with a stir of words and
clash of thought which corresponds to and portrays
the strong, deep agitation of the speaker's soul.

Shakespeare mixed not only metaphors, but
metaphors and plain language. He unites even
the material and the spiritual; and yet his image
loses neither strength nor beauty, because its head
is of gold and its feet of clay. When Hamlet
says,

> "and bless'd are those
> Whose blood and judgment are so well co-mingled
> That they are not a pipe for Fortune's finger
> To play what stop she please,"

what a union of weight and edge is given to the passage by the welding of the physical idea of blood with the moral idea of judgment! Yet the rhetoricians have forbidden the banns of such unions. But the period as a whole, no less than the first member of it, is obnoxious to their denunciation. For the last half is as apparently incongruous with the first, as the elements of the first are with each other. How can the commingling of blood and judgment make a pipe? But Shakespeare did not write for men who read after this mole-eyed fashion. Nor did he here mean that blood and judgment make a pipe. Blood and judgment make the man, and the man is then compared to a pipe in the hands of fortune. This is discovered not by an analysis, however rapid, but apprehended at once by the understanding of every reader who can and does admit the entrance of more than one idea into his mind at the same time. So in Hamlet's speech, against which there was an outcry all through the last century, —

> "To take arms against a sea of troubles," —

Shakespeare does not put his moody prince in the attitude of a military Mrs. Partington, using arms instead of broom against the ocean. It is against the troubles that the man is to struggle, and it is the troubles which are to be ended. Had Shakespeare written a "host of troubles," or any equivalent phrase, the line would have been within the capacity of a poet of the second rank; but by writing "sea," he with one word brings to mind the tumultuous, ever succeeding woes, which seeming innumerable, like the multitudinous seas, sometimes overwhelm the soul. It is to his faculty of combining the expression of an impressive truth or a genuine human feeling with fancies which by themselves would seem extravagant, that Shakespeare's style owes its peculiar and never failing charm, — a faculty which in its action transcends all law, except that of its own being. He has, in the height of his hyperbole, and even in the occasional inflation of his imagery, a keeping which makes his expressions seem those of simple though elevated nature. He possesses, also, in its highest manifestation, the correlative power of giving, by the reflected light of his intellect, beauty to that which is in itself repulsive. Not only passion, guilt, and woe, but even inhumanity and baseness, are presented to us so tempered and elevated through the medium of his genius, that we are not wounded or repelled by the picture, while we mourn over, or condemn, or even loathe, that which it represents. We may say of his genius, as Laertes says of the crazed Ophelia,

> "Thought and affliction, passion, hell itself,
> She turns to favor and to prettiness."

Thus Shakespeare furnishes us with the very
language in which we can pass critical judgment
upon himself; so that it is possible that the best
and completest expression of his genius could be
culled from the works which that genius has produced.

Shakespeare, from the height to which he
soars, can overlook and disregard that which af-
fronts lowlier eyes; or, by the universal solvent
of his genius, he can compel the union of elements whose natural repugnance resists less po-
tent alchemy. Yet, with no material detriment to
his fame, it may be admitted that precisians and
purists, and all who admire, as Sampson fought,
only when the law is on their side, can find a true
bill of extravagance against him. For what was
justly said of Plato, that "if he had not erred he
would have done less," is quite as applicable to
the great dramatic poet as to the great philosopher; and the allowance may be more reasonably
made in the case of Shakespeare. If we will have
high-sounding poetry, we must risk an occasional
flight beyond the bounds of reason. Genius has
produced some bombast which is really grand, and
some tinsel that will shine forever.

Much more objectionable than such extravagance as that into which Shakespeare sometimes,
though rarely, fell, are the opposite faults of style,
an elaboration of nice conceit, and a proneness to
verbal quibbling, into which he was led by a con-

formity to the taste of his period. These trivial blemishes, easily discernible, were just of the kind to provoke the censure of the last century's critics, who were never tired of pecking at Shakespeare for the readiness with which he sprang at an opportunity for a pun; and there can be no doubt that some fine passages of his poetry are less purely beautiful than they would have been, were they not spotted with this labored use of words in a double sense. This fault is like those fripperies of dress which are generally an ungraceful and elaborate affectation in the fashion of a day, and which it is better indeed that the painter of a picture in the grand style should omit from the costume of his figures. But should a great master introduce them, who that can comprehend and rightly admire the essential parts of his work will waste much time in grieving? Of the kindred fault, which did not take the form of an absolute pun, but which is hardly less offensive, the Lucrece furnishes the following perfect specimen : —

> " Even here she sheathed in her harmless breast
> A harmful knife, which thence her soul unsheathed."

Conceits like this, which abound in all departments of the literature of the Elizabethan age, are mere labored verbal antitheses corresponding to parallel antitheses of thought. The humorous side of this conceit in style is a pun, in which there is correspondence of words but incongruity

of thought.   The development of taste has taught
us that in serious writing these antitheses are im-
pertinent; but the pleasing surprise of a certain
lack of pertinence, which yet seems pertinent,
forms no small ingredient in our enjoyment of
wit.   Of this kind of wit, no less than of that subtler comic quality which we call humor, Shakespeare has shown himself in Falstaff the matchless master.   And thus we find that his most
objectionable and most noticeable fault is nearly
related to one of his most exquisite and charming
graces.   All Shakespeare's faults of the kind just
noticed are found united in the following passage
from *Henry the Fifth*, the most offensively thus
deformed in all his works : —

> " A many of our bodies shall, no doubt,
>   Find native graves, upon the which, I trust,
>   Shall witness live in brass of this day's work ;
>   And those that leave their valiant bones in France,
>   Dying like men, though buried in your dunghills,
>   They shall be famed ; for there the sun shall greet them,
>   And draw their honors reeking up to heaven,
>   Leaving their earthly parts to choke your clime,
>   The smell whereof shall breed a plague in France.
>   Mark, then, abounding valor in our English ;
>   That, being dead, like to the bullet's grazing,
>   Break out into a second course of mischief,
>   Killing in relapse of mortality."

This is not the nodding of Homer : these sins
were committed with open eyes.   Such indeed
was Shakespeare's vivacity of mind, that he rarely
drowsed over his work.   But upon one or two oc-

casions he slumbered outright ; as when he made
Coriolanus say that·his "throat of war" should,
if he flattered the people, become like "the virgin
voice which babies lulls asleep," which is a rare,
almost an isolated instance of his misuse of epithet.   It is interesting to know that, while he
conformed to the fashion of his day in this matter
of conceits and quibbles, he saw how petty and
injurious it was, and visited it with open condemnation.   In *Twelfth Night,* after making the
Clown quibble for three speeches, to Viola's be-
wilderment, upon two words, he makes the same
character exclaim : "To see this age!   A sentence
is but a cheveril glove to a good wit.   How quick-
·ly the wrong side may be turned outward !"   To
which Viola replies, "Nay, that's certain ; they
that dally nicely with words may quickly make
them wanton."   This is one of the very few passages in his plays which may safely be accepted as
a mere expression of his own opinions.

Another mark which his period set upon Shakespeare's style — his reference to subjects and his
use of words which are excluded from polite society by modern notions of decorum — may be passed
by with slight attention.   Within certain wide
limits, which seem to be set by nature, decency in
word and deed is determined absolutely by custom.   What is decent in one age or under certain
circumstances, may be indecent in another age or
under other circumstances.   ·The defying of cus-

tom is the essence of indecency. This is notably exemplified in the history of language. For
in language the tendency is to the degradation
and consequent exclusion of words from polite
usage, while the idea maintains its place. Thus
we do not hesitate to speak, if it be necessary to
do so, of the stomach or bowels; but in Elizabeth's time the best-bred people designated those
parts of the body by words the first of which is
now heard only among boys, and the second
never among decent people. It has been before
remarked, that Shakespeare is less obnoxious to
our modern code in this respect than any other
dramatic writer of his period. He has some passages which are not to be read in general society now-a-days; but there is no moral taint in
any of his works,—nothing that can debauch the
mind of the pure and innocent. It is only as a
concession to the fancies of the weak-minded, or
as a provision for the needs of those who find it
agreeable to read Shakespeare aloud in mixed
company, that Bowdler's mutilations are at all
defensible.

But one fashion of his day, at Shakespeare's
conformity to which we must chiefly rejoice, was
that of using blank verse instead of rhyme in dramatic compositions. His choice doubtless went
with his conformity; but that he yielded in this
respect to fashion is plain from the facts that his
earlier plays abound in rhymed passages, a great

part of one of them, *The Comedy of Errors*, being
in complete or alternate rhyme, and that he used
blank verse only in his plays. Blank verse had
been slowly growing in favor with our English
poets ever since Surrey used it for his translation
of the fourth book of the Æneid, forty years before Shakespeare entered upon his career. At
the latter period it was coming into vogue upon
the stage; and Shakespeare, who in all that he
wrote to set forth as poetry chose rhyme, soon
became in his dramas the greatest master of English heroic measure. Not much can be said, and,
if there could, not much need be said, in an attempt to appreciate Shakespeare's genius, of the
beauty of his versification. Criticism can do no
more than record its various and surpassing beauties. The mere structure of verse is mechanical. It can be, it has been, made perfect by rule.
Much good sense has been written in lines composed of five feet of two syllables, with accent
duly disposed and tastefully and correctly varied,
which are unexceptionable verses, quite as perfect
as any that Shakespeare ever wrote; but they are,
most of them, weariness to the flesh, while his
delights our ears forever. The reason of this difference it is impossible to set forth. We can no
more say why it is, than we can say why, when
one composer writes a succession of notes which
follow each other in perfect conformity to the rules
of music, and the canons of taste, as well as the laws

of composition, we may say with Sly, "A very excellent piece of work, would 't were done!" and when Mozart writes conforming to no other laws, he ravishes our souls with melody. Power over sound, whether of words or musical notes, is a personal gift, which, unlike other personal gifts, such as wisdom, logical power, imagination, the mastery of form, as in sculpture and architecture, or of color, as in painting and decoration, is exercised (within certain general limits) purely according to the personal fancy, the spontaneous and intuitive preference of the possessor. Thus, for instance, the sculptor and the painter must represent something in nature, by the form or color of which they are limited: the architect must adapt his structure, not only to certain mechanical and æsthetic laws, but to the purpose for which his building is intended. But the musician has no such limit to the exercise of his faculty. Within himself alone he finds both guide and motive for the flow of his melody and the progression of his harmony. He adapts his melody to his words, if he write to words; but, within the limitation of poetic rhythm, that determines not its form, only its spirit. And so the poet in the sensuous expression of his verse is guided only by his own sense of what is fit and beautiful. We can see that he attains this purpose by the variation of his pauses, the balance of his sentences, and his choice and arrangement of words in regard to sound. But why he does this as he does it, we cannot tell; nor could he tell himself. Haydn could give no other reason for writing a certain passage in a certain way, than that he thought "it would sound best so." We can test one of Shakespeare's characters by the laws of our moral nature; but we have no law, except those before mentioned, which refer to the rudiments and mechanism of the art, by which we can test the sensuous beauties of his poetry. Except in his songs, he wrote almost entirely in one kind of verse; and he wrote that as he willed, his variations of style in this respect resulting only from the greater or less freedom which he allowed himself, guided only by his innate, exquisite sense of the beautiful. The dissertations upon his versification written by critics of past generations, who discovered that he had furnished us admirable instances of different kinds of verse with very imposing names, trochaic dimeter brachycatalectic, for instance, are in my judgment only lamentable instances of the waste of learning and of ingenuity. The freedom of dramatic writing at his day allowed him to be very irregular in his verse. He had no criticism to fear (it cannot be too constantly kept in mind), and the success of his plays was not with a public who read, but with an audience who listened. Therefore he allowed himself defective and redundant lines, the alternation of verse with prose, and of rhyme with blank verse;

conscious that, so long as the dialogue ran easily and naturally on, the audience would concern themselves with the situations, the thoughts and feelings of the personages, indifferent to niceties of versification, which indeed only a reader could detect.

In respect to the strict laws of versification, the dramatic poet of the days of Elizabeth was a chartered libertine. This is plain enough to any critical reader. But contemporary testimony is not lacking to the entire freedom from rhetorical restraint in this respect, as in all others, with which the Elizabethan dramatists labored.

> "Too popular [i. e. vulgar] is tragic poesie,
> Straining his tiptoes for a farthing fee;
> And doth beside in nameless numbers tread;
> Turbid iambics flow from careless head."
>
> Bishop Hall's *Satires.*

Shakespeare availed himself of this freedom to the full; and we can see that as he grew older he allowed himself greater license; the effect of which relaxation was counterbalanced and modified by his greater mastery of the material in which he worked and his more refined perceptions of beauty. The plays which we know were his latest productions, such as *The Winter's Tale*, *Coriolanus*, and *Henry the Eighth*, are notably freer, free almost to carelessness, when compared with *The Two Gentlemen of Verona* and *King Richard the Second* for instance, which we know were of his early writing. In some of the Roman plays and in *King Henry the Eighth* he reaches the point of almost failing to mark his verse by any cæsural or final pause whatever ; very often allowing the place of the last accent to be filled by a syllable, frequently a monosyllabic word, which cannot be accented.

> " The king's majesty
> Commends his good opinion of you to you, *and*
> Does purpose honor to you no less flowing
> Than Marchioness of Pembroke."
> *Henry VIII.*, Act I. Sc. 3.

> " Sir, I desire you to do me right and justice,
> And to bestow your pity on me ; *for*
> I am a most poor woman and a stranger."
> *Ibid.*, Sc. 4.

> " Because that now it lies in you to speak
> To th' people ; not by your own instruction,
> Nor by the matter that your heart prompts *you*,
> But with such words that are but voted *in*
> Your tongue," &c.
> *Coriolanus*, Act III. Sc. 2.

> " My name is Caius Marcius, who hath done
> *To thee particularly and to all the Volsces*
> Great hurt and mischief ; thereto witness *may*
> My surname, Coriolanus. . . . . Only that name remains :
> The cruelty and envy of the people,
> Permitted by our dastard nobles, *who*
> Have all forsook me, hath devour'd the rest ;
> And suffered me by th' voice of slaves to *be*
> Whoop'd out of Rome.   Now, this extremity
> Hath brought me to thy hearth : not out of hope —
> Mistake me not — to save my life ; for *if*
> I had fear'd death, of all the men i' the world
> I would have 'voided thee."
> *Ib.*, Act IV. Sc. 5.

> "You are they
> That made the air unwholesome, when you cast
> Your stinking, greasy caps, in hooting *at*
> Coriolanus' exile."
>
> *Ib.*, Act IV. Sc. 6.

It is true that the rhythm of all modern poetry depends merely upon accent, and that the English language has among its happy distinctions that of containing no word which is unfit for poetry. But the facility given by these traits is shared in the first instance by all modern poets, in the second by all English poets. Yet of all English, as well as of all modern poets, Shakespeare, in respect to his versification, as well as in all other respects, is the supreme master. The rhythm of his verse and the cadence of his periods is determined by an exquisite sense of the beauty of verbal form, working with an intuitive, though not unconscious, power in the adaptation of form to spirit.

One point in regard to the history and structure of our language is particularly worthy of notice in connection with the present topic. As the rhythm of English verse is dependent solely upon accent, a permanence of accent in pronunciation is necessary, not only to the continued enjoyment of verse during many generations, but actually to its continuing to be verse; while the completest change in the vowel sounds of the words of which a verse is composed will not deprive it of its rhythmical, and scarcely of any musical quality.

Shakespeare's poetry is no less verse and no less beautiful to the Englishman born north of the Tweed, who calls himself a Lowland Scot, or to the Englishman born in Ulster, who calls himself an Irishman, than to the native of London or Boston. Yet each of the two former, however well educated, will pronounce the words of which that verse is composed, with vowel sounds, and in a measure with an articulation, peculiar to himself, and different from that of the educated man born in the Old England or the New. But the latter themselves give to a very large proportion of words vowel sounds quite different from their common forefathers, for whom Shakespeare wrote, and whose pronunciation was more like that of the so-called Irishman than that which they have adopted. These facts make it the more worthy of note that the changes of accent in our language since its maturity, about three hundred years ago, have been so extremely few as to leave it, to all intents and purposes, the same in this respect that it was in the Elizabethan era ; although the changes in many vowel and some consonant sounds have been so great, that, if the wits who met at the Mermaid could hear their descendants of to day read their writings, they would surely smile and wonder, even if they could understand. Accent furnishes to the body of our language its bones and articulations, and preserves its form and determines its movement, although its softer and

apparently more vital parts are changed by time
and circumstance.   To this characteristic we owe,
and our posterity will owe, the inestimable advantage of reading Shakespeare's poetry with no less
pleasure than it gave to his contemporaries.

Like in the irresponsibility and absoluteness of
its operation to the faculty of melodious versification is that faculty which we call fancy, touching Shakespeare's exercise of which somewhat has
necessarily been said already.   Fancy is defined
by Johnson as "the power by which the mind
forms to itself images of things, persons, or scenes
of being," and he gives imagination as its synonyme and first definition ; by Webster, as "the
faculty by which the mind forms images or representations of things at pleasure"; by Worcester,
as "the faculty of combining ideas"; and some
metaphysicians, attempting to draw a distinction
between fancy and imagination, have attributed to
the former faculty the power of forming images or
representations of things in the mind, — to the latter, that of combining and modifying them.   If
these definitions were correct and sufficient, fancy
could not with propriety be considered as a trait
of style, which is in poet, painter, or musician the
mode of expression.   It would belong to the substance of an author's work, — that which style
expresses.   But the definitions in question, to
which all others known to me conform with un-
essential variation, must be set aside as express-

ing neither the idea of fancy which is presented by our best writers of any age, nor that which has determined the general use of the word among intelligent people.

This is not the place in which to go into extended dissertation upon the characteristic traits and differences of fancy and imagination ; but it may be briefly said, that if "fancy" were ever correctly used as a synonyme of "imagination," which is more than doubtful, or as the name of a creative image-forming faculty, that usage has long since passed away ; and that the needs of intelligent people have effected a distinction between the two words similar in kind to that which has been made between "talent" and "genius." Carlyle, for instance, is celebrated as a writer of vivid and powerful imagination ; but no person of ordinary discrimination would speak of fancy as one of his characteristic mental traits. So the style of *A Midsummer Night's Dream* is peculiarly rich and brilliant in fancy ; but, except in the personages of Puck and the clowns, it is not distinguished among Shakespeare's plays for imagination, which as exhibited in his works finds its highest manifestation in *King Lear, Macbeth*, and *The Tempest*.

Imagination works upon the substance or material of a writer of fiction or history, producing his personages, with their traits, actions, and surroundings ; fancy, upon the style in which he en-

11*

forces and adorns his thoughts. And thus Sheridan, satirizing an opponent, said that he drew upon his imagination for his facts, not upon his fancy. In truth the sense of the world has for ages regarded the fancy as a faculty so peculiarly individual, and having to do with that which passes within a man's own mind, that it has applied the word "fancy" to love between the sexes,* to any personal predilection, to an eccentric notion, a dress adopted by an individual, or a fashion prevailing among a few. The poor, abandoned girl still has her fancy-man, the costumer makes fancy dresses, even the baker fancy cake; and every one has his own fancies, for which he is held altogether irresponsible. But what need to go about for definition and illustration, when Shakespeare himself, all-discerning, has given them? Miranda says to Ferdinand,

> "I would not wish
> Any companion in the world but you;
> Nor can imagination form a shape
> Besides yourself to like of."

And Theseus tells Hippolyta, in a famous passage of *A Midsummer Night's Dream*, that "imagination bodies forth the forms of things unknown." On the other hand, the King of Navarre in *Love's Labour's Lost* calls an eccentric personage, who

---

* "Tell me where is fancy bred?" — *Mer. of Ven.*

"In maiden meditation, fancy free." — *M. N. Dr.*

"All fancy-sick she is and pale of cheer. — *Ibid.*

"hath a mint of phrases in his brain," Armado, "this child of fancy"; and Holofernes, a sound and acute critic, though a pedant, speak of "the odoriferous flowers of fancy, the jerks of invention," which furnish not the substance, but "the elegance, facility, and golden cadence of poesy"; and he sends the love-born Orlando through the forest of Arden, "chewing the cud of sweet and bitter fancy." It is quite impossible to make fancy and imagination change places in these passages; or to suppose that the poet had in mind faculties of which one, fancy, furnishes representations of things which the other, imagination, combines and modifies. In brief, imagination is that creative faculty of the mind by which images of men and things, and their relations, are conceived and brought forth with seeming reality. It is a correlative of faith, which is the substance of things hoped for and the evidence of things not seen. Fancy is the faculty which illustrates, enriches, and adorns a person, a thing, or a statement of fact or truth, by association, by comparison, and by attributed function or action. Thus sexual love is rightly called fancy, because the loved is endowed by the lover with all that charms that lover in the other sex, though often having few or none of those endearing qualities. And thus Ariel is a creature of Shakespeare's imagination; but when he makes Ferdinand say of Ariel's song,

> "This music crept by me upon the waters,
> Allaying both their fury and my passion,"

he exhibits in one of its most entrancing manifestations his exquisite and peerless fancy. So when the Duke in *Twelfth Night* exclaims,

> "O when mine eyes did see Olivia first,
> Methought she purged the air of pestilence,"

Shakespeare at once exhibits his own fancy as a poet and portrays the fancy of a lover.

Never did intellectual wealth equal in degree the boundless riches of Shakespeare's fancy. He compelled all nature and all art, all that God had revealed, and all that man had discovered, to contribute materials to enrich his style and enforce his thought; so that the entire range of human knowledge must be laid under contribution to illustrate his writings. This inexhaustible mine of fancy, furnishing metaphor, comparison, illustration, impersonation, in ceaseless alternation, often intermingled, so that the one cannot be severed from the other, although the combination is clearly seen and leaves a vivid impression upon the mind, is the great distinctive intellectual trait of Shakespeare's style. In his use of simile, imagery, and impersonation, he exhibits a power to which that of any other poet in this respect cannot be compared, even in the way of derogation; for it is not only superior to, but unlike, that which we find in any other. He very rarely institutes a formal comparison, — rarely uses the word "like,"

which is so common with other poets. Nor does
the condensation of simile called metaphor, or
the attribution of will called impersonation, furnish a medium quite sufficient for his fancy. He
does not set off his thought and his image against
each other, or formally illustrate one by the other.
He fuses a thought or a feeling and an image together. They are not even twins, but a single
birth; thought giving soul to image, and image
embodying thought. When Milton, in a passage
of justly celebrated beauty, would exhibit the
bashfulness of a modest, new-made wife, he makes
Adam say,

> " To the nuptial bower
> I led her blushing like the morn."

But Shakespeare makes Posthumus say that in
like circumstances Imogen showed

> " A pudency so rosy the sweet sight on 't
> Might well have warmed old Saturn."

In the epic poet there are two ideas, not only distinct, but severed. The dramatist presents one
which suggests two. Again, Milton, in a passage
yet more beautiful than the last quoted from him,
describing the dawn, says,

> "Now Morn, her rosy steps i' th' eastern clime
> Advancing, sowed the earth with orient pearl."

This is nearer, especially in the rosy steps; but
still there is a severance between morn and the
eastern clime, between morn and the orient pearl.

Shakespeare, describing the same event, says, in his compact way,

> "Morn, in russet mantle clad,
> Walks o'er the dew of yon high eastern hill."

This is the production of no acquired art, but of an inborn faculty. Shakespeare displayed the fulness of its strength in his earliest plays. Who has not already thought of Romeo's announcement of the dawn, —

> "Night's candles are burnt out, and jocund day
> Stands tiptoe on the misty mountain-top"?

But this is mere description of natural phenomena. Shakespeare's peculiar power in this respect is the vividness with which his fancy illustrates thought, action, and emotion. The highest exercise of that faculty appears in the following passage, which has never been surpassed in the grandeur of its imagery or the felicity of its illustration. Queen Margaret, taunting York after the battle of Sandal Castle with his disappointed ambition, says,

> "Come, make him stand upon this mole-hill here
> That raught at mountains with outstretched arms,
> Yet parted but the shadow with his hand."

Yet this passage is from a speech in *The True Tragedy of Richard, Duke of York*, which was written when Shakespeare was but about twenty-five years of age, and an unknown dramatist, working in company with others. He transferred the speech bodily to his *Third Part of King Henry the Sixth.* It is of his writing. Its mere excellence does not alone stamp it as his; but no other poet has made such a use of imagery.

It has been already remarked, that the richness of Shakespeare's style is due in great measure to the variety of his allusions and the extended knowledge from which he draws his illustrations. His knowledge of man and of nature was chiefly intuitive, although it was developed and perfected by observation and reflection. But so intimate is the acquaintance which he exhibits with certain arts and occupations, and certain departments of learning, that on this hypotheses have been framed, and supported by argument, that he passed some of his early years in the professional acquirement of the knowledge which he afterward put so dexterously to use. A dangerous foundation for such a supposition in regard to any author of quick observation and a lively fancy, — most dangerous with regard to Shakespeare. Johnson's dictum, that Nature gives no man knowledge, is, to say the least, too general in its terms to be true in all its bearings. It is hardly less safe to limit the power of genius in expressing emotions by the bounds of individual experience, than to assume that it cannot describe actual occurrences which it has not witnessed, or places which it has not seen. And although it is clear that genius cannot furnish its possessor with knowledge of facts, or with technical knowledge, men whose faculties do not rise to the plane of genius may, by powers of keen observation, quick perception, retentive memory, and ready combination, acquire in the ordinary intercourse of life, without special study, a technical knowledge which, up to a certain point, shall be real, and, dexterously deployed, seem thorough. It is not derogatory to Shakespeare's genius, but rather the reverse, to believe that in his works much of what appears to be the fruit of special knowledge was acquired in this man- . ner. Of all men known to the history of literature, he seems to have had the most subtle and sensitive intellectual apprehension. What he casually heard, and what he saw by side glances, he seems to have understood by intuition, and to have made thenceforth a part of his intellectual resources. The very management of the ship in *The Tempest*, which satisfies naval critics, may have been the fruit either of casual observation, or of what men of letters call "cram," rapidly assimilated by his genius.

As to book knowledge it is certain that, although he was not what scholars call a scholar, he had as much learning as he had occasion to use, or even more. His plays and poems teem with evidence that he devoured books, and that he assimilated what he read with marvellous celerity and completeness. Even when we can trace in his poetry the very passages of the authors to whom he was indebted, they reappear from the mysterious recesses of his brain transmuted and glorified. When we see what it was that he absorbed, and how he reproduced it, we are reminded of Ariel's song : —

> " Full fathom five thy father lies;
> Of his bones are coral made ;
> Those are pearls that were his eyes ;
> Nothing of him that doth fade
> But doth suffer a sea change
> Into something rich and strange."

His early plays are full of allusions to ancient classic literature, showing no great learning indeed, but a mind fresh from academic studies such as they were. But he soon discontinued this school-boyish habit. The fulness of his brain with his own thoughts left no room for second-hand lumber. He imbibed the spirit of Greek and Roman history, through whatever channel he received it, although he sometimes violated chronology and costume to the annoyance of some critics hardly worthy to have been his readers. Where, even in Plutarch's pages, are the aristocratic republican tone and the tough muscularity of mind which characterized the Romans so embodied as in Shakespeare's Roman plays? Where, even in Homer's song, the subtle wisdom of the crafty Ulysses, the sullen selfishness and conscious martial might of broad Achilles, the blundering courage of thick-headed Ajax, or the mingled gallantry and foppery of Paris, so vividly portrayed as in *Troilus and Cressida?* What

matter is it that he committed such an error in
costume as to make Aufidius say to Coriolanus,
that he joyed more at welcoming him a friend and
ally of Corioli, than when he first saw his wedded
mistress bestride his threshold, — the fact having
been that the newly married wife of the Latin race
was carefully lifted over the threshold on her first
entrance to her husband's house? What, that he
made Hector cite Aristotle, who lived eight hundred years after the siege of Troy? He did not
care; nor did his hearers; and why should we
be troubled? Must our little learning so cripple
our imagination? Shakespeare's genius could not
have taught him the relations which Greek literature bore to that of Rome; but he having acquired that knowledge, his intuitive perception of
higher relations taught him what function the
Greek language would perform for an accomplished Roman orator, statesman, and philosopher; and his dramatic imagination of the scene
when Cæsar fell into a fit after having refused the
crown, showed him Cicero speaking Greek, so
that "those that understood him smiled at one
another and shook their heads." But when, in
Henry the Fifth, the Bishop of Exeter makes his
comparison of government to the subordination
and harmony of parts in music, —

> "For government, though high and low and lower
> Put into parts, doth keep in one consent,
> Congruing in a full and natural close
> Like music," —

it were more than superfluous to seek, as some
have sought, in Cicero *De Republica*, the origin of
this simile; for that book was lost to literature, and
unknown except by name, until Angelo Mai discovered it upon a palimpsest in the Vatican, and
gave it to the world in 1822. Cicero very probably borrowed the fancy from Plato; but it was not
Shakespeare's way to go so far for that which lay
near at hand. Music, and particularly vocal part-
music, was much cultivated by our forefathers in
Shakespeare's time; and he seems to have been a
proficient in the art. The comparison is one that
might well occur to any thoughtful man who is
also a musician; but it is not every such man who
would use it with so much aptness and make it
with so much beauty.

No less noticeable than this display of knowledge, more or less recondite, yet no less easy to
understand, is Shakespeare's use in illustration of
natural phenomena which must have been beyond
his personal observation. Of all negative facts in
regard to his life, none perhaps is surer than that
he never was at sea; yet in *Henry the Eighth*, describing the outburst of admiration and loyalty
of the multitude at sight of Anne Bullen, he says,
as if he had spent his life on shipboard,

> "Such a noise arose
> As the shrouds make at sea in a stiff tempest;
> As loud, and to as many tunes."

We may be very sure that he made no special

study of natural phenomena ; and indeed no condition of his life seems surer than that it afforded
him neither time nor opportunity for such studies.
Yet in the following lines from his sixty-fourth
sonnet, an important geological fact serves him for
illustration : —

> " When I have seen the hungry ocean gain
>   Advantage on the kingdom of the shore,
>   And the firm soil win of the watery main,
>   Increasing store with loss and loss with store. . . . ."

Where and how and why had Shakespeare observed a great operation of nature like this, which
takes many years to effect changes that are perceptible ?   Yet we may be sure that Shakespeare
had this knowledge in no miraculous way, though
his possession of it might be remarkable to the
many who did not possess it themselves.   For we
find that his knowledge of that which he could
not learn of his own soul, which could teach him
everything with regard to man, but nothing with
regard to material nature, was limited to what he
had observed, and to the knowledge of his time,
even in the simplest matters.   He knew that Cicero would be likely to veil a sententious comment
upon an important political event in Greek ; he
knew that the shrouds of a ship howled dismally
in a tempest ; he even knew that a compensating
loss and gain are going on between the great
waters and the continents ; but he did not know
what every lad fit to enter college now knows,
and what it would seem that any intelligent man

who considered the subject must have discovered
for himself, that the sparks produced by flint and
steel are minute pieces of steel struck off and
heated to redness by friction. Like all his contemporaries, he supposed that the fire was in
the flint. Thersites says that Ajax's wit "lies as
coldly in him as fire in a flint, which will not
show without knocking."

But the limits of Shakespeare's knowledge did
not mark the scope of his genius, and his ignorance or his learning is of small account in estimating the quality of his poetry, or the truth
and interest of his dramatic conceptions. Would
either of two passages from which lines have just
been quoted have been more impressive, if Aufidius had spoken of his new-married wife being
lifted over his threshold, or if Shakespeare had
known that steel was burned by collision with
flint? It matters little what naturalists and scholars think of the material which Shakespeare used
for the illustration of his thought, and less whence
those materials were derived. Of no more importance is it that he has transferred thoughts from
forgotten wastes to his own blooming pages.
What matter that he has taken some from Lilly?
It is he alone who makes those thoughts admired.
Those which he did not take, the world has quite
forgotten. The glory is not in the cloud, but in
the eternal light that falls upon the fleeting exha-
lation. Even in regard to the special knowledge

which is most strikingly exhibited in Shakespeare's writings, that of the law, of how little real importance is it to establish the bare fact that Shakespeare was an attorney's clerk before he was an actor. Suppose it proved, what have we learned? Nothing peculiar to Shakespeare, but merely what was true of a great number of other young men, his contemporaries. It has a naked material relation to the other fact, that he uses legal phrases oftener than any other dramatist or poet; but with his plastic power over those grotesque and rugged forms of language it has naught to do whatever. That was his inborn mastery. Legal phrases did nothing for him; but he did much for them. Chance cast their uncouth forms around him, and the golden overflow from the furnace of his glowing thought fell upon them, enshielding and glorifying them forever. The same fortune might have befallen the lumber of any other craft; it did befall that of some others, — the difference being one of quantity and not of kind. The certainty that Shakespeare had been bred in the law, would it even help us to the knowledge of his life, — of what he did for himself, thought for himself, — how he joyed, how he suffered, what he was? No more would it help us to understand his genius.

Whatever Shakespeare may have learned, he did not learn his dramatic art, in which he had,

not only no instructor, but no model. By dramatic
art is not here meant the principles which guided
him in the *construction* of his plays. In that he
had teachers who were also his examples. The
form and the action of all his dramas, whether
comedies, histories, or tragedies, were determined
by laws over which he had, or at least exercised,
no control. At the time of his arrival in London
the English drama had attained a recognized, if
not an established form, which was not an imitation of an elder type or the invention of an individual, but an outgrowth of the national character. As the physical traits and moral qualities of
men are determined by those of their forefathers,
and the growth which produced the political institutions of a country upon which such institutions
have not been forcibly imposed can be traced
through its history, so the form, and in a certain
measure the spirit, of the English drama (in this
respect, as in all others, so unlike those of France
and Spain) were the result of centuries of spontaneous development. The English drama sprang
from English soil.* Shakespeare accepted this
form with entire acquiescence, and during the
whole of his career confined the exercise of genius within its limitations. Not only was the
form of plays thus determined, but the manner of
writing them. It was the settled practice of the
dramatic writers of that day, most of whom were

---

* See the *Account of the English Drama*, &c., pp. 315, et seq.

connected with one theatre or another, either as
actors or retained playwrights, to take plots wher-
ever they could find them, — from popular novels,
old plays, or well-known passages of history, — and
to work these up as quickly as possible into an ef-
fective play, which, by its story and its characters,
would interest the public.   Preference was given
to the plots of old plays or the stories of novels
which already had a hold upon popular favor.   In
those days the theatre supplied in a great measure, even to those who could read, the place now
filled by literature.   This we know from the fact
that readers and books were then comparatively
scarce; but it also appears from the very construction of the plays of that period.   If the story of the play were fictitious, the people wished
to enjoy the story, as well as the presentation of
the characters.   They were not bound up, as we
are, in sentiment, character, style, and stage effect.
They liked to have a complete narration of all the
events of the story, without reference to dramatic
climax ; and therefore, after that climax had been
reached, they did not resent, as we do, a continuation of the action.   They were even pleased with
a relation by some of the characters of the occurrence of events not represented, but connected
with the story.   Thus, for instance, the dramatic
interest of *Hamlet* ceases with the death of the
prince, when our managers very properly drop the
curtain ; but the audiences of Shakespeare's day

liked to have Fortinbras and the English ambas-
sadors come in and tell the fate of Rosencranz
and Guildenstern, and to hear that Hamlet would
be buried in princely style and with a funeral ora-
tion by Horatio. So also, as few could then read
the history of their own country, they liked to see
history, to have it "lively presented" to them
upon the stage. They asked in these historical
entertainments for the spirit and the essential
facts and leading characters of the period represented, rather than details or strict chronological
accuracy. They seem to have been quite indifferent as to a gradual culmination of the action ;
although, of course, it was natural to expect that
the end of the play should coincide with the accomplishment or defeat of some great purpose.
To supply this want, and guided only by these
demands, Shakespeare wrote his Histories. Indeed, almost every play that bears his name bears
also evidence of his conformity to the require-
ments of the audience for which he wrote, as well
as to the practices of contemporary playwrights.

To another well-known custom of his day, that
of engaging two or more writers upon one play,
he also conformed. He did so certainly at the
beginning and the end, if not occasionally during
the whole of his career.* He rewrote old plays,

* See the Introduction to the *Taming of the Shrew, Titus Andronicus, Romeo and Juliet*, and Essay on *Henry the Sixth*, in the
author's edition of Shakespeare's Works.

12

got his plots out of popular novels, and even took English history just as he found it in the Chronicles, and Greek or Roman history just as it was told in North's Plutarch, appropriating the very language of the chronicler or the translator, — as sometimes he did that of an old playwright, with a difference, — but what a difference! — and wrote in company or alone, just as best suited the theatre's purpose and his own convenience. It is worth while to bring to mind these well-established facts in regard to Shakespeare's dramatic writing, because it is the fashion of some critics to regard him as writing, like Sophocles or Euripides, to a listening nation, conscious that its fame was partly involved in his productions, the judgment of which was worthy of the grave consideration of gravest men, and because much superfine subtlety and ingenuity have been exhibited in tracing his purposes and in providing him with psychological theories, according to which he gave certain traits to certain personages, and led them through such and such experience, when in fact he was but following the old play or the old story to which he had gone for the framework or the material of his drama. Even his historical pieces, which all the evidence shows were written at haphazard as far as regards their order, or at least only with the public taste in view, have been solemnly resolved into tetralogies and cycles, with a central thought and a ruling purpose, as if Shakespeare meant in writing them to give the world a philosophy of history. This indeed can be extracted from them by the thoughtful reader for himself; but only because they are an idealized picture in little of real life. And what wonderful psychological knowledge has one of Shakespeare's later critics found in the bringing Romeo upon the scene enamored of Rosaline, to have this passion supplanted by the purer and tenderer one for Juliet! which, on the contrary, critics of the last century regarded as a great fault in the amorous Veronese's character. But the truth which these critics did not know is, that in this transfer of affection Shakespeare merely followed the novel and the poem to which he went for his plot. There he found the incident of Romeo's earlier love; there, too, he found the Old Nurse, and even her praise of Paris to Juliet, and her underrating of Romeo after his banishment, with her counsel to the second marriage; all of which have been lauded as exquisite and subtly drawn traits of nature. Which, again, indeed they are; and Shakespeare could doubtless have invented them: but the truth is that he found them. So in the tale which he dramatized and called *Othello* he found Iago, with his craft and his spontaneous and almost superfluous fiendishness, the reason and the right of which have been the occasion of so much profound psychological discussion. There is ground for believing the sudden changes in the feelings of lovers and tyrants in some of

Shakespeare's plays, and such unaccountable acts, for instance, as Valentine's willingness to resign his mistress to Proteus, would be accounted for, though perhaps not explained, by the discovery of some lost play or novel. In plays thus written as daily labor by a man whose sole object in writing was to please a promiscuous audience, — by a playwright who worked merely as one of a company or partnership, his part of the business being to furnish words for others to speak, who composed sometimes in joint authorship, and who worked over the old material which lay nearest to his hand and was best suited to his money-making purpose, always saving time and trouble as much as possible, — in such plays, so produced, what folly to seek, as some have sought, a central thought, a great psychological motive ! Shakespeare, like all men of creative genius, "builded better than he knew," knowing right well, however, what, though not how greatly, he was building. But although genius destined to empire may seek asses and find a crown, genius cannot have a purpose great or small unconsciously. For will is the soul of purpose ; and from all that we know of Shakespeare and his circumstances, and all that can be extracted from his plays without torture, we may be sure that the great central thoughts and inner motives which have been sought out for his various dramas by critics of the German school, could he but come back and hear them, would

excite only his smiling wonder. In the mere construction of his dramas, although Shakespeare
sometimes displays great skill, not only in the
working of the plot, but in the manner in which
he conformed his genius to the taste and the
dramatic fashions of his day, he exhibits nowhere
a conformity to principles of art unknown before
his era.

Every thoughtful reader of Shakespeare must
see that his peculiar power as a dramatist lies in
his treatment of character. The interest which
distinguishes his plays, as plays, from all others,
is that which centres in the personages, in their
expressions of thought and emotion, and in their
motives and modes of action. *This* was his dramatic art, and this it was in which he had neither
teacher nor model. For at the time when he began
to write, character, properly so called, was almost,
if not quite, unknown either to English literature
or even to that of the Latin races. In English
dramatic literature Marlowe alone had attempted
character, but in a style extremely coarse and
rudimentary. The Italian and French novelists
who preceded Shakespeare, including even Boc-
caccio himself, interest by mere story, by incident,
and sentiment. Their personages have no character. They are indeed of different kinds, good
and bad, lovers, tyrants, intriguers, clowns, and
gentlemen, of whom some are grave and others
merry. But they are mere human formulas, not
either types or individuals.

It has been much disputed whether Shakespeare's personages are types or individuals.
They are both. Those which are of his own
creation are type individuals. So real are they
in their individuality, so sharply outlined and
completely constructed, that the men and women
that we meet seem but shadows compared with
them; and yet each one of them is so purged .
of the accidental and non-essential as to become typical, ideal. He made them so by uniting and harmonizing in them a variety of traits,
all subordinated to, yet not overwhelmed by, one
central, dominating trait, and by so modifying
and coloring the manifestation of this trait that
of itself it has individuality. Othello and Leon-
tes are both jealous, and unreasonable in their
jealousy, as all the jealous are. But the men
are almost as unlike as Lear and Hamlet; and
their jealousy differs almost as much as the fierce
madness of the old king from the young prince's
weak intellectual disorder. Iachimo and Iago
are both villains, who would pitilessly ruin a
wife's reputation for their selfish ends; but the
former is a rude and simple villain, who seems to
lack the moral sense; the latter, one who has a
keen intellectual perception of that moral beauty
which he neither possesses nor heartily admires.
Shakespeare's personages are thoroughly human,
and therefore not embodiments of single traits or
simple impulses, but complicated machines; and

the higher their type, the more complex their organization. He combines in one individual and
harmonizes qualities apparently incongruous, his
genius revealing to him their affinities. Thus
Angelo is no mere hypocrite, but really a precisian. He is sincere in his austerity, and has pride,
or rather an inordinate secretly enjoyed vanity, in
his power to restrain his strong passions in the
face of weak temptation. But he is intensely
selfish, as most precisians are, and there comes a
time when his passions and a great temptation
join their forces. Before these his artificial restraint gives way, and he consciously sets out
upon a course of monstrous crime, which he yet
shrinks from whispering in the solitude of his
own chamber. Iago, another hypocrite, on the
contrary, dallies with his villany, places it in various lights, and stands off, smiling admiration upon
the honest fellow who is working death and ruin.
Yet Iago was a good soldier and a brave man,
and, had he been promoted instead of Cassio,
would have made the better lieutenant to Othello,
for the very lack of a certain weak amiability
which beset Cassio off the battle-field. His victim, poor Othello, who in his relations toward
women is one of the most delicate and sensitive
of men, in the bitterness of his soul *pays* his
wife's own maid as he leaves the former's bedchamber; not either to reward or to offend Emilia,
but that he may torment his own soul by carrying

out his supposition to its most revolting consequences.

It is this complication of motive which causes
the characters of Shakespeare's personages to be
read differently by different people. This variety
of opinion upon them, within certain wide and
well-determined limits, is evidence of the truthfulness of the characters. Not only does their complex organization give opportunity for a different
appreciation of their working, but, as in real life,
the character, nay, the very age, of those who pass
judgment upon them is an element of their reputation. Not only will two men of equal natural
capacity, and equally thoughtful, form different
opinions of them ; but the judgment of the same
man will be modified by his experience. Unlike
the personages of the world around us, some of
whom pass from our sight while others come forward, and all change with the lapse of time, those
of Shakespeare's microcosm, by the conditions of
their existence, remain the same. But our view of
them is enlarged and modified by advancing years.
As we grow older, we look upon them from a higher
point, and the horizon of our sympathy broadens.
We lose little and we gain much. For manhood's
eye, ranging over its wider scope, finds that the
eminences which were the boy's bounds of admiration do not pass out of sight, but become parts of
a grander and more varied prospect, while dis-
tance, in diminishing their importance, casts upon

them the tender light of that happy memory
which ever lingers upon pure and early pleasures.
But, as in real life again, Shakespeare's characters, during their mimic existence, depend upon
and develop each the other. We see how they are
mutually worked upon and moulded. And in this
interdependence and reciprocal influence, more
than in mere structure of plot, consists the unity
of Shakespeare's plays as organic wholes. His
personages are not statuesque, with sharp, unchanging outlines. His genius was not severe
and statuesque, as for instance Dante's was. His
men and women are notably flexile ; and not only
so, but they seem to have that quality of flesh
and blood which unites changeableness with iden-
tity, — as a man's substance changes, and his
soul grows older, year by year, and yet he is the
same person. It is not only the story in Shakespeare's dramas which makes progress, but the
characters of the personages. Lear, Romeo, Macbeth, Othello, are, as the phrase is, not the same
men at the end of the play as at the beginning.
Their experience has modified their characters.
Yet they are the same, though *quanto mutatus !*
This it is which exhibits Shakespeare's supreme
peculiar power. What he did, for instance, for
Iago, was not to make him a villain, but to provide the ready-made villain with a soul. He
worked out in poetry a great psychological prob-
lem. Given such and such hellish deeds, what

kind of a man is he who does them? and how
does he think, and feel, and act? So as to the
incident of Romeo's sudden transfer of his love
from Rosaline to Juliet; Shakespeare found that
in the old story. But it was he who, in using that
incident and in working out the lover's character,
drew a distinction not indicated in the story, and
which until then had, I believe, not been drawn
in any work of imagination, and made Romeo's
first love that fierce desire for possession into
which sometimes the whole strength of a man's
nature is diverted, while his second is that union
of passion, tenderness, respect, and self-devotion
which is the highest type of love between the
sexes. Shakespeare indicates the nature of this
distinction in the quaint phrase of the chorus at
the end of the first act.

> "Now old desire doth in his death-bed lie,
>   And young affection gapes to be his heir."

The same distinction is drawn between the two
loves of the Duke in *Twelfth Night*, the earlier of
which was love at first sight. He says of his first
meeting with Olivia,

> "That instant was I turned into a hart;
>   And my desires, like fell and cruel hounds,
>   E'er since pursue me."

And when he finds his mistress has bestowed
upon Cesario the love she refused to him, he turns
upon her in wrath, and threatens the object of her

affection. Romeo is enamored of Rosaline, as Orsino is of Olivia; so he is enamored of Juliet; but in the first passion of neither is there any element of self-devotion. It does not fill, although it usurps, his entire nature; and therefore it is easily driven out by one which has all its strength, and what it has not,—completeness. This distinction is much more carefully made in *Twelfth Night* than in *Romeo and Juliet;* partly because of the different courses of the two plots, but partly also because the comedy was the fruit of maturer powers than those which produced the tragedy.

Shakespeare *made* souls to his characters: he did not give them his own. It is now the most commonly recognized truth in regard to him, that he is a self-oblivious poet. But this is not true of him without important qualification. In his sonnets, whether they were written in his own person or another's, he was not oblivious of self. On the contrary, his own thoughts, his own feelings, constantly appear. He pours out his own woes with a freedom in which he equals, but with a manliness in which he far surpasses, Byron. It is as a dramatist that he is self-oblivious; and he is so to a degree too absolute, it would seem, for the ever-conscious people of the world to apprehend. Else we should not hear, as we continually do hear, an opinion or a course of conduct sustained with an air of triumph by the citation of Shakespeare's opinion in its favor. For there is hardly a course of conduct or an opinion upon a moral question which cannot be thus supported. Shakespeare disappeared in his personages; and it is they who speak, and not their creator. The value, nay, the very meaning, of what his creatures say, must be measured by their characters and the circumstances under which it is spoken. It is not William Shakespeare who says, even in jest, that a perfect woman is fit only "to suckle fools and chronicle small beer," — it is that coarse, jeering villain, Iago. Nor is it he who says that "to be slow in words is woman's only virtue," — it is a cynical clown called Launce. It was not Shakespeare who called the first Tudor "shallow Richmond." We may be sure that no one knew better than he that the man who became Henry the Seventh was deep, prudent, and far-seeing, although not greatly wise. It was Richmond's enemy, Richard, who said that; and said it not to himself, but to one of his own followers. Let no one who delights in rich garments complacently think that Shakespeare commends a habit as costly as the purse can buy. That advice was given by a shrewd old courtier, at a time when sumptuous apparel was the recognized sign of a certain social standing.

Attempts have been made, on the one hand, to show that Shakespeare was an infidel, and, on the other, that he was a Roman Catholic. Both might have been equally successful. A Bishop has, by

ingenious and elaborate collation of passages of
the player's works, set forth certain religious principles and sentiments derived from the Bible as
Shakespeare's.   But by a like process just the
opposite might have been shown with equal certainty.   In this regard, as in all others, what
Shakespeare wrote was the outgrowth of character and circumstance.   Religious subjects could
not be treated with more solemnity than by some
of his personages, as the reader of *Henry the
Eighth, Richard the Second,* and *Measure for Measure* will remember ; nor, on the other hand, could
the most imposing dogmas of divinity be touched
with more daring or more disrespectful hands
than are laid upon them in *King Henry the
Fourth, Cymbeline, Macbeth,* and *Much ado about
Nothing.*

It is thus upon every question.   Because a
usurper, wishing to build up in himself a belief
that he rules by the grace of God, says,

> "There's such divinity doth hedge a king
> That treason can but peep to what it would,
> Acts little of his will,"

it no more follows that Shakespeare believed in
the absolute and divine right of kings, than, because one of Jack Cade's followers lays it down
that the command, labor in thy vocation "is as
much to say as let the magistrates be laboring
men, and therefore should we be magistrates,"
it follows that he was a radical democrat.   For

he made both the usurper and the demagogue. Shakespeare's entire absorption in his personages, and his substitution of their consciousness for his own, are perhaps most remarkable in *Antony and Cleopatra*, in which the passion of the queen for her new lover is manifested with a feminine consciousness of sex which approaches the miraculous. In the fourth scene of the second act of this play Cleopatra addresses to a messenger from Italy a few words which, although but an eager demand for his news, are of such intense sexuality that in these days the passage, although really harmless, is not quite quotable out of its setting. Her sex and that of him of whom she is enamored are constantly in this woman's mind and on her tongue. And here I will remark that in this tragedy there is not one worthy character; which is evidently by the author's design. Shakespeare's dramatic instinct kept even Octavia more out of sight than she is in the story which he followed, because he knew that otherwise Cleopatra might become despicable, and so lose all her interest. He meant that we, no less than Antony, should abandon ourselves entirely to the fascinations of the serpent of old Nile, and that we should sympathize with his wanton queen in her sneer at "the married woman," and resent her "still conclusion." I confess that, when I read *Antony and Cleopatra*, I look with cold aversion upon Octavia, — Octavia, beautiful, wronged, and noble. In her uneasy jealousy of her married rival Cleopatra inquires minutely as to her personal traits, and among other questions asks, "Is she shrill-tongued or low?" In this query Shakespeare either indicates a very subtle knowledge on the part of Cleopatra, or uses her to express one of his own strong personal tastes. For a sweet voice, one of woman's chiefest charms, is yet one of the last she thinks of enumerating either in her own attractions or another's. But Shakespeare makes Coriolanus meet his wife with the greeting, "My gracious silence!" and we all remember poor broken-hearted Lear sobbing over his dead Cordelia,

> "Her voice was ever soft,
> Gentle, and low, — an excellent thing in woman."

Indeed, from all of Shakespeare's plays we can gather little more as to his personal tastes than that he had a great aversion to high voices, false hair, and painted cheeks in women. Yet this is an indication, not of his individuality, but of his manhood.

It would seem as if in all Shakespeare's thickly peopled plays we might at least find one character which he meant should represent his own. But the longer and the closer our study of those plays, the more clearly it appears that of all his creatures none think his thoughts or express his preferences, except his fools. And perhaps the Fool in *King Lear* more nearly represents Shakespeare's tone of mind and view of life than any

other of his personages. All Shakespeare's fools
are wise; but this one has wisdom enough to
teach prudence to men of the world, and to set up
·a college of philosophers. A tinge of sadness,
almost of melancholy, tempers all the sallies of
his wit. He is as true as Kent and as tender as
Cordelia. Comparison to him were a compliment
to any other man than Shakespeare. His use
of the Jester exhibits in a striking manner two
marked traits of Shakespeare's method; one, the
ease with which he adapted himself to circumstances and bent his mighty genius to the little
needs of his profession; the other, the profusion
with which he poured out his thoughts and the
impartiality with which he bestowed his labor.
He seems never to have husbanded his resources,
or thought any work beneath his dignity. It is
a poor workman who complains of his tools; and
Shakespeare, finding the fool in possession of an
established place upon the stage, and thus essential
to the popularity of his plays with a mixed audience, instead of rebelling against or fretting at his
necessity, made him the vehicle of his sentiment,
his fancy, his practical wisdom, and even of his
pathos. That modification of the Jester called
the Clown appears even in *Hamlet*, although not
until the last act. We may not unreasonably
suppose that, had Shakespeare's motive in writing
his plays been to develop a "central thought,"
he would have composed such a play as *Hamlet*

without clowns. But the new tragedy comes to be talked over in the green-room, and Burbadge says: "Why, Master Shakespeare, this is an excellent play, — a right masterful tragedy. But methinks that some of our people will not know what your prince would be about; and moreover, although the play be somewhat overlong, there is no part for the Clown. People when they come to the Black-friars expect to see Kempe or Armin, above all them that stand in the yard; and I need not tell so thrifty a fellow as thou art, that pence count in the long run as well as shillings." And old Philip Henslow, if he happen to be present, says: "Right, Master Burbadge, I put out little money on a play that hath in it neither Clown nor Jester." Then Shakespeare takes his manuscript home again, and adds the Grave-diggers; working them in without remorse and with little trouble. Thus it was that Shakespeare labored. In the mere construction of his plays, although he sometimes exhibited great skill, as for instance in *The Tempest, Othello*, and *The Merchant of Venice*, he neither conformed to nor elaborated any principles of art not known before he entered upon his career.

Shakespeare has minor personages, but no slighted characters. They all have individuality, and he will waste on a messenger a sentiment or a simile that would grace a hero's tongue or add dignity to a royal proclamation. The *personnage prostatique* of the pseudo classic French stage has no place in Shakespeare's drama. This completeness of his minor characters is the more remarkable, because he has whole scenes which were manifestly written merely to meet the exigencies of stage management. Such for instance is the second scene of the third act of *Othello*. It consists of but six lines, and merely gives a glimpse of Othello as he goes to walk upon the works. But it separates two others, in both of which Cassio appears, at the end of the first and the beginning of the second; and it tells us that Iago is to meet Othello upon the works, from which they afterward enter together, the latter already made a little sensitive upon the subject of his lieutenant's nearness to his wife. And in *The Merry Wives of Windsor* the first scene of the fourth act, in which Sir Hugh Evans plays pedagogue to William Page, has nothing whatever to do with the plot, but it serves to separate the scene in which Falstaff receives his second invitation from that which exhibits the entertainment to which he is invited. These are mere contrivances to preserve the appearance of probability in action, which, when it has its formal name, is called the unity of time and place. It would have been well, for instance, in this respect, if a scene could have been thrown in between the first and second of the first act of *All's Well that Ends Well*, which present one of the most striking examples of Shakespeare's disregard of that unity. For although one is at Rousillon and the other at Paris, Bertram and Parolles appear in both; the latter's entrance before the King in his palace being separated by only seven short speeches from his exit at Rousillon to accompany Bertram on his journey. But of how small importance is such discrepancy! No dramatic interest is broken by it; no essential propriety violated. It would be open to no objection in a story; and in regard to their construction English plays are only acted stories. But in fact Shakespeare, as we have just seen, was put to shifts in common with the merest journeyman playwright that ever wrote to-day to get him bread to-morrow. Yet these straits only ministered occasion to his genius. He went to his work like a faithful servant; but he did it like a king. The very superfluous scene in *The Merry Wives of Windsor*, just cited, one of the least important its author wrote, bears unmistakable marks of his hand, and for its character and humor will always be read with pleasure.

Hardly less remarkable than Shakespeare's vigorous and vivid style of dramatic portraiture are the range of his subjects and the variety of his characters. He left no department of his art untried, and sounded the dramatic lyre from its lowest note to the top of its compass. The same hand that struck from it the woes of Lear and the troubled harmonies of Hamlet's soul drew

forth also its most fantastic strains, and left us in
The Comedy of Errors a farce equally extravagant
and jocular. No other writer has so run through
the scale of humanity. In this respect it is safe
to say that Shakespeare will never be surpassed,
because he left no important type of character
untouched. From Hamlet to Abhorson, from
Imogen to Mistress Quickly, what a descent!
Yet between these extremes the full gradation is
maintained. Nay, the lower extreme is passed.
Caliban bridges the gap between the human creature and the brute ; and Crab stands upon the
other side, with cur-like thanklessness for a character as sharply drawn as his master's.

Whence did Shakespeare draw the characters of
such a multitude of various and well-defined personages ? From models ? Did he, as some would
have it, keep watch upon the world around him,
and, seizing upon the individuals that suited his
purposes, put them into his dramas ? Great paint-
ers have thus filled their canvases ; and dramatists of high rank have manifestly drawn their
characters from people whom they saw around
them. Hence it is that we find the same face
doing duty for like character in the works of paint-
ers from Raphael to Leech, so that we recognize
their pictures by traces of some lovely woman
or some strongly marked man whose traits have
seized upon their imaginations. Hence, that
throughout Beaumont and Fletcher's and Jon-

son's plays, and much more in those of inferior dramatists, the men and women who fulfil certain functions, good or bad, have an unmistakable resemblance. But among Shakespeare's personages there is not this familiar likeness. There is no likeness whatever, except in the style of their portrayal. These are plainly from the same mint, but do not, like those, seem to have been struck with the same die. Gustave Doré is the only painter who shows a similar fecundity. Had Shakespeare, working as he did merely to make money, drawn his characters from models, he surely must have fallen into a habit which would have saved him much labor and have satisfied his audience. He would have had his stock of models; and those, worked into each new plot as they were needed, speaking his fancy, his wisdom, his wit, and his humor, and dressed in different costume, would have filled the eye and ear of his public. It is true that he must have observed; he was probably the most observant of men, as well as the most reflective; and his works had of necessity the advantage of his observation, as well as of his reflection and his imagination. Nor did the greatness of his mind absolve it from the law of development and progress common to humanity. Although wise in his youth, — and his early plays show wisdom, — he must, by the very exercise of his faculties and the habit of introspection, have grown wiser as he grew older. But if we may judge by the ruling

sentiment of his plays, while he seems early to
have understood the world, he seems also to have
long retained the hope and trustfulness of youth.
When we consider that *The Merry Wives of Windsor*, *King Henry the Fifth*, and *Hamlet* were written within two years, we shall see that it is difficult, if not impossible, to mark his periods by sentiment, choice of subject, or manner of treatment.
It is only by his literary or external style that we
trace his passage from youth to maturity.   Otherwise Shakespeare seems to have had moods, not
periods.   Age, too, although it brings more acquaintance with mankind, does not necessarily
bring better knowledge of human nature.   That
knowledge is not an aggregation, but a growth; its
germ is born with him who has it, and it spreads
from within.   Individuals are mere opportunities
for its development, occasions for its manifestation.   That Shakespeare availed himself of all
such opportunities and occasions, that he tested
his judgments by experiment and his conceptions by comparison, that he watched in the men
and women around him the operation of those
laws to which his creations must conform, cannot
reasonably be doubted.   It is probable, too, that
he found here and there a trait, or even a character, which, though not a model, was a suggestion.
His women especially show the fruit of this kind
of study.   A painter of mere talent, but of fine
taste and dexterous hand, may elaborate a perfect

figure from models none of which are perfect; but
a painter of great genius, constantly studying and
observing, makes his knowledge a part of himself,
and produces many figures, not by various combi-
nations of remembered forms, but by independent
creations instinct with the knowledge which he
has assimilated and the laws which he has mas-
tered. Of the latter kind was Shakespeare's
study and Shakespeare's knowledge. That he did
not draw his personages from life is manifest from
the facts that all the principal of them, those the
creation of which made his fame what it is, are
such as he could not possibly have seen, except in
mental vision, and that the experiences through
which they pass, and by which their living proto-
types most have manifested their intellectual and
moral traits to him, are such as he could not have
had the opportunity of observing. Did Shakespeare ever meet a mad king, a king whose conscious kingliness is supreme even in his madness,
but whose dawning madness tinges the first manifestations of his kingly power? As well suppose
that he had met a Caliban. Shakespeare's mind
contained, but it had not received, his characters.
In that play so marvellously full of thought, *Troilus and Cressida*, perhaps the most thoughtful of
his works, Ulysses rises to the full height of our
idea of the wandering Ithacan. Whence came
this Ulysses? Not from Homer's brain; for although Homer tells us that the king of Ithaca

was "divine" and "spear-renowned," and "well
skilled in various enterprise and counsel," the
deeds and words of the hero as represented by
the great poet hardly justify these epithets. Here
we see that Shakespeare was even wiser than the
Homeric ideal of human wisdom. For Shakespeare made our Ulysses. It was but his name
and his reputation that had come down from antiquity. It was the character that corresponded
to and justified these that Shakespeare supplied,
in this instance as in many others. He did not
restore a limb, or even supply a head ; but, as if
catching and filling the outline of a shadow van-
ished for centuries, he surmounted with the speaking substance of that shadow an inscribed and
empty pedestal.

Shakespeare thus used the skeletons of former
life that had drifted down to him upon the stream
of time and were cast at his feet, a heap of mere
dead matter. But he clothed them with flesh and
blood, and breathed life into their nostrils ; and
they lived and moved with a life that was individual and self-existent after he had once thrown it
off from his own exuberant intellectual vitality.
He made his plays no galleries of portraits of his
contemporaries, carefully seeking models through
the social scale, from king to beggar. His teeming
brain bred lowlier beggars and kinglier kings than
all Europe could have furnished as subjects for his
portraiture. He found in his own consciousness

ideals, the like of which for beauty or deformity neither he nor any other man had ever looked upon. In his heart were the motives, the passions, of all humanity; in his mind, the capability, if not the actuality, of all human thought. Nature, in forming him alone of all the poets, had laid that touch upon his soul which made it akin with the whole world, and which enabled him to live at will throughout all time, among all peoples. Capable thus, in his complete and symmetrical nature, of feeling with and thinking for all mankind, he found in an isolated and momentary phase of his own existence the law which governed the life of those to whom that single phase was their whole sphere. From the germ within himself he produced the perfected individual, as it had been or might have been developed. The eternal laws of human life were his servants by his heaven-bestowed prerogative, and he was yet their instrument. Conformed to them because instinct with them, obedient to, yet swaying them, he used their subtle and unerring powers to work out from seemingly trivial and independent truths the vast problems of humanity; and standing ever within the limits of his own experience, he read and reproduced the inner life of those on the loftiest heights or in the lowest depths of being, with the certainty of the physiologist who from the study of his own organization recreates the monsters of the ante-human world, or of the astrono-

mer who, not moving from his narrow study, announced the place, form, movement, and condition
of a planet then hid from earthly eyes in the abyss
of space.

Shakespeare thus suffered not even a temporary
absorption in his personages ; he lost not the least
consciousness of selfhood, or the creator's power
over the clay that he was moulding. He was
at no time a murderer at heart because he drew
Macbeth, or mad because he made King Lear.
We see that, although he thinks with the brain
and feels with the soul of each of his personages
by turns, he has the power of deliberate introspection during this strange metempsychosis, and
of standing outside of his transmuted self, and
regarding these forms which his mind takes on
as we do ; in a word, of being at the same time
actor and spectator.

This wonderful duality in unity is perhaps most
striking in Shakespeare's representation of insanity. It is comparatively easy to understand
how the normal action of one mind is taken on
by another ; because sane men think and act
in accordance with known and unchanging laws.
The union in the dramatist of a thorough knowledge of human nature with the dramatic faculty
insures, therefore, a natural development of character in his personages. But in the creation
of a personage whose faculties are supposed to
be deranged, and thus absolved from the opera-

tion of the laws of our common nature, how is the dramatist to keep true to that which itself has no keeping? Attempts to represent insanity usually produce only a repulsive extravagance of word and action, which neither provokes mirth nor excites sympathy. But Shakespeare seems not to have found even this limit to his power of thinking and feeling with the creatures of his imagination. He has portrayed insanity in nearly every form in which it is known to the students of psychological pathology; and so true do they find him to nature, even in disorganization, their analysis only discovering that his intuition has been beforehand, that they, like all other observers of mankind, from testing him by nature have come to studying nature in him. With delicate and unerring discrimination he distinguishes between the various kinds of mental derangement, and even follows the disorder in its advancing stages from the first unsettling of the reason until the mind lies wrecked before us, —as in Ophelia, a sweet flower crushed and perfumeless, or in Lear, a grand and awful ruin.

Our inability to follow or to comprehend the working of Shakespeare's mind in no way diminishes our capacity of apprehending or appreciating its creations. Man conceives, or receives, the very idea of God, because there is in him some Divine capacity; and his god, that which he worships, is ever the measure of his moral and intellectual elevation. This axiom is of general application. But most especially in his appreciation of so lofty and universal an intelligence as Shakespeare's does a man show the elevation or the meanness, the richness or the poverty, the purity or the foulness, of his own soul. It is a vain notion, put forth by some who should know better, that much study, reflection, and earnest endeavor are required to understand Shakespeare rightly. Culture and discipline and natural powers of analysis are doubtless demanded for the explanation of motives and characteristic traits of Shakespeare's personages, and to the unravelling of some of his involved passages (which are very few), or following of some of his highest flights of fancy. But almost all of us must have something of Shakespeare latent in our souls, voiceless and unexpressed; else we should be incapable of that sympathetic comprehension of his thoughts and his characters, the existence of which among ever-increasing multitudes for many generations is the only possible condition of his peculiar and enduring fame. Some men, it is true, will never understand him in some passages, and some, happily for the world very few, will not be able to understand him at all by any study or reflection of which they are capable. This from no proneness of the poet to paradox, or to eccentric or sentimental views of life, or to over-subtlety of thought. For although of all poets he is most profoundly psychological, as well as most fanciful and most imaginative, yet with him philosophy, fancy, and imagination are penetrated with the spirit of that unwritten law of reason which we speak of as if it were a faculty, common sense. His philosophy is practical, and his practical views are fused with philosophy and poetry. He is withal the sage and the oracle of this world. Subjects which are essentially, and in other hands would seem, prosaic and almost sordid, are raised by him into the realms of poetry, and yet in language so clearly expressive of their essential character as to be adopted as shrewd maxims by the worldly wise.

In this constant presence and rule of reason in his most exalted flights, we recognize again a trait of the English origin and character of his genius, — a trait which is at the foundation of its eminence, even in the realm of imagination, but at which other people often jeer. Even in our passions we will ask, "Why?" and say, "Because." "*Voila,*" cries the French maid in one of the few passages of insight in Vanbrugh's *Provoked Wife,* — "*Voila un vrai Anglais! Il est amoureux, et cependant il veut raisonner.*"

Many people have given themselves serious concern as to the moral influence of Shakespeare's plays; and critics of great weight, fulfilling their function, have gone down far and stayed down long in the attempt to fathom the profound moral

purpose which they are sure must be hidden in the
depths of these mighty compositions.*   But the
direct moral influence of Shakespeare is nothing ;
and we may be sure that he wrote with no moral
purpose.   He sought only to present life ; and
the world which he shows us, like that in which
we live, teaches us moral lessons according to our
will and our capacity.   Johnson, meaning censure
of "his first defect," wrote Shakespeare's highest
praise in this respect, in saying of him that "he
carries his persons indifferently through right or
wrong, and at the close dismisses them without
further care, and leaves their example to operate
by chance."   That word "indifferently" is Shakespeare's eulogy.   He gives the means of study,
and leads insensibly to reflection.   Men resent or
turn away from conviction at the lips of others,
which they will receive and lay to heart if they
hear it from the lips of the inward monitor.   And
even children see through and despise the shallow
device which makes goodness always lead to happiness, and flout the stories which conduct them

* The feeling of the latter half of the last century, and of the
earlier years of the present, upon this subject, is well represented
by the following passage from the Dramatic Censor's article
upon *Richard the Third :* —

"Having now given a general delineation of the plot and
arrangement of the scenes, it becomes necessary to inquire for
the moral, without which no dramatic piece can have intrinsic
worth." — Vol. I. p. 9, ed. 1770.

This notion in a very stupendous form seems to have seized
hold of the Germans of the last and present generations.

through artificial paths to bring them out upon
a moral. Man, however gifted, can never teach
more than life and nature ; and among gifted men
there has been only Shakespeare who could teach
as much. The moral unity which distinguishes
his plays is not, as some, especially among the
Germans, would have it, the result of a moral purpose deliberately planned and well worked out;
but of the fact that those dramatic poems were
the spontaneous manifestation of one great, symmetrical mind, in complete and intimate accordance with nature. Shakespeare is able to teach as
much as nature, nay, even more than unmitigat-
ed nature does, for two reasons. One is, that he
presents us something which is not nature, but a
perfect reflex of nature. It is strange, but true as
strange, that imitation generally interests us more
than reality. The very reflection of a beautiful
landscape in a mirror wins our attention more,
nay, seems more beautiful, than the landscape itself. Seen in a Claude glass it becomes a picture,
a *quasi* work of art, which we study, over which
we muse, and to which we again and again recur ;
while the scene itself, if we see it often, may become
to us an unnoticed part of our daily life, like the
rising of the sun, that daily miracle. And so the
mirror which, following his own maxim, Shakespeare holds up to nature, is more studied by us
than Nature herself, and by means of it nature is
better understood. The phenomena are brought

by him within the range of our mental vision. Reduced in their dimensions, but kept perfect in proportion and true in color, they are transferred to and fixed upon his pages; and we can take down from our shelves these specimens of thought and passion, and muse and ponder over them at leisure. This is measurably true of all imaginative writing; but it is pre-eminently true of Shakespeare's.

But the chief reason of Shakespeare's ability to teach us as much as nature is a breadth of moral sympathy, a wide intellectual charity, which makes him as impartial as nature. His mirror tinges the scene which it reflects with no color of its own. The life-giving rain of his genius falls equally on the just and the unjust; and as the sunshine and the shower develop both tares and wheat according to their kind, so he never seeks to modify the nature or the seeming of that which he quickens into life; and he is never more impartial than when he is most creative. What viler or more loathsome creature than Parolles was ever spoken into being? who is never more disgusting, though he may be more irritating or ridiculous, than in his interview with Helena on his first appearance. Yet in this very dialogue, unquotable though it be, what insight, what wisdom, what practical sense, are developed through this wretch, though we detest the creature as Helena does, and as Shakespeare meant we should, for uttering

then and there the conclusions of his keen but
degraded judgment! Yet we look upon this
abominable creature with admiration; nay, he fas-
cinates us by his exquisite loathsomeness, which
is as proper to him as crawling to a reptile. As
Helena herself says in the words which Shakespeare furnished her, concentrating in these four
lines all that I have just tried to say, and elevat-
ing it into poetry with that apparently unconscious exercise of supreme mastery over expression which must make every man who holds a
pen despair, —

> "These fix'd evils sit so fit in him
> That they take place, when virtue's steely bones
> Look bleak in the cold air. Withal full oft we see
> Cold wisdom waiting on superfluous folly."

It was this quality of universal sympathy in his
mental constitution which enabled Shakespeare
to unite to the knowledge of man and of truth
that knowledge of men and of things which is
called knowledge of the world. He seems to
have had this latter knowledge in as great a degree as that more abstract knowledge which made
him a great dramatic and philosophical poet, and
to have been the most perfect man of the world
whose name appears upon the roll of literature.
All that we know of his life shows him in full possession of this great qualification of the perfect
social man, so rarely found in poets ; and his
works are pervaded with its exhibition. Consider

13*

well such characters as Angelo, Parolles, Faulcon-
bridge, Polonius, Jaques, Falstaff, such gentlemen
as Bassanio, Mercutio, Prince Henry, Cassio, Antony (in *Julius Cæsar*), and see what knowledge,
not only of the human heart, but of society, of
manners, of actual life, in short, to return to the accepted phrase, what knowledge of the world, these
characters display. It is this knowledge, this tact,
which enables him to walk so firmly and so deli-
cately upon the perilous edge of essential decency,
and not fall into the foul slough below, where the
elegant dramatists of the last century lie wallow-
ing. This he does notably, for instance, in Faul-
conbridge and Falstaff,— Falstaff, a gentleman by
birth and breeding, but coarse, gross, mean, and
selfish, a degraded castaway, yet, with consum-
mate tact and exquisite art never allowed to be
vulgar or repulsive, and whose matchless humor
makes his company delightful.

It has been objected to the assertion of the am-
plitude of Shakespeare's mind, and to the generosity of his character, that he always represents
the laborer and the artisan in a degraded position,
and often makes his ignorance and his uncouth-
ness the butt of ridicule. The charge is brought
by reformers and philanthropists of such narrow
views that they cannot see that art is not the
pioneer, but the landscape gardener, of society.
Shakespeare, although he thought as a philosopher, wrought as an artist; and art has to do

with the facts of the world before it, idealizing them, but not changing their nature. Three hundred years ago the husbandman and the mechanic were degraded in the world's eyes; and Shakespeare, the healthiness of whose understanding is as remarkable as any trait of his genius, knew that the world's appreciation is generally right of men in mass, and that these hard-handed men had all the consideration that was their due, though not all the rights or advantages. It is always so. Individual men may fail to receive a just appreciation; but as surely as water finds its level, classes of men always rise to the standing that they can maintain. It is because the workingman, whether his labor be rude or skilled, has raised himself, has in fact become another man, that the world now awards him a consideration which he did not receive in the days of Queen Elizabeth. Shakespeare, although he represented the world as he saw it, was no panegyrist of things as they were, no mere *laudator temporis acti*. He was no sycophant to power. Whatever might have been the faults of others in this regard, (and they seem to have been fewer and less in the mother country in those days than in the present,) Shakespeare did not hesitate to tell kings and nobles all the truth, and even to put it into their own mouths. In bitterness of soul King Richard II. utters in the following passage at once a sarcasm and a confession : —

" For within the hollow crown,
That rounds the mortal temples of a king,
Keeps Death his court : and there the antic sits,
Scoffing his state, and grinning at his pomp ;
Allowing him a breath, a little scene
To monarchize, be fear'd, and kill with looks;
Infusing him with self and vain conceit,
As if this flesh, which walls about our life,
Were brass impregnable, and, humor'd thus,
Comes at the last, and with a little pin
Bores through his castle wall, and — farewell, king !
Cover your heads, and mock not flesh and blood
With solemn reverence : throw away respect,
Tradition, form, and ceremonious duty,
For you have but mistook me all this while :
I live with bread like you, feel want, taste grief,
Need friends.   Subjected thus,
How can you say to me, I am a king ? "

And Shakespeare's favorite among his kings,
Harry the Fifth, says, when disguised as a common
soldier, " I think the king is but a man,
as I am ; the violet smells to him as it doth to
me ; the element shows to him as it doth to
me ; all his senses have but human conditions ;
his ceremonies laid by, in his nakedness he appears
but a man." One passage of *Cymbeline* is
too remarkably in point to be passed by ; for
although it is addressed by a princess to, as
she supposes, two mountaineers, it unites an assertion
of the most catholic and radical equality
with a quiet, cutting satire upon the conventional
distinctions of rank and privilege. Arviragus
asks Imogen, " Are we not brothers ? " and the
princess answers,

> " So man and man should be ;
> But clay and clay differs in dignity,
> Whose dust is both alike."

Shakespeare himself, in his personal opinions and inclinations, is so little traceable in his works, that we can only judge of his feeling toward the wretched and oppressed by the intimate sympathy which he shows with their privations and their sufferings, and also their lowly pleasures. Could this be better shown than in these lines spoken again by King Henry the Fifth ?

> " Not all these, laid in bed majestical,
>   Can sleep so soundly as the wretched slave ;
>   Who, with a body fill'd, and vacant mind,
>   Gets him to rest, cramm'd with distressful bread,
>   Never sees horrid night, the child of hell,
>   But like a lackey, from the rise to set,
>   Sweats in the eye of Phœbus, and all night
>   Sleeps in Elysium ; next day, after dawn,
>   Doth rise, and help Hyperion to his horse,
>   And follow so the ever-running year,
>   With profitable labor, to his grave :
>   And but for ceremony, such a wretch,
>   Winding up days with toil, and nights with sleep,
>   Had the fore-hand and vantage of a king."

Again, in *King Lear*, Edgar's disguising himself as an Abraham man gave Shakespeare an opportunity, which so thrifty a householder as he was might well have seized, to hold up those tramping pests of our forefathers to condemnation, or at least to ridicule. But his picture presents the sufferer's side of the case, and tells us how he "eats the swimming frog, the toad, the tadpole, the wall-newt and the water, swallows the old rat and the ditch-dog, drinks the green mantle of the standing pool, and is whipped from tything to tything, and stocked, punished, and imprisoned." Shakespeare must have well known the ways of the begging impostor; but he chose to show us in this most touching manner the dreadful extremities and sufferings of the vagrant pauper.

The little that remains to be said is of a general nature.

Shakespeare's art was not simple, its manifestation was not serene. Simplicity and serenity are the highest ideal in the arts of design. The Greeks attained it in their sculpture and their temples; Raphael, in his Madonnas; and even in landscape art, the highest style is that which, rising above the representation of phenomenal effects, presents the ideal of Nature in her wonted phases. But this limitation does not hold in literature; and especially in dramatic literature, in which action, complication, intensity, and variety approaching incongruity, are compatible with, if not essential to, the attainment of the highest excellence. Grecian architecture is simple and severe, but not therefore the highest type of architecture. And Shakespeare's genius may be well compared (and possibly the comparison is not new) to a Gothic cathedral, vast, grand, and solemn in its general aspect, and single in its total impression, yet on closer view seen to bear the stamp of various periods, and to be filled with airy, light, upspringing columns, and minutely decorated with delicate tracery, and grotesque, humorous, and even indecorous details, correspondent to each other, yet all unlike though seeming like, and, to an eye capable of the great whole, blending into rich harmony.

There are these three, — Homer, Dante, and Shakespeare. And these three have pre-eminence in right of their imaginations. Homer saw with placid mental eye the people and the deeds that he describes, as clearly as if they had passed before him in the flesh; Astyanax shrinking from his father's flashing helm and threatening crest; Hector striding across the battle-field, his huge shield rattling, as he walked, against his neck and ankles; the opposing hosts, assembled upon the plain, whose swaying spears and waving plumes, seen from afar, showed dark broad ripples, like cat's-paws on the water. Dante, with more incisive word-touch, if not more penetrating vision, puts before us Ugolino and his boys dying one by one of hunger; the Centaur with an arrow parting his beard upon his jaws before he speaks; or those two tormented alchemists who leaned against each other like pans set up to dry, and scraped the scales from their leprous bodies in prurient agony. But Shakespeare's imagination was more than this. Homer and Dante saw:

he not only saw, but was. His art is more than imagination, more than fancy, more than philosophy, more than their aggregation. It is their union in one nameless faculty. Indeed, it is only after recurring to Homer and Dante, and to Milton, Virgil, and Horace, that we know how far, how immeasurably far, is the step from the lofty cumulation of all their qualities to Shakespeare's quality. It is almost like that from the finite to the infinite. As we add number to number, until numbers cease to have significance, and then at last spring to the idea of the infinite, to which we cannot otherwise approach, so we put together all the qualities of all other poets, and then, seeing our failure to reach the Parnassian summit by heaping Pelions upon Ossas, we break off and leap to Shakespeare.

Shakespeare worked all his wonders with the lordliness of a supreme master; yet, we may be sure, not without labor. Certain men have higher tasks, and for them higher faculties, than others: he, highest. But nothing is attained by human powers, however transcendent, without paying for it man's price,—toil. There is no such thing as real impromptu. There is only the ready use on present occasion of the fruits of past exertion;—

> "Che, seggendo in piuma,
> In fama non si vien, nè sotto coltre." *

But may not the time arrive when the world

* *Inferno*, Canto XXIV. l. 47.

will say, We have had enough of Shakespeare?
May not men become pardonably weary of hearing of this one matchless man, and so ostracize
him for his very excellence? It might possibly
be so, if men lived forever; but generation suc-
ceeds to generation, and to each one he is new,
and so will be new as long as the tongue in which
he wrote is spoken. To each fresh reader Shakespeare brings more than one life can exhaust, and
those who have studied him longest are they who
are best assured that no man ever laid his head
so close upon the great heart of Nature, and
heard so clearly the throb of her deep pulses.
For this reason the man who studies Shakespeare
and attempts the unfolding of his characters is
not engaged in mere literary criticism, is not a
literary parasite; he is dealing with the most hidden and elemental truths of man's knowledge of
mankind; and for this reason, too, it is, that he
who has really any thoughts of his own upon
Shakespeare to give to the world is sure of a
kindly disposed audience. For very few, even of
the most sensitive souls and penetrating intellects,
have felt for themselves and perceived for themselves all the beauty and the strength and the
wisdom of those marvellous works that were written with the immediate purpose only of drawing
full houses to the Black-friars Theatre in London
in the days of Good Queen Bess.

All that I have inadequately said is true, and
yet it is no less true that Shakespeare revealed to
the world no new truth in ethics, in politics, or in
philosophy. He was not an intellectual discov-
erer. If the plague had not spared him in his
cradle, the great movements of the world would
have been deprived of no direct impulse coming
from his mind. They would have gone on without him, much as they have gone on under the
influence of his writings. No social or political
development of his race or of mankind would
have been checked, except in so far as a diffusion
of intellectual and moral culture and refinement
might have been retarded. For man's knowledge
of himself would have been very much more limited, because of the lack of those works which afford at once the most alluring temptations to the
study of human nature and the best field and
school for its pursuit. The English, or, if we
choose to call it so, the Anglo-Saxon race, both
in Europe and in America, would have lacked a
certain degree of that general elevation of mental
and moral tone, and that practical wisdom, which
distinguish it among the peoples. A source of
pleasure more exquisite and more refining than is
elsewhere to be found, of instruction more nearly
priceless than any except that which fell from the
lips of Jesus of Nazareth, would not have been
opened. Thus, though Shakespeare exercised no
direct influence upon the world's progress, that

which he has exercised indirectly is large and is constantly increasing, and it will increase with the diffusion of our race, and an acquaintance with its literature.

It has been before remarked, that the dramatists of Shakespeare's time, writing only to please the people, had only to consult the general taste, and were free from any restraint except that imposed by their own judgment. Some of them did attempt to work, measurably at least, according to classical formulas, and these failed entirely to attain the ends which they had in view, — popularity and profit. Of the rest, all, with one or two exceptions, being without a trusty monitor, external or internal, fell into monstrous extravagance, coarseness, conceit, and triviality. But Shakespeare, save for his conformity to mere outside fashion, was entirely unlike his contemporaries. He is among them, but not of them. Their minds run in the same channel, but do not mingle. The powerful and pellucid current of his thought flows swiftly and clearly side by side with their sluggish and turbid outpourings, leaving them behind, and taking no tint or taint from its surroundings. To him there was gain instead of loss in the disregard of formulas. Creative genius is mostly great, not by means of formulas, but in their despite. Almost inevitably it provokes censure by breaking through established rules; a truth which has at last obtained

such recognition that defiance of rule is sometimes ignorantly set up as evidence of genius,—
of which only individuality and inherent vitality
and strength are witnesses. The so-called extrav-
agances of genius establish its claims by themselves becoming formulas for minds of lower
rank; and thus schools are formed, of which no
one is really great except the founder. Yet the
highest order of poets, the seraphs of the art, do
not have followers, because they soar too high
in the empyrean for the manner of their flight
to be observed and imitated. It is the second-
rate men, great yet second, who form schools.
For their way of working is discernible, compre-
hensible, imitable. But the supremely divine is
ever a mystery. This is especially true of Shakespeare. As he worked in the manner of no
school, so he founded none. He adopted the old
forms indeed, and he labored with the same ar-
tistic motive, as well as the same material objects,
as his contemporaries and immediate predecessors
and successors. But this produced no living likeness between their offspring. His plays and those
of Marlowe, Jonson, Massinger, Marston, Middleton, Ford, and Field have neither in their dramatic nor their poetical traits the least family likeness; none, in fact, except a certain affluence and
strength of diction, and certain colloquial tricks
of expression, characteristic of the period. The
mistakes which have been made upon this subject

by writers of mark are so great as to cast a doubt
upon the soundness of all critical judgment. Although Shakespeare worked not only among a
throng of dramatists and poets, but even occasionally with some of them, there is in truth no more
striking fact in the history of literature than the
solitary position and peculiar character of his genius. Beaumont and Fletcher, and all that crew,
who came after him, although more brilliant than
Peele and Marlowe, and all that crew, that went
before him, caught no fire from his soul, no light
from his intellect. He rose upon the world eclips-
ing a few twinkling stars and one fitful meteor;
and after his grand career he sank like a midsummer sun, in full splendor, leaving no moon behind
him to prolong his reign by shining with his reflected glory.*

May the world expect another Shakespeare?
Not unless circumstances corresponding to those
which produced this Shakespeare should occur
again. Shakespeare marked a stage in the world's
progress, or at least in the history of a race which
since his time has more than any other influenced
that progress. He appeared at the period when
the English character, slowly forming through
centuries, had attained its typical development;
when the English language had assumed a form

* Yet I remember seeing in a bookseller's catalogue, at the
end of a book published at the beginning of the last century, the
announcement of a tragedy, *Jane Shore* I believe, "in Shakespeare's style, by N. Rowe."

from which it has not varied sensibly for three
centuries, and when our race, having freed itself
from the restraints of feudalism, had attained the
most symmetrical and harmonious social development possible to it under an established gradation
of classes. The English nobleman three centuries
ago, whether called by herald lord or gentleman,
was a spontaneous product of a healthy soil, a
goodly tree nourished by fibres that pierced the
mould of centuries. But he had flourished his
appointed time; and before the prerogative of
the Tudor his root began to perish, and under
the sun of the Reformation his branches to with-
er; and since then aristocracy in England has
been living, year after year, a fictitious life, and
year after year has needed more props to keep
its sapless form above the ground, which its decay and fall will enrich for another spontaneous
outgrowth. It was to express the spirit and give
form to the ideas of such a completed period in
the history of the English people, as well as to
utter the eternal truths, or rather it was to speak
those truths with the voice of that period, that he
who *was* "of an age" as well as "for all time"
appeared. A new Shakespeare may be born to
us; but only as the fruit of new conditions. He
can only appear when essential civilization, not
mere outward refinement, has advanced so far as
to have established radically new relations among
men, and when our language has so far changed

as to be the fitting vehicle for the expression of a new philosophy, a new worldly wisdom, a new range of sympathy, new sentiment, both high and homely, and a new cast of thought. For in him of whom we speak the old has had its full expression. It may be doubted whether these conditions will, even in the new England, ever be fulfilled. But should they be, then Nature, at once chary and inexhaustible, never working in vain, but ever prompt and able to supply the needs which she creates, will produce another Shakespeare, because then, and not till then, another will be required.

AN ACCOUNT

OF THE RISE AND PROGRESS OF

THE ENGLISH DRAMA

TO THE TIME OF SHAKESPEARE.

THE ENGLISH DRAMA.

THE remains of our early drama may be regarded from two principal points : one, that of the lover of what is old for the mere sake of its antiquity ; the other, that of the critical student of this department of English literature. The labor, or the pastime, of the former investigator may be protracted almost at his pleasure ; for the material is ample, although it is probable that not one in ten of the English plays written before the time of Shakespeare have escaped destruction. But the task of the latter, weary and endless although it seems at first, soon shortens by its very lack of interest. For it does not take long to discover that, with two or three exceptions, the existing English plays written before the year 1580 offer to the modern reader only an unvarying succession of platitude, triviality, coarseness, and bombast, rarely relieved even by traits which indicate the manners and the customs of the people to please whom they were produced. The practised student soon learns to take in the qualities of one of these performances at a rapid glance. The

dreariness of a desert, seen at first sight, is not
known the more surely by an examination of the
grains of sand which form its dry, interminable
waste ; nor is it necessary to a knowledge of the
English drama before the time of Shakespeare
sufficient to the appreciation of the state in which
he found it, that the reader should be dragged
step by step over the ground which his guide has
previously explored.   Therefore, as this historical
sketch regards the literary rather than the antiquarian aspect of that drama, it may well be brief,
even while it seeks to present all that, either by
intrinsic or relative interest, can illustrate its
theme.

The English drama, like the Greek, has a purely religious origin.   The same is true of the drama of every civilized people of modern times.   It
is worthy of particular remark, that the theatre,
denounced by churchmen and by laymen of eminently evangelical profession as base, corrupting,
and sinful, not in its abuse and its degradation, but
in its very essence, should have been planted and
nourished by churchmen, having priests for its first
authors and actors, and having been for centuries
the chief school of religion and of morals to an
unlettered people.   The taste for dramatic representation seems to be innate in man.   He loves
to simulate and to see others simulate character,
and seem, without deceit, other than they are.   He
finds pleasure in the consciousness that the per-

sonage before him, still more that he himself, is both John Smith and Julius Cæsar. No people, however rude and savage, except some of the more degraded tribes of Africa, have been yet discovered with whom dramatic performance of some kind, although coarse and rudimentary, was not a customary amusement. And when the great showman of the day exhibits a dwarf, he shrewdly takes advantage of this craving, and, not trusting to the mere monstrosity of his little monster, he sends him before the people in the character of Achilles or Napoleon ; nay, even ventures thus to show the Iron Duke himself his own picture in little. Theatrical representations have probably continued without interruption from the time of Æschylus. Even in the dark ages, which we look back upon too exclusively as a period of gloom, tumult, and blood-shedding, people bought and sold, and were married and given in marriage, and feasted and amused themselves as we do now ; and we may be sure that among their amusements dramatic representations of some sort were not lacking.

The earliest dramatic performances in the modern languages of Europe, of which we have any record or tradition, were representations of the most striking events recorded in the Hebrew Scriptures and in the Christian Gospels, of some of the stories told in the Pseudo Evangelium or spurious Gospel, and of legends of the saints.

On the Continent these were called Mysteries; in
England, both Mysteries and Miracle-Plays. When
miracle-plays were first performed, it seems quite
impossible to determine; and indeed, from the
universality of the taste for dramatic representations, there can hardly be a more perplexing or
fruitless task than the attempt to discover the
time and place of their origin. The ancient Hebrews had at least one miracle-play. It was founded upon the exodus of their people from Egypt.
Fragments of this play, in Greek iambics, have
been preserved to modern times in the works of
various authors. The principal characters are
Moses, Zipporah, and God in the Bush. The author, one Ezekiel, is called by Scaliger the tragic
poet of the Jews. His work is referred by one
critic to a date before the Christian era; others
suppose that he was one of the Seventy Translators; but Warton, my authority in this instance,
supposes that he wrote his play after the destruction of Jerusalem, hoping by its means to warm
the patriotism and revive the hopes of his deject-
ed countrymen.

The Eastern Empire long clung to all the glories to which its name, its language, and its position gave it a presumptive title; and the tragedies
of Sophocles and Euripides were performed after
some fashion at Constantinople until the fourth
century. At this period, Gregory Nazianzen, arch-
bishop, patriarch, and one of the fathers of the

Church, banished the pagan drama from the Greek stage, and substituted plays founded on subjects taken from the Hebrew or the Christian Scriptures. St. Gregory wrote many plays of this kind himself; and Warton says that one of them, called Χριστὸς πάσχων, or Christ's Passion, is still extant.* In this play, which, according to the Prologue, was written in imitation of Euripides, the Virgin Mary was introduced upon the stage, making then, as far as we know, her first appearance. St. Gregory died about A. D. 390. Gregory's religious plays more than rivalled his other theological writings in the favor of the people; for, as Warton also mentions, St. Chrysostom, who soon succeeded Gregory in the see of Constantinople, complained that in his day people heard a comedian with much more pleasure than a minister of the Gospel. St. Chrysostom held the see of Constantinople from A. D. 398 to A. D. 404. In this quarter, also, another kind of dramatic representation, that of mummery or masking, developed itself in a Christian or modern form. It is known that many of the Christian festivals which have come down to us from the dark ages were the fruits of a grafting of Christian legends upon pagan ceremonies; a contrivance by which the priests supposed that they had circumvented the heathen, who would more easily give up their re-

---

* History of English Poetry, Sec. XXXIV., Vol. II. p. 517, ed. 1840.

ligion than their feasts and their holidays. And the introduction of religious mumming and masking by Theophylact, Patriarch of Constantinople, about the year 990, has been reasonably attributed to a design of giving the people a Christian performance which they could and would substitute in place of the bacchanalian revels. He is said by an historian of the succeeding generation to have "introduced the practice which prevails even at this day, of scandalizing God and the memory of his saints on the most splendid and popular festivals, by indecent and ridiculous songs and enormous shoutings, ... diabolical dances, exclamations of ribaldry, and ballads borrowed from the streets and brothels." The Feast of Fools and the Feast of Asses, the latter of which was instituted in honor of Balaam's beast, had this origin. Such mingling of revelry and religion as these feasts, and of amusement and instruction in the faith as the mysteries, suited both the priestly and the popular need of the time; and they soon found their way westward, and particularly into France. Here, not long after, the Feast of Asses was performed, and in this manner. The clergy walked on Christmas-day in procession, habited to represent Moses, David, the prophets, other Hebrews and Assyrians. Balaam, with an immense pair of spurs, rode on a wooden ass, which enclosed a speaker. Virgil was one of the procession, which moved on, chanting versicles and dialoguing in character on the birth of Christ, through the body of the church, until it reached the choir.* The fairs of those days, which were the great occasions of profit and amusement, offered opportunities for the performance of these "holy farces," or of the soberer mysteries of miracle-plays, of which the priests did not fail to avail themselves; and thus this rude form of religious drama spread gradually, but not slowly, throughout Europe.

With regard to one country alone, Italy, is there question as to the early prevalence of the miracle-play. In all departments of art and literature the Italians imitated the Greeks. Voltaire supposed that they soon adopted the religious drama from Constantinople; but Riccoboni, who is the chief authority upon this subject, held the contrary. We have seen that Gregory introduced the performance of Christian plays at Constantinople in the latter part of the fourth century. But in Italy the pagan, or Latin, theatre held its own, or what we must call its own, for centuries afterward, even by the side of the Christian drama. Riccoboni indeed seems to have thought that only the pagan drama, in a gradually degenerating form, was known in Italy for seven or eight hundred years later; and he will have it that the very pied and patched dress of the modern Harlequin is a remnant of the cos-

* Warton's *History of English Poetry*, Sec. VI., Vol. II. p. 29, ed. 1840.

14*   U

tume of the mimes of the Latin stage. It would seem rather a perpetuation of the party-colored dress of the Fools of the chivalric period. But be this as it may, Warton and his editor Price found that religious plays were performed in Italy at a period very much earlier than either Riccoboni or Crescembini supposed; in fact, that they were common as early as 1250. And it is, in my judgment, improbable to the verge of impossibility that this form of the drama, (in the creation of which priests were the chief agents,) should not have been known in Italy before it came into vogue in countries farther west, and more remote from the spring, at that time, of all religious and intellectual movement. Indeed, it is to the free-masonry of the priesthood, and to the fact that the priests travelled much from country to country, and communicated freely with each other, and especially upon religious and public matters, that we may attribute the universal prevalence of the religious drama in all Christian countries throughout the later feudal ages. In the natural order of things this species of performance would pass from Italy to France, and from France to England; and the supposition that it was brought into the latter country across the Channel is supported by the fact, that there is evidence that the first religious plays performed in England were translations from the French. Some yet extant have passages in that language scattered through

them ; a fact which can be most reasonably accounted for by the supposition that these isolated passages are parts of the original, left un-
translated in the manuscripts which have come
down to us. It has even been supposed that the
first miracle-plays produced in England were performed in French. Possibly this supposition is
well founded ; but we may be sure that these
plays soon received an English dress. For the
miracle-plays were used by the priesthood for the
religious instruction, not only of those who could
not read, among whom were the Norman nobles
who could understand French, but also, and chiefly, of the middle and lower classes, to whom
French was almost as incomprehensible as the
Latin in which their prayers were vicariously
mumbled. Miracle-plays seem to have been, in
some measure at least, the fruit of the same lau-
dable desire on the part of the Roman Catholic
priesthood for the instruction of their people in
religious truth, to which we owe the rhymed
homilies or Gospel paraphrases of the thirteenth
century, in which the lesson of the day, read of
course in Latin, was translated, amplified, and illustrated in octosyllabic rhymes, which were read
to the people by the priest. Six ancient manuscript collections of these homilies are known to
exist ; and in the prologue to the oldest one of
them, which is of the fourteenth century, and
which has recently been printed, the writer ex-

pressly says that he has undertaken his task of
thus preaching in English that all may understand what he says; because both clerks and ignorant men can understand English, but all men
cannot understand Latin and French.*

* Here follows the passage above cited: —

"Forthi suld ilke precheour schau,
The god that Godd hauis gert him knau,
For qua sa hides Godes gift,
God may chalange him of thift.
In al thing es he nouht lele,
That Godes gift fra man wil sele,
Forthi the litel that I kanne,
Wil I schau til ilke manne,
Yf I kan mar god than he,
For than lif Ic in charite,
For Godes wisdom that es kid,
And na thing worthe quen it is hid,
Forthi wil I of my pouert,
Schau sum thing that Ik haf in hert,
On Ingelis tong that alle may
Understand quat I wil say,
For laued men hauis mar mister,
Godes word for to her,
Than klerkes that thair mirour lokes,
And sees hou thai sal lif on bokes,
And bathe klerk and laued man,
Englis understand kan,
That was born in Ingeland,
And lang haues ben thar in wonand,
Bot al men can noht, I wis,
Understand Latin and Frankis,
Forthi me think almous it isse,
To werke sum god thing on Inglisse,
That mai ken lered and laued bathe,
Hou thai mai yem them fra schathe,

The earliest performance of a miracle-play in England of which any record has been discovered took place within about ten years previous to 1119. The play, founded upon the legend of St. Catharine, was written by Geoffrey, afterward Abbot of St. Alban's, before he became abbot, and was performed in Dunstaple. So says Matthew Paris in his *Lives of the Abbots*, which was written before 1240. Geoffry, a Norman monk and a member of the University of Paris, became Abbot of St. Alban's in 1119. But his miracle-play was no novelty; for Bulæus, the historian of the University of Paris,* tells us that it was at that time

> And stithe stand igain the fend,
> And til the blis of heuen wend."
>
> *English Metrical Homilies, from MSS. of the Four-teenth Century.* 4to. Edinburgh, 1862.

The particular manuscript collection from which this passage is taken has special philological interest, as its editor, Mr. John Small, remarks, because, as indeed the passage above shows, the homilies which it has preserved were composed in the North of England at a very early period, when the Anglo-Saxon was passing into English, and when the Anglo-Norman French was yet in use among the higher classes. Its special interest is enhanced also by the fact that it shows that the same broad dialect of English was common at that period to Scotland south of the Grampians and to the North of England. The manuscript contains internal evidence that the homilies were read by the priests to the people; for in the midst of the second homily are some Latin hexameters with this rubric: "*Isti versus omittantur a lectore quando legit Anglicum coram laycis.*"

* I have seen neither Mathew Paris's *Historia Major*, &c., nor Bulæus's *Historia Universitatis Parisiensis*. Both are cited by Markland and Warton, who are here my authorities.

common for teachers and scholars to get up these performances. Fitz-Stephen, Thomas à Becket's contemporary and biographer, also records that in London, during or soon after the life of that stiff-necked priest, who was put to death in 1170, there were performed in London religious plays representing the miracles wrought by saints or the sufferings and constancy of martyrs.* These miracle-plays, or mysteries, derived their name from the fact that, whether founded upon the Old or the New Testament, the spurious gospel attributed to Nicodemus, or church tradition, they almost without exception represented a display of supernatural power. Made the means of teaching not only religious history but religious dogmas, these miracle-plays often represented a display of supernatural power in the support of those dogmas; and naturally that one most in need of such extra-rational aid, transubstantiation, received the most of this bolstering. One of the oldest manuscript miracle-plays extant, the manuscript being, in the judgment of experts, as old as 1460–70, is upon this subject. It is called *The Play of the Blessed Sacrament*, and dramatizes a miracle said to have been worked in the forest of Aragon in the year 1461; but doubtless

---

* "Londonia pro spectaculis theatralibus, pro ludis scenicis, ludos habet sanctiores, representationes miraculorum, quæ sancti confessores operati sunt, seu representationes passionum quibus claruit constantia martyrum." — Fitz-Stephen's *Description of London,* ed. Pegge, 1773, p. 73.

the tradition is older. Among the characters are
Christ, five Jews, a bishop, a curate, a Christian
merchant, a physician, and his man. The merchant, whose name is Aristorius, in the crude style
of these plays thus describes himself:

> "Ffor off all Aragon I am most myghty of sylver and of gold,
> Ffor and yt wer a countre to by now wold I nat wond.
> Syr Arystory ys my name;
> A merchante myghty of a royall araye;
> Fful wyde in this worlde spryngyth my fame,
> Fere kend and knowen the sothe for to saye."

The last line of this extract is noteworthy as indicative of the existence, even in remote times, of
the merchant's pride in his mercantile honor, in
having his word as good as his bond, however
questionable may be the character, in other respects, of some of his transactions, as in the case
of this Aristorius. The principal Jew, whose
name is Jonathas, induces Aristorius to steal the
Host and sell it to him for one hundred pounds.
Then Jonathas and his Hebrew companions take
it to his house for experimental purposes. They
stab it; it bleeds. They are about to plunge it
into a caldron of boiling oil; but Jonathas goes
mad with the Host in his hand. He still keeping
his hold, the rest nail the wafer to a post, and attempt to drag him away. They accomplish their
purpose with the loss of his hand, which comes
off and clings to the wafer. The physician is sent
for, and his man entering first makes sport by a

burlesque laudation of his master, who is not
forthcoming, and as to whom he makes the following proclamation : —

> "Yff ther be eyther man or woman
> That sawe master Brundyche of Braban,
> Or owyht of hym tel can,
>   Shall wele be quit hys mede.
> He hath a cut berd and a flatte noose,
> A therde bare gowne and a rent hoose,
> He spekyth never good matere nor purpoose,
>   To the pyllere ye hym lede."

The physician arrives and offers his services ; but
both master and man are driven out as meddling
quacks. Jonathas's hand with the Host in it is
then thrown into the caldron, which immediately boils up with blood. The Jews then heat an
oven red-hot, and cast in the wafer. The oven
bleeds at the chinks and bursts asunder, and the
figure of Jesus issues from it, before which the
Jews prostrate themselves and become Christians
on the spot. The bishop then forms a religious
procession, enters the Jew's house, and addresses
the figure, which changes to bread again. Aristorius confesses his crime, and is ordered, by way
of penance, to give up buying and selling. The
bishop then "improves the occasion" offered by
this comic-pantomime-like performance, and closes
the play by a rhymed homily upon the doctrines
of the Trinity and Transubstantiation. Certain
peculiarities of language indicate that the author
was a North of England man ; and there are

traces in the composition of the old Anglo-Saxon alliterative verse. There is more art in the construction of this play, rude as it is, than in any other of the early English plays of its kind.

There were neither theatres nor professional actors in England, indeed in Europe, at the period when miracle-plays first came in vogue. The first performers in these plays were clergymen; the first stages or scaffolds on which they were presented were set up in churches. Evidence that this was the case has been discovered in such profusion, that it is needless to specify it more particularly in this place, than to remark that councils and prelates finally found it necessary to forbid such performances either in churches or by the clergy. But it is worthy of remark, that evidence of the ecclesiastical character of the first actors of our drama is preserved in dramatic literature to this day in the Latin words of direction, *Exit* and *Exeunt*. The stage directions in the miracle-plays (like the direction to the priest as to reading the metrical homily quoted on page 324) were partly, and at first it would seem entirely, in Latin, which it is needless to say no layman, and not all clergymen, could then understand. Even in Shakespeare's day Latin held its own in the headings of the acts and scenes, — *Actus Primus*, *Scœna Secunda*, and so forth. After the exclusion of the clergy from the religious stage, lay brothers, parish clerks, and the hangers-on of the priesthood naturally took the place of their spiritual fathers, under whose superintendence, or, to speak precisely, management, the miracle-plays were brought out. Excluded from the church itself, like the strange *Danse Macabre*, or Dance of Death, like that dance the miracle-play found fitting refuge in the church-yard. But it was finally forbidden within all hallowed precincts, and was then presented upon a movable scaffold or pageant, which was dragged through the town, and stopped for the performance at certain places designated by an announcement made a day or two before. At last the presentation of these plays fell entirely into the hands of laymen, and handicraftsmen became their actors; the members of the various guilds undertaking respectively certain plays which they made for the time their specialty. Thus the Shearmen and Taylors would represent one; the Cappers another; and so with the Smiths, the Skinners, the Fishmongers, and others. In the Chester series, Noah's flood was very appropriately assigned to the Water-dealers and Drawers of Dee. It is almost needless to remark, that female characters were always played by striplings and young men. Women did not appear upon the English stage until the middle of the seventeenth century. It would seem that the priests appeared only as amateurs, and that their performances were gratuitous. But when laymen, or at least when handicraftsmen undertook the busi-

ness, they were paid, as we know by the memorandums of account still existing.*

With regard to one place of performance and
one play, though not in England, there has been
preserved a record full of interest. Riccoboni gives
in his catalogue of old printed Italian plays the
following as the title-page of an ancient miracle-
play: "*Della Passione da Nostro Signore Giesu
Christo, rapresentata il Giovedi santo nel Coliseo di
Roma*," — by which we see that the Coliseum, itself the scene of many a Christian martyrdom,
the place where many a disciple of Paul fought
with wild beasts, as his teacher had fought at
Ephesus, became in the course of a few hundred
years the theatre on which were represented the
life and sufferings and death of the Greatest
Teacher, to their faith in whom those martyrs
offered up themselves, a bloody sacrifice, in that
vast human slaughter-house.

Writers of chronicle and history, and sometimes

---

* The following items of account are taken from one of many
memorandums discovered by Mr. Sharp in the archives of Coventry, and published in his Essay on the Coventry Mysteries : —

"Md. payd to the players for corpus christi daye

Imprimis, to God	ij⁴
Itm to Cayphas	iij⁴ iiij⁴
Itm to Heroude	iij⁴ iiij⁴
Itm to Pilatt is wyff	ij⁴
Itm to the Bedull	iiij⁴
Itm to one of the knights	ij⁴
Itm to the devyll and Judas	xviij⁴ "

even of family genealogy, in the Middle Ages,
disdained to skip to the deluge, and take creation
for granted; and the writers of miracle-plays were
in this respect like-minded. The disposition to
go back to the beginning of all things is a trait
of rude and unlettered periods. Stowe records
the performance at London, in the year 1409, of
a play "which lasted eight days, and was of matter from the creation of the world," — a dramatic
protracted meeting which quite puts to shame
the assistance at the famous representation of
Monte Christo in Paris; and Lidgate wrote a series of miracle-plays, also beginning with the creation. Indeed, that event is the starting-point of
two of the three great collections of English miracle-plays which have come down to us. But we
may be sure that the writers set out from there
only because of the difficulty of getting back farther; and in fact the third series, the Chester,
does begin with the fall of Lucifer, and the authors of the other two contrive to work that incident into the play on the Creation.

The most ancient manuscript of an English
miracle-play yet discovered is that of one called
The Harrowing of Hell, which very formidable
title, however, merely signifies the harrying, the
invasion and spoliation of hell by Christ, — the
event alluded to in the Apostles' Creed by the
words, "He descended into Hell." This play is
founded upon a passage in the apocryphal Gos-

pel of Nicodemus, and represents the descent of Christ into Hell to set free Adam and Eve, Abraham, Moses, John the Baptist, and other holy persons. In it Satan enters into a discussion with Christ as to the injustice of carrying off his, i. e. Satan's, property. But Christ accomplishes his purpose without resistance, and binds Satan until the day of judgment. Indeed, in spite of its title, this play is of a most peaceful character, and is filled with words rather than action. Both language and versification are very rude, as may be seen in the following lines spoken by Christ: —

> " Helle gates y come nou to,
> And I wolle that heo un do.
> Wer ys nou this gateward?
> Me thunketh he is a coward."

There are a prologue, an epilogue, and nine speakers. The manuscript is supposed to have been written about 1350.* But that date does not of course help us to determine when the play was composed, or give it priority in this respect to others which have been preserved in more modern writing. *The Harrowing of Hell* is supposed with probability to have formed part of a series; and its subject has its place in collections which from their completeness have greater interest and importance.

The three sets of miracle-plays above men-

---

* It is among the Harleian MSS. in the British Museum, and has been printed by Mr. Halliwell.

tioned are known as the Towneley, the Coventry, and the Chester Collections. The Towneley Collection is supposed to have belonged to Widkirk Abbey, and is hence sometimes called the Widkirk Collection. The manuscript, in the opinion of Mr. Collier, is of the time of Henry VI.* The Coventry Collection is so called because there is reason to believe that it was the property of the Gray Friars of Coventry, who were famous for the performance of miracle-plays at the feast of Corpus Christi. The principal part of the manuscript copy extant was written in the year 1468, as appears by that date upon one page of the volume.† The Chester Collection, of which there

* The following are the subjects of the thirty plays in the Towneley series. I. The Creation and the Rebellion of Lucifer. II. Mactatio Abel. III. Processus Noæ cum filiis. IV. Abraham. V. Jacob and Esau. VI. Processus Prophetarum. VII. Pharao. VIII. Cæsar Augustus. IX. Annunciatio. X. Salutatio Elizabethæ. XI. Pastorum. XII. Alia eorundem. XIII. Oblatio Magorum. XIV. Fugatio Josephi et Mariæ in Egiptum. XV. Magnus Herodus. XVI. Purificatio Mariæ. XVII. Johannes Baptista. XVIII. Conspiratio Christi. XIX. Calaphisatio. XX. Flagellatio. XXI. Processus Crucis. XXII. Processus Talentorum. XXIII. Extractio Animarum. XXIV. Resurrectio Domini. XXV. Peregrini. XXVI. Thomas Indiæ. XXVII. Ascensio Domini. XXVIII. Judicium. XXIX. Lazarus. XXX. Suspensio Judæ.

† The Coventry series contains forty-two plays upon the following subjects : — I. The Creation. II. The Fall of Man. III. The Death of Abel. IV. Noah's Flood. V. Abraham's Sacrifice. VI. Moses and the Two Tables. VII. The Genealogy of Christ. VIII. Anna's Pregnancy. IX. Mary in the Temple. X. Mary's Betrothment. XI. The Salutation and the Concep-

are three existing manuscript copies, the oldest
only of the year 1600, belonged to the city of
Chester.   Their author was one Randle, a monk of
Chester Abbey.*   They were played upon Whit-
sunday by the tradesmen of that city ; and Mr.
Markland, one of the earliest, and, in the phrase

tion.   XII. Joseph's Return.   XIII. The Visit to Elizabeth.
XIV. The Trial of Joseph and Mary.   XV. The Birth of Christ.
XVI. The Adoration of the Shepherds.   XVII. The Adora-
tion of the Magi. XVIII. The Purification.   XIX. The Slaugh-
ter of the Innocents.   XX. Christ Disputing in the Temple.
XXI. The Baptism of Christ. XXII. The Temptation. XXIII.
The Woman taken in Adultery.   XXIV. Lazarus.   XXV. The
Council of the Jews.   XXVI. The Entry into Jerusalem.
XXVII. The Last Supper.   XXVIII. The Betraying of Christ.
XXIX. King Herod.   XXX. The Trial of Christ.   XXXI. Pi-
late's Wife's Dream.   XXXII. The Crucifixion.   XXXIII. The
Descent into Hell. XXXIV. The Burial of Christ. XXXV. The
Resurrection. XXXVI. The Three Maries.   XXXVII. Christ
appearing to Mary Magdalen. XXXVIII. The Pilgrim of Emaus.
XXXIX. The Ascension. XL. The Descent of the Holy Ghost.
XLI. The Assumption.   XLII. Doomsday.

   * We have the testimony of the "Banes" (i. e. banns or prologue), that this Chester series of miracle-plays was written by
"Done Randall, moonke of Chester Abbey," with the intention
of instructing the people in the Bible, and also of affording them
merry entertainment.

   "This moonke, not moonke-like, in scriptures well seene,
      In storjes travilled with the best sorte ;
      In pagentes set fourthe, apparently to all eyne,
      The old and newe testament with livelye comforte ;
      Intermingling therewith, oncly to make sporte,
      Some things not warranted by any writt,
      Which to gladd the hearers he would men to take yt."

This prologue was written some time, possibly a century or more,
after the production of the plays themselves.

of his day, most ingenious writers upon this subject, has pretty clearly established that they were
first produced in 1268, four years after the establishment of the feast of Corpus Christi, under the
auspices of Sir John Arneway, Mayor of Chester.*

A brief analysis of some of the plays of the
Coventry series will give a correct notion of the
characters of these queer compositions. A prologue in stanzas, spoken alternately by three vex-
illators, tells in detail the subjects of the forty-two
plays. The first, *The Creation*, is opened by God,
who, after declaring in Latin that he is Alpha
and Omega, the beginning and the end, goes on
in English to assert his might and his triune existence, and then announces his creative inten-
tions. A chorus of angels then sing in Latin the
Tibi omnes angeli, &c. of the *Te Deum*. Lucifer
next appears, and asks of the angels whether they

* The Chester series contains but twenty-four plays, upon the
following subjects : — I. The Fall of Lucifer. II. De Creatione
Mundi. III. De Diluvio Noæ. IV. De Abrahamo, Melchise-
dech et Lotte. V. De Mose et Rege Balak, et Balaam Propheta.
VI. De Salutatione et Nativitate Salvatoris. VII. De Pastoribus
greges pascentibus. VIII. De tribus Regibus Orientalibus. IX.
De Oblatione Tertium Regum. X. De Occisione Innocentum.
XI. De Purificatione Virginis. XII. De Tentatione Salvatoris.
XIII. De Chelidomo et Resurrectio Lazari. XIV. De Jesu in-
tranto domum Simeonis Leprosi. XV. De Cœna Domini. XVI.
De Passione Christi. XVII. De Descensu Christi ad Inferos.
XVIII. De Resurrectione Jesu Christi   XIX. De Christo ad
Castellum Emmaus. XX. De Ascensione Domini. XXI. De
Electione Matthiæ. XXII. Ezekiel. XXIII. De Adventu An-
tichristi. XXIV. De Judicio extremo.

sing thus in God's honor or his, asserting that he is the most worthy. The good angels declare for God; the bad, for Lucifer. God then dooms him to fall from heaven to hell. Lucifer submits to his sentence without murmuring, and expresses his emotion only in a manner most likely to deprive the scene of any semblance of dignity it might otherwise have exhibited.*

The second play, *The Fall of Man*, opens with a speech by Adam, and a reply by Eve, in which they set forth their happy condition and the command concerning the tree of knowledge of good and evil. The serpent then appears and tempts Eve to violate this command. The action, if action it must be called, follows in the most servile manner, and with no expansion, the narrative in Genesis; and

* "*Deus.* Thu Lucyfere ffor thi mekyl pryde,
  I bydde the ffalle from hefne to helle;
And alle tho that holdyn on thi syde,
  In my blysse nevyr more to dwelle.
At my comawndement anoon down thou slyde,
  With merthe and joye nevyr more to melle,
In myschyf and manas evyr xalt thou abyde,
  In byttyr brennyng and fyer so felle,
      In peyn evyr to be pyht.
"*Lucyfer.* At thy byddyng thi wyl I werke,
And pas fro joy to peyne smerte,
Now I am a devyl ful derke,
      That was an aungelle bryht.

"Now to helle the wey I take,
  In endeles peyn ther to be pyht.
ffor fere of fyre a fart I crake,
  In helle doonjoone myn dene is dyth."

15   V

Adam and Eve are expelled from Paradise.*   It is
clear that the representatives of the types of mankind appeared upon the stage innocently free from
"the troublesome disguises that we wear"; and
that they afterward very faithfully followed the
Hebrew lawgiver's´ narrative in the use of fig-
leaves.†   It has been urged that the nakedness in
this scene was a supposed nakedness; that shame
could not have been so utterly disregarded as it
must have been had these speeches and these
directions a literal significance.   But the manners
of the time, as they are shown in old books and
prints, justify the acceptance of these passages in
their plain and simple meaning.   We are apt to
forget how much of what we call shame is purely
conventional, — as purely so as the horror of a
Turkish woman at uncovering her face before a

---

* Here is Eve's lamentation :

> "*Eva.*   Alas ! alas ! and wele away,
>   That evyr towchyd I the tre ;
>   I wende as wrecche in welsom way,
>   In blake busshys my boure xal be.
>   In paradys is plenté of pleye,
>   ffayr frutys ryth gret plenté,
>   The ȝatys be schet with Godys keye,
>   My husbond is lost because of me.
>   Leve spowse now thou fonde,
>   Now stomble we on stalk and ston,
>   My wyt awey is fro me gon,
>   Wrythe on to my necke bon,
>   With hardnesse of thin honde."

† In the Chester miracle-play the stage direction is, "*Then
shall Adam and Eve stand nackede, and shall not be ashamed.*"   In

strange man. It is related in the Life of William Blake, the painter, a pure and good man, that a Mr. Butts on visiting him found him and his wife sitting entirely naked in the summer-house in their garden. He shrank back astounded; but "Come in," cried Blake, "it's only Adam and Eve, you know." They had been reading the *Paradise Lost*, and like the actor who blackened himself all over that he might more thoroughly enter into the character of Othello, they, to realize the situation of Adam and Eve in Eden, had adopted the costume worn previous to the temptation. And this was no solitary instance. Blake frequently went naked; so in her own room did Mrs. Blake; and the children went about the house and to the door to admit friends naked. It may be said that Blake was crazy; but his wife was not, nor were his children.

the Coventry play, Adam speaks thus, immediately after he has eaten the apple: —

> "*Adam dicet sic.*
>
> Alas! alas! ffor this fals dede,
>   My flesly frend my fo I fynde,
> Schameful synne doth us unhede,
>   I se us nakyd before and behynde.
> Oure lordes wurd wold we not drede,
>   Therfore we be now caytyvys unkynde,
> Oure pore prevytés ffor to hede,
>   Summe ffygge-levys fayn wolde I fynde,
>   ffor to hyde oure schame.
> Womman, ley this leff on thi pryvyté,
> And with this leff I xal hyde me,
> Gret schame it is us nakyd to se,
>   Oure lord God thus to grame."

In the third play, *Cain and Abel*, the only noteworthy points are, first, that Cain speaks very dis-
respectfully of Adam and his counsels, saying that
he cares not a haw if he never sees him ; and
next, that, when Abel's offering is accepted and
consumed by fire, Cain breaks out into abuse of
him, calling him a "stinking losel." * This, by
the way, is one of the few representations of contemporary manners furnished by these miracle-
plays. If we accept them as truthful in this regard, we must credit our forefathers with a ready
resort to foul language when they were angered.
Afterward, in the play on *Noah's Flood*, Lamech
calls a young man "a stinking lurdane" ; and
in that on *The Woman taken in Adultery*, the
Scribes and Pharisees call her forth to be taken
to judgment in language far more pharisaic than

---

* Cain's speech, which follows, will give a notion of the language and action of the play at its point of highest interest.

> "*Caym.*   What ? thou stynkyng losel, and is it so ?
>   Doth God the love and hatyht me ?
> Thou xalt be ded, I xal the slo,
>   Thi Lord thi God thou xalt nevyr se !
> Tythyng more xalt thou nevyr do,
>   With this chavyl bon I xal sle the,
> Thi deth is dyht, thi days be go,
>   Out of myn handys xalt thou not fle,
>   With this strok I the kylle.—
> Now this boy is slayn and dede,
> Of hym I xal nevyr more han drede ;
> He xal hereafter nevyr ete brede,
>   With this gresse I xal hym hylle."

decent.* The Towneley mystery, which represents the first fratricide, is even more grotesque
and indecent than that in the collection which we
are examining. Cain comes upon the stage with
a plough and team, and quarrels with his plough-
boy for refusing to drive the oxen. Abel enters,
bids speed the plough to Cain, and in reply is
told to do something quite unmentionable. After
Abel is killed, the boy counsels flight for fear of
the bailiffs. Cain then makes a mock proclamation, which his boy blunderingly repeats; and after
this clownish foolery, Cain bids the audience farewell before he goes to hell.

The personages in the fourth play, *Noah's Flood*,
are God, Noah and his wife, his three sons and their
wives, an angel, Cain, Lamech, and a young man.
Noah and his family talk pharisaic morality for
about the first third of the play. God then declares
his displeasure, and that he "wol be vengyd";
to which end he will destroy all the world except
Noah and his family. The angel announces the
coming flood to Noah, and bids him build a ship to
save himself, his household, and "of every kyndys

---

* "*Scriba.* Come forthe, thou stotte ! com forthe, thou scowte !
   Come forthe, thou bysmare and brothel bolde !
  Come fforthe, thou hore, and stynkynge byche clowte !
   How longe hast thou suche harlotry holde ?
 "*Phariseus.* Come forth, thou quene ! come forthe, thou scolde !
   Com forth, thou sloveyn ! com forthe, thou slutte !
  We xal the teche with carys colde, .
   A lytyl bettyr to kepe thi kutte."

bestes a cowpyl." Noah and his family go out to build the ship, and Lamech enters blind, and conducted by a young man. In spite of his infirmity, at the suggestion of his guide, he shoots at a supposed beast in a bush; but, like another hapless person known to rhyme who "bent his bow," he hits what he did not shoot at, and kills Cain, who mysteriously happens to be in the bush. Aroused to wrath, and moved by fear of the fate predicted of him who should slay Cain, Lamech kills the young man who had misled him into shooting at the beast. He goes out, and Noah comes in with his ship,—"*et statim intrat Noe* cum *navi cantantes.*" This ship, as we learn from the direction in the corresponding play of the Chester Mysteries, was customarily painted over with figures of the beasts supposed to be within, as if they had struck through and come out like an eruption.* In that play, too, and also in the corresponding Towneley play, Noah's wife refuses to enter the ark. Indeed, in these plays she is represented as an arrant scold. In the first scene she berates Noah,

---

* "Then Noe shall goe into the arke with all his familye, his wife excepte. The arke must be boarded round about, and uppon the bordes all the beastes and fowles hereafter rehearsed must be painted, that there wordes maye agree with the pictures." To Noah's request that she will come into the ark, his wife, in the Chester play, thus replies:—

"Yea sir set up your saile,
And rowe forth with evil haile,
For withouten anie saile
I will not out of this toune.

who gives her as good as she sends, and both swear roundly by the Virgin Mary; and as to going into the ark, the patriarch, "the secunde fathyr," as he styles himself, edifies the female part of the audience by fairly flogging his wife into it with a cart-whip. The flood comes on, (we have returned to the Coventry plays,) Noah and his family speak thirty lines of dialogue, and then he says:—

> "Xl.ᵗⁱ days and nyghtes hath lasted this rayn,
>   And xl.ᵗⁱ days this grett flood begynnyth to slake;
> This crowe xal I sende out to seke sum playn,
>   Good tydynges to brynge, this massage I make."

The crow does not return, and the dove is sent, "*qua redeunte cum ramo viride olivæ*," as the stage direction says, Noah and his family leave the ark, singing, "*Mare vidit et fugit*," &c.

The fourteenth play, which represents the *Trial of Joseph and Mary* on accusations based upon the latter's mysterious pregnancy, is opened by a crier, who summons the jurors, and people who

> "But I have my gossepes everich one,
>   One foot further I will not gone;
> They shal not drown by St. John,
>   And I may save ther life.
>
> "They loved me ful well by Christ;
>   But thou will let them in thi chist,
> Ellis row forth, Noe, when thou list
>   And get thee a newe wife."

But Noah neither lets them in his chist, nor gets him a new wife.

have causes, to come into court. Although the trial is supposed, of course, to take place in Palestine before the Christian era, it is presided over by "my lorde the buschop," and the people summoned are Englishfolk of the lower class, whose surnames have plainly been given to them on account of their occupation or their personal traits. The crier lets us into a judge's secret, by warning those who have causes to be tried to put money in their purses, or their cause may speed the worse.* In the next play, which is entitled *The*

---

* "*Den.* Avoyd, seres, and lete my lorde the buschop come,
And syt in the courte the lawes ffor to doo;
And I xal gon in this place them for to somowne,
Tho that ben in my book the court ȝe must com too.
I warne ȝow here alle abowte,
That I somown ȝow alle the rowte,
Loke ȝe fayl, for no dowte,
At the court to pere.
Bothe John Jurdon, and Geffrey Gyle,
Malkyn Mylkedoke, and fayr Mabyle,
Stevyn Sturdy, and Jak at the Style,
And Sawdyr Sadelere.

"Thom Tynkere and Betrys Belle,
Peyrs Potter and Whatt at the Welle,
Symme Smalfeyth and Kate Kelle,
And Bertylmew the Bochere.
Kytt Cakelere and Colett Crane,
Gylle Fetyse and fayr Jane,
Powle Pewterere and Pernel Prane,
And Phelypp the good Flecchere.

"Cok Crane and Davy Drydust,
Luce Lyere and Letyce Lytyltrust,

Birth of Christ, Mary, as she and Joseph are on
their way to Bethlehem, longs for cherries from a
tree which they pass. Joseph is old, lazy, and
huffish, and tells her that the tree is too high,
and that he may get her cherries who got her
with child. Whereupon Mary prays for the cherries, and the boughs bend down to her; at which
sight Joseph repents.* Plainly there were prop-

> Miles the Myllere and Colle Crakecrust,
> > Bothe Bette the Bakere, and Robyn Rede.
> And loke ȝe ryngewele in ȝour purs,
> ffor ellys ȝour cawse may spede the wurs,
> Thow that ȝe slynge Goddys curs
> > Evyn at myn hede, ffast com away.
> Bothe Boutyng the Browstere, and Sybyly Slynge,
> Megge Merywedyr and Sabyn Sprynge,
> Tyffany Twynkelere, ffayle ffor nothynge,
> > The courte xal be this day."

* "*Maria*. Now, my spowse, I pray ȝow to behold,
> How the cheryes growyn upon ȝon tre;
ffor to have therof ryght ffayn I wold,
> And it plesyd ȝow to labore so meche for me.
"*Joseph*. ȝour desyre to ffulfylle I xal assay sekyrly,
> Ow to plucke ȝow of these cheries; it is a werk wylde,
ffor the tre is so hyȝ it wol not be lyghtly,
> Therfore lete hym pluk ȝow cheryes begatt ȝow with childe.
"*Maria*. Now, good Lord, I pray the graunt me this boun,
> To have of these cheries, and it be ȝour wylle:
Now, I thank it God, this tre bowyth to me downe!
> I may now gaderyn anowe, and etyn my ffylle.
"*Josephe*. Ow, I know weyl I have offendyd my God in Trinyté,
> Spekyng to my spowse these unkynde wurdys;
ffor now I beleve wel it may non other be,
> But that my spowse beryght the kyngys son of blys;
> > He help us now at oure nede!"

erties, and even machinery, upon the stage at this rude and early period; and indeed the lists of properties (for they seem always to have been so called) which have been preserved, show that no small pains were taken to portray the glories and the horrors of the various scenes presented, and especially in the imitations of such miraculous events as that of the bowing down of the branches of the cherry-tree.

The seventeenth play, *The Adoration of the Magi*, introduces the most famous character in these dramas, Herod. He is always represented in them, not only as wicked and cruel, but as a tremendous braggart. He raves and swaggers and swears without stint; his favorite oath being by Mahound, i. e. Mohammed; for in all respects these miracle-plays set chronology at defiance. The speeches put into his mouth more than any others are written in the old Anglo-Saxon alliterative style, of which *Piers Ploughman's Vision* is a well-known example.* Herod, in spite of

---

* Perhaps the most characteristic speech of his, in every respect, is the following from *The Slaughter of the Innocents.*

"*Herodes Rex.* I ryde on my rowel ryche in my regne,
    Rybbys fful reed with rape xal I sende;
Popetys et paphawkes I xal puttyn in peyne,
    With my spere prevyn, pychyn, and to-pende.
The gowys with gold crownys gete thei nevyr ageyn,
    To seke tho sottys sondys xal I sende;
Do howlott howtyn hoberd and heyn,
    Whan here barnys blede undyr credyl bende;
        Sharply I xal hem shende!

his heathenism, his cruelty, his profanity, and his
braggadocio, perhaps by reason of them, used to
be a favorite character with young men of spirit
and parts who were stage-struck. Chaucer, it

> The knave childeryn that be
> In alle Israel countré,
> Thei xul have blody ble,
>   ffor on I calde unkende.

> "It is tolde in Grw,
> His name xulde be Jhesu
>   I-fownde.
> To have hym ʒe gon,
> Hewe the flesche with the bon,
>   And gyff hym wownde !
> Now kene knyghtes, kythe ʒour craftys,
>   And kyllyth knave chylderyn and castyth hem in clay;
> Shewyth on ʒour shulderes scheldys and schaftys,
>   Shapyht amonge schel chowthys ashyrlyng shray;
> Doth rowncys rennyn with rakynge raftys,
>   Tyl rybbys be to rent with a reed ray;
> Lete no barne beleve on bete baftys,
>   Tyl a beggere blede be bestys baye
>   Mahound that best may;
> I warne ʒow my knyghtes,
> A barn is born I plyghtys,
> Wolde clymbyn kynge and kyknytes,
>   And lett my lordly lay.

> "Knyghtys wyse,
> Chosyn ful chyse,
> Aryse ! aryse !
>   And take ʒour tolle !
> And every page
> Of ij. ʒere age,
> Or evyr ʒe swage,
>   Sleythe ilke a fool.

will be remembered, says, in the Miller's Tale, of
his "Absolon that joly was and gay":

> " Sometime to shew his lightness and maistrie
> He plaieth Herode on a skaffolde hie." *

But more than by the indecency, the coarseness, the bombast, and the vapidity of these miracle-plays, we are astonished and repelled by the
degrading familiarity with which they treat the
most awful and most moving incidents of the
Gospel history. The Last Supper was actually

> " On of hem alle
> Was born in stalle,
> ffolys hym calle
>> Kynge in crowne.
> With byttyr galle,
> He xalle down falle, —
> My myght in halle
>> Xal nevyr go down."

---

* Absolon was parish-clerk; but the costume and habits of
some of the lay gallants who played Herod is set forth in the following passage, spoken by the Devil in the twenty-fifth play, *The
Council of the Jews*. It has no dramatic significance, but is an
interesting and doubtless a truthful portraiture of the period,
even as to the side-locks that "harbor quick beasts that tickle
men."

> " Byholde the dyvercyté of my dysgysyd varyauns,
>> Eche thyng sett of dewe nateralle dysposycion,
> And eche parte acordynge to his resemblauns,
>> ffro the sool of the ffoot to the hyest asencion.

> " Off ffyne cordewan a goodly peyre of long pekyd schon;
>> Hosyn enclosyd of the most costyous cloth of crenseyn;
> Thus a bey to a jentylman to make comperycion,
>> With two doseyn poyntys of cheverelle, the aglottes of sylver
>> feyn.

played; the Crucifixion was actually played; and even the Resurrection was not too sacred or mysterious a subject to be represented. Conforming both to the religious spirit and the taste of the time, the clerical dramatist spared his audience the sight of no indignity, of no torture, suffered by Christ; but took delight in representing all the physical circumstances attending his death with gross and audacious particularity.*

> "A shert of feyn Holond, but care not for the payment;
>   A stomachere of clere reynes the best may be bowth;
> Thow poverté be chef, lete pride ther be present,
>   And alle tho that repreff pride, thou sette hem at nowth.

> "Cadace wolle or flokkys, where it may be sowth,
>   To stuffe withal thi dobbelet, and make the of proporcyon;
> Two smale legges and a gret body, thow it ryme nowth,
>   ʒet loke that thou desyre to an the newe faccion.

> "A gowne of thre ʒerdys, loke thou make comparison,
>   Unto alle degrees dayly that passe thin astat;
> A purse withoutyn mony, a daggere for devoscyon;
>   And there repref is of synne, loke thou make debat.

> "With syde lokkys I schrewe thin here to thi colere hangyng
>   downe,
>   To herborwe qweke bestys that tekele men onyth;
> An hey smal bonet for curyng of the crowne,
>   And alle beggeres and pore pepyll have hem in dyspyte.
> Onto the grete othys and lycherye gyf thi delyte;
>   To maynteyn thin astate lete brybory be present;
> And yf the lawe repreve the, say thou wylt ffyth,
>   And gadere the a felachep after thin entent."

* The following passage, it will be seen, shows that the Crucifixion was represented even to the minutest of its attendant circumstances : —

And as we close our examination of the miracle-plays a reflection of their mingled childishness

" *Than xul thei pulle Jhesu out of his clothis, and leyn them to-gedyr ; and ther thei xul pullyn hym down and leyn along on the cros, and after that naylyn hym thereon.*

" *Primus Judæus.*   Come on now here, we xal asay
    Yf the cros for the be mete ;
Cast hym down here in the devyl way,
    How long xal he standyn on his fete ?

" *Secundus Judæus.*   Pul hym down, evyl mote he the !
    And gyf me his arm in hast ;
And anon we xal se
    Hese good days thei xul be past !

" *Tertius Judæus.*   Gef hese other arm to me, —
    Another take hed to hese feet ;
And anon we xal se
    Yf the borys be for hym meet.

" *Quartus Judæus.*   This is mete, take good hede ;
    Pulle out that arm to the sore.
Primus Judæus.   This is short, the devyl hym sped,
    Be a large fote and more.

" *Secundus Judæus.*   ffest on a rop and pulle hym long,
    And I xal drawe the ageyn ;
Spare we not these ropys strong,
    Thow we brest both flesch and veyn !

" *Tertius Judæus.*   Dryve in the nayle anon, lete se,
    And loke and the flesch and sennes welle last.
Quartus Judæus.   That I graunt, so mote I the ;
    Lo ! this nayl is dreve ryth wel and fast.

" *Primus Judæus.*   ffest a rope than to his feet,
    And drawe hym down long anow.
Secundus Judæus.   Here is a nayl for both good and greet,
    I xal dryve it thorwe, I make a vow !

" *Here xule thei leve of and dawncyn abowte the cros shortly.*"

and temerity must be uppermost in the mind of
every reader. Had it not been done, it would
seem almost impossible that such subjects could
be so unworthily treated by men of sense and education, which the better class of Roman Catholic
priests were, even in the days when these plays
were written. Here were the grandest themes
handled by authors to whom they were matters
of religious faith and supreme concern ; and all
that was done was to degrade, to belittle, and to
make ridiculous. The rudeness of the people for
whose instruction and pleasure the miracle-plays
were produced, and the gross and material character of religion at that day, account, in a great
measure, for this shocking contrast between subject and treatment. But yet it would seem that,
though rude and simple, these compositions might
have preserved some touch of the spirit of the
Hebrew writers from whom their subjects were
taken, and who themselves wrote for a people
only a little advanced beyond the pale of semi-
barbarism. And one subject, by remarkable coincidence, was treated with a certain degree of
simplicity and pathos by the writers of all of the
three great collections of English miracle-plays.
This was the story of Abraham and Isaac. And
it is worthy of special remark, that it was a subject of which the interest is purely human, or at
least that part of the subject in question which
exhibited paternal love on the one side and filial

love and devotion on the other, which raised all
these writers out of their slough of coarseness and
buffoonery into the region of healthy sentiment.
The Coventry series, which we have been examining, offers the best treatment of this incident;
which in itself, and in the barest relation of it,
is, if one can repress an outbreak of rebellious
indignation and disbelief, the most pathetic and
heart-breaking told in all the Hebrew Scriptures.
With an extract from this composition, which I
shall put into modern language, I shall close this
notice of English miracle-plays.

> "*Isaac.*   All ready father, even at your will,
>   And at your bidding I am you by
> With you to walk over dale and hill,
>   At your calling I am ready.
> To the father ever most comely
>   It behoveth the child ever obedient to be;
> I will obey, full heartily,
>   To everything that ye bid me.

> "*Abraham.*   Now, son, in thy neck this fagot thou take
>   And this fire bear in thy hand,
> For we must now sacrifice go make,
>   Even after the will of God's command.
> Take this burning brand,
>   My sweet child, and let us go;
> There may no man that liveth upon land
>   Have more sorrow than I have woe.

> "*Isa.*   Father, father, you go right still,
>   I pray now, father, speak unto me.
> *Abra.*   My good child, what is thy will?
>   Tell me thy heart, I pray to thee.
> *Isa.*   Father, fire and wood here is plenty,
>   But I can see no sacrifice;

What ye will offer fain would I see,
That it were done at best advice.

"*Abra.* God shall that ordain that is in heaven,
My sweet son, for this offering;
A dearer sacrifice may no man name
Than this shall be, my dear darling.
Isa. Let be, dear father, your sad weeping,
Your heavy looks aggrieve me sore.
Tell me, father, your great mourning,
And I shall seek some help therefor

"*Abra.* Alas! dear son, for needs must me
Even here thee kill, as God hath sent;
Thine own father thy death must be,—
Alas that ever this bow was bent!
With this fire bright thou must be brent;
An angel said to me right so;
Alas! my child, thou shalt be shent!
Thy careful father must be thy foe."

Isaac yields to what Abraham tells him is the Divine command, which yet he says makes his heart "cling and cleave as clay."

"*Isa.* Yet work God's will, father, I you pray,
And slay me here anon forthright;
And turn from me your face away,
My head when that you shall off smite.

"*Abra.* Alas! dear son, I may not choose,
I must needs here my sweet son kill;
My dear darling now must me lose,
Mine own heart's blood now shall I spill.
Yet this deed ere I fulfil,
My sweet son, thy mouth I kiss.
Isa. All ready, father, even at your will
I do your bidding, as reason is.

"*Abra.* Alas! dear son, here is no grace,
But need is dead now must thou be.

w

With this kerchief I hide thy face ;
   In the time that I slay thee
Thy lovely visage would I not see,
   Not for all this world's good."

It is true that the incident here represented is
in itself the most touching that can be conceived ;
but the author of the play has amplified and
worked out the very brief account in Genesis in
a dialogue which, rude although it be, is natural,
simple, and touching.   The conditions of the
action are monstrous and incredible, if we leave
out the supernatural element ; and the situation,
unrelieved by the ever-present consciousness that
the sacrifice is not to be made, would be too heart-
rending for contemplation.   But an unquestioning
belief in the supernatural, even to the literal acceptance of the figurative style and extravagant
phraseology of the Orient, was assumed by the
writers of miracle-plays.   The son's love, sub-
mission, and self-devotion, and the father's anguish, are expressed with tenderness and truth.
Abraham's silent woe as they walk together is
exhibited with really dramatic power in Isaac's
exclamation, "Father, father, ye go right still" ;
and Abraham's reply, "Tell me thy heart," and
his after exclamation, "Alas that ever this bow
was bent!" are full of pathos.   And when at last
the child tells the father to do God's will, yet begs
him to turn away his face when he strikes, and
Abraham kisses his son and hides from his own

eyes the boy's lovely visage, the interest is wrought up to such a pitch that supernatural intervention is indignantly demanded by the holiest instincts of that very nature which supernatural intervention has so pitilessly outraged.

It is worthy of remark, that the most interesting story related in the Hebrew Scriptures, and that best suited for dramatic representation, the story of Joseph, appears in neither of the English series of miracle-plays. There is, however, a very formidable French play upon the subject, one ancient copy of which exists, printed in Gothic letter. It is entitled *Moralité de la Vendition de Joseph.* *

The personages of this drama are forty-nine in number. The list includes, beside Jacob, Joseph and his eleven brothers, Pharaoh, Potiphar and his wife, and the officers or attendants of their households, among whom of course are Pharaoh's

---

* "Moralite de la vendition de Joseph filz du patriarche Jacob, comment ses freres esmeuz par envye, sassemblerent pour le faire mourir, mais par le vouloir de Dieu apres lavoir piteusement oultrage le devalerent en une cisterne, et enfin le vendirent a des marchans gallatides et ysmaelites, lequelz de rechief le vendirent a Putifard en egypte ou il fut au prez de Pharaon Roy dudict egipte. Lequel fut tempte de luxure par plusieurs jours de sa maistresse a laquelle il laissa son manteau et senfouit, dequoy il en fut en prison, mais peu de temps apres il interpreta les songes de Pharaon, Et a faict si bonne puision en egipte qil a este dict et appelle le saulveur de tout le pays, comme plus amplement est escript en la saincte bible au trenseptieme et douze aultres chapitres en suyvant du livre de genese. Et est ledict Joseph figure de la vendition de nostre saulueur Jhesucrist."

chief butler and chief baker, a certain King Cordelamor, unknown to the Hebrew story, with his
attendants, and also three allegorical personages,
Envy, Pity, and Justice, and finally God himself.
This play was produced about the end of the fifteenth or the beginning of the sixteenth century.
The only ancient copy known to exist was printed
about 1530. Ninety copies were printed in fac-simile, in 1835, at the expense of the Prince d'Essling.
The introduction of King Cordelamor indicates a
great advance by the author of this play in the
art of dramatic construction. The story as it is
told in Genesis gives no reason, either for the im-
prisonment of Pharaoh's chief butler and chief
baker, or for the hanging of the latter and the
pardon of the former,—the very incidents upon
which the whole story turns, and by which Joseph's elevation is brought about. This reason
the author of the French play furnishes; or, in
other words, he undertakes to supply a motive for
the action of his drama. King Cordelamor opens
the play by announcing, with an amusing confusion of geographical lines, that he has for a long
time desired to conquer and destroy Babylon,
which, with all the realm of Egypt, is justly his,
although it is held by the usurper Pharaoh, who
obtained it Cordelamor does not know exactly
how.

> "Tout le pays egipcien
> Selon raison doubt estre mien
> Pharaon la possession

> En tient, et le dit estre sien
> Par ie ne scay quel fol moyen
> Quil a par usurpation
> Car par droicte succession
> Je doy la domination."

A Centurion, in whose hearing he utters his complaints, says that he knows a way of accomplishing the desired end, which, although quite proper, is not strictly honorable.

> " Je scay ung moyen conuenable
> Mais il nest pas fort honnorable."

Cordelamor takes the idea at once, and says that Pharaoh must be poisoned.

> " Il le faudroit empoysonner
> Et luy donner en trahison
> En son manger quelque poyson
> Qui tout le cueur luy creueroit."

But, says a Decurion, " Who will give it to him? there is the difficulty." The ready Centurion says that the usurper's baker and butler must be bribed to do the deed.

> " Il fauldroit a son pennetier
> Et a son bouteillier parler
> Et a segret les apeller
> Promettre les mons et les vaulx
> Or et argent chiens et oyseaulx
> Mais quilz vous voulsissent promettre
> A estre traistres a leur maistre
> Et luy bailler a son breuaige
> En son pain ou en son potaige
> Quelque grant poyson mortifere."

Cordelamor sends the Decurion into Egypt to

accomplish this purpose, and he goes, saying that
his master shall hear from him in two days. And
here the rudeness of the stage, and the ease with
which the imagination of the audience enabled
the dramatist to defy the unities of time and place,
appear. The previous dialogue has been spoken
upon the staging or pageant. Now the stage direction is, " Pausa. Reced. et dicat," — " A pause.
He comes down and says." — What he says is that
he sees one of Pharaoh's people near yonder door.
The person is the chief baker ; who, being tempted, consents. After the conference, another pause
and the ascent of the Decurion are directed.
" Pausa. Decurion ascend." The Decurion re-
ports his success, and Cordelamor promises the
Decurion and the Centurion that, if he ever possess Egypt, they shall be his best rewarded friends
and counsellors. Then a little pause, " Pausa par-
va," is directed, and the Chief Baker soliloquizes,
saying that he must get the Chief Butler into the
plot. Pharaoh then appears and gives his "Mais-
tre d'hotel" orders for a great feast to all his lords
and chivalry. Then Jacob and his sons appear.
Jacob has a long speech, beginning,

> "O haulte deite
> Parfaicte auctorite
> Plaine de dignite
> Humblement je rends grace
> A vostre majeste
> Qui mon antiquite
> Par grand felicite
> Comforte en ceste place."

In this speech the patriarch, with a knowledge of geography rivalling that of King Cordelamor, recounts the incidents of the dream and the angels' ladder, which took place as he was on his way to "the city of Mesopotamia." In this scene the jealousy of Joseph and Benjamin on the part of their ten brothers is developed, and Jacob gives the former the coat of many colors, — "la robe polimite." Another pause is directed, with the descent of all the sons to the ground, except Joseph and Benjamin, who are directed to remain. Then, apparently upon another scaffold, Pity and Justice have a long conference with God, in which God, who acts through the play as a sort of chorus, announces that he intends that Joseph's experience and fate shall typify that of Jesus Christ. Another pause; and Judah soliloquizes his envy of Joseph on account of "la belle robe polimite."

> "Une robe que le grant diable
> y ait sa part est bien donne."

Again a pause; and God commands dreams to visit Joseph.

> "Des songes pour clariffier
> Mes sainctes predications
> Grandes sermociations."

After another pause, Joseph tells his dream. The consequences are of course those told in the original story. Judah exclaims:

> "Quoy, faire Roy de ce garson
> Le grant dyable denfer memport

> Se mieulx nameroys estre mort
> Quant a ma part que ie lendure."

Joseph and his brothers go home by remounting the scaffold. "Les filz montent es eschaffaulx et ioseph remonte." Envy soon afterward appears, and thus describes herself as a mingling of covetousness, malice, and slander, in a passage of no little delicacy and spirit: —

> " La haine ie croistray bien souef
> Car ie scay bien tourner la clef
> De tout vetil
> Dequoy il en viendra meschef
> Car de tous maulx ie suis le chef
> Par mon babil.
>   Jen ay fait mourir plus de mil
> Et mettre plusieurs en exil
> Quant ie me fume.
> Il nest homme tant soit subtil
> Qui osast leuer le sourcil
> cest ma coustume.
>   Il nest homme que ie ne plume
> Amours damys ie boy et hume
> comme brouet.
> Legiere suys comme une pleume
> Et pesant comme une enclume
> Eu vng paquet.
>   Quant il deslye mon caquet
> Ma langue va comme vng traquet
> Sans nul arrest.
> Plustost elle tourne que vng rouet
> Plus souple que nest vng fouet
> Quant il me plaist."

Envy approaches Joseph's brethren, and in a long interview, and with much subtlety, incites them to Joseph's destruction, and they all, except Reuben, agree to slay him. Jacob sends his son with "la belle robe polimite" to seek his brethren. The student of language will observe in these lines evidence of the great antiquity of this composition:—

> "Touteffois ioseph il te fault
> Aller en sichen bas ou hault
> Scavoir ou ilz sont, car ie craing
> Quil ne leur soit venu besoing
> Vaten veoir comme tout se porte."

So also, in the following speeches upon Joseph's appearance among his brethren, like indications:—

> " *Juda*   Ho bon guet, voicy le songeart
> Que tout lemond se evertue
> Davoir bon cueur
>
> " *Ruben*   Jay graut regart
> Ad ce fait
>
> " *Juda*   Il fault quon le tue
> Remyde nya
>
> " *Ruben*   Sang a me mue
> Car le cas est fort inhumain
> Humanite me redargue
>
> " *Juda*   Chya chya cest a demain
> A luy premier mettray le main
> Nostre conclusion est telle."

Joseph is enthroned in mockery; his scoffing brethren bow down to him; he is buffeted by each in turn, and, having been bound to a column, scourged. The Ishmaelites, who are accompanied by their Prince, now enter, not upon the scaffold,

16

but the ground; for they come with beasts laden with merchandise. The stage directions are very particular: "Nota que icy ilz ont des cheuaulx et bestes chargez de marchandises. Ilz charge leur cheuaulx." Afterward, when the Prince is about to appear, "Icy fault que le prince soyt prest"; and again, when the bargain for Joseph is struck, "Il fault icy vingt deniers." Pharaoh gives his feast; but the dishes are hardly placed upon the table when the King's physician detects poison in some of them. The Chief Baker is accused, and he accuses the Chief Butler; and both are put under guard, and afterward thrown into prison. The Ishmaelites, arriving in Egypt, sell Joseph to Potiphar for thirty pieces of silver. Here Joseph's boyhood is brought to a close by a stage direction: "¶ La fin du petit ioseph." Thus far the part was doubtless played by a lad; afterward by a man, when the direction is given, "¶ Joseph le grant commence." Potiphar soon expresses to Joseph before his wife his entire confidence in him, and then goes on a short journey. Here a pause is directed, because, it is said, Joseph should absent himself from the barrier, i. e. the front of the staging, — "Pausa, car ioseph se doibt absenter de la barriere," — the occasion being a confession in soliloquy, by Mrs. Potiphar, how much she is enamored of her husband's steward. Hereafter the play follows the story with great exactness, but also with great expansion. King

Cordelamor, having fulfilled his function, on learning the miscarriage of his plot, disappears from the scene. Joseph is tempted by his mistress in the bluntest possible language, and with much repetition, and in reply preaches to her in the most edifying manner. When he is taken to prison, the sergeant who has him in charge tells the jailer of what he is accused, upon which the latter slanderously remarks:

> "Sil est vray ce seroit mal fait
> Mais ainsi que ie puis comprendre
> Femmes peuent donne a entendre
> Des faulcetez aulcuneffoys."

The baker is hanged before the eyes of the audience upon a gallows, "en forme de croix potencer," and afterward cut down. Joseph's triumph and the gathering in of the corn seem to have been represented with great care for what may be called scenic effect, if we may judge by the particularity of the stage directions; and much help to the imagination of the audience was plainly looked for from the separation of the actors by the staging. The directions, "Estant a terre dit," and "Il remont en hault," are of very frequent occurrence. The play follows the events of Joseph's life down to the burial of Jacob. Its length is enormous. It contains nearly eight thousand lines; twice as many as *Hamlet.*

An examination of this French *moralité,* so called, is not strictly in place in an account of the

English stage, upon which it was not presented
either in translation or by imitation.   But the nature of its subject connected it with the miracle-
plays, from which we are about to part; and the
peculiarity of its construction, its interesting and
novel admixture of character, the particularity of
its stage directions, and the evident splendor and
faithfulness to reality with which it was performed, connect it also with that period of our
drama to the consideration of which we are about
to pass, and have induced me to bring it — and it
is here brought for the first time, I believe — to
the attention of the English reader.

II.

Rude, gross, and childish as the miracle-plays
were, they yet contained the germ of our drama;
and from them its development, slow but never
checked, can be traced up to the sudden and
splendid maturity of the Elizabethan era.   The
Coventry series, which we have just been examining, differs from the Towneley and the Chester
series by the introduction of allegorical characters
into some of the plays.   In the earlier miracle-
plays the personages all belonged to the religious
history the course of which they were written
to teach; and the author confined his work to
the putting of Scriptural story or saintly legend

into the form of dialogue and soliloquy. But as
time wore on, virtues, vices, and even modes of
mental action, were impersonated, and mingled
upon the pageant or the scaffold with patriarchs,
apostles, and saints. Thus the eighth of the Coventry series, *The Barrenness of Anna*, is opened
with a kind of prologue or introductory chorus
by Contemplation, a character which reappears
in the series; and in *The Salutation and Conception*, the Virtues, collectively embodied, with
Truth, Pity, and Justice, perform functions like
those of the Greek chorus. At last, in *The
Slaughter of the Innocents*, Death (*Mors*) takes
part in the action; and in some of the other
plays, impersonal Detractors, Accusers, and Con-
solers also appear. In the three Digby miracle-
plays * there is one founded upon the life of Mary
Magdalen, which is interesting in this respect.
And in the first of the set, which represents the
conversion of St. Paul, it is noteworthy that, of
two devils who are among the characters, one is
named Belial and the other Mercury! The first
is instructed to enter thus: "Here to enter a
Dyvel with thunder and fyre, and to avaunce hym
selfe, saying as folowyth; and his spech spoken, to
syt downe in a chayre." While he is thus making
himself comfortably at home in a devilish way,

---

* So called because they are preserved among the Digby
MSS. in the Bodleian Library. See Collier's *Annals of the
Stage*, &c., Vol. II. p. 230.

and complaining of the lack of news, his attendant or messenger comes in, according to this direction: "Here shall entere a nother devyll, called
Mercury, with a fyering, coming in hast, cryeing
and rorying." After a consultation as to the
bad way their friend Saul appears to be in, to
wit, peril of salvation body and soul, they both
"vanyshe away with a fyrye flame and a tempest." * The play on the *Life of Mary Magdalen*,
rather a late miracle-play, was intended to be a
spectacle of unusual attraction. It required four
pageants or scaffolds. Tiberius, Herod, Pilate,
and the Devil, personages of apparently equal
dramatic dignity, had each his own station before
the audience, and the entrance of the last is thus
directed: "Here shal entyr the prynce of dev-
ylls in a stage, and hell onder neth that stage."
Indeed, the representation of hell, or of hell-
mouth, into which demons and their victims were
sent, was ·a standing, and, it would seem, a much
prized, scenic effect in the performance of the
miracle-plays. In the account-books of the expenses of the Coventry plays there are many
charges for "the repayring of hel-mought." † To
return to the play of *Mary Magdalen*, — a ship appears between the scaffolds ; the mariners spy the
castle of Mary, which the Devil and the Seven
Deadly Sins besiege and capture. Lechery ad-

---

* Collier, as above.
† Sharpe's *Dissertation on the Coventry Mysteries.*

dresses the heroine in a speech, the following extract from which will give a notion of the style of the composition :—

> "Hayl, lady, most lawdabyll of alyauns!
> Heyl, orient as the sonne in his reflexite!
> Much pepul be comfortyd be your benygnant affyauns;
> Brighter than the bornyd is your bemys of bewte:
> Most debonarius with your aungelly velycyte."

The appearance of the Seven Deadly Sins and of the Kings of the World, the Flesh, and the Devil in this play, as ten distinct characters, is not only very curious, but is a noteworthy step toward the next stage of our drama, which now took the allegorical form of the Moral-Play. Of character and action, in a true dramatic sense, the miracle-plays, with one or two exceptions to be noticed hereafter, had really none. The personages came upon the stage and described themselves, giving a dry catalogue of their qualities, conditions, and relations, and then went formally through the speech and action prescribed for them in Scripture or legend. But when allegorical personages began to multiply, as they did, in the miracle-plays, they began also to interfere with and modify this slavish adherence to Scripture story and Church tradition; until finally these personages, who, it will be seen upon a moment's reflection, represent an extraneous human element, and are in fact a clumsy embodiment alternately of the mental conditions of the other characters and of the audience, obtained possession of the stage, and completely expelled the angels, saints, and patriarchs, in aid of whose waning power to interest the people they had been created.

In a moral-play pure and simple, the personages are all embodiments of abstract ideas, and the motive of the play is the enforcement of moral truth as a guide of human conduct. The abstract ideas may be virtues, as Justice, Mercy, Compassion; or vices, as Avarice, Malice, Falsehood; or a state, condition, or mode of life, as Youth, Old Age, Poverty, Abominable Living; or an embodiment of the human race, as in the character Every Man in the moral-play of that name; or of a part of it, as in the play of *Lusty Juventus;* or of the end of all men, for in these compositions Death itself is not unfrequently embodied. But there were two permanent, and, so to speak, stock characters, which were as essential to a moral-play as Harlequin and Columbine to an old pantomime. These were the Devil and the Vice; the former being an inheritance from the miracle-plays, but the latter a new creation. Exactly why and how this personage came into being with the moral-play, we do not know; but may it not have been with the purpose of having ever present an embodied antithesis to the motive of the play, — morality? That the name was derived from the nature of the character would seem manifest without a word, were it not that other and fantastic derivations have been suggested.* The Devil was represented as the hideous monster evolved by the morbid religious imagination of the dark ages, having horns, at least one hoof, a tail, a shaggy body, and a visage both frightful and ridiculous. The Vice wore generally, if not always, the costume of the domestic fool or jester of the period, which is now worn by the clown of the circus. He was at first called the Vice; but as the Vice became a distinct line of character, as much as walking gentleman on our stage, or *père noble* on the French, his name and his functions were afterward those of Infidelity, Hypocrisy, Desire, and so forth. Sometimes the part of a gallant or a bully was written for the Vice, and was named accordingly; and sometimes he was called Iniquity. When he bore this name, he would seem to have been not a mere buffoon or clown, making merriment with gibes and antics, but a sententious person with all his fun; for Shakespeare makes the following descriptive mention of this kind of Vice:

> "Thus, like the *formal* Vice, Iniquity,
> I moralize two meanings in one word."
> *Richard the Third*, Act III. Sc. 1.

But the Vice generally performed the mingled functions of scamp, braggart, and practical joker.

* The reader who cares to see them may find them stated and confuted in Douce's *Illustrations of Shakespeare*, Vol. I. p. 466.

There was a conventional make-up for his face. Barnaby Rich, in his *Adventures of Brusanus*, published 1592, says that a certain personage had " his beard cut peecke a devant, turnde uppe a little, like the Vice of a playe." He was armed with a dagger or sword of lath, with which he beat the Devil, — that personage having his revenge, almost invariably, at the end of the play, by taking his tormentor upon his back and running off with him into "hell-mought." There has been a notable and mysterious moral significance discovered in this beating of the Devil by the Vice, of the master by the servant. I cannot see it. It seems plainly that the object of the performance was merely to make coarse fun for coarse people ; the contrivers, to be sure, not lacking wit so utterly as to fail to make both the temporary annoyance and the final retribution fall upon the supremely bad personages.

In one of the Clown's songs in *Twelfth Night*, Shakespeare describes in a few words the function of the Vice, his quickness of movement, his weapon, and his tormenting of the Devil.

> " I am gone, sir,
>   And anon, sir,
>   I 'll be with you again,
>   In a trice,
>   Like to the old Vice,
>   Your need to sustain ;
>
> " Who with dagger of lath
>   In his rage and his wrath
>   Cries, Aha ! to the Devil."

Moral-plays were at first performed upon the pageants or scaffolds from which they were driving the miracle-plays. But at last it was thought that people might better go to the play than have the play go to them ; and it was found that barns and great halls were more convenient for both actors and audience than movable scaffolds. Yet later, people discovered that best of all available places were inn-yards, where windows and galleries and verandas commanded a view of a court round which the house was built. Sometimes moral-plays were written to be played in the interval between a feast or dinner and a banquet ; the banquet having corresponded to what we call the dessert, and having been usually served in another room. Hence the name of "Interlude," which was frequently given to these plays. Yet the name "Interlude" came to be almost confined to a kind of play shorter than a moral-play, and without allegorical characters or significance, and so better suited to the occasion for which it was intended. John Heywood was the master of this kind of play-writing, if, indeed, he were not its inventor ; but his proper place is at a later period of our little history.

The oldest English moral-play yet discovered exists in manuscript, and is entitled *The Castle of Perseverance*.* It was written about 1450. The

* Once in possession of Dr. Cox Macro ; it passed into the collection of Mr. Hudson Gurney, who submitted it to Mr. Collier. See that gentleman's *Annals of the Stage*, &c., Vol. II. p. 278.

principal character is Humanum Genus, an embodiment of mankind, whose moral enemies, the
World, the Flesh, and the Devil (Mundus, Caro,
and Belial), open the play by a conference, in
which they boast of their powers.* Mankind (Humanum Genus) then appears, and announces that
he has just come into the world naked, and immediately a good and a bad angel present themselves,
and assert their claims to his confidence. He
gives himself up to the latter, who through the
agency of the World places him in the hands of
Voluptuousness and Folly (Voluptas and Stulti-
tia ; but let it suffice to say that all the charac-

---

* This triad was a great favorite with the authors of moral-
plays. There is extant a unique copy of a French moral-play
with the following title : "Moralite nouvelle, de Mundus : Caro :
Demonia. En laquelle verrez les durs assautz et tentations quilz
font au Chevalier Chrestien : Et comme par conseil de son bon
esprit, avec la grace de Dieu, les vaincra, et a la fin aura le Roy-
aume de paradis. Et est a cinq personnages. Cest a savoir. Le
chavalier chrestien, Lesprit, La chair, Le monde, et le Dyable."
Notwithstanding the assaults mentioned in its title, this moral-
play has none of the life and action of the English play upon
the same subject. It is a dull talk between the five personages, in which Lesprit rarely speaks without quoting Saint Paul
with great particularity. The French miracle-plays and moral-
plays are always much more "talky" than ours. So early appeared that difference between the dramatic taste of the two
peoples, — the one inclining to action, the other to speech. The
single existing ancient copy of this moral-play (which is accompanied by a farce, *Les deux savetiers*) is printed in Gothic letter,
and evidently came from the press in the early part of the sixteenth century. Like others of the printed plays of that period,
it is in a very singular form, the page being in height about four

ters have Latin names). Backbiter then makes him acquainted with Avarice and the other deadly sins, of whom Luxury — in these plays always a woman — becomes his leman. The good angel sends Confession to him, who is told that he is come too soon, he having then more agreeable matters in hand than the confessing of sin. But at last, by the help of Penitence, Mankind is reclaimed, and got off into the strong Castle of Perseverance, in company with the Seven Cardinal Virtues. Belial and the Deadly Sins lay siege to the castle; the leader having first berated and beaten his forces for having allowed his prey to escape him.* Belial and the Sins are defeated,

---

times its width. This form was adopted as most convenient for the play-lovers of that day to carry to the theatre. Ninety facsimile copies of this singular and interesting play-book, and also of *La Vendition de Joseph* and *Les Blasphemateurs de Dieu*, which were originally printed in the same form, at about the same time, and of each of which but a single ancient copy exists, were printed at the expense of the Prince d'Essling.

* Belial thus incites his followers to the assault: —

> "I here trumpys trebelen all of tene:
> The wery world walkyth to werre . . . .
> Sprede my penon upon a prene
> And stryke we for the now undyr sterre.
> Schapyth now your sheldys shene
> Yone skallyd skouts for to skerre . . . .
> Buske ye now, boys, belyve,
> For ever I stond in mekyl stryve
> Whyl Mankind is clene lyve."

Mr. Collier, from whom I copy them, justly remarks upon a certain degree of life and spirit in these rude lines.

chiefly by the aid of Charity and Patience, who
pelt them with roses from the battlements. But
Mankind begins to grow old; and Avarice under-
mines the castle, and persuades him to leave it.
Garcio (a boy) claims all the goods which Mankind
has gathered with the aid of Avarice, when Death
and the Soul appear; and the latter calls on Pity
for help. But the bad angel takes the hero on
his back and sets off with him hellward. The
scene changes to heaven, where Pity, Peace, Justice, and Truth plead for him with God, and we
are left to infer that Man is saved. God speaks
the moralizing epilogue. A rude drawing on the
last leaf of the manuscript shows the Castle with
a bed beneath it for Humanum Genus, and five
scaffolds for God, Belial, the World, the Flesh,
and Avarice.

Mr. Collier is of opinion that so carefully constructed and varied an allegory "must have had
predecessors in the same kind"; but this supposition seems to me by no means necessary.
An allegorical purpose once formed, the miracle-plays furnished all the necessary precedents
for the development of the idea. In another
play in the same collection, called *Mind, Will,
and Understanding*, Anima, the soul, also appears, and, having been debauched by the three
personages who give the play its name, she "ap-
perythe in most horribul wyse, fowlere than a
fend," and gives birth to six of the deadly sins

according to this direction: "Here rennyt out from undyr the horrybull mantyll of the Soule six small boys in the lyknes of devyllys, and so retorne ageyn." Conscious of her degradation, she goes out with her three seducers, and it is directed that "in the going the Soule syngyth in the most lamentabull wyse, with drawte notes, as yt ys songyn in the passyon wyke." In the end, Mind, Will, and Understanding are converted from their evil ways, to the great joy of Anima.

John Skelton, poet laureate to Henry VII. and his son, wrote two moral plays, *The Necromancer* and *Magnificence*. A copy of the latter still exists; and one of the former was seen and described by Collins, although it has since been lost. The characters are a Necromancer, the Devil, a Notary, Simony, and Avarice; and the action is merely the trial of the last two before the Devil. The Necromancer calls up the Devil and opens the court. The prisoners are found guilty, and are sent straightway to hell. The Devil abuses the Conjurer for rousing him too early; but in the end they have a dance together in hell, at the end of which Sathanas trips up the Conjurer and disappears in flame and smoke. This play, which was played before King Henry VII. at Woodstock on Palm Sunday, was printed in 1504. When *Magnificence* was produced we do not know, as its title-page is without date; but Skelton mentions it in a poem printed in 1523.

Its purpose is to show the vanity of Magnificence. The hero, Magnificence, eaten out of house and home by a rabble of friends called Fancy *alias* Largess, Counterfeit-countenance, Crafty-conveyance, Cloked-collusion, Courtly-abusion, and Folly, falls into the hands of Adversity and Poverty; and finally is taken possession of by Despair and Mischief, who persuade him to commit suicide, which he is about to do, when Good-hope stays his hand, and Redress, Circumspection, and Perseverance sober him down to a humble frame of mind. The piece is intolerably long, and much of it is written in that wearisome verse called Skeltonic.* To relieve it, some fun is introduced, which is of the coarsest kind, but which was probably more to the taste of all the poet's audience, high and low, than his heavy moralizing.†

* Of which the following passage is an example : —

"For counterfet countenaunce knowen am I:
 This worlde is full of my foly.
 I set not by hym a fly
 That cannot counterfet a lye,
 Swere and stare and byde thereby,
 And countenaunce it clenly,
 And defende it manerly.
 A knave will counterfet now a knyght,
 A lurdayne lyke a lorde to fyght,
 A mynstrell lyke a man of myght,
 A tappyster lyke a lady bryght.
 Thus make I them wyth thryft to fyght;
 Thus at the last I brynge hym ryght
 To tyburne, where they hange on hyght."

† As, for instance, the following passage quoted by Mr. Collier,

Of pure moral-plays the reader has probably had quite enough ; but two others may well be noticed, on account of traits peculiar to them. In one, called *The Longer thou Livest the more Foole thou art*, the chief character is Moros, a mischievous fool, who enters upon this direction : " Here entreth Moros, counterfaiting a vaine gesture and a foolish countenance, synging the foote of many songes, as fools were wont." This brings to mind Shakespeare's fools and clowns, who are always singing the foot of many songs ; and we see that the making them do so was no device of his, but a mere faithful copying of the living models before him ; though the lyric sweetness and the wit and the wisdom which he puts into their mouths were in most instances, we may be sure, his own. The other moral-play in question, *The Marriage of Wit and Science*,* is remarkable, not only for its very elaborate and ingenious, though equally dull

---

in which Folly wins a wager that he will laugh Crafty-conveyance out of his coat.

"[*Here foly maketh semblaunt to take a lowse from crafty conveyaunce shoulder.*]
Fancy. What hast thou found there ?
Foly. By god, a lowse.
Crafty-convey. By cockes harte, I trow thou lyste.
Foly. By the masse, a spanyshe moght with a gray lyste.
Fancy. Ha, ha, ha, ha, ha, ha !
　　　　　　[*Here crafty convaunce putteth of his gowne.*
Foly. Put on thy gowne agayne, for now thou hast lost.
Fancy. Lo, John a bonam, where is thy brayne ? "

* Reprinted by the Shakespeare Society.

and wearisome allegory, but for the fact that it is
regularly divided into acts and scenes, which is
not the case with even many of the early comedies
and tragedies by which the miracle-plays were
succeeded. One of the very latest of the moral-
plays was *The Three Lords and Three Ladies of
London,* which was written after 1588, and printed
in 1590. But, as its title would indicate, this is in
reality a kind of comedy ; and it is also remarkable as being written for the most part in blank-
verse.

III.

As allegory had crept into the miracle-plays,
and, by introducing the impersonation of abstract
qualities, had gradually worked changes in their
structure and their purpose which finally produced the moral-play, so personages intended as
satires upon classes and individuals, and as representations of the manners and customs of the
day, year after year took more and more the place
of the cold and stiff abstractions which filled the
stage in the pure moral-play, until at last Comedy,
or the ideal representation of human life, appeared
in English drama. Thus in *Tom Tyler and his
Wife,* which, according to Ritson, was published
in 1578, and which contains internal evidence that
it was written about eight years before that date,
the personages are Tom Tyler, his good woman,

who is a gray mare of the most formidable kind,
Tom Tailor, his friend, Desire, Strife, Sturdy,
Tipple, Patience, and the Vice. In *The Conflict
of Conscience*, written at about the same date,
among Conscience, Hypocrisy, Tyranny, Avarice,
Sensual-suggestion, and the like, appear four historical personages, Francis Spiera, an Italian lawyer, who is called Philologus, his two sons, and
Cardinal Eusebius. Mr. Collier also mentions a
political moral-play, written about 1565, called *Albion Knight*, in which the hero, a knight named
Albion, is a personification of England, and the
motive of which is satire upon the oppression of
the commons by the nobles. But before this
date, and probably in the reign of Edward VI.,
Bishop Bale had written his *Kynge Johan*, a play
the purpose of which was to further the Reformation, and which partook of the characters of a
moral-play and a dramatic chronicle-history.* Indeed, neither the reformers nor their opponents
were slow to take advantage of the stage as a
means of indoctrinating the people with their peculiar views ; and as the government passed alternately into the hands of Papists and Protestants,
plays were suppressed, or dramatic performances
interdicted altogether, as the good of the ecclesiastical party in power seemed to require.† In the

* See the Introduction to *King John*, Vol. VI. p. 10 of the
author's edition of Shakespeare's Works.

† The curious reader will find in Hawkins's *Origin of the Eng-*

very first year of Queen Mary's reign, 1553, a po-
litico-religious moral-play, called *Respublica*, was
produced, the purpose of which was to check the
Reformation. The kingdom of England is impersonated as Respublica; and, by the author's own
admission, Queen Mary herself figures as Nemesis,
the goddess of redress and correction.*

John Heywood, whose interludes have been
already mentioned, produced his first play before
the year 1521; yet, in turning our eyes back two
generations to glance at his compositions, we may
obtain perhaps a more correct view of the manner
in which the English drama was developed, than
if we had examined them in the order of time.
Heywood was attached to the court of Henry VIII.
as a singer and player upon the virginals. His
interludes were short pieces, about the length of
one act of a modern comedy. Humorous in their

---

lish Drama a reprint of *Lusty Juventus*, which was written in the
reign of Edward VI., and which is sufficiently thoroughgoing in
its denunciation of the corruptions of the Church of Rome to
satisfy the straitest Puritan. The personages quote Scripture,
and in the midst of their speeches give chapter and verse with a
merciless particularity which rivals that of Mause Headrigg.
One of them is actually named God's Merciful Promises. May
not the extraordinary names sometimes given by the Puritans to
their children, rising from Thankful and Submit to Fight-the-
good-fight-of-faith and Through-much-tribulation-thou-shalt-en-
ter-into-the-kingdom-of-Heaven (called "for short" Trib), have
been at first taken from favorite characters in moral-plays, written in support of the Reformation?

* Described in Collier's edition of Shakespeare's Works, 1843,
Vol. I. p. xviii.

motive, and dependent for all their interest upon extravagant burlesque of every-day life, upon the broadest jokes and the coarsest satire, they were indeed but a kind of farce. That which is regarded as Heywood's earliest extant production is entitled *A Mery Play betwene the Pardoner and the Frere, the Curate, and Neybour Pratte.* The Pardoner and the Friar have got leave of the Curate to use his church, the former to show his relics, the latter to preach ; both having the same end in view, — money. They quarrel as to who shall have precedence, and at last fight. The Curate, brought in by this row between his clerical brethren, attempts to separate and pacify them ; but failing to accomplish this single-handed, he calls Neighbor Pratt to his aid. In vain, however ; for the Pardoner and the Friar, like man and wife interrupted in a quarrel, unite their forces and beat the interlopers soundly. After which they depart, and the play ends. In *The Four P's,* another of Heywood's interludes, the personages are the Palmer, the Pardoner, the Poticary, and the Pedler. In this play there is little action ; and the four worthies, after gibing at each other's professions for a while, set out to see which can tell the biggest lie. After much elaborate and ingenious falsehood, the Palmer beats by the simple assertion that he never saw a woman out of patience in his life ; at which his opponents "come down" without another word. The satire in these plays is found in the inconsistency between the characters of the personages and their professions, and particularly in the absurd and ridiculous pretensions of the clergymen as to their priestly functions and the nature of their relics. In *The Pardoner and the Friar*, the Pardoner produces "the great too of the holy trynyte," and

> " of our Ladye a relyke full good,
> Her bongrace, which she ware with her French hode
> Whan she wente oute al wayes for sonne bornynge ";

also, " Of all helowes the blessed jaw-bone"; and in *The Four P's*, there is " a buttocke-bone of Pentecoste." And yet Heywood was a stanch Romanist.

Another of Heywood's interludes, *Johan, Tyb, and Sir Jhan*, is equally severe upon the clergy of his day. Johan pretends to be master of his own house, and, in Tyb's absence, threatens to beat her when she comes home. She returns and overhears him ; calls him to account, and he backs out. She brings home a pie and orders Johan to go and invite Sir Jhan, the priest, to eat it in their company. He believes all is not right between the priest and Tyb, but he is obliged to obey. The priest comes, and Johan is sent out to get water. While he is gone, it becomes plain that Sir Jhan and Tyb understand each other. He returns without water, the pail having leaked ; and while he is mending it with wax, the precious pair eat up the pie in spite of his complaints. At last he dashes down the pail in a rage, when they fall upon him and beat him till the blood runs, and go out together. He assumes the airs of a victor, until it occurs to him that they have gone "to make hym a cokwolde," which catastrophe he rushes out to prevent, and the curtain falls.

There are certain passages in Heywood's plays, which, considering the period at which he wrote, are remarkable for genuine humor and descriptive power, as well as for spirited and lively versification ; * and coarse and indecent as his produc-

* See the following description of an alleged visit to hell by the Pardoner, in *The Four P's :* —

> "Thys devyll and I walket arme in arme,
> So farre, tyll he had brought me thyther,
> Where all the devylls of hell togyther
> Stode in a ray, in suche apparell
> As for that day there metely fell.
> Theyr hornes well gylt, theyr clowes full clene,
> Theyr taylles well kempt, and as I wene,
> With sothery butter theyr bodyes anoynted ;
> I never sawe devylls so well appoynted.
> The mayster devyll sat in his jacket,
> And all the soules were playinge at racket.
> None other rackettes they hadde in hande,
> Save every soule a good fyre brand ;
> Wherewith they played so pretely,
> That Lucyfer laughed merely ;
> And all the resedew of the feinds,
> Did laugh thereat ful wel like freends.
> But of my frende I sawe no whyt,
> Nor durst not axe for her as yet.
> Anone all this rout was brought in silens,
> And I by an usher brougt in presens

tions must be pronounced, they exhibit more real
dramatic power than appears in those of any other
playwright of the first half of the sixteenth century.

Heywood founded no school, seems to have had
no imitators: there is no line of succession between him and the man who must be regarded
as the first writer of genuine English comedy.
We have seen that plays in which characters
drawn from real life mingled with the allegorical
personages proper to moral-plays were written as
late as 1570. Such were *Tom Tyler and his Wife*
and *The Conflict of Conscience*, mentioned above.

> Of Lucyfer: the lowe, as wel I could,
> I knelyd, whiche he so well alowde,   .
> That thus he beckte, and by saynt Antony
> He smyled on me well favouredly,
> Bendynge his browes as brode as barne durres,
> Shakynge hys eares as ruged as burres;
> Rolynge his eyes as rounde as two bushels;
> Flastynge the fyre out of his nosetryls;
> Gnashinge hys teeth so vaynglorously,
> That me thought tyme to fall to flatery,
> Wherewith I tolde, as I shall tell.   .
> O plesant pycture!   O prince of hell!
> Feutred in fashyon abominable,
> And syns that is inestimable
> For me to prayse, the worthyly,
> I leve of prayse, as unworthy
> To geve the prays, besechynge the
> To heare my sewte, and then to be
> So good to graunt the thynge I crave."

But as early as the year 1551, Nicolas Udall, who became Master of Eton and afterward of Westminster, had written a play divided into acts and scenes, with a gradually developed action tending to a climax, and the characters of which were all ideal representatives of actual life ; a play which was, in short, a comedy. The play is named, after its hero, *Ralph Roister Doister.* The scene is laid in London ; and Ralph, who is a conceited, rattle-pated young fellow about town, and amorous withal, fancies himself in love with Dame Custance, a gay young widow with " a tocher," as he thinks, of a thousand pounds and more. But upon this point Matthew Merrygreek,* his poor kinsman and attendant, a shrewd, mischievous, timeserving fellow, remarks to him, that

> " An hundred pounde of marriage-money doubtlesse,
> Is ever thirtie pounde sterlyng, or somewhat less;
> So that her thousande pounde, yf she be thriftie
> Is much neere about two hundred and fiftie.
> Howbeit, wowers and widowes are never poore."

Which shows that our ways, in this respect at least, have not changed much from those of our forefathers three hundred years ago. When the play opens, Custance is betrothed to Garvin Goodluck, a merchant who is then at sea. But Merrygreek crams his master with eagerly swallowed

---

* " Merry-Greek " was slang, three hundred years ago, for what we now call a jolly fellow. " Then she 's a merry Greek indeed." *Troilus and Cressida*, Act I. Sc. 2.

flattery, and puts him in heart by telling him
that a man of his person and spirit can win any
woman. Ralph encounters three of Custance's
handmaids, old and young; and by flattering
words and caresses tries to bring them over to
his side. He leaves a letter with one of them for
Custance, which is delivered, but not immediately opened. The next day Dobinet Doughty,
the merchant's servant, brings a ring and token
from Master Goodluck to Dame Custance; but
Madge, having got a scolding for her pains in delivering Ralph's letter, refuses to carry the ring
and token. Other servants entering, Dobinet introduces himself as a messenger from the Dame's
betrothed husband; and they, especially one Ti-
bet Talkapace, being delighted at the idea of a
wedding, and mistaking the man who is thus to
bless the household, fall out as to who is to deliver .
Ralph's presents. But Tib triumphs by snatch-
ing the souvenirs and running out with them to
her mistress. A reproof to Tib, in her turn, ends
the second act. The third opens with a visit by
Merrygreek to Dame Custance, that he may find
out if the ring and token have worked well for
his master's interest. But he only learns from
Dame Custance that she is fast betrothed to Goodluck; that she has not even opened Ralph's letter,
but knows that it must be from him, —

"For no man there is but a very dolte and lout
  That to wowe a widowe would so go about."

She adds, that Ralph shall never have her for his wife while he lives. On receiving this news, Ralph declares that he shall then and there incontinently die; when Merrygreek takes him at his word, pretends to think that he is really dying, and calls in a priest and four assistants to sing a mock requiem. Ralph, however, like most disappointed lovers, concludes to live; and Merrygreek advises him to serenade Custance and boldly ask her hand. So done; but Custance snubs him, and produces his yet unread letter; which Merrygreek reads to the assembled company, with such defiance of the punctuation that the sense is perverted, and all are moved to mirth, except Ralph, who in wrath disowns the composition. Dame Custance retires; and Merrygreek, again flattering his master, advises him to refrain himself awhile from his lady-love, and that then she will seek him; for as to women,

"When ye will, they will not; will not ye, then will they."

Ralph threatens vengeance upon the scrivener who copied his letter; but when the penman reads it with the proper pauses, he finds out who is the real culprit; and thus the third act ends.

The fourth opens with the entrance of another messenger from Goodluck to Dame Custance. While he is talking to the lady, Ralph enters, ostentatiously giving orders about making ready his armor, takes great airs, calls Custance his spouse, and tells the messenger to tell his master

that "his betters be in place now." The angered
Dame summons maid and man, and turns Ralph
and Merrygreek out of doors; but the latter soon
slips back and tells her that his only purpose is to
make sport of Ralph, who is about returning
armed "to pitch a field" with his female foes.
Roister Doister soon enters, armed with pot, pan,
and popgun, and accompanied by three or four
assistants. But the comely Dame, who seems to
be a tall woman of her hands, stands her ground,
and, aided by her maids, "pitches into" the enemy,
and with mop and besom puts him to ignominious
flight; in which squabble the knave Merrygreek,
pretending to fight for his rich kinsman, manages
to belabor him soundly. At the beginning of the
fifth act Garvin Goodluck makes his appearance,
and Sim Suresby tells him of what he saw and
heard at his visit to Dame Custance. Goodluck
is convinced of the lady's fickleness. She arrives,
and would welcome him tenderly; but of course
there is trouble. Finally, however, on the evidence of Tristram Trusty, she is freed from suspicion; and Ralph, petitioning for pardon, is invited to the wedding supper, and the play is at an
end. It is rather a rude performance, but it contains all the elements of a regular comedy of the
romantic school; and it must be confessed that
many a duller one has been presented to a modern audience.*

* The following extract from the opening of the third scene
of Act IV. of this comedy is a fair example of its style : —

Yet ruder and coarser than *Ralph Roister Dois-ter*, and less amusing, is *Gammer Gurton's Needle*, which until 1818 was supposed to be the earliest extant English comedy ; but which was not writ-ten until about thirty years later than Udall's play, it having been first performed, as Malone reasonably concludes, at Christ College, Cam-bridge, in 1566. Its author was John Still, after-ward Bishop of Bath and Wells, who was born in

"*C. Custance.* What meane these lewde felowes thus to trouble
       me still ?
Sym. Suresby here, perchaunce, shal thereof deme som yll,
And shall suspect me in some point of naughtinesse,
And they come hitherward.
Sym. Suresby. What is their businesse ?
Cust. I have nought to them, nor they to me, in sadnesse.
Sure. Let us hearken them ; somewhat there is, I feare it.
Ralph Royster. I wil speake out aloude best, that she may
      heare it.
Merrygreek. Nay, alas ! ye may so feare hir out of hir wit.
Royster. Nay by the crosse of my sworde, I will hurt hir no whit.
Merry. Will ye doe noe harme in deede ? Shall I trust your
      worde ?
Royster. By Roister Doister's fayth, I will speak but in borde.
Sure. Let us hearken them : somewhat there is, I feare it.
Royster. I will speake out aloude, I care not who heare it.—
Sirs, see that my harnesse, my tergat, and my shield,
Be made as bright now as when I was last in fielde,
As white as I shoulde to warre againe to morrowe :
For sicke shall I be but I worke some folke sorrowe.
Therefore see that all shine as bright as sainct George,
Or as doth a key newly come from the smith's forge.
I woulde have my sworde and harnesse to shine so bright
That I might ther with dimme mine enemies' sight :
I would have it cast beames as fast, I tell you playne,

1543. The personages in this play are all, with two or three exceptions, rustics, and their language is a broad provincial dialect. The plot turns upon the simple incident of Gammer Gurton's loss of her needle while she is mending her servant Hodge's breeches. Sharp is the hunt through five acts after this needful instrument; Hodge even pretending to have an interview with the Devil upon the subject. But the needle is

> As doth the glittryng grass after a showre of raine.
> And see that, in case I should have to come to armyng,
> All things may be ready at a minute's warning.
> For such a chaunce may chaunce in an houre, do ye heare ?
> *Merry.*   As perchaunce shall not chaunce againe in seven
>   yeare.
> *Royster.*   Now draw we neare to hir, and heare what shal be
>   sayde.
> *Merry.*   But I woulde not have you make hir too much afrayde.
> *Royster.*   Well founde, sweete wife (I trust) for al this your
>   soure looke.
> *Cust.*   Wife !   Why cal ye me wife ?
> *Sure.*   Wife ! this gear goeth acrook.
> *Merry.*   Nay Mistresse Custance, I warrant you our letter
> Is not as we redde e'en nowe, but much better ;
> And where ye half stomaked this gentleman afore,
> For this same letter ye wyll love hym nowe therefore ;
> Nor it is not this letter though ye were a queene
> That shoulde breake marriage betweene you twaine, I weene.
> *Cust.*   I did not refuse hym for the letter's sake.
> *Royster.*   Then ye are content me for your husbande to take.
> *Cust.*   You for my husbande to take !   Nothing lesse, truely.
> *Royster.*   Yea, say so sweete spouse, afore strangers hardly.
> *Merry.*   And though I have here his letter of love with me,
> Yet his rings and his tokens he sent keepe safe with ye.
> *Cust.*   A mischief take his tokens, and him and thee too."

not found until Hodge, having on the mended
garment, is hit "a good blow on the buttocks" by
the bailiff, whose services have been called in;
when the Clown discovers that Gammer Gurton's
needle, like Old Rapid's in the *Road to Ruin*,
does not always stick in the right place. The
second act of this farrago of practical jokes and
coarse humor opens with that jolly old drinking-
song, beginning,

> "I cannot eat but little meat,
>   My stomach is not good,"

which may be found in many collections of lyric
verse.

IV.

Whether it was that moral-plays satisfied·for a
long time our forefathers' desire for serious entertainment, and furnished them sufficient occasion
for that reflection upon the graver interests and
incidents of human life which it is tragedy's chief
function to suggest, or whether the public, wearied
by the sententious gravity of the moral-plays,
(which, however, their authors had often sought
to relieve by humorous character and incident,)
demanded, on the introduction of real life into
the drama, that only its light and merry side
should be presented, it is certain that Comedy entered upon the English stage much in advance of
her elder sister. It is barely possible that a play

upon the story of Romeo and Juliet was performed
in London before the year 1562;* but the earliest
tragedy extant in our language is *Ferrex and Porrex*, or *Gorboduc*, all of which was probably written by Thomas Sackville, Earl of Dorset, but to
the first three acts of which Thomas Norton has
a disputed claim.　This play is founded on events
in the fabulous chronicles of Britain.　The principal personages are Gorboduc, King of Britain
about B. C. 600, Videna, his wife, and Ferrex and
Porrex, his sons.　But nobles, counsellors, para-
sites, a lady, and messengers make the personages
number thirteen.　The first act is occupied with
the division of the kingdom by Gorboduc to his
sons, and the talk thereupon.　The second, to the
fomenting of a quarrel between the brothers for
complete sovereignty.　The third, to the events
of a civil war, in which Porrex kills Ferrex.　In
the fourth, the Queen, who most loved Ferrex,
kills Porrex while he is asleep at night in his
chamber; and the people rise in wrath and
avenge this murder by the death of both Videna
and Gorboduc.　The fifth act is occupied by a
bloody suppression of this rebellion by the nobles,
who in their turn fall into dissension; and the
land, without a rightful king and rent by civil
strife, becomes desolate.　This tragedy was written for one of the Christmas festivals of the Inner

---

* See the Introduction to *Romeo and Juliet*, in the author's
edition of Shakespeare's Works.

Temple, to be played by the gentlemen of that society; and by desire of Queen Elizabeth it was performed by them at Whitehall on the 18th of January, 1561. It is plain that the author of this play meant to be very elegant, decorous, and classical; and he succeeded. Of all the stirring events upon which the tragedy is built, not one is represented; all are told. Even Ferrex and Porrex are not brought together on the stage, and Videna does not meet either of them before the audience after the first act. Each act is introduced by a dumb show, intended to be symbolical of what will follow, — a common device on our early stage, which was ridiculed by Shakespeare in the third act of *Hamlet;* * and each act, except the last, is followed by a moralizing and

---

* "*The Order and Signification of the Domme Shew before the fourth Act.*

"First the musick of howeboies began to playe, during which there came from under the stage as though out of hell, three furies, Alecto, Megera, and Ctisiphone, clad in blacke garmentes sprinkled with bloud and flames, their bodies girt with snakes, their heds spred with serpentes in stead of heire, the one bearing in her hand a snake, the other a whip, and the third a burning firebrand; ech driving before them a king and a queene, which moved by furies unnaturally had slaine their owne children. The names of the kings and queenes were these, Tantalus, Medea, Athamas, Ino, Cambises, Althea; after that the furies and these had passed about the stage thrise, they departed and than the musick ceased: hereby was signified the unnaturall murders to follow, that is to say Porrex slaine by his owne mother; and of King Gorboduc and Queen Videna, killed by their owne subjects."

17*

explanatory chorus recited by "four ancient and sage men of Britain."

Ferrex and Porrex is remarkable as being the first English play extant in blank verse ; and probably it was the first so written. It is to be wondered at that, even in this respect, it was ever taken as a model. For although Sir Philip Sidney in his *Defence of Poesie*, finding fault with *Ferrex and Porrex* for its violation of the unities of time and place, admits that it is "full of stately speeches and well-sounding phrases, climbing to the height of Seneca his stile, and full of notable morality, which it doth most delightfully teach," yet it may be safely said that another play so lifeless in movement, so commonplace in thought, so utterly undramatic in motive, so oppressively didactic in language, so absolutely without distinction of character among its personages, cannot be found in our dramatic literature. From *Ferrex and Porrex* we turn even to the miracle-plays and moral-plays with relief, if not with pleasure. Some notion of its tediousness may be gathered from the fact, that it closes with a speech one hundred lines in length, and that the first act is chiefly occupied with three speeches by three counsellors, which together make two hundred and sixty verses.*

---

* Of its style, the following passage, in which its most exciting incident, the murder of Porrex, is announced, is a favorable specimen.

"*Marcella.* O where is ruth, or where is pitie now ?
Whether is gentle hart and mercy fled ?

This play demands notice because it is our first tragedy, our first play written in blank verse, but

> Are they exil'd out of our stony brestes,
> Never to make returne? is all the world
> Drowned in bloud, and soncke in crueltie?
> If not in women mercy may be found,
> If not (alas) within the mother's brest
> To her owne childe, to her owne flesh and bloud;
> If ruthe be banished thence, if pitie there
> May have no place, if there no gentle hart
> Do live and dwell, where should we seeke it then?
>   " *Gorboduc*. Madame (alas), what meanes your wofull tale?
>   " *Marcella*. O silly woman I! why to this houre
> Have kinde and fortune thus deferred my breath,
> That I should live to see this dolefull day?
> Will ever wight beleve that such hard hart
> Could rest within the cruell mother's brest,
> With her owne hand to slaye her onely sonne?
> But out (alas) these eyes behelde the same,
> They saw the driery sight, and are become
> Most ruthefull recordes of the bloody fact.
> Porrex (alas) is by his mother slaine,
> And with her hand a wofull thing to tell;
> While slumbring on his carefull he restes,
> His hart stabde in with knife is reft of life.
>   " *Gorboduc*. O Eubulus, oh draw this sword of ours
> And pearce this hart with speed! O hatefull light,
> O loathsome life, O sweete and welcome death,
> Deare Eubulus, worke this we thee besech!
>   " *Eubulus*. Pacient your grace, perhappes he liveth yet,
> With wound receaved but not of certaine death.
>   " *Gorboduc*. O let us then repayre unto the place
> And see if Porrex live, or thus be slaine.
>   " *Marcella*. Alas, he liveth not it is to true,
> That with these eyes, of him a pereless prince,
> Sonne to a king, and in the flower of youth,
> Even with a twinkle a sensless stocke I saw."

for no other reason.   It had no perceptible effect
upon, and marks no stage in, the progress of the
English drama.   In that regard it might as well
have been written in Greece and in Greek, or
in ancient British, by Gorboduc himself; for, in
either case, its motive and plan could not have
been more foreign to the genius of English dramatic literature.   And here it is proper to say, that
translated plays, and plays adapted from Greek
and Latin authors, of which there were many
performed in the earlier part of Elizabeth's reign,
are passed by without notice in this account, not
merely because they were translations and adaptations, but because, not being an outgrowth of
the English character, they were entirely without
influence upon the development of the English
drama, in an account of which they therefore have
no proper place.   They were not seeds that took
root ; but lifeless foreign bodies cast upon the
ground, to bury themselves by their own weight,
in the process of time, out of sight and out of
memory.   Nor do the translations and adaptations
of Italian plays, of which not a few were made
at about the same period, seem to have had any
more vitality or assimilative power ; although
one of them, *The Supposes*, translated from Ariosto by George Gascoigne, and acted at Gray's
Inn in 1566, must be mentioned as the earliest
extant play in English prose.   The fact is significant, indeed, that none of the many plays espe-

cially written for the court, and for the learned
societies and the elegant people of that day, have
left any traces even of a temporary influence
upon our stage. Our English drama, unlike that
of France, had its germ in the instincts, and its
growth with the growth, of the whole English
people.

It must be confessed that up to, and even past,
the beginning of the Elizabethan era,* the plays
which were produced to satisfy the taste of our
forefathers were rude, gross, unsymmetrical, and
heterogeneous; and that their apparently discordant elements were rarely bound together by any
stronger bond of unity than the mere scenic succession of events. Of character there was little;
of keeping, no more; probability was defied, decorum violated. The individual traits of the personages in a play were rather described by each
other, or even by themselves, than developed;
and the feelings which the poet deemed proper
to any dramatic situation were enumerated rather
than expressed. The more cultivated people of
that time saw all these defects, except the last;
and yet, as cultivated people often do, devised for
them the wrong remedy.† Not seeing or not re-

---

* The era which bears the name of Elizabeth, because the men
who made it illustrious were her contemporaries, commenced
after the beginning, and stretched beyond the end, of her reign.
Its limits may be taken as 1575–1625.

† George Whetstone, in the dedication of his *Promos and Cas-*

garding the fact that our drama was a new and
native growth, they judged it by a foreign standard, and would have conformed it to an effete and
foreign type.　In this English drama, rude, coarse,
and confused as it appears, there was yet a native,
inherent vitality.　Supported by the strong Eng-.
lish imagination, it could defy the unities of time

sandra, the incidents of which Shakespeare used in his *Measure
for Measure*, and which was published in 1578, gives us the following criticism upon the English drama of that day:—

"The Englishman in this quallitie is most vaine, indiscreete,
and out of order: he first groundes his worke on impossibilities:
then, in three howers, ronnes he throwe the worlde: marryes,
gets children, makes children men, men to conquer kingdomes,
murder monsters, and bringeth Gods from Heaven, and fetcheth
divils from Hel.　And (that which is worst) their ground is not so
unperfect as their workinge indiscreete; not waying, so the people laugh, though they laugh them (for their follies) to scorn.
Manye tymes, to make myrthe, they make a clowne companion
with a Kinge: in theyr grave Councils they allow the advise of
fools: yea, they use one order of speach for all persons, a grose
Indecorum," &c.

Sir Philip Sidney, in a passage of his *Defence of Poesie*, (written about 1583,) which has been often quoted, but which is too
important to be omitted here, says:—

"Our Tragedies and Comedies are not without cause cried out
against, observing rules neither of honest civilitie nor skilfull Po-
etrie.　Excepting Gorboduck (againe I say of those that I have
seene) which notwithstanding, as it is full of statelie speeches, and
well sounding phrases, climing to the height of Seneca his stile,
and as full of notable moralitie, which it doth most delightfully
teach, and so obtaine the verie end of Poesie, yet in truth it is
very defectious in the circumstances, which grieves me, because
it might not remaine as an exact modell of all Tragedies.　For it
is faulty in place and time, the two necessarie companions of all
corporall actions.　For when the Stage should alway represent

and place ; but in obedience to the English love of
moral truth, it struggled after that greater unity,
the unity of dramatic interest. With a contempt
of the conventional peculiarly English, it sought
the presentation of an idealized picture of real
life, which life is neither pure tragedy nor pure
comedy, and in which mirth and sadness, kings

but one place, and the uttermost time presupposed in it, should
be, both by Aristotle's precept and common reason, but one day,
there is both many dayes and manie places artificially imagined.
But if it bee so in *Gorboduck*, how much more in all the rest, where
you shall have *Asia* of the one side, and *Affrick* of the other, and
so many other under-kingdoms, that the Player, when he comes
in, must ever begin with telling where he is, or else the tale will
not be conceived. Now you shall have three ladies walke to
gather flowers, and then we must believe the stage to be a garden. By and by we hear newes of a shipwrack in the same
place ; then, we are to blame if we accept it not for a rocke.
Upon the backe of that comes out a hideous monster with fire
and smoke, and then the miserable beholders are bound to take
it for a cave ; while, in the meantime, two armies flie in, represented with four swords and bucklers, and then what hard hart
will not receive it for a pitched field ? Now, of time they are
much more liberal ; for ordinarie it is that two young Princes fall
in love : after many traverses she is got with child, delivered of
a fair boy ; he is lost, groweth a man, falleth in love, and is ready
to get another child, and all this in two houres' space : which
how absurd it is in sense, even sense may imagine, and art hath
taught, and all ancient examples justified, and at this daye the
ordinarie players in *Italie* wil not erre in. . . . . But besides these
grosse absurdities how all their Playes be neither right Tragedies
nor right Comedies, mingling Kings and Clownes, not because
the matter so carieth it, but thrust in the Clowne by head and
shoulders, to play a part in Majestical matters with neither de-
cencie nor discretion ; so as neither the admiration and commis-
eration, nor right sportfulness is by their mongrell Tragi-comedy
obtained."

and clowns, do mingle.* It clung to its confused collocation of heterogeneous materials, because it was striving to work them together into a natural symmetry, — a symmetry not austere, limited, and geometrical, like that of a Doric temple, in which one half is the exact counterpart of the other, and the details are the repetition of a single form, but large and free, yet true, like the symmetry of mountains and of trees, in which the masses are irregular and the details unlike, while yet there is perfect balance, and a harmony the more satisfying that it is not constant concord and repeated sameness.

Our drama, advancing through centuries, had slowly reached this stage of growth, where if its development had been stayed its history would have been utterly without interest, except to the literary antiquarian, when suddenly its homely, uncouth bud burst into flower so sweet, of beauty so glorious, so perennial, as ever after to gladden, to perfume, and to adorn the ages. The rapidity of this transition is astonishing. It is almost like magical transformation. In less than twenty

---

* There is conventionality enough and to spare in the everyday life of people of English race in the United States, and still more in that of the same race in Great Britain. But they see, and, more, they feel, the unnatural restraint of pure conventionalism. They act under it with an awkward self-consciousness. They scorn it, and have some contempt for themselves for their conformity to it. Whereas the people of the continent of Europe believe in it, accept it without a question, enter into it heartily, and act under it unconsciously.

years from the time when the best plays yet produced by English authors were intrinsically unworthy of a place in literature, the English stage
had become illustrious. This change was brought
about by the great and increasing taste of the
day for dramatic performances, which called into
the service of the theatre every needy hand that
held a ready pen. A crowd of young men left
the learned professions in London, or, abandoning
rustic homes, flocked thither, to make money by
writing plays. Among these men seven attained
distinction ; and yet not only so inferior, but of
so little intrinsic, enduring interest was the work
of six of them, that, with one, and hardly one,
exception, their names would not have been
known outside of purely literary circles but for
the seventh. They were Thomas Kyd, John Lilly,
George Peele, George Chapman, Robert Greene,
Christopher Marlowe, and William Shakespeare.
Of the six, the oldest whose age is known to us
was only ten years the senior of the seventh; and
the most eminent, Marlowe, was born but two
years before him.* Shakespeare got to work in
London very early in life. He was using his pen
there as a dramatic writer before he was twenty-
four years old.† These men were therefore in

---

* Lilly was born about 1553, Peele about the same year, Chap
man in 1559, Greene about 1560, Marlowe about 1562, Shakespeare in 1564. The date of Kyd's birth can only be conjectured.

† See Section XII. of the Essay on the Authorship of *King*

z

both the strictest and the broadest sense his contemporaries, — his contemporaries as men and as
authors. The mere fact that he found four of
them, Kyd, Peele, Greene, and Marlowe, in the
front rank of dramatic writers on his arrival in
London, does not properly entitle them to consideration as his predecessors in the English drama.
Being so absolutely contemporaneous with him in
age, they could be justly regarded as his predecessors only as having been the founders of a
school of which he was an eminent disciple, or to
which he had established a rival or a successor.
But he stood to them in neither of these relations.
He and they were all, with a single exception, of
one school, of which neither one of them was the
founder. With this one exception, these men
were all striving to do the same thing, at the
same time, in the same way. The time had come
when it was to be done, and the time brought the
men who were to do it, each according to his
ability. And not only were their aims identical,
but there is the best reason, short of competent
contemporary testimony, for believing that four
of them, including Shakespeare, were co-laborers
upon still existing works.*

Henry the Sixth, Vol. VII. of the author's edition of Shakespeare's Works.

* See the Introduction to the *Taming of the Shrew*, and the
Essay upon *King Henry the Sixth*, in the author's edition of
Shakespeare's Works.

The exception to this unity of purpose was John Lilly, the Euphuist. Lilly is known in dramatic literature as the author of eight comedies written to be performed. at the court of Elizabeth.* They are in all respects opposed to the genius of the English drama. They do not even pretend to be representations of human life and human character, but are pure fantasy-pieces, in which the personages are a heterogeneous medley of Grecian gods and goddesses and impossible colorless creatures with sublunary names, all thinking with one brain and speaking with one tongue, — the conceitful crotchety brain and the dainty, well-trained tongue of clever, witty John Lilly. They are all in prose, but contain some pretty, fanciful verses called songs, which are as unlyric in spirit as the plays in which they appear are undramatic. From these plays Shakespeare borrowed a few thoughts, but they exercised no modifying influence upon his genius, nor did they at all conform to that of the English drama, upon which they are a mere grotesque excrescence.

Chapman, one of the elder and the stronger of the six above named, is not known as the author, even in part, of any play older than Shakespeare's

---

* Lilly's plays are *Endimion, Campaspe, Sapho and Phao, Gallathea, Mydas, Mother Bombie, The Woman in the Moone,* and *Love's Metamorphosis. The Maid's Metamorphosis,* which was published anonymously in 1600, has been attributed to him, as also has *A Warning for Faire Women,* which was published anonymously in 1599; but neither of them bears traces of his style.

earliest performances. He probably entered upon
dramatic composition at a somewhat later period
in life than either of the others; and as a dramatist is properly to be passed over in this place as
not having been Shakespeare's predecessor in the
mere order of time by even that very brief period
which may be admitted in the cases of Peele,
Greene, and Marlowe. Upon the styles of these
three dramatists I have remarked elsewhere * that
I cannot entirely assent to the opinion entertained by many persons, that Marlowe's talents
were very far superior to those of the two others,
at least as far as Peele is concerned. Marlowe
was indeed the most gifted dramatic writer of his
time, in our language, except Shakespeare. His
imagination sometimes shaped out living forms,
though monstrous; and from the murky clouds
of his bombast there shoot fitful gleams of real
poetic fancy. Peele's plays, it is true, lack some
of the fire and fury of Marlowe's; but they are
also without much of his fustian. His characters are less strongly marked than Marlowe's, but
they are also less absurd and extravagant, and in
my opinion they are equally well discriminated;
but that is little praise. Peele's *David and Bath-
seba* is a play which, for the genuineness of its
feeling, if not for the harmony of its verse, Marlowe might have been glad to own; and *The Battle of Alcanzar* is in the same furious, savage vein

* Essay upon the Authorship of *King Henry the Sixth.*

with his *Tamburlaine,* and equal, if not superior,
to it in sense and keeping. It is also noteworthy
that the prologue to Peele's *Arraignment of Paris,*
which was published in 1584, when Marlowe was
but twenty years old, and before he had taken his
Bachelor's degree at Cambridge, is, for union of
completeness of measure with variety of pause,
unsurpassed by any dramatic blank verse, that
of one play excepted, written before the time of
Shakespeare. In forming a comparative judgment as to Marlowe, it must be borne in mind that
there is good reason for believing that *Edward
the Second,* his best play in versification, no less
than in style, sentiment, and character, was written after 1590, and after the production of *The
First Part of the Contention,* and *The True Tragedy
of Richard, Duke of York,* in which he had some
lessons in dramatic versification from Shakespeare.*

With regard to these dramatists there only remains to be noticed the claim which has been set
up for one of them,† Marlowe, that he was the
first who used blank verse upon our public stage,
and "the first who harmonized it with variety of
pause." As to which I will only say briefly, that
although it is probably true that he in his *Tam-*

---

* See the Essay on the Authorship of *King Henry the Sixth,*
before mentioned.

† By Mr. Collier in his History of English Dramatic Poetry,
&c., and Mr. Dyce in his Life of Shakespeare.

burlaine made one of the earliest efforts to bring
blank verse into vogue in plays written for the
general public, and to substitute the roll and flow
of measured rhythm for the feebler and more mo-
notonous music of rhyme in dramatic poetry intended for uncultured as well as cultured ears, I
cannot find in this endeavor reason for giving him
the credit due to an innovator, much less that
which belongs to an inventor. Blank verse, as
we have seen, was used in plays produced for
special occasions and audiences many years before Marlowe wrote; and he, writing only for the
general theatre-going public, seems merely to
have used and somewhat improved an instrument
which he found made to his hand.

Among the dramatists who preceded Marlowe
in the use of blank verse on the public stage is
one who, in my judgment, wrote it with a spirit
and freedom which Marlowe himself hardly ex-
celled. This dramatist is the unknown author of
Jeronimo. A continuation of this play, called
The Spanish Tragedy, or Hieronimo is mad again,
was one of the most popular dramas of the Elizabethan era. It was written, as we know on the
testimony of Thomas Heywood, by Thomas Kyd;
and hitherto it has been maintained, perhaps I
should rather say assumed, that Kyd was also the
author of *Jeronimo*. But it seems to me very
clear that the fact that Kyd did write *The Spanish
Tragedy* is conclusive against his authorship of

the elder play. It is hardly possible that they are by the same writer. And as *Jeronimo* is a typical play of the transition period between the pre-Elizabethan and the Elizabethan drama, the question as to its authorship may be here opportunely examined. There is no contemporary testimony, direct or indirect, upon this subject. Heywood's evidence is limited to the authorship of *The Spanish Tragedy*.* Ben Jonson, who makes the only other contemporary allusion to Kyd's performance, refers only to the same play. In the Introduction to *Cynthia's Revels*, where he indulges his cynical humor at the expense of his immediate predecessors and his contemporaries, Jonson makes one of the interlocutors, speaking of the critics in the audience, say: "Another, whom it hath pleased nature to furnish with more beard than brain, prunes his mustachio, lisps, and with some score of affected oaths, swears down all that sit about him, 'That the *old Hieronimo, as it was first acted,* was the only best and judiciously penn'd play of Europe.'" And in the immediately preceding speech, he makes this allusion: " O, (I had almost forgot it, too,) they say the *umbræ* or ghosts of some three or four plays departed a dozen years since have been seen walking about your stage here." Now the ghost of the lover in *Jeronimo*

---

* Heywood says: "Therefore Mr. Kyd in the *Spanish Tragedy*, upon an occasion presenting itself, thus writes:

'Why, Nero thought it no disparagement,'" &c.

is brought in as chorus in *The Spanish Tragedy;*
and this circumstance, coupled with the proximity
of the two speeches above cited, makes it plain
that Jonson had the latter play in mind, as principal among the three or four to which he refers.
Cynthia's Revels having been produced in 1599,
this gives us 1587 as the date, not at which "the
old *Hieronimo*" was first acted, as hitherto it
has been somewhat strangely assumed, but about
which it had become old and worn enough for a
playwright, cynical and vain like Jonson, to place
it among those which had "departed," although it
was often acted during the dozen years which he
had in mind. We know that it is *The Spanish
Tragedy* to which Jonson refers as "the old *Hieronimo,*" not only because he uses the name
Hieronimo, instead of *Jeronimo,* but because he
refers to it "as it was first acted"; which shows
that in 1599 the play in question was not performed as Kyd had left it, but had been "newly
revived and polished according to the decorum of
these days," as *Tancred and Gismunda,* written in
1568, is announced to have been, on its title-page,
printed in 1592. It was a common practice at
that time thus to revive and polish old plays
which had achieved and retained public favor.
Now of the two plays before us *The Spanish
Tragedy* was the popular favorite; and that we
know, from Henslowe's Diary, was twice added
to by Jonson himself between the time of his

gibe at it and 1602. But *Jeronimo*, although not published until 1605, when at least four editions of *The Spanish Tragedy* had been issued, including two which contained, as their title-pages announced, the "new additions" which Jonson made,* shows no trace of alteration or addition, and no announcement of any appears upon the title-page, which absence we may take as more than a negative pregnant.† Ben Jonson was not alone in his contempt of *The Spanish Tragedy*. It is jeered at by many writers of the Elizabethan era, including Shakespeare. The great favor with which it was popularly regarded seems to have nettled the dramatists of that day, and justly; for it is a very feeble and ridiculous performance, which probably owed its theatrical popularity to the murder and suicide which plentifully enliven

---

* "The Spanish Tragedie, containing the lamentable ende of Don Horatio and Bel-imperia : with the pittiful death of old Hieronimo. — Newly corrected and amended of such grosse faultes as passed in the former impression. At London, Printed by William White, dwelling in Cow lane, 1599."

"The Spanish Tragedie, containing the lamentable ende of Don Horatio and Bel-imperia : with the pittifull death of olde Hieronimo. Newly corrected, amended, and enlarged, with new additions of the Painter's part and others, as it hath of late been divers times acted. Imprinted at London by W. W. for T. Pavier, and are to be solde at the signe of the Cat and Parrots near the Exchange. 1602."

† "The First Part of Jeronimo. With the Warres of Portugall, and the Life and Death of Don Andræa. Printed at London for Thomas Pavyer, and are to be solde at his shop, at the entrance into the Exchange. 1605."

its action,* and to the extravagance of its situations. *Jeronimo* escaped such gibes as those which were levelled at *The Spanish Tragedy;* and well it might; for it is a very much better composition than its successor : in construction, though rude, at least not inferior, and far superior in dramatic and poetic power.†

In the absence of testimony as to Kyd's authorship of *Jeronimo*, internal evidence must decide the question, if it can be decided. For as to subject and personages, (which are, so to speak, identical in that play and in *The Spanish Tragedy*,) they, and not only they, but in a certain degree

---

* Nine several extinctions of life by hanging, stabbing, and shooting, and in one case by both, take place before the audience in *The Spanish Tragedy.* They are thus recounted with gusto by the Ghost at the end of the play : —

"Aye, now my hopes have end in their effects,
When blood and sorrow finish my desires,
Horatio murdered in his father's bower ;
Vile Serberine by Pedringano slain ;
False Pedringano hang'd by quaint device,
Fair Isabella by herself misdone,
Prince Balthazar by Belimperia stabb'd ;
The duke of Castile and his wicked son,
Both done to death by old Hieronimo ;
My Belimperia fallen, as Dido fell ;
And good Hieronimo slain by himself,
Ay, these were spectacles to please my soul."

† But Mr. Collier says, "As a dramatic production *Jeronimo* is in every respect below *The Spanish Tragedy*," which he calls "a very powerful performance." — *History of Dramatic Poetry,* Vol. III. pp. 208, 209.

plot, and even language, were looked upon as common property in the early part of the Elizabethan
era, when play-writing was a trade and plays were
patchwork. A comparison of the play which we
know Kyd did write with that which we do not
know he wrote, shows that they are utterly unlike
in construction, in characterization, and in every
distinctive quality of style. Both are defiant of
the unities, and even of the possibilities, of time
and place; but the action of the elder play, *Jeronimo*, is direct, spirited, and manly; that of the
later, *The Spanish Tragedy*, is confused, languid,
and childish. In characterization both are weak
when compared with Shakespeare's, or even Marlowe's works; but compared with each other,
the elder is the stronger and more original, the
later at best feebly copying the traits of the elder.
But it is in style that their unlikeness is most
striking. Blank verse and rhyme are mingled in
both, *Jeronimo* containing a larger proportion of
the latter. But so far is this from being an indication that *Jeronimo* is the earlier and *The Spanish Tragedy* the later work of a man who was
ridding himself of the trammels of rhyme, and
gaining freedom of versification by practice and
example, that the very rhymed couplets of the
former are freer and more varied than the blank
verse of the latter, which is formal and monoto-
nous, with a pause in sense and rhythm at the end
of almost every line; while the blank verse of

Jeronimo has often an ease and breadth and variety never attained by the author of *The Spanish Tragedy*, or by any other dramatist before Shakespeare, except occasionally by Marlowe.* In merely interlocutory passages, where speeches consist of but a few words, the author of the elder play composes his verses of the speeches of various characters, or disregards the completion of a verse, and writes merely in measured rhythm. Kyd, on the contrary, gives a perfect line or two to each speaker.† One peculiarity of the versifi-

---

* "Come, valiant spirits; you peers of Portugal
That owe your lives, your faiths and services,
To set you free from base captivity:
O let our fathers' scandal ne'er be seen
As a base blush upon our free-born cheeks:
Let all the tribute that proud Spain receiv'd
Of those all captive Portugales deceased,
Turn into chafe, and choak their insolence.
Methinks no moiety, not one little thought
Of them whose servile acts live in their graves,
But should raise spleens big as a cannon-bullet
Within your bosoms: O for honor,
Your country's reputation, your lives freedom,
Indeed your all that may be termed revenge,
Now let your bloods be liberal as the sea;
And all the wounds that you receive of Spain,
Let theirs be equal to quit yours again.
Speak Portugales: are you resolved as I,
To live like captives, or as freeborn die."

† The following brief passage from *Jeronimo* exhibits the author's manner in such passages as are above referred to.

"*Jeron.*   What! have I almost quited you?
Andrea.   Have done
Impatient marshal.

cation of *Jeronimo* is very striking: this is the frequent insertion of a hemistich in the midst of a speech in blank verse of several lines. Eighteen instances of this occur in that short play, but not one in the much longer *Spanish Tragedy*. The student of Shakespeare will remember many such in *Macbeth*, *King Lear*, and *Hamlet*. Marlowe does not use them. The supposition that this peculiarity in *Jeronimo* may be due to imperfection of the manuscript, or the carelessness with

> *Balth.*   Spanish combatants,
> What! do you set a little pigmy marshal
> To question with a prince?
> *Andrea.*   No, Prince Balthezar
> I have desired him peace that we might war."

This presents a striking contrast to the following passage from *The Spanish Tragedy*, which shows Kyd's style in like circumstances.

> "*Lorenzo.*   Sister, what means this melancholy walk?
> *Belimperia.*   That for a while I wish no company.
> *Loren.*   But here the Prince has come to visit you.
> *Bel.*   That argues, that he lives in liberty.
> *Balthazar.*   No, madam, but in pleasing servitude.
> *Bel.*   Your prison then, belike, is your conceit,
> *Balth.*   Ay, by conceit my freedom is enthralled.
> *Bel.*   Then with conceit enlarge yourself again.
> *Balth.*   What if conceit have laid my heart to gage?
> *Bel.*   Pay that you borrowed and recover it.
> *Balth.*   I die if I return from whence it lies.
> *Bel.*   A heartless man, and live? a miracle!
> *Balth.*   Ay, lady, love can work such miracles.
> *Loren.*   Tush, tush, my lord, let go these ambages,
> And in plain terms acquaint her with your love.
> *Bel.*   What boots complaint when there 's no remedy?"

which the only existing edition was printed, is precluded by the fact that these hemistichs generally rhyme with the following line. Fifteen of the eighteen instances in question have this peculiarity, — in itself a remarkable trait of style.* *The Spanish Tragedy* is filled with classical allusions, its author having brought the Greek mythology constantly into his service. *Jeronimo* is absolutely free from this cheap exhibition of schol-

---

* Of this rhymed hemistich, and also again of the freedom and harmonious variety of pause which distinguish the blank verse in *Jeronimo*, the following brief passages are examples.

> " *Lorenzo.* Andrea's gone embassador :
> Lorenzo is not dreamt on in this age :
> Hard fate,
> When villains sit not in the highest state !
> Ambition's plumes, that flourish'd in our court,
> Severe authority has dash'd with justice ;
> And policy and pride walk like to exiles
> Giving attendance, that were once attended."

> "'T is said we shall not answer at next birth
> Our father's faults in heaven ; why then on earth ?
> Which proves and shows that which they lost
> By base captivity,
> We may redeem by honor'd valiancy :
> We borrow naught : our kingdom is our own :
> He 's a base king that pays rent for his throne."

> " And thou long thing of Portugal, why not ?
> Thou that art full as tall
> As an English gallows, upper beam and all,
> Devourer of apparel, thou huge swallower,
> My hose will scarce make thee a standing collar.
> What, have I 'quited you ? "

arship, if we except a single mention of Mars, and
the introduction of Charon, whose names and
functions were familiar to the general public of
that period. But *The Spanish Tragedy* is not
only distinguished by this trait ; it has Latin quo-
tations in the midst of its speeches. An entire
speech of one of the personages is in Latin. Italian and Spanish are also quoted. This use of foreign language occurs sixteen times in the play.
In one instance, and that where the situation is
most touching, the principal personage quotes
from the Æneid fourteen lines of Dido's last dying speech and confession. But in *Jeronimo*, although it is about half as long as its continuation,
not one word of Latin, Spanish, or Italian occurs.
This peculiarity of *The Spanish Tragedy* Shakespeare ridicules in *The Taming of the Shrew ;*
and it is one which might be expected in Kyd,
who was a scholar and a translator more than a
poet. The difference in the spelling of the name
of the principal personage common to both plays
becomes, under these circumstances, significant.
It has been supposed that this was due to the discovery by Kyd, in the interval between the production of the two plays, "that Jeronimo was rather
Italian than Spanish." But a mistake like the
one supposed is exactly the one into which the
author of *The Spanish Tragedy* and the translator of Garnier's *Cornelia* would not be likely to
fall. Who wrote *Jeronimo* we do not know.

But can there be a doubt that Kyd was not its author?

The Spanish Tragedy had been written, as we have seen, long enough before 1587 to be then an old story. We may be equally sure that the play of which it is a continuation had preceded it some years. In structure *Jeronimo* bears strong traces of the pre-Elizabethan era. It opens with a dumb show, explanatory of the situation of the characters before the action commences; * the action does not "grow to a point," and the play consequently reads less like a tragedy than an episode of history, dramatized with little constructive art. Quite one half of the play is in rhyme; and among its *dramatis personæ* one is allegorical, — Revenge. This personage and the Ghost of Andrea, the slain lover, who appears with him in the last scene of *Jeronimo*, are also used by Kyd in *The Spanish Tragedy;* but in that they merely form a chorus, and neither mingle in nor influence the action. The traits of *Jeronimo* just mentioned, and particularly the first and last, are indicative of a period earlier than that known as the Elizabethan

---

* "Sound a signet, and pass over the stage. Enter at one door the King of Spain, Duke of Castile, Duke Medina, Lorenzo, and Rogero; at another door, Andrea, Horatio, and Jeronimo. Jeronimo kneels down, and the King creates him Marshal of Spain. Lorenzo puts on his spurs and Andrea his sword. The King goes along with Jeronimo to his house; after a long signet is sounded, enter all the Nobles with covered dishes to a banquet. *Exeunt omnes.* That done, enter all again as before."

era ; while the versification and characterization
belong to that era, and indeed would disgrace
none of its dramatists except Shakespeare himself, and are hardly unworthy of his prentice hand.
Dumb shows went out as the Elizabethan dramatists began to occupy the stage ; and allegory
is the distinctive trait of the period of the moral-
plays, although, as we have seen, it yielded place
gradually to real life. The use of dumb show,
and especially the introduction of an allegorical
character among the *dramatis personæ* of a tragedy of real life, written in blank verse, of which
no other example is known to me, distinctly mark
the transitional type of *Jeronimo;* which may
be regarded as a fine and characteristic example
of English tragedy in the stage of its development immediately preceding that which produced
Shakespeare. And indeed this play and its continuation, in spite of the crudeness of both and
the childishness of the latter, seem to have left
stronger traces of influence upon Shakespeare's
works than any other or than all others written
by his predecessors or his contemporaries.*

* A critical examination and comparison of these two tragedies would be an interesting and perhaps not unfruitful task ; but
enough of these pages cannot be spared for that purpose. The
reader who desires to examine them for himself will find both
Jeronimo and *The Spanish Tragedy* among Dodsley's *Old Plays*,
and the latter in Hawkins's *Origin of the English Drama*. It is
my intention to undertake, in an Essay supplementary to this
volume, a critical examination of these two tragedies and their
relations to Shakespeare's works.

18.*   .   A A

The English drama, and not the theatre and the stage, before the time of Shakespeare, is the subject of this account; but it may be fitly closed with a very brief description of the play-houses and the theatrical management of his early years. The general use of inn-yards as places of dramatic amusement has been already mentioned in the course of remark upon the moral-play; and when Shakespeare arrived in London at least three inns there, the Bull, the Cross Keys, and the Bell Savage, were thus regularly occupied. But, by a striking coincidence, with the Elizabethan era of our drama came theatres proper,—buildings specially adapted to the needs of actors and audiences. Shakespeare found three such in the metropolis,—four, if to The Theatre, The Curtain, and The Black-friars, we are to add Paris Garden, where bear-baiting shared the boards with comedy. All the theatres of Shakespeare's time were probably built of wood and plaster. Of the three above mentioned, the Black-friars belonged to the class called private theatres, we know not why, unless because the private theatres were entirely roofed in, while in the others the pit was uncovered, and of course the stage and the gallery exposed to the external air. A flag was kept flying from a staff on the roof during the performance. Inside, there was the stage, the pit, the boxes and galleries, much as we have them now-a-days. In the public theatres the pit, separated from the stage by a paling, was called the yard, and was without seats. The price of admission to the pit, or yard, varied, according to the pretensions of the theatre, from twopence, and even a penny, to sixpence; that to the boxes or rooms, from a shilling to two shillings, and even, on extraordinary occasions, half a crown.

The performance usually commenced at three o'clock in the afternoon; but the theatre appears to have been always artificially lighted, in the body of the house by cressets, and upon the stage by large, rude chandeliers. The small band of musicians sat, not in an orchestra in front of the stage, but, it would seem, in a balcony projecting from the proscenium. People went early to the theatre, for the purpose of securing good places, and while waiting for the play to begin, they read, gamed, smoked, drank, and cracked nuts and jokes together; those who set up for wits, gallants, or critics liked to appear upon the stage itself, which they were allowed to do all through the performance, lying upon the rushes with which the stage was strewn, or sitting upon stools, for which they paid an extra price. Pickpockets, when detected at the theatre, seem to have been put in an extempore pillory on the stage, among the wits and gallants, at whose tongues, if not whose hands, they doubtless suffered. Kempe, the actor, in his *Nine Daies Wonder*, A. D. 1600, compares a man to "such a one as we tye to a poast on our stage for all the people to wonder at when they are taken pilfering."

Certain very peculiar dramatic companies of Shakespeare's time should not be passed by here entirely without notice. They were composed entirely of children. The boys of St. Paul's choir, those of Westminster school, and a special company called the Children of the Revels, were the most important. The first two companies acted under the direction of the Master of St. Paul's choir, and of the school, the last under that of the Master of the Revels. Their performances were much admired, and the companies of the adult actors at the theatre were piqued, and perhaps touched in pocket, by the public favor of these younkers. Shakespeare shows this by the complaint which he puts into Rosencrans's mouth, in *Hamlet*. Their audiences were generally composed of the higher classes, and they acted plays of established reputation only. This appears from the following passage in *Jack Drum's Entertainment*, published in 1601, which was itself played by the children of Paul's, as appears by its title-page.

"*Sir Edward.* I sawe the children of Pawles last night,
And troth they pleas'd me prettie prettie well.
The Apes in time will do it handsomely.
  "*Planet.* I faith I like the audience that frequenteth there,
With much applause : A man shall not be choakte
With the stench of Garlicke, nor be pasted
To the barmy Iackett of a Beer-brewer.
  "*Brabant ju.* Tis a good gentle audience, and I hope the Boys
Will come one day into the Court of Requests.

" *Brabant Sig.* I, and they had good playes, but they produce
Such mustie fopperies of antiquitie
As do not sute the humorous ages backs
With cloathes in fashion."

Sig. H. 3. b.

The performance was announced by three flour-
ishes of trumpets. At the third sounding, the
curtain, which was divided in the middle from top
to bottom, and ran upon rods, was drawn, and,
after the prologue, the actors entered. The prologue was spoken by a person who wore a long
black cloak and a wreath of bays upon his head.
The reason of which costume was, that prologues
were first spoken by the authors of plays themselves, who wore the poetical costume of the Middle Ages, such as we see it in the old portraits of
Ariosto, Tasso, and others. When the authors
themselves no longer appeared as Prologue, the
actors, who were their proxies, assumed their professional habit. Poor Robert Greene, the debauched playwright and poet, begged upon his
miserable death-bed that his coffin might be
strewed with bays; and the cobbler's wife at
whose house he died respected this clinging of
the wretched author to his right to Parnassian
honors, and fulfilled his request.

In the early part of the Elizabethan era, it was
common for all the actors who were to take part
in the play to appear in character and pass over
the stage before the performance began. This
was a relic of the days of the miracle-plays and
moral-plays.

In the course of the piece, he who played the clown would favor the audience with outbreaks of extemporaneous wit and practical joking, in virtue of a time-honored privilege claimed by the clowns to "speak more than was set down for them." Indeed, extempore dialogue seems to have been permitted to, if not expected from, the representatives of comic characters. Such directions as the following, in Greene's *Tu Quoque*, A. D. 1614, are not uncommon : —

"*Here they two talke and rayle what they list; then Rash speakes to Staynes.*

"*All Speake.* Ud's fool dost thou stand by and do nothing? Come talke and drown her clamors.

"*Here they all talke and Joyce gives over weeping and Exit.*"

Between the acts there was dancing and singing; and after the play, a jig; which was a kind of comic solo, sung, said, acted, and danced by the clown, to the accompaniment of his own pipe and tabor. Each day's exhibition was closed by a prayer for the Queen, offered by all the actors kneeling.

The stage exhibited no movable scenery. It was hung with painted cloths and arras; and when tragedy was played, the hangings were, sometimes at least, sable. Over the stage was a blue canopy, called "the heavens." But although there was no proper scenery, there was ample provision of rude properties, such as towers,

tombs, dragons, pasteboard banquets, and the like.
Furniture was used of course, and was in many
cases the only means of indicating a change of
scene; which indeed, in most cases, was left to the
imagination of the audience, helped, it might be,
as Sir Philip Sidney says, if the supposed scene
were Thebes, by "seeing *Thebes* written in great
letters on an old door."* Machinery and trap-
doors were freely used, and gods and goddesses
were let down from and hoisted up to the heavens, in chairs moved by pulleys and tackle that
creaked and groaned in the most sublunary and
mechanical manner. At the back of the stage
was a balcony, which, like the furniture in the
Duke Aranza's cottage, served "a hundred uses."

* Such stage directions as the following show how very rude
were the devices for indicating a change of scene in the latter
part of the sixteenth and the early part of the seventeenth centuries : —

"*Enter Sybilla, lying in childbed, with her child lying by her.*"—
Heywood's *Golden Age*, 1611.

"*Enter a Shoemaker sitting on the stage at work. Jenkin to
him.*"—Greene's *George-a-Greene*, 1599.

In the following passage the audience were evidently expected
to "make believe" that a few steps across the stage were a going
to the town's end : —

"*Shoemaker.* Come, sir, will you go to the town's end now, sir ?

"*Jenkin.* Ay, sir, come. — Now we are at the town's end ;
say you now ?"—*Idem, ut supra.*

In the plays of that period, after a murder or killing in combat,
the direction is generally to the survivor, "Exit with the body."
There was no device by which the dead body could be shut out
from the audience, that the next scene might go on without its
presence.

It was inner room, upper room, window, balcony,
battlements, hillside, Mount Olympus,—any place,
in fact, that was supposed to be separated from
and above the scene of the main action.   It was
in this balcony, for instance, that Sly and his attendants sat while they witnessed the performance of *The Taming of the Shrew.*

The wardrobes of the principal theatres were
rich, varied, and costly.   It was 'customary to buy
for stage use slightly worn court dresses and the
gorgeous robes used at coronations.   Near the
end of the last century, Steevens tells us, there
was "yet in the wardrobe of Covent Garden
Theatre a rich suit of clothes that once belonged
to James I."   Steevens saw it worn by the per-
former of Justice Greely in Massinger's *New Way
to pay Old Debts.*   The Allen Papers and Henslowe's Diary* inform us fully upon this point.
In the latter there is a memorandum of the payment of £4 14*s.* (equal to $120) for a single
pair of hose; and by the former we see that £16
(equal to $400) was paid for one embroidered vel-
vet cloak, and £20 10*s.* (equal to $512) for an-
other.   Costume of conventional significance was
also worn; for Henslowe records the purchase, at
the large price of £3 10*s.*, of "a robe for to goo
invisibell."   •   .

A comparison of the prices paid for dresses
with those paid for the plays in which they were

---

* Both printed by the Shakespeare Society.   .

worn shows us that the absence of scenery and of stage decoration, to which it has been supposed we owe much of the rich imagery in the Elizabethan drama, was due only to poverty of resource, and not to the higher value set by the public, and consequently by the theatrical proprietors, upon the intellectual part of their entertainment. The highest sum which Henslowe records as having been paid by him before 1600 as the full price of a play is £8, not half what was given for a cloak that might have been worn in it; the lowest sum is £4, not as much as the hero's hose might have cost. By 1613 theatrical competition had raised the price of a play by a dramatist of repute to £20, which, being equal to $500 of the present day, was perhaps quite as much as the proprietors could afford, and was not an inadequate payment for such plays as went to make up the bulk of the dramatic productions of the day. Happily, nearly all of these have perished, and of those which have survived, the best claim the attention of posterity only because Shakespeare lived when they were written.

THE END.

Cambridge : Stereotyped and Printed by Welch, Bigelow, & Co.